WHAT BAD MEN DO

Ramos' Reign

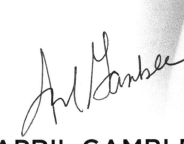

APRIL GAMBLE

For information regarding permission, call 941-922-2662 or
contact us at our website:
www.peppertreepublishing.com or write to:
The Peppertree Press, LLC.
Attention: Publisher
715 N. Washington Blvd., Suite B
Sarasota, Florida 34236

ISBN: 978-1-61493-928-3
Library of Congress: 2023924521
Printed: January 2024

the Peppertree Press
www.peppertreepublishing.com

To
Ted

Thank You

To my son Jeff.
Once, when having difficulty getting me away from
my characters to join a family dinner, he sat
the Bad Men a place at the table.

Dear Readers,

Making up the characters and the actions in What Bad Men Do has been a blast. Any real persons or events are taken straight from the pages of the press or Google. They are used to establish time frames, political climate, and public sympathies over several decades.

There are no *safe spaces* in these volumes. The title, What Bad Men Do, prepares you that these individuals are not kind or politically correct. It is a peek at an ugly world from a safe distance.

You may believe you find grammatical and spelling errors, but as the stories are set in England, the author has intentionally written in the language of that nation.

In The Canterville Ghost (1887), Oscar Wilde wrote: "We have really everything in common with America nowadays except, of course, language".

Winston Churchill, "Americans and British are one people separated by a common language."

Enjoy the tales,
April Gamble

WHAT BAD MEN DO - VOLUME III
Ramos' Reign

## CHAPTER 1

ANGEL DOWN

"What the fuck!" Ramos entered the seventh-floor flat, previously the Tower home to Sir John Kohl, London Mega-Face and international hero. Currently, where Kohl's son, Johnnie, the second John Kohl resides. These were hardened men, but when walking in to find Johnnie fucking his sad strung-out younger sister Julie, it turned Ramos's stomach. So goddamn unnecessary.

Once the protected angel of Sir John Kohl Senior, Julie is now broken and drugged up. Her mother died years earlier. Her father, the Legend, died during COVID, though not of COVID. In a shocking turn soon after her father's death, Julie's much-loved husband Ross, an architect, was killed in a freak crane accident on a skyscraper construction site he was managing for her brother Johnnie, who had inherited control of their father's vast fortune and businesses.

Weeks later, she delivered their second child, a stillborn son. Julie, a once upbeat, joyous young woman, was destroyed. The tragedies, the disappointments, and the loneliness left scant hope for the sad young woman at the mercy of her brother.

Julie was unable to care for her young daughter, Annie. The house staff of her sprawling fifth-floor home was left to raise the little one.

Johnnie stood and tossed the duvet over his sister's inert body. "What?

Johnnie is the eldest son of the late Sir John Kohl, for decades, the most powerful and feared underworld figure in England. Maybe all of Europe, which includes some very bad men.

Kohl Senior was a handsome, charismatic rock star villain. Between his legitimate and non-taxable enterprises, he amassed a fortune in the billions.

At Kohl's death, his son and mini-me, Johnnie Kohl, took the reigns. A young man well prepared with years of dirt and evil on his hands. The transition seemed seamless at first, but he began a downward slide.

Johnnie was a dashing, charismatic young man with confidence and brains. His wit and charm were welcome in the hearts and beds of London. The most *eligible bachelor in the world* said the tabloids. Drugs and liquor were not an issue before his father's death, but currently, he demonstrates the paranoia and anxiety you see in junkies. And the crude and boorish behaviour seen in drunks. A man entirely without checks and balances.

Kohl Senior knew how to use cultivated elegance and make people fall in love with him to cover his malign intentions. Movie star handsome, hundreds of millions to charities, and spent a year in hellish captivity as he sought revenge on a Russian villain. In an unexpected *twist of fate*, he ended up saving children from Chechen sex traffickers. He received the George Cross and a Knighthood, real hero stuff. These are the *hand-made shoes* Johnnie Kohl was expected to fill with ease. No one quite knew what to do with the mess he was in.

Not yet thirty; maybe it was Johnnie's age? His actions were far from wise. Everyone hoped it was his way of dealing with grief and would pass. The clock was ticking.

# #

Ramos Santiago is the number two man in Kohl Enterprises. For many years, he was a loyal and skilled villain whose physical presence said *Don't Feed the Bears, or you will get hurt*. He remained silent at Johnnie's question, refusing the bait.

Both were in Belgravia for a meeting at the seven-story structure John built and used as a base camp for his business and home. The Tower, as it was known, balked convention where baddies were creepy characters in decaying mansions with hidden rooms and creaky staircases. Kohl instead had chosen for his lair an unwelcoming black glass and unyielding steel monolith to convey his power and danger.

Being one of the crew based at the Tower was considered the highest order of protection and enforcement, one of the elite team.

Ramos oversaw all of the crew and the off-the-books businesses. Loans, protection, drugs, gambling, and the always-in-demand pussy were varied and shockingly profitable. Additionally, he handled significant portions of related and crossover legal business. Clubs, trucking, and highly lucrative parking garages. He curated an impressive army of monsters to do whatever it took.

The Kohl domain was far more than thugs and drugs. It was all measures of vice and villain but included a vast legitimate empire of property and international business worth billions, all handled by professionals in the city.

Johnnie's father, John Senior, was a malevolent genius at villainy. He was estimated to have billions more hidden offshore, and still, it rolled in.

Years earlier, he branched out all over the globe. Kohl Defence Industries built and operated private prisons in twenty-six countries, including the US. Also, security and mercenaries contracted out to US, UK, and Euro concerns in forty-one countries. John's favourite; worldwide, he provided weapons of every kind to dictators, despots, drug dealers, and wealthy wannabes.

John Kohl Senior was not the Chairman of the Board. He was god, and it never bodes well to piss-off god. But he lived a dangerous life, and danger sometimes wins.

Jimmy Redmond, a man at Seniors' side for decades, was onboard for the day's meet in the third-floor offices. He was a brilliant legal mind and considered the Consiglieri and family fixer. His years of contributions and loyalty to John had made him a rich man. Jimmy was the father-in-law of the young woman molested by her brother. His son was the one recently killed in a crane accident. Johnnie Kohl was not sorry about his demise. Like his father, he tightly controlled Julie and did not want her to have any option other than him.

Johnnie and Ramos were once as close as family, favourite *Uncle and nephew*. Ramos was there the day Johnnie was born and always the one of his father's animals who took a moment to stop and treat him well. As a child with a distant father, Johnnie loved Ramos. Now with eyes locked in hate. "She needs it." Johnnie zipped up. "She can't feel anything else."

You are the one who can't feel anything, thought Ramos. Since John's death, Johnnie has been a fucking zombie. His once impeccable manners and elegant style morphed into brutality, cruelty, and erratic whims.

John was Johnnie's God. His daily goals were to please, surprise, idolize, best, and impress him. His life goal was to be his father. Now that he was, he lost the fucken plot.

# # #

CHAPTER 2

DANNY

Danny, Ramos' adopted son, was accepted into the prestigious MIT University in America. Almost impossible to get in, but Danny sailed through the gruelling international admission process. He was to study Astrophysics and mathematics; the family's Steven Hawkins. Ramos stepped up to pay the seventy-five thousand Dollar annual tuition plus all other expenses. He knew Danny was a fucking genius and was happy for him to prove it.

Danny was excited to be on his way to the challenging studies, but his mother, Ramos's wife, Alice, was sad and worried, as all mothers feel when a child is ready to leave home.

Billie, Danny's twin brother, was not going anywhere. He was at Ramos's side, a bad man in training and all it implied. He told his mother he wanted her blessing when he was headed to the outlaw life. If not, he would go off and find his way but still seek what he believes is the exciting, dangerous, powerful life of a gangster.

Alice knew he was safer with her husband Ramos, but her heart was broken. He would be a liar, a thief, a whoremonger, a thug, and maybe even a killer, and it was her fault. She brought him into the criminal world when she accepted Ramos' offer to be part of his life.

For the first time, the twin boys were about to be separated. Sissy, the sister of Tyler, one of Ramos's top men, would watch Luna and Stella, their young daughters. Alice wanted the trip to be only her and Danny. To get him familiar and settled in Boston. She secretly gave him one last chance to change his mind and return to England; Brunel or Oxford. Both wanted him, though she knew it would not happen. She was also worried he might not return from America.

# #

With Tyler and Axel following, Ramos walked in and could see goodbyes underway. He planned to be home earlier, but as usual, business shit was hard to get off his shoe.

"Oi, my man. You ready to conquer America?" said Tyler, "the fucking red, white and blue." Alice flinched. "Ah, sorry, Alice.

"Tyler said a bad word." Reported Luna, Ramos, and Alice's eldest daughter. Tyler reached down and scooped up the child in his muscular arms. "Me bad, Cupcake." He called her the nickname Ramos's previous right-hand man Joe had given her. Joe came to a harsh end. It was *ancient history*; a matter of sloppy work and loyalty issues, but justice in a bad man's world.

Ramos looked at Danny and thought how random life could be. A gentle kid with no street smarts, only a brilliant view of math and science. He will probably invent something essential and end up wealthier than anyone.

"OK, nerd, remember what I told you?" Billie placed his hand on his brother's shoulder as the family gathered to say final goodbyes before heading to the airport. Despite their glaring differences, the boys had always been close.

"Ah. What was that? I'm crap at video games?" he smiled at his brother.

"No. Your IQ exceeds your weight, so let me know if anyone gives you shit. I will beat the hell out of um." Billie is dark, 6'3, muscular, and far larger than his 5'6, pale, skinny twin. He looked him right in the eye. "I got you, bro. No matter where, no matter when."

Luna piped up, "Billie said a bad word." She recently took on the task of the family bad-*word-police*. She held her arms wide, palms up, "Daddy, Billie and Tyler have to go to the naughty chair; they say bad words." Emotions were high, and everyone laughed, breaking the tension.

The car was waiting. Axel would see them to Biggin Hill Airport and accompany them across the pond. Ramos arranged a private jet and a five-star hotel in Boston. A home had been purchased to ensure Danny's security. A driver and local hardman, Naill, would keep them safe. The family of a Face of the power and stature of Ramos Santiago would always be in danger and require strict security. The old adage of a villain's family being off-limits was an outdated notion in the 21st century.

Ramos is an immensely wealthy man. Alice is what they call a *homebody*, and what a magnificent home it is. A Surrey property with 24 acres, a stately main home with outbuildings for security, a gym, pool, tennis courts, guest houses, and garages.

Alice appreciated her home and privacy. She was particularly happy to be out of the spotlight, where the intense glare blazed on Ramos.

A voracious non-fiction reader, Alice was the unlikely woman of a thug. She wrote children's books, played classical piano, grew vegetables, and lived quietly on the estate surrounded by her children and hardmen who protected them 24/7.

A few years earlier, three opportunists attacked Alice and Luna in their former home in the suburb of Baylor. Since that time, Ramos kept them close and fiercely guarded. After the attack, he married her and adopted her twin sons to make a statement that harm to her would be met with severe consequences. Alice loved being a mother, and to no one's surprise, she was not done having babies.

⚜ ⚜

Ramos and Alice lounged in bed following a comfortable fuck. They were familiar and relaxed as couples together for many years. Their sex life was less than exotic.

Ramos fucked whom he wanted when he wanted and always had. Alice felt that with dozens of beautiful Escorts and club whores close at hand, he would be unlikely to wander far. She knew because years earlier, when a desperate mother, for a brief time, took sex work at one of the many clubs her husband controlled for John Kohl. He regularly fucked the whores without the slightest emotion. He never picked her to fuck during her three months and four days. She was too sweet and not his type. Instead, she was seen at the club as unexciting but valuable by caring for the shoe salesmen and school teachers, not the hardmen or the rough fuckers.

A year after she left the club, they ran into each other in a discount market, and *the rest, as they say, is history*.

The humiliation was difficult early on, but now she learned to live with what he did with his big dick. She was far more concerned about his heart. Assuming he had one, he had not given it to her. She hoped he would not give it to anyone else. It's not ideal, but one of many compromises needed to love and live with a very bad man.

⚜ ⚜ ⚜

## CHAPTER 3

SANDI

Alice and the children lived a country life, and the weeks passed with infrequent visits from Ramos. He gave them little thought and no time. He arrived for a rare daylight visit, and the little ones playing outside ran to him. "Daddy, Daddy!"

"We are going to the park for a picnic and games. Come with us," said Luna. The little girls were all smiles. He knew they rarely left the estate, and he would rather have his crack and sack waxed than join them.

"We are going to feed the ducks," said Stella, holding up a half bag of old bread.

"Not today. I have business." He patted Luna's shoulder and tried to make his way to the men's quarters they called the zoo. Thinking his men must hate this detail. He also knew their job was to do anything he told them to do. No one would dare grumble.

Alice gave him a slight wave, and he nodded. I wish to hell she would stay on the property, as always concerned for their safety. She hoped he would spend a few moments with his daughters.

Two more cars passed through the gates. As usual, Alice had no idea who was coming or going. Long ago, she quit trying to guess.

Rio noticed a woman making her way near Alice as she stood on the edge of a playing field at the park. Rio nodded to Wyatt, and they moved in.

The girls and a dozen other children played an impromptu footie game with four balls and loads of shoving and laughter.

Wyatt and Rio stood near when the woman finally positioned herself beside Alice. The woman wore a huge hat and sunshades; she almost appeared in disguise. "They have such energy," she remarked.

Alice smiled, "Yes, they do. It exhausts me just watching."

Rio pushed right between the women. Alice gave the woman a look of apology, and then Rio spoke. "Sandi."

"Hello, Rio," her reply was casual.

"You two know each other?" Alice felt better believing Rio was not rude, only anxious to say hello to the elegant woman.

She seemed not in the least intimidated by Wyatt or Rio. "Yes, I used to work for the Kohl organization before I married."

"Perhaps you know my husband, Ramos Santiago? I'll tell him you said hello." Alice was her usual friendly self, and it did not cross her mind that the chic woman was a whore.

Rio gave Sandi a stern look. "The boys have the details." Turning, the beauty stepped toward the playing children, "Come along, Johnnie." Turning back toward Alice and Rio.

A tall, dark-haired boy ran to his mother. She held him close as they walked away.

Sandi and Mindy were the top requested Smoke Escort before their departure a few years earlier. If you like sultry, Sandi was your pick; if you wanted sparkle, Mindy was your go-to. Both fucked their way to fame and fortune and were missed by the unquenchable big spenders who could never get enough of the two beauties.

#

For a Tuesday night, the Sahara was heaving with business. More than the usual number of ass-wipes lined up to beg the indulgences of Ramos and waste his time. No, no, and hell no, his repeated reply.

First up were personnel problems. Not a favourite way to occupy his time, and he was cranky. "What the fuck happened to Boomer?" He and Cody were supposed to go to Peckham and install a new area distro. Cody was here instead, requesting "sick days for Boom," unheard of unless you were shot.

"Ah, boss, we were killing time before the meet. We stopped at the Lone Star," an east-end Texas-themed Kohl club, "for a few cool ones and bitches in boots," mumbled the news bearer. "They got one of the mechanical bulls, and ah...." Cody looked for empathy, but Ramos returned none. "Boom stayed on the damn thing a long time. We cranked it higher, and he landed on his balls. Let out a scream from hell you could have heard in Dallas.

Took him to Casualty." Ramos continued his silence. "Poor bastard's sack is the size of a rugby ball. He has to keep um on ice," Cody grimaced, "it's painful as hell; he can't walk."

Ramos shook his head, "Get Billie and get your ass to Peckham." Nothing interfering with business is funny, but Ramos silently chuckled after Cody departed. "Fucking animals."

#

Tyler pressed Ramos for a moment. "Make it fast. My balls or my gun will go off in about five minutes."

"Today at the park, your wife..."

"No way, I am not in the mood. Send in Vicki and get out."

Ramos was foul and short-tempered as Tyler continued. "Your wife met Sandi." Tyler let it hang in the air.

"Sandi? Sandi from Smoke?" A bit puzzled, "I thought she married some billionaire and moved to Australia?"

"Seems she's back." Tyler wasn't sure how Ramos would take the rest of the news but didn't hesitate, "Back with a son named Johnnie."

"That fucking cunt." Ramos shot up, his eyes fury-filled as he slammed his hand hard on his desk. Jimmy walked in.

"Saw Sandi out front. I hope she is looking for work." Looking at the stony faces of the men, he slowly asked, "Have I stepped in it?"

"That bitch is looking for something." Jimmy shook his head as if to say, what's up?

Ramos looked at Tyler. "Keep her the hell away from Johnnie. If she asks, tell her I am unavailable tonight. Follow her home, find out where she lives."

He looked at his watch past midnight. To Jimmy: "Get our best investigator up and on it now."

Jimmy made the call to Devon, the best snoop on staff. "That fucking cunt is up to something."

"Have you seen her? Has she asked for anything?"

Ramos gave Jimmy a hard look. "That bitch made a move on Alice."

"Let's see what Devon comes up with. What time is it in Sydney?" Said Jimmy, trying to cool the situation. Ramos is furious but willing to hear out the investigators.

Since the death of his father, Johnnie Kohl is a fucking disaster, and Sandi and her little Johnnie would be an unwelcome complication.

The Intel gathering undertaken was fast and thorough. By eleven the following morning, Ramos had the information he wanted. Sandi, a top Smoke escort, married an Australian billionaire and moved to Sydney. Six weeks after the wedding, she announced her pregnancy.

At this *joyful* news, he savagely beat her. He revealed he had testicular cancer and was sterile. An intelligent man taken for a chump; the baby wasn't his, and he didn't much give a damn whose it was.

Sandi signed a standard prenup and non-disclosure document. He annulled the marriage and sent her from Australia with fifty thousand dollars.

Her first stop was in New York; she had her baby and worked for several years. She returned to London when she was almost out of money and homesick. Ramos didn't know if she had returned for work or to squeeze the Kohls.

He didn't much give a shit what she wanted. John Kohl was dead, and his children were a fucking mess. Ramos would not allow some cunt to step in and create further chaos. Nothing was allowed to interfere with business.

# #

Two nights later, looking beautiful, Sandi returned to the Sahara and enjoyed the Golden Bar's attention. Rio walked to her. "Follow me." The same asshole, she thought.

Ramos was behind the office desk reading the Times headlines. Sandi, all friendly and sexy, "Hello, you're quite the big shot these days. And this is still the place to go in London." She was right. With John dead and Johnnie an unstable piece of shit, managing the Kohl empire had fallen to Ramos Santiago. Once a soldier, but now the unnamed General.

"Business is fine. It seems married life agrees with you." Sandi did not believe for a moment; Ramos knew nothing about her short marriage.

"It didn't work out." It had been six years. "I came home."

"You looking for work?" His dick was warming up. Sandi was always a great fuck.

"Never work with you."

"Let's take a ride." Sandi knew he meant let's go to the Dorchester to a fuck-pad he kept there.

Thirty minutes later, both lay exhausted. Ramos fucked her hard. Sandi, a real pro, had no trouble keeping up. "You don't seem to have lost any of your fine skills. When can you start?" Ramos took a drink of his whiskey.

"I need a few days to get settled. Then I'm all yours."

"I understand you have a son. Johnnie." He looked right into her eyes. She hesitated. She planned to tell John about his son, but by the time she returned to London, John was dead.

Ramos' gaze turned harder. She felt she needed to get out. "Yes, I do, and I better get home." Fumbling for her clothes, she moved to get out of bed. Ramos grabbed her arm and bent it behind her. "You can't believe John would have a whore as the mother of his children?"

What a hypocrite, she thought. She knew that Ramos' wife and mother of his children had been a whore, but to mention it would be dangerous.

"I didn't plan it. I didn't know until I got to Sydney."

"Fucking cunt." Shoving her out of bed with his foot, she fell to the floor. Ramos stood and grabbed his pants as he towered over her.

"Don't hurt him. I am not asking for anything, only a job." Scrambling to get dressed, she picked up her handbag and opened it. Removing an envelope, she laid it on a table.

"He's Johns. The DNA reports if you're interested." Sandi collected DNA from a whiskey glass she paid three hundred to a Dorchester maid to retrieve from Johnnie's suite.

Ramos grabbed her neck, "I don't give a fuck what it says. He's nothing to John, the Kohl family, or me." Ramos reached into his pocket and pulled a clip of money. Peeling off a thousand and throwing it on the bed. "Take it for the fuck and get out."

Sandi didn't feel brave but nearly broke, "Am I back at Smoke?"

He looked at her and grinned, *up in smoke*. "Absolutely."

In Ramos' world of very bad men, emotional stability demanded indifference to the suffering of others and willingness to do whatever it took. That night, Boomer, the crew explosives expert, created a gas leak, and Sandi's small rented house burnt to the ground.

The papers reported one female body and a badly burnt child in critical condition. He died the following morning.

To the bad man Ramos Santiago, the boy was not a child or anyone's son. He was an overdue abortion.

# # #

CHAPTER 4

FIRST Kill

Walking into Johnnie Kohl's office on the Tower's third floor for a strategy meeting, Ramos thought he was viewing a tender moment between Johnnie and his sister's angelic three-year-old daughter, Annie. She sat on her uncle's lap in her pink party dress and pigtails with ribbons.

Inside the room, the tableau faded fast. The little girl looked frightened. When Ramos threw a steely look at Johnnie, his response was a laugh.

"Ok, princess, Uncle Johnnie has to go to work. You run along."

Johnnie stood her beside him, adjusted his pants, and poked his dick back through the open zipper. She had been sitting on his penis in her pretty dress.

Ramos was a hardened man with much evil in his history, but it provoked. Not long ago, he walked in on Johnnie raping his sister, Annie's mother. Hardmen do not question the morals or actions of other hardmen. But right now, Ramos wanted to get out of there before he killed the degenerate who spiralled into this debauched existence and stood grinning at him.

Reaching for the child, Ramos carried her out of the room to her nanny waiting in the hall.

⚓ ⚓

In the basement garage, Ramos was seething and tried to reframe his focus back to business. He checked his watch, giving time for his emotions to subside. Perhaps because of his young daughters, but the abuse of Annie Kohl needed to stop.

Ramos viewed his men gathered, some with him years, others younger. Hardman was a gruelling life. The energy of youth was in high demand. His adopted son Billie emerged from the subbasement firing range.

Earlier, Ramos and Billie were in the gun range below the garage in the Tower. Billie was proceeding nicely, and his gun skills were exceptional.

As an outlaw, his training was no less demanding than his brothers would be at MIT. Ramos ensured he was prepared for what it meant to live in this world. Boxing lessons, karate, knives, guns, surveillance, and endless hours in the gym. Billie loved it.

Mix-race, like Ramos, Billy, at twenty-two, is already 6'3. He was not yet as large as his dad, but no one would be surprised if he grew even larger.

Against his mother's wishes, Billie followed Ramos into the world of villainy. "Hi, boss," he said, grinning with a gun in his hand. "I tried the new Glock..." He went quiet. He could see his dad's thoughts were elsewhere. Something was happening. Even as the newest member of the Tower elite crew, he knew something was amiss but was unsure what.

The lift door pinged open. Johnnie should have known to keep his mouth shut as he stepped into the massive garage where the men were gathered. Hate and danger exploded into the room as he shouted at Ramos, a first.

He sounded drunk or stoned as he slurred. "Ramos, you have something to say? You out here plotting on me?" The air was thick and intense as the hardmen nearby froze.

Titus, Johnnie's top henchman, leftover from John Senior's closest crew, went on point and waited for a signal or any sign from Johnnie. His eyes bore into Ramos. He hated Ramos and his superiority over him and would relish the job of killing him right then and there.

After arriving at the Tower for a meeting, Jimmy Redmond emerged from his car and immediately felt the tension. His driver moved a hand to his weapon.

Ramos remained silent and clenched his hands into enormous fists at his side.

"No? Nothing to say? Don't pussy up on me, big man. Say what's on your mind," prodded Johnnie, but Ramos would not play.

Ramos knew Johnnie since the day he was born. A favourite uncle of sorts, he taught him the business of the criminal world. He always liked the kid, but the man who stood there goading was unknown to him and filled him with disgust.

Johnnie, wanting a fight, went on. "You animal, you evil fucking bastard, you judging me?" He turned all the way around, looking at the men. His eyes landed on Billie. "Does Billy-boy know what sick shit you've done? He know about Sandi? Her boy was what, six?"

Swallowing hard, Ramos stood tall but remained silent as Johnnie continued to provoke, "He know you killed Joe?" His vile revelation was meant to taunt. "Hell, does he know your wife; his mother is a whore?"

Without hesitation, Billie, an unblooded rookie raised his gun and fired a shot right through the head of Johnnie Kohl. In astonishing swiftness, Tyler, Ramos' number one man, dropped Titus, a man few could get the drop on. Both men lay dead.

As they say, the silence is deafening as the men stand in stunned disbelief. The fifty-plus-year dynasty of the *Emperor of Evil*, Johnathan Bryce Kohl, and his namesake son had ended in a startling flash.

Jimmy, a man near seventy, raised his hands in surrender. No one among the hardmen left standing moved, but all gave a silent sigh of relief.

Unlike his crewmates with tattoos of skulls, snakes, spiders, and bitches with big tits, Billie's first tat was his mother's name over his heart. Sure, he took a lot of shit about it, but it should have been a hint that it might not be a good idea for anyone, even the all-mighty Johnnie Kohl, to call his mum a whore.

Previously, unknown to Billie, his mother had been a prostitute, but it was no surprise. Ramos was a dangerous gangster, and she had to meet him somewhere. Billie was born of rape, which he did not know. But he did know that a mum does what she has to do to care for her babies.

Billie and his twin brother were not identical except for their love of Mum. While Danny was in America at a prestigious University for the exceptionally brainy, Billie was a gangster. It was his first kill and a hell of a first kill. Ramos wanted to ask if he was okay but knew it would disrespect him in front of the men, so he remained silent.

Looking at his son, he remembered their first meeting at a shabby market in Hackney. Billie was ten or twelve at the time. The first thing he asked Ramos was for help with kicking a neighbour who hurt his mother.

"Put your hands down, Jimmy. You're in no danger." Said Ramos, who instantly became the head of a multi-billion Pound empire.

Ramos turned to the men standing at attention. "As for the rest, your job security depends on you. If any of you have a problem with the change in leadership, raise your hand. Tyler here will help you with your severance package." Each man knew those who demurred would be killed.

"No one wants to resign? Good."

"*The King is dead. Long live the King!*" shouted Frankie as the others joined in.

The years with John Kohl had made Ramos an exceedingly wealthy man. Now, he had the absolute power to go with it. "Time for business." Ramos did not foresee the fast-moving changes, but now, here, he was ready.

"Ah, boss, what do you want to do about...," Tyler jerked his head toward the bodies."

Ramos reached over, took Billie's gun, and handed it to Tyler. "Drop the gun at Vauxhall. Get these two in Johnnie's car. After dark, take them to Brixton, where the blood bath occurred a few weeks ago." There is about to be another house guest at the Glenwood location.

Glenwood was the location of the Kohl family mausoleum, which interned John Kohl senior and his wife Annie, Johnnie's parents. It also held Julie Kohl's husband and Jimmy Redmond's son, Ross Redmond.

⚹ ⚹

Alice took it hard when her son Billie told her he wanted to work with Ramos. It made her sick with worry but with few other regrets for bringing her children into his world. It was more than a decade since Ramos rescued them from a dump in a dangerous area of the city. He moved them into luxury homes and cared for and protected them since.

Ramos lacked tenderness or romance. He never once said he loved Alice. Did he? A man takes care of his family, and their security is intense. Is this what passes for love in a badman's world? From the beginning, he spent little time at home, kept his own schedule, and fucked whomever he wanted, but primarily, his focus was business. The John Kohl business empire took Kohl fifty years to build. In an astonishing change of circumstances, it would all now be controlled by hardman Ramos Santiago.

Countless numbers of women threw their cunts at Ramos. He was an enormous muscular beast, scarred and dark, and while not ugly, he was the exact opposite of pretty. A well-known Face in the UK. Rich, powerful, and smart as hell. The women who loved the bad boys knew Ramos Santiago was the baddest and biggest catch of them all. His wife Alice was the unlikely winner of the big prize, but it did not keep others from trying to unseat Mrs. Santiago.

⚹ ⚹

Jimmy poured two whiskeys as Ramos sat behind his desk in the Tower's third-floor offices. Ramos's immediate priority was to ensure normal patterns of business. The currency of the day was strength. Other Faces might see the change in command as a weakness and make a move. He would need to make a few swift and bold moves to survive unscathed.

"Billie certainly knows how to handle…." Jimmy did not finish.

"Handle business?" said Ramos. "He does." Both men chuckled but did not say Billie did them all a huge fuckin favour.

"Jimmy, I need your help to get all of it legally into my hands. Also, the sale of the Arms business. For that, I will give you 5%."

"I will do what I can, but it might take a while. We will need to devise trusts and business partnerships filed offshore."

Because of their importance to Johnnie Kohl, Ramos and Jimmy knew every business detail, except perhaps the twenty-six plus alphanumeric characters of Johnnie's Bitcoin wallet.

"You wouldn't happen to know the Bitcoin password," asked Jimmy.

"No," said Ramos with an utterly unreadable face. "You?"

"No." Both men took a brief second to digest the answers each had given. They failed to acknowledge if either knew the address. If so, they were not telling.

There were bound to be hundreds of millions, perhaps billions, in the accounts, though crypto had taken a dramatic plunge in the last few months. Figuring out the password in a limited number of tries would be a devilish puzzle. But it was a problem for another day. There were still billions close at hand. If Johnnie took anything else to the grave, neither Ramos nor Jimmy knew what.

"The most urgent item is to sell the Arms division. Axel is well qualified with his German military background and is doing a superb job running it. But it's too time-consuming, and I don't have the desire for world domination." The men laughed together, knowing the quest for world domination summed up the life of the late Sir John Kohl.

"Expect offers to start coming in as soon as it is known for sale."

"And attacks. Why spend two billion for something you can steal?" John Kohl did not purchase the arms division he called KDI, Kohl Defence Industries. He took it through bloodshed and theft, and Ramos had been at his side that day. Then, turning it into a multi-billion Pound global juggernaut.

"What about Julie, Miles, and Nathan?" asked Jimmy of Sir John Kohl's remaining children.

"Nathan is a turnup since his car wreck, and Miles spends much of his time in rehab." These were Johnnie Kohl's younger twin brothers and the youngest of John's children. "Get me a financial conservatorship."

"It's already in place. You might consider setting aside a hundred million each for the three remaining heirs."

"It's a hell of a lot of money," said Ramos.

"Not out of billions, plus at least another two billion offshore. It will establish that you are not making money or a power grab, just honouring commitments to John to look after them. I would suggest a tontine. When each dies, their share goes directly to the remaining siblings."

"Make it happen. Make sure they each have wills which reflect the intent." Jimmy nodded in agreement. Both men knew Julie inherited fifty million dollars from her late husband Ross, plus twenty million in life insurance. He was Jimmy's son, and the fifty was a wedding gift from Jimmy. Money Jimmy earned working for John. All of the lives and vast riches were interconnected. Jimmy Redmond and Ramos Santiago's riches can circle back to the wealth created by the mega-thief and genius businessman Sir John Kohl.

"As for Julie, I want her cleaned up," said Ramos, who did not mention the abuse of Jimmy's granddaughter Annie.

Jimmy and his wife Renee loved Julie. She was married to his late son Ross and the mother of his grandchild. He had known Julie since her birth. He tried to convince Johnnie to get her help, but Johnnie refused. He wanted to control her, and her addiction allowed it.

"A tall order. It's tragic what has happened to that sweet girl. What do you suggest?" asked Jimmy.

"I'll take her and the little one to Surrey."

"I should take her home with me. My Renee loves them, but I can't. She is still waiting for a kidney." Said Jimmy with a sad shake of his head. "She can barely get out of bed."

Years earlier, in retaliation for Jimmy, in a moment of anger, putting his hands on Annie, Kohl's wife, John Senior hired French thugs to brutally beat Jimmy's wife, Renee. She lost a kidney and has been in precarious health in the years that followed.

The families of villains have plenty of money and lives of luxury, but the tolls can be high in their violent world.

Jimmy, an extremely wealthy man from his years in the criminal world, put a five-million worldwide black-market bounty out for a kidney match. It was a long process, but he remained hopeful it would happen before she was too weak to tolerate the transplant.

Known only to a very few, Renee Redmond killed the arrogant misogynist John Kohl. It was a shock and a surprise to everyone, especially to John. She told Jimmy to leave the day it happened and not come near her again. As her health deteriorated, he moved back to her side.

"Alice will work her magic. Julie deserves a chance."

# # #

CHAPTER 5

CRANE

"Boss, there's a wanker who wants to see you and.." said Tyler as his voice faded.

It was a long evening of irritating intruders, and Ramos was ready to move on. "Sounds *lovely*, but remind me why the hell I would give him two minutes?" His sarcasm is thick.

"He has been showing up, and I kept telling him to fuck off, but he said he has some information about the crane accident." Ramos sat up in his chair.

"He say what?"

"Naw, said he will only talk to you."

Jimmy's son, Julie's husband Ross, had been killed in a crane accident the previous year. There has never been a whiff of intrigue or scandal.

When Jimmy's wife, Renee, had been badly hurt by John Kohl's hired thugs, it had been years before the culprit was revealed. Revenge and grudges can fester for decades.

"Pat him for weapons and wires, then bring him in." Ramos sighed heavily. Kohl's men had wondered if Johnnie had arranged the accident, but there was no hint of proof. The thought kept resurfacing because these men knew Johnnie and his obsession to keep his angel, his sister, in his absolute control.

When Julie had eloped with Ross, the crew believed Redmond's days were numbered. No one was surprised when an accident occurred, and Ross was conveniently pruned from the Kohl family tree.

The man Tyler escorted in was not what Ramos was expecting. Dressed in a quality suit and tie, he carried himself like an educated man. Tyler handed Ramos the man's identification.

"Mr. Kirby, what brings you by?" Asked Tyler.

"Call me Evan. What shall I call you?" said Kirby as he addressed Ramos with the smile of an uninvited salesman.

Ramos was not interested in making new friends and other bullshit time wasters. Ramos remained silent. Kirby shuffled from foot to foot and then continued. "We have a shared interest in the unfortunate crane accident. You know, the one that killed the guy married to the Kohl girl." Kirby sounded much less confident. "I understand you run things." Ramos assumed he read the Tabloids stories that ran regularly in the press. The stories always stressed how powerful and wealthy Ramos Santiago had become.

"Not sure if you remember, but Redmond was not the only one killed that day. So was my brother. I am certain he was murdered. They were murdered." Ramos remained silent. "My brother was a bit of a loser, and he had a few run-ins with the law, but he never hurt anyone."

Ramos was not in the least interested in Kirby's testimonial of his brother and was about to end the conversation when Kirby added, "He left me a letter."

Kirby reached into his inside jacket pocket and pulled out an envelope. Inside was a copy of a handwritten letter.

Dear Evan,

I'm really sorry. Please tell Mum I was not a bad man. I have some debts I can't pay and must do something terrible. They said they would hurt Mum and our sister Kay if I didn't. I might not make it back.

You have always been a good brother to me.

Love,

Cillian

Ramos reads the letter. "What do you think he meant?"

"I don't know, but I found the letter in his car after the accident. It sounds like maybe he had something to do with it?"

"What do you want, Mr. Kirby? Why are you here?"

"I want to know who killed my brother. And the Kohl girl's husband and the other two men who died that day. Then I am going to sue them."

"So, what you want is money?"

"Yeah, that too, but don't you think that letter means something? If I gave it to the police, they might open an investigation."

"Why didn't you take it to the police?"

"Ah, sometimes the police mess things up, and I...."

"Want the money." Ramos finished his sentence.

"Yes, but I told you I want to know what happened to my brother. Will you help me, or do I go to the newspaper?"

"That sounds like a threat," said Tyler in a low, calm voice.

"It's not! Do I look stupid to you?" Ramos's reputation as a dangerous man was well known.

"How much?" Ramos let it hang.

"Don't get me wrong. I need the money to take care of my brother's family."

"How much?"

"Three hundred thousand."

"No."

"He has three children and a wife. Ok, two hundred thousand, but it can't be less than that." Evan showed a bit more aggression, but Ramos remained cool with an almost bored demeanour.

"Where is the original letter? This is a copy."

"I got it at home."

"It seems a bit reckless to leave such valuable information unguarded in your home with your wife and children," said Tyler. The threat was implicate, Evan's face filled with fear, which he tried to hide.

"Just forget I dropped by." Evan turned to leave, but Tyler stood before the door.

"Sit down, Evan," said Tyler. Kirby no longer looked self-assured. He was about to shit himself.

"We have established why you're here: the money, but not why I would care. It doesn't sound like your brother was a victim; he was the murderer. Why would I pay blackmail to keep that quiet?"

"Blackmail? No, not blackmail. That's not what I meant." Evan was near panic. "I just thought you would want to know the truth."

"And now I do." Said Ramos, who had always known. He arranged the crane disaster in an ultra-secret order from Johnnie Kohl.

Ramos believed Johnnie was in error wanting Ross gone. Julie was happy and occupied with her husband and child. But Johnnie Kohl valued control, and his sister's happiness was a far lesser consideration.

When the accident was executed, Ramos was the top General in Kohl's army of villains, but even a General is a soldier, and soldiers follow orders. Johnnie was pleased with the results of the discrete crane accident; his sister was once again entirely his and only his.

"Tyler, show Mr. Kirby out."

Kirby stood ready to depart but took a last stand. "I don't want any trouble with you, but I will have to go to the papers because they will pay, and I need the money."

"Fifty thousand and an NDA. The offer expires in ten seconds."

With a surge in courage, Kirby countered. "One hundred."

The late step-up made Ramos laugh out loud. "Ok, Evan, seventy. Done?"

"Done."

"Tyler will take you home to get the original letter, meet the family, and pay you." Ramos wanted him to know he would know where his family lived and that there would be consequences if any new theories about the crane accident surfaced.

Tyler pushed a document toward Evan. "Sign this." It was a non-disclosure agreement, which didn't mean much, but law-abiding civilians always seemed intimidated by them.

#

When Tyler returned, unrushed, he poured a whiskey and sat in a leather club chair across from Ramos's desk.

He shoved the letter and a stack of cash toward the boss, "Bit more to the story. Evan decided to share. He wants to marry his brother's widow. Her youngest child, a son, is his. He needs the money to dump the one he already has." He took a deep drink from his glass.

"I met her; she's a fat toad. And his daughter is as ugly as her mum. The letter was Evan's ticket to paradise."

"Was?"

"Yeah, tragic. On the way back, he accidentally fell out of the car and got run over by the Number 32 bus."

"The Kirby family is accident-prone. Now can we wrap up this cunting day?"

#

CHAPTER 6

BAD WORDS

The intoxicating aromas of roasted meat and baked goods filled the house and served as appetizers.

Alice loved to cook, and four or five men from Ramos' crew typically joined the family for Sunday lunch. Ramos made it home to Surrey most Sundays. Julie, while fragile, was improving daily and came downstairs to join them.

"Hi, Julie," said Billie. She and her daughter Annie had lived in his parent's Surrey home for several months while she got clean. He rarely saw her, and it was a first at Sunday lunch. "I hope you're hungry. Mum is the best cook ever."

"I know. I believe she is trying to fatten me up." The drug addiction and her mental state resulted from the death of her father, brother Johnnie, beloved husband Ross, and a stillborn baby in a short time. She was skin and bones, though her face was still soft and pretty. "Can I sit by you?"

"Sure," Billie patted the seat next to him and stood to help her be seated.

"Look at the little monkeys," Billie laughed, looking at his sisters and Julie's daughter Annie. All of them were under the age of six and giggling.

The crew at the table seemed slightly subdued by the presence of Julie Kohl, her first time sharing a meal with them. John Kohl had been their god and his stunningly wealthy heiress daughter, his most untouchable treasure. At one time, she was full of light and joy; today, she sat, broken and frail.

"More Yorkshire pudding?" asked Alice as Tyler seemed to be eyeing-balling the platter.

"Yes, mam; I'm just getting started." Everyone laughed.

"I saw a program on telly which said men like to eat what their mum fixed when they were children. I guess your mothers made a fine Sunday roast?" Alice smiled as she added more warm rolls to the basket on the table.

Ramos and his men exchanged discreet glances. "Something like that," said Wyatt. These were men with mothers who cared only about whoring, and the next fix it would buy them if they had stuck around at all. Hateful women for whom their children's only worth is for child benefit checks or rounding up men to fuck. Alice's parenting style of encouragement, kindness, and love was new to them and a fucking source of wonder.

"Billie," said Ramos, "after dinner, I want you to get your things and move out to the Zoo," the term the men used for the outbuildings that held the animals, his crew. "I don't want anyone thinking you are getting special treatment living in the big house."

"But he is, he is special?" Alice added. She wanted to believe Ramos was protecting him. Ramos' men stayed quiet, eyes down during the exchange.

"Mum. I got this." Billie knew it was difficult for his mother, but his choice to be an outlaw was made. Her incipient anxiety over his decision had been building for several years, but she needed to get used to it. "Ok, Boss, I'm on it."

"Boss, not Dad?"

The look on Ramos's face said, "Enough." He knew it would undermine Billie's respect and position if she kept on. Things hardmen could not compromise.

In a rare spurt of profanity, Alice raised her hands in frustration, "Oh hell."

The swear word did not go unchecked. Luna was about to call her on it when the crew at the dinner table piped up in unison, "That's a bad word," which gave the table a much-needed laugh.

Earlier, Billie asked Ramos permission to move into the men's quarters. He did not want his Mum to know when he came or went. Or what condition he was in, if and when he came home. Ramos was pleased with his request and agreed it was a positive move. The conversation was a setup. Closely following Danny's departure, Alice felt the loss, but it needed to be done.

Frankie interrupted in an attempt to end the conversation, which was clearly distressing Alice. "Any puddings?"

# # #

CHAPTER 7

AJAX

Ajax Ngcobo was a formidable man in the universe of Ramos in brains and brawn, and few were. His terrifyingly jacked physique pissed off the crew, who could not recall seeing him in the gym. Working in London for Kohl for years, he maintained ties in Africa. It wasn't a horrible life in Yaounde, Cameroon, but he wanted more excitement and more money, a great deal more money.

First, he found his way as a mercenary for hire in Nigeria and Angola. He protected oil company executives and their families. His route was similar to Ramos and Carlos, who were *senior citizens* in contrast. When given the opportunity to relocate to London and be a part of John Kohl's empire, Ajax never looked back.

Ajax trained at his mentor's side, Ramos Santiago, a legend in the world of bad men. Loyal and efficient, his specialty was creative killing, which made him valuable. His reward was massive. Though he chose to live a non-showy life. Sleeping at the crash houses provided by Kohl and fucking the free pussy at mid-level Kohl clubs. His was a simple life, but he was not a simple man.

Like many members of Ramos' teams, he sent money to his family. Many men joined the outlaw life because of personal or family concerns and no other skills to meet those obligations. Other men were in the life because they loved grit, physicality, and danger. All of the above appealed to Ajax.

"Jax, you got a letter," said a voice behind a tittie magazine in the War Room.

"My fan club, huh? Hope they sent pussy shots." Ajax took the letter as the men laughed. He knew the writing was from his grandmother in Cameroon, who raised him. He tried to call her once a month but couldn't remember the last time he had, though he never failed to send money.

My Good Boy,

You have been naughty. You must tell your Mamma you are ok. News in England is terrible: gangs, blowing up things, and many unhappy politicians.

I have good news. Our neighbour, your friend Sheera, is living in London. She knows no one. You must see her and make sure she is ok.

I'm sharing her phone number. Do it, and I will forgive you for forgetting me. Thank you for the money. You are my favourite grandson.

Love Mamma Ngcobo

Oh, hell, three thousand miles away, she is trying to fix me up. He tucked the letter into his pocket. "Let's roll he said and headed for the door.

As head of the drug division for Ramos, his was a hazardous sector of the company, but Ajax proved himself worthy of the title. His cut from the pie from drugs an exceedingly profitable sector. After all, money was the motivator for these beasts.

♯ ♯

Close to a month after receiving his grandmother's letter, and tired of moving the letter from jacket to jacket, he punched in the number on one of his phones.

"Bonjour," Sheera spoke in French, Cameroon's most commonly spoken language.

"Hello, Sheera. It's Jax."

"Oh my, oh my, I am so happy."

"Mamma wanted me to see how you are doing?"

"It is a big city. Very busy. Yes, I am happy."

"I will let her know," said Ajax, ready to hang up.

"Please, can we have coffee?" She asked.

Oh, fuck thought Ajax. She's a nice girl, but he was not in the market for a woman. He wanted to say no, but he couldn't. Funny, a beast of a man, feared by many, but he could not let his grandmother down.

"Sure. Tomorrow?"

"No. I work late tomorrow, but Tuesday?"

"Four o'clock? Where do you live?"

"In Brixton." Oh hell, thought Ajax, probably a rough area. He would need to find her a better place. "We can meet at St. Thomas Hospital Gardens near the fountain. It is where I work."

"Tuesday at four. My business is on call. If I cannot make it, I will let you know." He hung up with even less enthusiasm than when he placed the call.

#

The Tuesday date did not happen. Dealing with North London yardies, it was late when he remembered Sheera. He could almost hear his *Nii* telling him off. "Sheera, it's Jax. Sorry, I couldn't make it. I will, can we," he stumbled as he left the message. He hung up and saw she was trying to call him.

"Allo,"

"Sorry about today," frustrated by the social task his grandmother initiated. "You ok for tomorrow?"

"Yes, but do not believe you must see me because Mamma Ngcobo tells you."

He laughed, "No, it would be nice to see someone from home. Same place. Tomorrow." When he hung up, he thought it might be a pleasant change, for a minute, to think of something other than druggies and assorted pieces of shit.

#

Sitting on a bench near the fountain, Sheera watched the steady stream of people walking by and wondered if she would recognize Ajax. He was 19 and she 15 when he left the neighbourhood and went to work in Angola. One of many schoolgirls with a crush on him, but even as a teenager, he was a man with no time for girls, only women, the loose kind.

When he neared her, the crowd parted. He looked amazing. She tried to hide her delight. What a big, handsome man, and he looked important.

"Hello, Sheera."

She couldn't help herself. She jumped up, smiling, and hugged him. Oh my, he felt warm and strong, a real man. Sheera caught herself and backed up.

"Sorry. I am so happy to see you." She had taken care with her hair and face but was wearing her uniform as her shift began at six.

"You grew up," said Jax as he sat on the bench beside her. Sheera had dark, ebony skin with a full-rounded African body. Her smile was genuine and pretty; unexpectedly, he felt his dick awaken.

"You look successful. You are happy in England?" she asked.

Ajax was not one to answer questions, a technique he learned from Ramos. His reply was vague, "It's all right." He didn't want to talk about himself and turned the table. "What brings you to London?"

"I needed a change. I saw an advertisement saying London welcomes nurses, so I came. St Thomas is a nice place. I have a permit to work for one year."

"How is your family?"

"My foolish brother is in prison. He will die there." She shook her head. "He joined the Boma gang and was caught with drugs and a dead body."

"Where?"

"In Douala."

"No, which prison?" An important question. All of the prisons in Cameroon were hellish, but some even more so.

"Kondengui." Her face looked sad, and it should. It was a harsh place. "My father and mother died in Covid." Sheera was alone, and Jax was unsurprised that his Gran was looking out for her.

"You ever marry?" he asks as young Cameroon girls typically wish to marry.

"Yes, five years ago. My husband was killed."

"What happened?"

"I stabbed him."

The answer caught him off guard, and he suppressed a chuckle. "Oh, I see."

"Every night, he comes home drunk and wants sex. But not able, he hit me and fell asleep; the next night, the same happened. One night, he returned home and wanted sex but was not able; he did not hit me; he hit our little boy. I wait for him to go to sleep; I stab him. I am a nurse; I know the best place to stick the blade." She showed no joy and no remorse.

"So, you needed a change." He smiled at her.

"Did you marry? Perhaps a skinny blond English girl?"

Ajax chuckled. "No. Is your boy here?"

"Oh yes. Isaac, he is my heart. Mamma Ngcobo spoils him. All of the children on the street go to Mamma's house. She gives them Puff-Puff," a tasty West African pastry.

She offered no further information on her husband. "If you come to dinner, you can meet him. I will fix your favourite Cameroon food."

It was a surprise to Ajax, but he said yes. Sheera was pretty and stirred feelings of home.

#

Ajax and Sheera were married now with two more boys, plus Isaac. Ramos was the only guest at the registry wedding. Ajax's private life was like Ramos', separate from the violence and vice of business. Sheera and his sons lived in a detached, high-quality, peaceful house in Wandsworth.

Sheera accepted the limitations of loving a gangster. She made a happy home for him on the intermittent occasions Jax could join the family. It is a difficult or impossible life for many women. Those marriages full of drama and disappointment would falter. A few women, like Alice and Sheera, would survive.

#

CHAPTER 8

BALLET

Julie dressed Annie, Luna, and Stella in matching Burberry dresses, new shoes, and bonnets. Alice told them they were invited to a concert and tea. Down the stairs they came holding hands and giggling.

Chairs were lined up in rows in the music room, most filled with dolls, bears, and other large soft toys. The girls were told they were in for a special treat. Sissy joined in. Once seated, the concert began.

Alice prepared a piano collection of light and happy children's songs. Recently, she began working with each of the girls in pre-piano lessons. Her big dream was to teach them to love the piano as she does.

After each song, Julie led the applause. Alice stood and bowed, and the children gave her flowers at the end of the short performance. "Bravo!" said Julie. "Time for our lovely tea and cakes. The girls scrambled for the garden where the fancy-laid table was waiting.

# #

"Julie, it was such a good idea. The girls seemed to enjoy the music and behaved fairly well. I didn't know those little jitter-bugs could sit still that long."

"Almost still. Annie lost her shoe, and Stella desperately needed a tissue." Laughing with pride, the experiment worked, and she hoped it would not be too long until they would be ready for real-world shows directed at children. COVID had kept the theatres and concerts dark.

"Alice, I have an idea for a gift, and I hope you like it. You have been so kind and generous to Annie and me. I want to build a ballet studio on the property and teach the girls. I am not competent at much, but ballet, I know. What do you think?"

"What a wonderful idea and extravagant gift. I danced too, but I was much better at the piano. How old were you when you first began to dance," asked Alice.

"Younger than I can remember. I suppose the same is true for you for piano?"

"It helped that my mother was passionate about piano and a loving teacher.

"I, too, have a building project in mind: a chapel," said Alice. She had been dreaming about one for a while.

"That would mean so much. I was raised in the church and at Sacred Hearts school," said Julie. "I am too well known now to go to any church."

"A place for prayer would be a real luxury. We could ask the Parish Priest to come and give us communion. I'll check with Ramos for the best locations." Both were excited, and both women knew Alice meant she would ask his permission, and both believed he would say yes.

Three girls gleefully shouted, "Daddy, Daddy," and interrupted the conversation. Alice and Julie turned to see Ramos approach. He had been watching for a while. His world outside was harsh and ugly. It was like being on another planet when he stepped into his Surrey home. He was committed to keeping his innocent daughters from becoming bait to the bad men outside the gates.

"Daddy, we hear songs," said Luna.

"See my pretty dress," said Stella, holding out her hem to show him.

"Daddy, we have cake," said Annie softly. Alice heard Daddy, looked at Julie, and smiled, hoping it wasn't painful for her. It was not. Julie wanted Annie to have a family. After her mother died, she was lonely and desperate for a family until she met Ross. She would never let her daughter forget her father, but Annie needed a daddy now.

"Yes, we have cake and sandwiches. Care to join us?" asked Julie, smiling.

Ramos could not recall the last time he had seen the frail young woman smile. "Looks tempting, but I have business." Ramos turned back into the house, and Julie thought of her father, John Kohl, with no time for his children and always business first. Ramos was the same man.

"You go on, Alice. Spend some time together. I've got the girls," said Julie.

"Thank you. I will."

She started into the house as Sissy asked, "Who needs more tea," which today was milk served in a flowery teapot?

#

Ramos' study door stood open, but Alice tapped lightly as if waiting for an invitation before crossing the threshold. "You busy?"

"Come on in," he said from his desk. It was early in the day, and he rarely stayed the night when he came home early. She shut the door behind her.

He pushed back his chair, which she took as an invitation. She raised her long skirt and straddled him. It's not easy with her protruding baby bump. Ramos was hard in an instant.

Alice moaned softly as she rocked. Her husband was not much of a kisser or toucher, but he gave her neck a soft nibble, which she loved. The chair gave a loud squeak as they finished, which caused both to laugh. "We're asking a lot of this chair," said Alice as she patted her belly and started to stand. Pausing, she asked, "if there is anything you want that I don't do, please tell me."

"You are doing fine."

"A girl doesn't want to hear that when she is trying to be sexy."

"No worries, you aren't competing with anyone." He sought to assure her and end the conversation. But he knew problems with another woman were looming and, if unable to contain them, would hit Alice hard.

"Fat lot, you know." She smiled. "I'm competing with everyone. They all want what I have: a big, strong man to keep you safe, a beautiful place to live, nice things, money to spend." Ramos could tell she thought about it. "They would scratch my eyes out if they could."

"Sounds rough out there," he smiled and tried to lighten the moment, but since the death of Johnnie Kohl, Ramos has been exceptionally busy, and the strain and exhaustion were beginning to show on his usually unreadable face.

Alice was pleasantly surprised to see him today, but he seemed to have little conversation in him. She tried, "How's Billie doing? That rascal doesn't come by often."

"He's working." No chat was forthcoming; Alice wondered what was on his mind. A great deal, but Ramos is not a man to share.

"Danny called and told me he's cold. Boston gets more snow than we do." It felt stupid to talk about the weather, so she didn't continue. She tried something else. "Julie is doing so well. She has offered us a special thank you gift if you say, OK?"

"What's up?" His voice sounded disinterested, but Alice pushed on.

"A ballet studio, and she will teach the girls. She tells me she loved to dance."

"She spent hours at it. She could usually be found on the fourth floor."

"Yes, she said. But it isn't practical to take the children back and forth. It would be a real luxury to have a home studio. We could also use it for yoga. Is it ok? To build?"

"Sure." Ramos would not allow Alice and the girls to go to the Tower, but it would not be necessary to say so with a new home studio.

"Is there room for a chapel somewhere? It's time to get the girls familiar with the rituals, and when things are less public, we can start attending a local church for Mass. I was surprised, but there is quite a number in Surrey."

"Plenty of space for both; I'll check into it." He liked the ideas; another way to keep his vulnerable family on-site and protected from the outside world. Ramos knew it was unlikely his wife would ever be able to attend Mass as she had previously. Unknown to Alice, he recently purchased seventeen additional acres adjoining the current Surrey twenty-four, and a twelve-foot high stone fence to match the existing property was already being constructed. Forty-one acres are more than enough for any expansion.

"It will be wonderful for the girls, for all of us." She could see his mind was not on her, sex, ballet, or God, and he was already back to business. She stood and went for the door. "Can I get you anything?"

"Huh, ah no." She looked at her watch as she closed the door behind her. It had been seventeen minutes.

 # # #*

CHAPTER 9

MESSY

"Daddy home," squealed Luna as she stood up from her mud pile. Ramos leaned against the door frame, watching his wife and little ones in a walled garden off the breakfast room. Alice turned to look as their two daughters ran toward their father.

"Girls, you are a muddy mess. Don't touch Daddy." In an expensive bespoke suit, Ramos scooped them both in his arms and held them close for a cuddle as he kept his eyes on Alice. The cuddling and affection did not come naturally, but he went through the motions for his wife. Today's effort was even less sincere than most, which did not escape Alice's notice. His idea of being a father meant protection and nice things for their whole life. He would never trust other men to care for them.

"Daddy, I make a pretty flower." Said Luna with pride.

"Me too," said Stella, trying to copy her adored older sister.

"You missed Julie. Billie is driving her back to the Tower. He has been wonderful with her. I guess she enjoys being with someone her age?" Julie was clean and sober, making small steps to get on with her life. Her daughter Annie loved it in Surrey with the other little girls, and Julie regularly let her stay in Surrey when she returned briefly to the Tower. Alice made it clear that both were always welcome at the Surrey home.

Ramos made no reply as Alice lumbered up. Eight-plus months pregnant and losing her usual bounce. Laughing at her clumsy self, "You must be tired of seeing me fat. I sure am."

Ramos was not a man turned on by the *beauty* of a pregnant woman. In his world of vice and fuckery, getting laid is a given. Sex with Alice was never what brought him home.

Alice had the odd sense that she was talking to herself and became concerned. Something was wrong, but she continued her attempt at casual conversation. "Turning your daughters into gardeners is more like mud wrestling." She caught her husband's serious face, and hers flooded with concern when she saw Sissy walk up.

Sissy was the sister of Tyler, Ramos's top man. She was a simple but sweet girl who helped with the children. She took her time with them seriously and gradually moved into the large Surrey property.

"Sissy, take them in and get them cleaned up." Said Ramos.

Worry hit as Alice's breath shortened. "Is everything okay?" she asked but knew it wasn't. After a dozen-plus years together, she could read him. No easy task. His business made him intentionally unreadable. "Is it Billie?" A mother's fear rushed to the surface.

"Billie's fine. Come inside. We need to talk."

"Can I get cleaned up first?" She wanted a few minutes to compose and prepare herself.

Nodding his reply, but he didn't want to wait. "I'll be in my office."

Alice's mind raced. She knew he did many illegal things and, through the years, grew able to put it mostly out of her mind. Was he going to prison? Was Billie? Was Danny OK? Was her husband sick? She braced for bad news as she stood in the shower, and the water washed away the mud but not the dirt. Hers was a life built on dirty deeds and dirty money, and she knew someday there would be a reckoning.

Clean, fresh, and dressed in a simple but pretty, pale, floaty cornflower blue maternity dress. Alice entered Ramos's elegant *gentleman's* office. With thick Persian rugs, warm walnut cabinets, and shelves of leather-bound books, suddenly, the grandeur of it repulsed her. She tried to regain herself, for she would need her strength for what was sure to come.

⚜ ⚜

Ramos stood and went toward her. Stopping short, she looked up with a forced smile. "What's going on?" she asked, knowing it could be anything.

Not moving to be seated, he addressed her in the middle of the room. "A great deal is going on, and tomorrow it will all become public. I want to prepare you." She replied with a cautious nod.

"There is a money laundry and bribery case under investigation. It has been in the works for close to a year. I tried to get ahead of it, making contact with one of the investigators. I am hitting it from multiple fronts, and what I've done will probably get it tossed, but it will be messy until then."

In 2020, London was named the *world's money laundry capital*, a title they didn't want to own and one which energized the Crown Prosecution.

Silent, Alice's heart was thumping, but she kept her gaze steady. "The press will have their version of the story tomorrow, which will probably be in the papers for weeks or months."

Alice knew there was more to this. It was not unusual for stories to run. Stories, good or bad, they used Ramos to sell papers. The reason she wanted none of the limelight to shine in her direction. "How can I help? Can we just leave here? Tonight? Get the children and vanish? Surely there are places we can go they can't find you?" She was all in and ready to do whatever it took.

She paused as she looked at her husband's unemotional face. Her fear spiked, "You wouldn't leave without us, would you?"

Ramos would protect and provide for them, but both knew that if he fled, he would leave them behind. He spent his whole life on high alert and in extreme defence mode. If under attack, no one would be safe or spared from hurt or annihilation. He ignored the question. Looking at his intelligent, gentle, loyal wife, he knew he had squandered her trust. It was very personal now, and he was about to smash it all in her face.

"The detective is a woman, Marita Baez, half English, half Portuguese. She started showing up at the clubs and mixing it with the crew." Thousands of people feared Ramos or relied on him financially and did precisely what he told them to do, but he felt ill at ease as he attempted to explain. "Trying to meet me and get close. I believed it to my advantage because Baez started dropping useful things about the investigation."

Ramos knew at their first meeting that he had seen Marita before.

⚜ ⚜

Ramos and his men rolled up on a meet to find two cars on fire, four marked and unmarked police vehicles, and a fire and ambulance. "What the fuck?" said Ramos. "Ride on."

All four men in the Bentley kept their eyes straight ahead and did not look toward the scene as a street cop waved the traffic through. Ramos made eye contact with the WPC as they crawled by with the torch, giving directions. She looked right back at him and winked. What the fuck thought Ramos. He had more urgent matters, but she made him curious.

The meet was an Afghan connect. The supplier was on a short leash. The batch of heroin had been stepped on with shit, possibly Fentanyl, and was putting people in Casualty and the grave, the drama you never want in the drug game.

Ramos already ordered two more batches and upfronted close to seven hundred thousand. He wanted his money back and was not known as a patient man.

The three soldiers with him: Frankie, a big tough Irishman. Tyler, a seasoned right-hand man since the death of Joe, a hardman who made a wrong choice, and a newbie to the elite crew, Boomer. His real name is Bossley; he came on board as a demolition expert, and the name Boomer fit. The fucker loved to blow shit up.

Ramos did not do drug deals and low-level gangster meets, but it was on the way to Surrey and one of his wife Alice's historic Sunday Roasts. Cruising by in time to see the cluster-fuck in progress.

Ramos, usually impervious to flirting, later recalled the cop who winked. He was not a handsome man, but he needed no ego strokes. Women were plentiful in his world, plus he had a good woman at home. Was the cop sending him a signal, code, or clue?

Tyler discreetly took photos of the area as they rolled by. Ramos checked his phone and had her picture. Who the fuck are you, and why the hell were you trying to get my attention? This was a year earlier. He would later learn that in a diversity drive, the Met had made her an entry-level detective.

⌗ ⌗

"I guess a fuck isn't always just a fuck," Ramos told her this as a way of dismissing his routine infidelity. This a bold and unusual remark from Alice. From her brief days whoring at the Lightening Rod years earlier, she knew he meant it. Until now. It was the first time Alice knew her husband was fucking someone other than whores, though he had never promised it was whores only. It felt very different.

Ramos never blinked. "It's gone on longer than expected. The case is massive, and I need Baez on side." The position of explaining and justifying himself was beyond rare it was fucking historic. "It all blows up tomorrow. I am working on using her involvement to taint the case and get it thrown out," as unapologetic as always.

"Was she setting you up?"

"Yes, but not for the Filth." He halted; his wife was clever, and he knew he didn't have to explain.

She raised her eyes to his. "She's star-struck." Not a question.

"She says…," his voice faded. "She wants to be you."

"The money, the fame, the house?" The massive estate was featured in Hello magazine with the former owners.

"Yes."

"Has she ever been here?" Alice only occasionally left the property.

The question was unexpected. Ramos routinely lied to his wife but felt she deserved the truth. It might come out anyway. "Yes, early on for a meet. She insisted it be here. She knew valuable information I needed and…"

"Inside our home?" she struggled as she breathed deeply.

"You took the girls to the ice show, and …" He knew Alice would remember he grossly misled her by making plans to *surprise* her with the outdoor ice show trip. She helped the girls make glittery thank you notes to give him for their special treat.

"You got us out of your way." He remained silent; to Ramos, this was business, not personal. "Did you have sex with her in our home?" The tears were impossible to deny as she looked at her swollen belly.

"Don't do this. She's just a piece of ass." She caught his verb use: is not was. He was telling her the truth. He would kill the scheming bitch at the first opportunity, but it would be a while, maybe a long while.

Her lower lip trembled, "In our bed?"

"No." Marita tried to get him to fuck her in their bedroom while she was on the *house tour,* but Ramos moved her to the office and fucked her near where Alice now stood.

Eyes down and voice low, Alice could no longer look at him. "Is she young and pretty?" Alice was near forty.

Marita was a young beauty with a hard edge. There is no need to lie to Alice because pictures will appear in the papers tomorrow. Marita alerted the press on numerous occasions. She wanted to be Alice, with an elaborate plan to make it happen.

"Yes." Unused to interrogation and not liking it. He needed Marita, even if it meant hurting his wife. Staying out of prison was a fucking priority.

"Does Billie know?" She moved from hurt wife to concerned Mum.

"They all know. She used Billie to get to me. He's embarrassed at falling for her *Honeytrap.*" The other men knew not to introduce some *strange* to the boss. But Billie was excited about her and wanted to show her to his dad, a rookie mistake.

"And it's messy?" said Alice, referring to his earlier description.

Ramos knew it would crush her, but the story was about to get much worse, "She's pregnant."

"Oh," she squeaked. Alice went limp and slipped toward the floor. Ramos caught her and guided her to the large leather Chesterfield before a lit fireplace. Ramos was not a man to say please, thank you, or sorry, and he did not.

Breathing in sharp gasps, Alice tried to process the pretty young detective who wanted to be her, have her life, home, and husband, and was pregnant with his child. It was too much to take in. Her face drained of its usual joy, her voice flat. It wasn't self-pity but reality. "Do you love her?" She wanted to ask him if he loved her but was too afraid of his answer.

Ramos shook his head. "No."

Slowly and softly, she kept going. "Maybe you'll get your boy." They already knew Alice was expecting a third daughter. Ramos did not say he wanted a boy, but most men do.

"I have two sons," said Ramos, who legally adopted her boys.

"Do you have any other children I don't know about?" She knew her questions were pointless; he might just lie. He might get angry she had asked. He did.

Unmoved by her tears or pain, his frustration surged. He raised his hand as if to strike her, "No, goddammit." The shock on her face paused his action. He closed his fingers and punched his other palm instead. "No."

He destroyed this blameless woman and was unable to mitigate the damage. To a formidable man, being powerless to keep from hurting her was an alien feeling he did not like.

This was about business, the business of staying the hell out of prison. "You have been *in the life* for more than a decade. You know it's not traditional. It's complex and, at times, ugly. The stakes are high. It's no time for sloppy thinking or hurt feelings." His message was clear: This is serious. Keep your shit together.

Alice shook her head in disbelief at what he was saying. "If I had just told you I was expecting another man's child, you would kill him and probably kill me first. So please allow me a moment for my hurt feelings."

She tried to go on with more courage than she felt but spoke barely above a whisper. "For years, I have managed my expectations to be content with the tiniest portion of your life. I convinced myself that the security you provide and the nice surroundings for our family proved our value to you. It doesn't really when you get your face rubbed in it. You are forgiven for thinking I don't need self-respect; I guess I haven't really had any for a very long time."

"I'm a whore, after all. I traded all this and some money to spend for anything you want to do to me. That's a whore, right?"

"Baez means nothing to me, but the case is huge." He was trying to crash the case from numerous angles. He bribed the Organized Crime chief with photos of him and two underage bum boys. He paid the husband of the Solicitor General two hundred thousand and let her know it was all on video. "This will all be over. Give it some time."

"It will never be over. She is having your baby." Hot tears of regret and humiliation flowed down her face. "I know you are capable of horrible things, but I can't believe you would do this to our family. The one thing I thought I didn't have to share was my pride in being the mother of your children. But it doesn't make anyone special, and it's all I ever had." Her heart was beating so rapidly that she felt nauseous. Alice finally looked into his eyes again.

"I'll always love you, but tell her she can be me now. I don't want to be me anymore."

It was pointless to go on, so she didn't. Her husband could not understand the self-loathing she felt for the choices she made, which led to this day.

Leaning into the sofa, she pulled a cashmere throw around her shoulders and wrapped her arms around herself in search of comfort. Turning her face away, he knew she was no longer hearing him.

CHAPTER 10

SUNNY

On waking, Alice felt the weight of dread and shame. What kind of woman lets her man fuck anyone, come and go without explanation, and allows herself to be humiliated repeatedly in private and public? A whore, that's who.

At the bedroom window, she saw it was a bright Sunday, but there was no light in her heart until she heard the giggles of her little girls.

"Mummy, we made tea," said Luna.

"And biscuits," added Stella as she took a nibble. Sissy walked in behind, carrying the tea tray.

"How special, tea in bed, but perhaps at the table by the window." She turned to Sissy. "Please bring the papers up. I don't think I am ready for stairs just yet."

Sissy looked pained. A sweet simpleton, she was devoted to the children and Alice. "I don't know, I …" Alice knew she needed to see the tabloids and the sordid details.

"Please get them while I have my tea." She took a sip of the horrible, cold sugary tea. It was so sweet it could go on crepes. "How many sugars did you put in this?" She looked at her giggling girls.

"I am five. I put in five and…" said Luna.

"I three," said Stella as she held up two fingers.

"So, you put in three? It is perfect." Sissy entered the room, lay the papers on the end of the bed, and rushed out. Alice spread them across the table.

"My daddy," said Luna as she pointed to an enormous colour front-page photo. Alice could only see the beauty standing next to him, Marita Baez. A dam of unshed tears burst. Alice began to sob loud, uncontrolled sobs. Soon, Luna and Stella were crying, but Alice could not stop. Luna rushed from the room. When she returned with Sissy, both were sobbing.

"Please take the girls; I want to sleep. Please go." Sissy and the little ones left the grand bedroom.

Sissy was frantic and, after listening to Alice wail for over an hour, called her brother Tyler, Ramos right hand, and asked him for help. He sent Billie to see his mum.

Alice did not know how long she cried or slept but became aware she was not alone. The shame and self-hatred left her weak and exhausted. She did not turn to see who was sitting on the bed. She didn't want to know.

"Mum, it's me. Are you ok?" Billie moved quickly into the world of bad men who did terrible things, but he held a deep well of love for his mother. "Mum, are you ok? I am so sorry."

She looked at her son without rising. "No. I'm sorry. I brought you into this ugly world of crime and bad men. I was afraid and tired of being alone. I don't deserve anything good to happen to me." She was sobbing again; she had lost heart.

"No. You're the best Mum ever."

"Do you know how I met your dad?" Alice was consumed with guilt and self-contempt. She felt like a worthless whore.

"It doesn't matter. You're good, and I am so lucky you're my mum. Danny and the girls are lucky, and Ramos too. Please, mum, be ok?"

"Go, son, please go. I want to be alone. Please." She turned from him.

Billie, sad and angry, rushed down the stairs. He would go to the Zoo, get a gun and kill the bitch who hurt his mum. Tyler stood at the bottom of the stairs. "I'm going to kill her. She hurt my mum, and I am going to kill her."

Tyler, a muscular man, grabbed him. "No. You're a soldier. Your job is to do what you're told. No one orders a kill except the boss."

Billie fought to loosen his grip, but Tyler held tight.

"She ruined our family; she needs to die."

"That cunt is the *walking dead*, but your dad needs her for the case. He will know when the time is right; he alone will make the call."

Tyler liked Alice. All the men did. A good woman and these men met very few, but the women in the world of villainy knew anything could happen at any time. There would be no Sunday roast today.

# #

Three hours later, Alice went into Labour. She called her doctor, who told her to go to the hospital. It was her fifth live birth, and the delivery would be quick.

She called for a car and said she was going to London. Only later, riding along, she asked them to take her to Fulham Road. She didn't say she was in labour; she wanted it to be known for as little time as possible. Her plan was interrupted by a gripping contraction and a loud gasp. Dex, driving, and Frankie on shotgun looked back at her. Before they could ask if she was okay, she had another contraction, and her water broke. "Please take me to the Chelsea and Westminster Hospital." It wasn't far, but the cars were crawling along at a rush-hour pace as the weekend ended and people returned to London. It felt as if it took forever.

Dex pulled up to the Kensington Wing maternity entrance. Frankie reached in, picked her up in his massive arms, and carried her inside.

#

"It has been a busy Sunday; five babies so far," said the Doctor. As Alice gave her final push, she sighed and waited to hear her baby cry. "There she goes," said the Doctor as a shrill wail pierced the room. "She's beautiful," announced the nurse, which is the delivery room code for the baby was perfect. The nurse lay the baby in her mother's arms.

"I shall call her Sunday." She asked Ramos if he had any name preferences when his second daughter was born. He said she earned the right to name her as she did all the hard work.

A fabulously wealthy celebrity gangster and public figure, Ramos entering the hospital made big news, especially with the earlier editions and all their juicy details of villainy and scandal. The press was everywhere. Ramos put men on all the doors so Alice would not be disturbed. Billie and Julie were her only visitors.

Walking into Alice's flower-filled Platinum suite, the most expensive in the city, Ramos was unsure of his welcome. He knew Alice had other things on her mind.

Alice opened her eyes as he approached. She managed a weak smile. She knew at that moment there could be no benefit to her family to be hurt, angry, or self-loathing, but she was, and her feelings for Ramos felt numb.

"Can you have Billie drive us home?" Eyes and voice low, she shook her head in the shame of it all. "I'd like to leave right away," knowing everyone in the hospital was probably talking about the expose' in the press.

"He left with Julie. I'll take you." Which brought tears to her eyes, which she quickly brushed away.

Offering a slight nod, she asked, "Did you see her?"

"She's lovely, like her mother." Ramos was not a man for compliments; it was a gesture of peace.

##

One week after Alice and Sunday left the hospital, Marita Baez toured the Kensington Wing. She requested a more luxurious suite than Mrs. Santiago's but was told none were more significant. She made her maternity reservation with press and photographer contingents close at her side. The details appeared in the next chapter of Gangster & Detective.

###

CHAPTER 11

JET

"Oi, Jet, ride with me to the Tower. I have to scoop up Billie-boy."

"You mind waiting until I finish shaggin this fat ass?" Both men were upstairs at the Rod rocken some afternoon pussy.

"Sure, but what's taking you so damn long? You fall in love over there?" Cody laughed as he tucked his dick in his trousers and zipped up.

"You'll be the first to know." Jet finished with a grunt.

⚡⚡

Lei Wang-Hung was the newest member of the elite team and worked and trained for six years under the nurturing of Ajax. It was a cliché, but he was a martial arts expert, which gained him much respect. Standing considerably shorter than the rest of the crew and always a source of humour, but not so much for Wang.

From day one, the men called him Jet after the awesome Jet Li, and he was okay with that, considering the names some occasionally put on him: *Wanger*, Wonton, and Hung Low, to name a few.

Due to Jet's addiction to video games, the team gave him endless shit except when competing. He was a wizard with a respected international gaming name and following. When Ramos updated the War Room and Zoo electronics, he put Jet in charge. He put in water-cooled computers, top-of-the-line controllers, and gaming hardware. Jet would pass up opportunities to hit the clubs and fuck live bitches to stay in and play games.

⚡⚡

"What's up with the meet?" asked Billie, just making conversation on the ride to Soho.

"Boss didn't consult me; he consult you, Jet?" said Cody.

"No. Maybe he's inviting us to lunch?"

"Yeah, that must be it. Billie, your dad is such a warm and friendly guy."

"Yeah, good timing too. I'm hungry. You hungry, Billie?"

"Blow me," said Billie, wondering how these assholes made it through the day without a morsel of kindness. He wanted to be a hard man, but not hard. Was that even possible?

Soho looked like a deserted war zone. The Covid war. Shops boarded up, homeless, and a scattering of zombies in face masks. After nearly a year, the once tawdry sex zone, gay bars, after-theatre dining cafes, and clubs were mostly dark and probably roach and mould-infested. Getting them back up and running was taking time and money.

Not so at The Golden Triangle, the first club of the late John Kohl and now part of his enormous property empire controlled by Ramos. Frankie stood on the pavement at the door smoking. He flipped his splif into the street and, with a head jerk, turned to go in. As the three followed, Frankie said, "Not you, youngblood. Keep an eye on the door."

Billie stood on the pavement, looking at the closed door, and wondered what was up. He let that go because the life of a hardman was full of intrigue, secrets, action, need-to-know situations, and waiting. Billie didn't smoke cigarettes and was in no mood to blaze one. Instead, he leaned against the wall and polished his shoes on the backs of his pant legs.

That took thirty seconds. Looking around for something else to focus on, he saw a vandalized photo of a woman in trashy lingerie. Feeling his dick stir, he laughs at himself. Checking the score of Euro 2021 in Rome, England was up two. Jet stuck his head out the door and mumbled, "Inside."

Billie did not know that he was going to be a *staked goat*. Ramos was sure there was a grass. Maybe not in the top crew, but close. He figured they would see Billie as a weak link and privy to top information due to his relationship with the boss. They might approach him, try to make pals, and get info. He asked his men to watch for anyone showing interest in getting up close to Billie.

#

The life of a hardman was fast, dirty, and dangerous, but the beasts attracted to the life embraced all of grit, risk, and pleasure. Yes, there was plenty of enjoyment for these thugs. Ramos's elite crew had free housing, booze and blow, and unlimited pussy. At times, there could be a pleasure management problem.

The brutes gave Ramos absolute authority and loyalty in return for the goodies. Few men who made it to this level made an unforgivable misstep. But it did happen.

The men were required to be fit, which meant plenty of gym time and a reasonable diet. They needed to forgo the showboating and whose dick was biggest. Hell, everyone knew that Ramos's dick was. They needed to work as a team on call 24/7, but they could party hard when downtime came.

Occasionally, one of the crew would find it difficult to put away the toys and return to business. Showing up hungover or drunk was unacceptable; lately, Wyatt had lost his way and was pissing off everyone.

Even the whores protested that Wyatt couldn't play, and when that happened, he roughed them up. That's just fucking wrong.

These men knew each was there to protect Ramos, his family, and each other and get business done. You can only do that if you are at your best, at the very least, sober. Recently, Wyatt missed a couple of callouts, and everyone gave it a shrug, but when he sat in the War Room with a cold beer, whiskey shots, and laid out lines when the boss was due, the men stepped away.

"Wyatt, you dumb shit, we are heading to Ilford for some wet work."

"Fuck off; I'm just relaxing."

"I am fucking tired of you relaxing. You almost got Dingo knifed last weekend when you were too fucking shit-faced to drive."

Wyatt continues with his lines without concern for the complaints of his coworkers.

"If Tyler sees what you are up to, you'll need to book it back to the shithole you came from."

"What a bunch of wankers." Wyatt shook his head.

"Yeah, well, I am not riding with you," said Rio.

"Good idea," said Boomer. "Your sloppy shit will kill one of us."

"Or kill Ramos," sneered Wyatt as Billie walked through the door.

Kill Ramos was all it took. Billie had his gun out and aimed at Wyatt, ready to do whatever it took.

Wyatt was too high to worry. "Little boy, just cause Daddy is boss, you don't get to shoot who the fuck you want."

Billie did not react to the insult or lower his gun, "What's up?" he asked anyone standing there.

"This asshole is putting us all at risk, and it's getting fucking old," said Frankie, who had unofficially moved into the third-chair position after Tyler.

"You get my attention when someone uses the words *kill and Ramos* in the same sentence. I need more than "asshole" as an explanation." Billie was serious and was not ready to let it go.

"What the hell?" asked Tyler as he entered the lounge, seeing Billie with his gun high and aimed at Wyatt. The men talked trash but pulling a weapon was not done.

No one spoke. "What?" Barked Tyler. The men exchanged discreet looks, but no one spoke up. Being a snitch was way over the line.

"We have business to do. If there's trouble, I want to know right now."

"Wyatt, the windy bastard is stinking up the war room, and no one wants to ride with him," said Rio.

"Wyatt, stay behind and get cleaned up." Ordered Tyler.

"All's well that ends whatever," slurred Wyatt as he attempted to stand and sprawled on the floor.

"What the fuck is going on?" demanded Tyler. "He's fucking wasted. If the boss sees this shit, someone's ass will be …"

The men discreetly eyed one another and then began talking all at once. "He's a piece of shit."

"Drunken ass-wipe."

"Ah fuck you," said Wyatt as he stumbled to his feet.

"Hasn't been sober in days."

"Weeks."

"He threatened the boss," said Billie.

"Is it true?" Tyler's face was stone.

"Bunch of ponces can't take a joke," said Wyatt.

All of the men gave a nod. Without further discussion, Tyler bypassed the twelve-step program approach to addiction, pulled his weapon, and put one dead centre in Wyatt's forehead.

"Load up." Wyatt's drama and life were done; it was time for business.

⚡ ⚡

Billie got little private time with Ramos and was surprised when told to ride with his dad to Surrey. He wondered if it was something to do with

Wyatt and the War Room the previous night? They were not alone. Ramos required far more protection than Billie could provide. Frankie and Tyler were along. The Baez daily drumbeat kept Ramos a very high-profile target.

Pulling through the iron gates, Billie asks, "Do I have time to see Mum?"

"Yeah," said Ramos who would use the opportunity to let the men in the Zoo know about the suspected mole and Billie's possible role.

# #

Alice looked up to see her son, "let me guess, you're hungry?" They both laughed. "Good timing. I have a pork tenderloin about ready to serve."

"Whatever it is, it smells yummy." He leaned in and took a peek at his baby sister Sunny in her cradle. "Does she sleep all the time? Every time I stop by, she is snoozing away."

"She's a peaceful baby. Not at all like you and your brother. I don't believe I slept more than an hour at a time for your first year." Billie reached into the refrigerator for the milk.

"Oh no, you don't. Do not put your mouth on that jug. Sit down." She reached for a glass.

"Julie was here earlier; she will be sorry she missed you. I think she likes having someone her age to talk to. After all, I am old enough to be her mother."

"She loves you and loves having a mum. She sure misses hers, and it has been years."

"Here you go," Alice sat a heaving plate before her son and stood back. He did love his grub.

"I'll talk while you eat. Or do you have plenty of time?"

"Mmmm, mu…" Billie was pretending to talk with his mouth full.

"Oh, I hear the *giggle-gang* heading our way. Stella, Luna, and Annie ran into the room, all holding hands and dressed alike. Julie had taken to buying the girls expensive designer children's clothes, all matching they loved to wear.

Theirs was a safe, secluded existence, and a visit from Billie was always treated as a special event. "Billie, Billie!"

# # #

CHAPTER 12

REBECCA

It's always something: One of Ramos's men beat up his woman because she got a tat of her last boyfriend to piss him off. It did. He got arrested after the beating because she pressed charges. The man was of value to Ramos in the middle of a substantial drug deal.

Ajax bailed him out, and he returned to his woman and walloped her again. Ramos ordered two of his men to beat the hell out of the employee. When released from the hospital, the injured WAG was by his side. Ramos demoted and fined him five thousand, HR in the criminal world.

##

In between handling irritating personnel matters, there was actual business to do.

Tyler, Dingo, and Ramos headed to The Shock Wave. Billie would see them there. The next meet would be an excellent vice and treachery teaching moment for his son. Billie was a proverbial sponge at soaking up the inside-out of the criminal world, and as for danger or violence, the *youngen* never blinked, a real chip off the old block.

"Oi," said Billie as he approached the main bar in the Wave. "Where's the boss?"

"Upstairs tapping the fat ass of somebody's mother. Said let him know when you got here."

"Don't interrupt him; he'll be grumpy for the rest of the night," laughed Billie.

"That's where he gets it, huh?" Billie joined the laughter and spotted Tyler. "Hey, Ty, how many fucks does one man need? The boss planning to do some business tonight?" Ramos walked up.

"You bunch of pounces sound unusually interested in my dick. That's fucking disturbing." He reached for a whiskey; Dingo poured as the men laughed.

"Well, Sensei, what great wisdom do you have for me tonight," Billie teased.

"How to teach a douche-bag-bent Filth bastard how to fulfil his obligations."

"Sounds like fun; let's roll."

"No need. He's joining us here." Ramos looked at his watch, "anytime."

"Convenient." Said Billie.

Twenty minutes later, Dingo showed DI Thompson into the Wave Office, where Billie, Ramos, and Tyler waited. The moment he stepped through the door, Tyler hit him with a punch that would fell most men. Thompson gasped loudly and stumbled to the wall for support.

"You imagine I pay you five thousand to fix a fucking parking ticket? Hell no. I paid to make sure the piece of shit over-eager partner of yours stayed the hell out of Hoxton. You get one more opportunity to keep your end or expect that animal," he pointed to Tyler, "to visit with your lovely wife, Joanne."

"No, no, don't touch her. Please no. I'll fix it. Greene didn't tell me he was going to Hoxton and…."

"Shut the fuck up. I will find you the perfect collar for Tuesday's blood bath; until then, you better not piss me off again." Ramos set up a rival gang to take the fall for a bloody drug deal that went nuclear. Getting all the ducks in a row would take a little longer. "You clear?" Thompson nodded his head, rapidly turned to the side, and vomited.

Billie, standing nearby, got sick splashed on his shoe. Without asking or thinking, he kicked the DCI in the balls. "Ooof," foul air expelled from the detective, followed by a sharp intake and groan.

Ramos stood and walked toward the door. "Get one of the bitches to clean it up. Throw this toe-rag out the back door." He walked to the bar with his son close behind.

Billie, an eager pupil, is impressed by the *grownup's* way of doing business. He asks, "Will he do it?"

"Yeah, he will do it if he has to shoot the bastard himself." Most civilians fold like a soggy bag of chips when you mention their loved ones and rape. "No matter what degree of skank they married, for some reason, the most valuable possession these idiots have is their wife or daughter's pussy. Works every time."

#

Sometimes, the lines were not as clear and a bit more personal.

Rebecca, a Norwegian whore who worked at The Rod, played Carter. He was Carlos' right-hand man, with his easy access to plenty of dosh. So, taken with her *assets,* he forgot the cardinal rule of bad men: remember, your dick is not your brain, so don't try to think with it.

Carter didn't just love her pale pussy. He loved all of her, apparently making plans. Or he was until she gave him herpes.

These bad boys dipped in any hole, and some were pretty nasty. They wore condoms and took their chances. Rebecca assured Carter she had no funk to bother his junk, and he didn't need a condom. Her secret plan was to get pregnant, quit whoring and have Carter care for them. Lying bitch, it was about trust issues.

When Rebecca failed to turn up for work, Carlos figured just another unreliable whore, but his suspicions grew when he overhead Carter at the bar.

"Why do you give a shit what happened to my hand? Maybe I was fist fucking your sister, and it got rough?" Carter snapped.

"He's been shitty all day," Carlos said to Frankie and Tyler throwing back some morning shots nearby.

"You on your period, Carter?" chuckled Frankie. "Sounds like it." Ignoring the insults, Carter continued his pout.

"Thought you were saving the *crown jewels* for your Viking beauty?" said Tyler.

"Who?" Carter's nonchalance fooled no one.

"Rebecca? Oh, so the wedding is off?" goaded Frankie.

"Fuck you," said Carter.

"Cough to it mate, break your heart, did she?"

"Broke my fucking dick, cunt gave me herpes." Frankie and Tyler roared with laughter, and Carter eventually joined them. "My dick exploded; the fucking thing is on fire."

"When can we expect the Norski princess to get her ass back to work?" Carlos's expectations were low, but his ask was serious.

"She's going back to Oslo."

"No doubt," smirked Tyler. "Would the fair Rebecca be in a bin bag or on a plane?"

"How would I know? I was at the clinic getting my dick fixed, wasn't I?"

"And your hand." Added Carlos. They knew Carter beat the hell out of her but didn't know if she was still breathing.

"Fuck you," said Carter.

"Yeah, you already said," replied Frankie.

Tyler switched to managerial mode, "Any of that bitch gonna blowback on Ramos? You better let him know straight up." The men turned as Ramos walked over. He knew these men so well he could read their faces.

"Whose shit's about to irritate me?" he asked without humour. Tyler and Frankie looked at Carter, looking at his hand as Carlos shook his head and walked up the bar.

"She's sort of waiting in the car," mumbled Carter.

"I see." Ramos sighed deeply. In the boot dead, he guessed. "Get it done. Frank, help him out." Ramos was disgusted, and it was evident in his tone. "The bullshit ends by five; we have some actual business today." Ramos threw back a whiskey as the music for the next set of dancers began to pulse, and the hos hit the stage. The life of one more throwaway whore quickly concluded. Taken by bad men and easily forgotten.

Old grudges can linger: Looking down the bar, Carlos spotted a young red-haired man who had been in daily for the last several weeks. He came alone and bought a beer, which he drank slowly. He never bought pussy or even a chat with a fellow aficionado of the pole dance. You see all kinds in a tittie bar. Often, the weirder ones come in the daytime.

The boy surprised him. "You, Carlos?"

"Yeah." The man looked at Carlos like something was on his mind.

I'm Rusty. Remember a woman named Marina?"

"No." Without a moment of thought, Carlos said no because he didn't want to personalize the conversation and because he didn't give a shit about any of the women he knew now or ever knew.

"You sure you don't remember Marina?"

"Yeah. I don't remember the name of any woman, not even my own mother."

"Marina was my mother, and according to her, you're my father."

"She a whore?" Carlos, not the sensitive type, "I only fuck whores."

"She did what she had to do." The anger in his voice failed to rise to the level of danger, but nothing can turn ugly faster than family matters.

"I'm no one's father." Carlos probably fathered children over the years, but none he knew about. "Time for you to leave. Go find Daddy somewhere else." Carlos turned his back to walk away. He heard a scuffle and dropped to the floor in a split second.

"Pump your breaks, asshole," said Frankie, who stood beside the young man asking questions. Frankie's gun jammed in his ribs. Both men ginger appeared in an odd tableau.

Slow and awkward, Rusty fumbled to pull a blade. He froze when Frankie poked him, reached over, and took the knife. "Start stepping, asshole." The man stood and turned to Carlos.

"See ya later, Dad," Rusty said as Frankie walked him to the exit.

Casual gun ownership began drying up, and knife violence in the city was on the rise with punks. On the lookout for business opportunities, Kohl started a gun rental service. Twenty-four hours for five hundred, if fired, a thousand. Ramos men, all with access to guns but rent-a-guns, were usually hired for domestic or workplace disputes, what the Yanks called "*going postal.*"

Carlos returned to the bar and poured two more vodkas, "Janky ass fool."

"Think he'll be back?" Asked Frankie.

"Probably. Let the door know to block red." Carlos sighed deeply. Being the manager of decent clubs should not require combat training, but everyone these days seems to have a grievance. Maybe he wanted money, though he hadn't said.

Frankie would later mention the incident to Tyler. Ramos considered assigning a man to shadow Carlos but knew he would be pissed off. Carlos was once serious muscle and would be offended if Ramos believed he needed to be covered like some bitch.

"Marina, huh?" asked Frankie.

"I can't remember the name of the bitch who blew me in my office thirty minutes ago, and he's twenty or so?"

Dishonest. Carlos remembered Marina as a tremendous fuck with thick red hair. She crushed on him for months. Carlos bet Ramos would remember her. Marina and a tiny blond spinner had a duo act going. They worked together, and both could take a dick. Marina was not doing what she had to do; she was doing what she loved to do.

# # #

CHAPTER 13

GRASS

Ramos expected results on the possible grass sooner, but his hunch to use Billie as bait was spot on. Frankie noticed first.

"Boss, I am not a hundred percent, but a young guy on Ajax crew seems to be rather *enamoured* with Billie."

"How so?" asked Ramos.

"I saw him at the Rod approach Billie and hang a little longer than seemed right. He was leaving when Billie walked in, and he circled back, worked his way close, and ordered rum. Just a hunch."

"On Jax's crew? What's his name?"

"Jaheem. He walks around in a do-rag like thirty years ago and is some Tupac clone. Can't stand the little shit. Maybe I want a reason to gut him?" Frankie smiled.

"After the Rod, I put eyes on him for the last week, and yep, he found his way again. He offered Billie a ride to Surrey. Billie declined."

"Stay on him. Get me a photo."

"Get one today."

Ramos was surprised anyone got by Ajax Ngcobo, one of his most capable men. But the drug business required many foot soldiers and *brothers* on corners. It's impossible to watch them all, all the time.

Ramos didn't tell Frankie, but Billie previously spoke to Tyler about Jaheem. Tyler had taken it to the boss earlier in the day.

⚏⚏

"Guv got one of Jax's hanging a bit too close to Billie. He had a couple of casual meets, but he seems out of place. He has to come across town. The Rod is not handy to his patch. Just sayin," said Tyler.

56

Ramos was pleased Billie noticed the out-of-character character. He followed standard protocol and went to Tyler. Of course, there was a chance Jaheem was just ambitious and trying to move closer to power.

# #

Four hours later, Frankie sent a photo. Face did not register, but it was time to call in a pair of the Filth's finest.

"To what do we owe this summons," said Detective Leon.

"What he means to say is this lucrative summons?" Detective Bonne clarified.

Ignoring both, Ramos pushed a printed photo to the edge of his Tower office desk. "Know him?" Both men shook their heads. "Find out what he was done for. He works product in E6. What's he trading? Get to it and get the fuck out."

Tyler showed them the door and a fat wedge.

After they departed, Ramos picked up a stack of tabloids Rio had delivered. More fucking Baez shit. This time, Marita gave a *virtue-signalling* interview inspired by Harry and Megan, whom she quoted. She hoped to convince Ramos of the importance and urgency of making the clubs and businesses he controls more energy-efficient and eco-friendly. She was worried about Climate Change and their baby boy's future.

Tyler to Ramos, "Sustainable pussy?"

# #

Making the rounds with Dingo, Billie called for a time-out. "I am fucking running on empty let's grab something to eat." He was finishing his second Big Mac when no shit, it was Jaheem walking in. They were on the outskirts of Baylor near Ribizzi's garage, a long fucking way from E6.

Billie and Dingo exchanged looks and went quiet. "Hey, Billie, and uh, you're Dingo, right?" Jaheem threw a wide, toothy smile.

"What are you doing out here?" asks Dingo.

"Uh, my nana lives nearby," A weak ass reply. There was no chance his Gran lived in this upscale area.

"Nice area. Nana must be doing well," said Billie.

Jaheem realized his mistake. "She lives with a rich old lady. Cleans for her and stuff."

"Stuff?" Billie and Dingo were not buying it, and Jaheem could feel the tension.

"Oh, I better get in line. I am hungry as hell." Jaheem walked away.

Ramos's plan was coming together, but there was still no proof Jaheem had done anything wrong. His next move was a sit-down with Ajax.

# #

"Boss, I tried to get here earlier, but Customs delayed the shipment in Tilbury, and the fucking dockworkers wanted double to unload. I was there when you texted."

"Pour yourself a whiskey and tell me about Jaheem."

"Jaheem? How the fuck did that toe-rag come to your attention?"

"He is grooming Billie. I believe he's a grass."

"Whoa. I've not had any issues. Business in E6 is going along smoothly, *keeping it blessed*. Any details?"

"Yeah," Ramos pushed a sealed arrest warrant across his desk. "The Detectives came through. Jaheem was busted on the 7th. All I need to know is what he is trading?"

"Pushes small weight; he doesn't know much. He did have a bust-up with one of the other shits. I moved him to another location. Maybe he got sloppy or hum? What do you want me to do?"

"Have another whiskey. Frankie is bringing him in." Ajax took a long pull and sat back." Twenty minutes later, Rio buzzed up from the War Room.

"Bag him," cover his head, said Ramos.

"Already is," said Rio. "He's jumpy as hell. Don't know if he is on something or just ready to shit himself?"

"Bring him up."

# #

Rio pushed Jaheem through the door, and he stumbled into the desk. "Jaheem, tell the boss about your chats with the Filth. Remember, you have one chance to get this right before you make the biggest and last mistake of your punk-ass life. You clear?" said Tyler.

Jaheem nodded his head. "I, I didn't tell um anything. No. Well, nothing important. I told them I would help, but I didn't. Not yet. Honest. I don't know anything." He fidgeted so wildly that he looked like he was doing a hip-hop rain dance.

Ramos was about to crank up the pressure when Miles Kohl walked in. Miles was one of the twins, the youngest children of the late John Kohl. Both Miles and Nathan were morons. Nathan was now on extended life support after crashing his Lambo.

Miles, when not in rehab for his persistent love of heroin, would occasionally wander into a business meeting and fuck it up.

"Get the hell out," shouted Ramos as Frankie stood between Miles and the business at hand.

"Fuck you, Ramos. The Tower is my building." Miles's attempt at being a big shot was far off the mark. When he said Ramos' name and the Tower, he effectively killed the punk with the sack over his head.

"Ok, what can I do for you, Miles?" Ramos was seething.

"I want some cash. Twenty thousand should do," the smug idiot was clueless, but Ramos would do as John Kohl had done. Give him money, send him on his way, and return to business. Ramos nodded to Frankie. The men knew there was cash in the safe in the War Room. Frankie knew the combination; all of Ramos's top men did. Quick access to money was essential in an all-cash business.

"Downstairs," said Frankie to Miles. "Shall we?" He motioned to the door. The man whose head was bagged thought he meant for him to go and turned, and when he did, Rio laid one in his gut, and he doubled over.

The whole thing was fucked up, and Ramos expected nothing more from Jaheem when the bagged man spoke up. "They wanted me to work with K-man, and he is the one who told me to be friends with Billie."

It was potentially helpful information. "K-man? Who the fuck is K-man?"

"Kamal. Kamal works for Jax-man, but…" said Jaheem.

"If you say *man* again, I will cut your fucking tongue out. Where can I find Kamal?"

"He works at the NatWest on Rain Street. Can I take this thing off my head? It's hot and…," Ramos signalled Rio, who removed the sack.

The information was an unexpected twist. "A banker. You sure?"

"Yeah, I met him there a couple of times. He dress dope." Jaheem seemed to relax, believing he had given them something important and would now be safe.

"You're sure you never gave him any information at all?" Ramos was unconvinced.

"No, I was told to give him the money. You know, from my area and get close to Billie. I told him Billie didn't seem to like me, and maybe it would not happen?"

"Did you have a special account to put the money in? Or what?"

"Jax-ma, I mean Jax, the boss told me to give him the paper."

"What paper?"

"The account numbers."

"What account? Who?"

"Don't know for sure, but I think it's the hair place. Uh, can I have a bottle of water?" The men chuckled. This idiot did not realize he was about to die.

"Take him next door."

Jaheem instantly looked panicked when he saw Ajax sitting in a chair behind him. "That was the truth. I don't know nothing else." Ramos gave a head jerk, and Rio took the punk's arm and led him from the room.

"Let's get you some water," said Rio with a grin.

Ramos used hair, nail, and tanning salons, laundromats, pet groomers, and other small businesses across the city to clean money. This twist was about the case the Crown Prosecution was building, not some low-level drug deals. Marita told him their goal was to expand from bribery and money laundering to tax evasion. The Filth found that a paper trail was *golden* for seizing the assets of villains.

Ramos wondered if the Filth had plants in banks everywhere. How widespread was it? He did not need Jaheem for the information. It was too bad Miles opened his fucking mouth. Now the nobody Tupac wannabe snitch had to go.

# # #

## CHAPTER 14

FULL ENGLISH

"That fucker took his time dying," snorted Frankie.

"Inconsiderate bastard, I'm hungry." laughed Cody as he wiped the blood from his hands and tossed the rag into the furnace with the body. "Light him up." Frankie threw a match in and slammed the metal door. "Let's get something to eat."

"First, let me get some money to Gran." Said Frankie. Cody shook his head. All the men have heard endless stories of Frankie's Gran. He left her in Ireland and sent her cash every week. She raised him in Belfast after his parents died.

Frankie didn't drink because when he was fifteen, he made a bargain with God to save her. Gran was still going, as was the oath. A 6'3 ginger always caused a chuckle when he went into a tittie bar and ordered a grape Ribena.

Cody waited in the car in front of the Post Office. He intended to watch PornHub but was thirsty and spotted an Asian market. He returned to the Range Rover as a fat *Boot-Bastard* was clamping it. "Oi, stop." Shouted Cody.

"Too late, Thor," with a sneering reference to Cody's swole-ass frame. "Or you could try to tear it off with your bare hands." The clamper had heard every story, every excuse, and was immune. He took particular pleasure in clamping rich guys or tough guys.

"Hey, maybe we can work this out? How much will it cost me?" Cody held out two hundred. The clamper just chuckled. Sometimes, he did take the money, but Cody is a good-looking hunk who always gets the girls, and the clamper wanted to be in the power position just this once.

"No chance." He held the paperwork out. "Should be able to get it tomorrow or the next day." He started to return to his truck when Frankie walked up and stuck his weapon right in the folds of tubbies back.

"Unlock the fucking thing," said Frank. When the clamper hesitated, Frankie surprised the man by grabbing his wallet and then pushing him hard. "What do you say Cody? We visit the Brown family at Anstey House in lovely Hackney?" Frank was reading from the fatties' license.

"Sure, bet his wife is real pretty and friendly."

Cody and Frank were a formidable pair, and the clamper was beginning to get the message and rethink his position. "Ok," friendly now, "I could use the two hundred."

"Shit-for-brains, it's too late for that. Get the fucking thing off."

Frank tossed the driver's license on the pavement as they drove away. Cody had to give him the piss. "Your girlfriend working?" Frankie had taken to going to only one post office and waiting in line for the same girl each time. They had a few brief conversations, but the men said the big Irishman was *falling in love*.

"Yeah. What gave it away, my fecken boner? Or I did have one before your street buddy."

"Is she still saying no? Resisting your Celtic charm?"

"Naw, she loves me, just playing hard to get." Winnie was a petite girl from mainland China, and Frankie was smitten. At least to the extent a brutal killer can crush.

"Why not grab her on her way home and fuck her blind?"

"You're a pig, but it's not a bad idea." Frankie laughed as Cody parked the Range Rover at a small café with six tables, checked plastic tablecloths, and Breakfast All Day sign in the window. It said take-out only, and they were surprised to see someone seated. These small places were struggling back from COVID.

"Hello, ladies. Can we join you?" said Frankie, walking into the mostly empty café, except for one table with a young woman sitting with a cup of tea and a pretty young waitress chatting.

"It's almost closing time. Do you know what you want?"

Cody slid into the booth next to the seated girl. "Looking at you, I do." She glanced across the table at her friend and rolled her eyes as Frankie sat. The waitress, whose name tag read Kelsey, just shrugged.

"You pretty ladies allow us to buy your breakfast?"

"It's 3:45, a little past breakfast," giggled the girl next to Cody.

"Now, it would depend on what time you get up," said Frankie, looking up at the waitress.

"Don't you have to get to work?" asked the server as she poured two cups of coffee.

Cody and Frankie looked at each other. "Sure."

"What do you girls do?" asked Frankie.

"I'm a student. In four months and three weeks, I'll be a nurse."

"Me? The pinny and the coffee pot in my hand didn't give it away?" a sassy one. "I'm a waitress, but I plan to be rich and famous." They laughed, and Frankie patted the seat next to him. Kelsey joined them.

"How do you plan to do it?" asked Frankie.

"Not sure yet? Invent an app, rob a bank, or who knows?"

"Make a sex tape. It worked for Kardashian and Paris Hilton," said Cody.

"It may come to that, but in the meantime, I am working on my certification in medical coding."

"What about you two? You sleep late. You must work nights?" Asked Bree.

Frankie decided to play, "We're gangsters; we make our own hours."

"Sure, you are," said Kelsey. "Or maybe sad and unemployed?"

"Don't buy gangster, huh?" Said Frankie.

"Real badasses; probably already killed someone today," laughed Kelsey.

"Can't get by you." Said Cody as he glanced at Frank.

"You're hunky and fit. Are you personal trainers?"

"Yeah, you got something that needs training?"

Bree is getting flirty. "What is your area of specialty? Yoga, weights, cardio, hum?"

"Pussy." Said Frankie as both girls went quiet, then burst into laughter.

"I take it you are not a veterinarian?" said Kelsey.

"Or gynaecologists?"

"Ok, what are you having? Julio is about to leave, and you don't want my cooking."

"That right?"

"Full English," said Cody, and Frankie nodded in agreement.

"Julio, two Big Boys." The waitress shouted as she moved to lock the door and turn the sign to Closed.

"You lock us in? Should we be scared?" said Frankie.

"No, only be nervous if we drag you to the storage room." Said Bree. The girls looked toward a door labelled storage and laughed.

"Hey, a couple of tough-guy gangsters are afraid of a flimsy lock? I don't buy it," said Kelsey.

"Me either. Though I must admit you two don't look like choir boys."

The men ate their grub as Julio and the dishwasher exited the café. Only the four remained.

"Ladies," Frankie wiped his mouth and finished his coffee. "Ladies, how about you giving us a tour of the storage room?"

The girls laughed. "Do we look like the kind of girls who would just say yes?"

"Do we look like the kind of men who would let you say no?" Both men relaxed, but the question was direct and challenging. Bree, the soon-to-be nurse, looked anxious and tried to stand. Cody pulled her back into her chair.

"Hey, where you going?"

"Let's go, Kelsey." Said Bree.

"No need to rush away. Let's have some fun."

The men could see Kelsey was cautious but interested. She tried sounding casual. "The storage room is pretty small, and you two are big. Not sure there is room to party."

"Let's check and see. Cody stood, took Bree's arm, and pulled her toward the storage room.

"Please stop. Really, please. We were just flirting." Said Bree.

"Tell you what. Let's see. If you aren't having fun, I'll stop. OK?" Cody, a good-looking thug, gave her a broad, friendly smile.

Going through the storage area door, the only place in the café with no windows. Bree felt frantic and tried one more thing. "I'm on my period."

"That's why god invented blow jobs." Cody shoved her to her knees as Frankie pushed Kelsey through the door to join them. The storage room was not tiny more than enough room for a fuck.

Kelsey could see Bree was teary, but instead, she felt feisty. "Boy, do I have rotten taste in men? I was liking you."

"You're making me feel all warm and cuddly." Frankie pulled his dick.

"Oh no, you have a better chance of getting struck by lightning than a blow job from me," said Kelsey.

"Is that right," asked Frankie with a huge grin. "Tell you what, I am not an animal. You get to pick a fuck or a blowjob."

Kelsey started to fight him, but when he loosened his pants, she saw his gun. Franke caught her eyes as she flinched. "Told you I was a bad guy," he laughed but held her arm tightly. "Come on, honey, make your choice, or I will? He asked as he pushed her to her knees.

"Looks like you already did."

"Open wide. Lightning is about to strike." He pushed her head on his hard cock. "Don't worry about the gun. Distract me."

Both girls were smart enough to know that fighting these two beasts was not an option. Both girls hoped just a blow was all they wanted and would not hurt them further.

When the men finished, they laughed out loud. "Ladies, you have brightened our day."

"Remember in the future," said Frankie, "If a man tells you he's a bad guy, you might wanna run like hell."

Both girls were getting to their feet. Bree was teary and wiped her mouth on her sleeve. "You aren't gangsters; you're rapists." She looked satisfied with her retort.

"And thieves. You owe twenty-three for the food," said Kelsey.

Frankie and Cody reached in their pockets, and each pulled a few hundred and tossed it on a crate of tinned beans. "Satisfied customers."

The men walked toward the door laughing. Picking up a bottle of HP sauce, Kelsey hurled it, striking Frankie in the back of his arm. Without slowing or looking back, he said, "Yeah, me too Beautiful; I'll call ya."

# # #

CHAPTER 15

LINDSEY

"Yeah?" said Dingo from the War Room. It was uncommon, but someone just rang the JKE, John Kohl Enterprises bell from the Tower public lobby. Rare because few knew it existed. Next to the buzzer was a discreet but threatening notice. *Absolutely Do Not Disturb. It is a violation unless you have a Scheduled Appointment. CCTV in operation.* A violation of what?

John Kohl agreed to create retail and public space on the ground floor to get the seven-story Tower built in Belgravia. The ground floor contained a lobby atrium area, a small bank branch, a dry cleaner, a Kohl betting shop, and a Kohl Coffee café.

Few people who patronized the commercial businesses knew what happened above or below. However, the relentless tabloid reference to the Tower made the place more well-known. Today, a pretty young woman in a modest dress rang the bell at the lift area.

"Hello, I am Lindsey Evans, and I am here to see Mr. Santiago."

"You have an appointment?" asked Dingo.

"No, but please, can I see him?"

"No." Dingo hung up. He took a closer look at the monitor. She looked harmless but unlikely to have any business with Ramos. The bell buzzed again.

"Don't hang up. I need to see Mr. Ramos about Nathan." She hoped using the name of a Kohl would help her gain entry.

"Stay there." Dingo was unsure but thought he better run it by Tyler, who was up in the third-floor offices. Dingo explained, and Tyler cranked on the monitor. The girl looked about twenty and was a civilian.

"Boss, a little cutie wants to see you about Nathan." Ramos looked up from his work.

"Nathan?" One of Sir John Kohl's twin sons. He has been on life support for the last sixteen months. Anyone else would have pulled the plug following his car wreck, but twin brother Miles wanted to keep him going. He was on a machine in a third-floor bedroom under twenty-four-hour care.

Ramos set up, rotated his neck, and stretched his back. "Bring her up."

# #

Dingo escorted the young woman into Ramos's office, where Tyler sat in an oversized leather chair with a whiskey in hand. It was ten in the morning.

"Hello," she spoke softly. She knew he was Ramos because his picture appeared almost daily in the press. "I'm Lindsey." Her face was naturally pretty, as was her soft brown hair. Her dress was simple and modest but attractive.

"What can I do for you, Lindsey?" It was fucking historic for Ramos to allow a stranger to step into his life; Tyler and Dingo were curious. Dingo got a head tilt from Tyler and was dismissed.

"I am a friend of Nathan Kohl. I was. He used to be my boyfriend." Ramos remained silent, and she went on. "I know he was hurt. I called Miles right after it happened, but he said I couldn't see him." She was nervous but did not seem afraid. "He told me to go away."

"I was Nathan's girlfriend." Her use of the words boyfriend and girlfriend sounded naïve to men like Ramos and Tyler. He assumed she wanted money, but she didn't go there.

"Where did you meet Nathan?" Miles and Nathan spent their lives drunk, stoned, fucking whores, and always closely guarded. This gentle girl did not fit the environment.

"I was a receptionist in his Dentist's office. I was studying to be a Dental Hygienist. We started going out. On my birthday, he bought champagne, and well, we ended up, you know, together. In bed." She seemed embarrassed. "After that, we did it a lot." She was no whore, and Ramos was unsure what the visit was about?

"I got pregnant." Here comes the ask for money determined Ramos and Tyler. "When I told Nathan, he said he could not marry me, and I could not keep the baby because he and his brother Miles made a pact that neither would marry nor have children." It rang true to Ramos, though he had not previously heard it.

"I see," said Ramos.

"I don't believe in abortions, so I moved to Shropshire. I have an elderly aunt there or did. She died." She stood calmly before his massive desk and smoothed her unwrinkled skirt.

"Where's the baby?" Ramos asked.

"Our baby died before he was born. A boy."

"I was working at a bakery and Tea Shop in Shropshire. The man who owned the bakery was Larry. He was gay. He told me his parents were giving him a hard time about not being settled down and married. He proposed that, while I was still pregnant, we get married, and I would have a job and a place to live and might be able to return to my Dental Hygienist program. He could have his gay lifestyle, but his parents would be satisfied. It seemed to solve a lot of problems."

"Not all of them?" said Ramos, who remained skeptical.

"No. Last week, Larry was walking home from the Pub, and he fell into the Severn and drowned. I guess he had too much to drink. The police said it looked like he had been hit by a car and stumbled in the river. I was asleep in my room at home and didn't know anything about it. He was a good friend to me." Her eyes were glassy.

"Two days ago was the funeral. Larry's parents handled things. When I got home, I walked in, and everything in our apartment was gone. Everything. Clothes, furniture, even the toilet roll." Ramos would not be surprised at what came next. It seemed Larry owed someone money. It was likely no accident Larry ended up taking a swim.

"There was a letter on the kitchen counter. It said: The date. Ten PM, The Chambers, and ask for Hirsch. I didn't know what it meant. I googled The Chambers on my phone. It's an adult establishment near Manchester.

I was exhausted and didn't feel like going, but I thought they might have information on what happened to the contents. I went." She looked up to see if she should keep going. She was agitated, and her hands were fidgety.

"It was a horrible, sinister place. People were drinking, and the women were almost naked." Ramos and Tyler exchanged glances. "With Covid, I was surprised it was open. I told the man at the door that I was there to see Hirsh. He let me in and told me to go to the office." She seemed to be slowing down.

"The whole place was scary inside. You could hear people making awful noises; it was dark and smelly. I knocked on the office door, and a large man opened it. Inside, behind a desk, Hirsch said you must be Lindsey?" She was about to cry, but Ramos could not see what all of it had to do with him or any Kohl.

"He told me Larry owed him fifteen thousand Pounds, and now I did. He didn't show me any documents or proof, but I was too afraid to ask. I told him I didn't have any money, but I could possibly sell the bakery, and he said he already owned the bakery. He didn't show me any proof of that either."

Ramos knew there was rarely a paper trail in the world of underground loans. "Hirsh said I have to work for him until he's paid. He means, you know?"

"Lindsey, what is it you believe I might do for you? Why are you here?" This is your one chance, little girl. It doesn't hurt to ask.

"Because I couldn't think of anything else. Hirsch told me I have to start Friday, tomorrow. He stood up and opened his pants, as did the other two men." She was crying softly and began to tremble. "When he was finished, he, he…." She pushed up her sleeve and showed where she had been burnt. Probably a cigar. "He said if I wanted to run," her voice was catching, "to look at my arm and know he would find me."

Ramos was not a man with an open and generous heart, and her problems were not his. "I would work for you any way you wanted. I am just too frightened to go back there. Nathan told me he had known you his whole life." Ramos had been at John Kohl's side when he delivered his twin sons on the Tower garage floor when their mother, Ann Kohl, failed to leave for the hospital in time.

Tyler was surprised when Ramos didn't tell her to get lost. Taking a deep breath, Ramos ran his palm across his lower face, "I'll have a couple of my men drive you up to Chambers and pay off Hirsch tonight. This is not a gift. You now owe me twenty-five. You will work in my club, The Lightning Rod. No one will hurt you, but you will fuck and suck until I am paid. Is that clear?" Her head was low, but she nodded her reply.

Ramos turned to Tyler as if she wasn't there. "Give it to Frank and Billie."

Tyler stood and led Lindsey from the room. Before she cleared the door, she softly said, "Thank you."

⚜ ⚜

Frankie, Billie, and Lindsey were cruising up the M6 and heading for The Chambers, which the men knew was a rough sex club and pain-cave on the outskirts of Manchester. Eli Hirsch, a purveyor of perversion and a last-chance money lender, owned it. Lindsey was right to be frightened of him. More than a few women walked through the Chambers' doors and vanished.

Still unused to the *silent hard man* type, Billie started to gab. Lindsey was grateful. "I've never been to Shropshire," he said.

"It is a charming town with a hint of Welsh." She looked toward Frankie. "You have an Irish accent. Are you from Ireland?"

Typically, Frankie was ready to tell anyone about the attributes of the emerald isle, but he was miffed at this crap transport job which put him in a cranky disposition. He and Rio planned an evening with a couple of freaky bitches, and now that wasn't happening. "Belfast."

It was clear Frankie was not in a chatty mood. Usually, a delivery job was way below his pay grade. However, Ramos knew Hirsch would not let him take a *sweet treat* like Lindsey without a fight. Or at the very least, without some financial negotiation. Ramos would also run this by Manchester's top Face. He was not looking to start a war over one bitch and would use the connection to Kohl's son to establish his rights. There was no chance Hirsch was operating without *supervision* from above.

"Anyone hungry or thirsty?" Asked Billie. Frankie looked at his watch and wanted to keep going. They would drive back later, making for a long fucking night.

"I could use a bathroom," Lindsey admitted.

"It's not far. We'll keep going." Said Frankie, the shot-caller of the situation.

She spoke up, "I know this road pretty well. It's an hour and a half at least. Honestly, I'm not sure I can wait." Lindsey was sheepish, but a *girl gotta do what a girl gotta do*.

Frankie sighed and pulled off at the next town. Driving by a McDonalds and a Harvester, he stopped on the gravel in front of a dimly lit bar: The Tit-4-Tat. "A bit of refreshment it is."

Except for her brief visit to The Chambers, Lindsey had never been to a sex club. It all looked distasteful, but she was not frightened with the two big men escorting her. "Do we need masks?" She asked. Frankie didn't bother with a reply.

The place was smoky from machines as the pulsing ostinato of the dancers' tunes banged on, and nearly naked zombie women twirled slowly around greasy poles. Lindsey put her hand on Frankie as he pointed to a sign with an arrow: *Bitches*. "Do you think it will be clean in there?" She was hesitant.

"I positively guarantee it will not. We'll be at the bar."

# #

"Where the hell did she come from?" asked Billie.

"She was fucking Nathan," said Frankie, draining a second cold Guinness.

"Yeah? She doesn't look like she has ever been fucked."

Frankie grabbed the ass of a bitch who was making herself known. He gave a quick head nod to Billie and walked off, presumably for a quick fuck. Billie thought it was an excellent idea; Frankie had been grumpy the whole trip.

Lindsey approached the bar, trying not to notice what was happening around her as Frankie returned. "Thank you for stopping. Oh, and you were right. It was ghastly."

"You want anything," asked Billie.

"I'll have water. Wait, maybe a Sauvignon Blanc," she needed to relax and hoped the wine would do it.

"White or red, large or small." Frankie laid out the options.

"Oh, a small white, please." She reached in her handbag for a plastic bottle. "Anyone need hand sanitizer?" It gave Billie and even Frankie, whose mood had improved, a good chuckle.

# #

They made it back to Surrey by sunup. Billie took Lindsey to a guest house near the pool. "Stay inside until I come to get you." She nodded. Billie did not want to explain to his mother what she was doing there.

# #

The men were told to deliver her to The Rod and Carlos. Pulling into the club at about three, they were surprised to see Ramos's car with Dingo wiping the side mirror. Outside, the club seemed closed, but that was the

Covid restrictions and not what was happening inside. Boris or a deadly virus cannot stop man's natural unrelenting quest for pussy.

"Home Sweet Home," said Frankie as they headed inside. The Rod was where Lindsey would work off her debt. She would not allow herself to guess how long it might take. She reminded herself it was a much better place than The Chambers or the horrible place they stopped at last night. By comparison, the Rod was clean and fresh.

Lindsey stood shyly at the bar as Frankie and Billie had drinks. They stopped on the way over for a quick breakfast, and she figured she was about to begin her first day as a prostitute. She felt her eyes water and looked away. Her dream of being a Dental Hygienist seemed to mock her.

Time dragged, and the men had more to drink. Ramos and Tyler exited the office twenty minutes later, followed by Carlos. Ramos and Tyler walked right by without a word. Carlos stopped, "Looks like we have a Bambi."

Bambi was Alice's whore name years ago; when desperate for money to care for her young twin sons, she walked into the Rod and asked for work. Ramos was there that day and called her Bambi due to the frightened look in her eyes. The name stuck for her four months and three days of employment. Sometimes, life puts you in an untenable place, and difficult choices must be made.

When Ramos heard Carlos say "Bambi," he stopped abruptly, returned to the bar, and grabbed Lindsey's shoulder. "Come with me. I have a different job for you." Alice was too sweet for sex work, as was Lindsey Evans. Ramos was not planning to save the world, but he could save Bambi.

⚜ ⚜

Ramos delivered Lindsey to the Tower's fifth floor and introduced her to Julie as her new helper. Julie did not need additional help, but Lindsey looked near her age and sweet, and Julie was always lonely. Ramos instructed Lindsey to keep her mouth shut about knowing Miles and Nathan and how she came to work for him. In a short time, Lindsey replaced Annie's nanny and became a companion to Julie. It took her several months to quit asking Julie what she wanted her to do. All Julie really wanted was a friend, and Lindsey needed one too.

⚜ ⚜ ⚜

CHAPTER 16

Q&A

Ramos and Jimmy were in the third-floor Tower office. The paperwork was endless. Ramos was happy, when at all possible, to leave it in the capable hands of his chief of staff.

"Business is good. Too good," said Redmond. "We have vaults filled with cash, and with inflation, it is more than ever." He shook his head as if this was a bad thing. "The foundation is exploding. Probably should move a big chunk fairly soon."

"Julie is not up to a public appearance. Though Alice tells me she is improving." Now that Johnnie was no longer around to juice and fuck her, the girl had a chance.

"What about Alice laying some paper?" asked Jimmy. "Take some of your many children; it would make for a positive photo op."

"No chance. Alice prefers the shadows."

"We have to distribute money soon, or the tax bastards will start to take notice."

"How much?" asked Ramos.

"Ten Million."

The amount made Ramos laugh. Pointing at three huge duffles of cash on the office floor, "Have a couple of the men take that up to the roof terrace and start throwing it to the wind."

"Sounds fun, but too in your face. Shall I just write a check for ten to the Children's Hospital? You will need to present the check." Both men knew a bit of positive PR was much needed about now.

"Sure." The problem of philanthropy is resolved. "Anything else on the agenda?" Jimmy replied by shaking his head and putting paperwork in his briefcase.

After Jimmy departed, Ramos looked with disgust at the stack of Tabloids on his desk. He attempted to pay little regard to the Gangster & Detective stories; after all, he had a vast fucking business empire to manage.

However, today's new twist demanded attention. It's a cliché, but Ramos is a *man-of-action*. Currently, he is unable to take any regarding Marita, and his frustration level is being tested. After reading the latest tabloid installment, he wanted to beat the hell out of someone. Starting with Marita, but anyone would do.

Marita Baez's supposed half-sister had arrived from Lisbon, doing photo shoots and giving interviews freely to the press. "I would love to meet Ramos Santiago, my sister's future husband. I have to look after her. I understand he is rich and famous, which does not intimidate me, but I want to ask him some important questions and get some promises."

When asked what questions, "First, I want proof that he is getting a divorce. I also want to know what steps he is taking to ensure her financial security, a will, and homes in her name. I may sound cold, but Marita is too much in love to ask and needs to be practical when she is about to give him a son."

Boomer had the misfortune of entering Ramos's office just as the boss picked up a bottle of whiskey from his desk and threw it at the door. Blessed with the swift reflexes of youth, Boomer swerved his face and deflected the bottle before it crashed to the floor.

Not one for sorry, and oops, Ramos roared, "Fuck!" He grabbed his massive mahogany desk and flipped it over.

In a few hours, he had a meeting with a slimy invertebrate politician, never a happily anticipated event. First, he needed to clear his head. Two things came to mind; a fuck or the gym? He was at the Tower office, so the gym was nearby, and the fuck wasn't. Decision made.

# #

When Ramos entered the gym, it was buzzing. It was clear what their topic of discussion was when the chatter came to a halt. "Ok, ladies, which one of you wants the chance to beat the hell out of the boss." He reached for a pair of boxing gloves.

The boss is a fucking beast. Even with a couple of decades on the girls, he is challenging to beat when in a good mood. No one rushed to join him when he was not a *happy-camper.*

Billie and Frankie were late arrivals. Rio tossed a pair of gloves at Frankie. "You're up."

"First, I need to take a shit." He tossed the gloves to Billie and then headed to the loo.

"What is it with you, Frank? You're always off to take a piss or a shit?" asked Rio. "Is this some kind of Irish thing?"

"Blow me," said Frankie as he departed the gym.

"Boss, is this for money or fun?" Wearing a big smile, Billie held the gloves but had no time to sense the mood and read the room.

Ramos dropped his gloves to the floor and headed to the door. "Neither; the Dorchester. Come with me."

#

"What the fuck just happened," asked Rio?

"Probably doesn't want to bloody his kid."

"No, I think he wants to relax and figures a fuck is better than a beat-down."

"A fuck is always better than a beat down?" laughed Boomer.

"Hell, I want to go to the Dorchester."

"Yeah, well, don't get your dick excited. You're heading to Shoreditch with me to torch a derelict Blockbuster Video."

"Ok. It's not far from the Boobytrap. Let's hit that blond bitch with no teeth."

"Dibs, I'm first."

"First? My nigga, you need to be there by sun up to be first." The men laughed as they departed for the evening's work.

#

Billie had fucked alongside his dad numerous times but not at the Dorchester. As far as he knew, no one else did, except possibly Tyler. Jet was driving, and Billie wasn't sure if he would be the man on the door or what.

Ramos glanced at Billie. "Get Odette and Zuri over," two of Smoke Escorts' finest. He did not usually care which woman he fucked. All top pros and a paid-for service, nothing more, but he was in the mood for something different. These two beauties had been away on a yacht for a few weeks with Smoke clients. Ramos closed his eyes and made no further conversation on the 20-minute ride to the hotel.

#

Ramos was a formidable presence even in a place as luxurious and used to celebrity as The Dorchester. He is an enormous, fit man in a seven-thousand-pound bespoke suit and right now probably the most famous man in all of England. Billie followed Ramos inside and joined him as they sat in plush chairs in the Promenade, a first for Billie. A formally dressed waiter brought Ramos his usual whiskey without being asked and did not offer anything to Billie because the men never joined in unless it was Tyler.

Ramos took a long pull on the warm whiskey and leaned his head back in exhaustion. After a few deep breaths, he asked, "How is your mother doing?" He had never before asked Billie about her.

"I don't know. Mum says she's okay and not to worry, but she looks tired and real skinny." Billie hoped honesty was what his dad wanted. "Told me your dad won't let anything happen to our family." He hoped what his mum said was true.

Ramos sat up and looked at his son. "This will all be over. Give it some time." The same line he had been giving Alice, but even to Ramos, it was beginning to wear thin.

Zuri and Odette arrived, and every dick went on point as they passed through the lobby. These were stunning women who knew their job. They did not look at Ramos and instead went to the lift and headed to the familiar suite Ramos kept for fucking.

Billie was anxious; he was not sure what he was supposed to do. Being here was a significant upgrade. When Ramos stood, Billie followed him to the elevator. Billie tried to look cool as they approached the suite's double doors, but his heart was thumping.

Jet stood sentry and let the women in after a security check. He gave the boss a brief nod and moved to open the door.

"Out front," said Ramos, relieving Jet of his custodial duties. He was mindful of not allowing the crew to believe his son got special treatment. Billie would be on the door and not going inside.

Billie spoke up. "Dad, those are a couple of fierce women in there. You need backup; let me know."

It gave Ramos a much-needed laugh. "Will do."

# # #

CHAPTER 17

COWARD

It had been a while. Ramos walked into the massive kitchen of his Surry home wearing not his usual dark bespoke Saville row suits but black cargo pants, a tight black T-shirt, and a black leather jacket. The wardrobe of his crew and his attire before his move to full-blown Face. It had been a rough, hands-on night. Earlier, he beat to death a Bulgarian shit-bag who pushed him too far. Alice looked up and seemed not to notice the blood.

"Who are you?" she asked. "If you plan to rape me, you better get busy, my husband is due home soon."

"Don't you usually feed him first?" said Ramos.

"Like that is it?" She laughed and reached for a whiskey bottle and refilled her glass.

"Rough day?" he asked. He found her in her nightie, standing at the island, having a whiskey, a first. Alice was not a drinker and was still nursing Sunny.

"Looking for some courage," she blew hairs from her eyes. Then she raised the bottle and looked inside, "how far down do I need to go?" Laughing at herself, she clumsily set the bottle down.

"The girls and I planted tomatoes, and Stella found a worm. All three girls were crying and hysterical. It took ages to calm them down." Alice was rambling. "They felt frightened and helpless. I'm not sure I'll ever get them back in the garden?"

"Why are men and women so different?" She paused as if pondering her question. "It isn't fair. We're always afraid, and you're not?" It was a one-sided conversation, but it usually was with her husband.

Ramos knew women were wise to be fearful. Men held power and might. Clever women found a man to protect them, trading their freedom for safety. Men were inclined to abuse their power. Especially weak men in an attempt to feel and appear strong.

"What's up?" This wasn't about worms. He wasn't much for feelings or conversation but made a slight effort since the Baez story broke.

"You probably don't know what it feels like to be a coward?" said Alice. "Are you ever afraid? You know, like wetting your knickers because there are so many frightening things."

The whiskey must be kicking in; she was in *danger* of making him laugh out loud. "You work so much at night." She felt he was constantly in danger but never seemed afraid. It puzzled her.

"Am I afraid of the dark?" Bad men used the fears of others to their advantage. "No."

"A lot of bad things happen at night." Derrick, the man who raped her, entered her room in the dark.

Ramos knew many bad things happen at night but spoke to lighten the conversation. "You mean monsters under the bed?"

Alice chuckled. "Even with those big gates and men out there, I want to be home with locked doors and lights on when it's dark outside."

"I noticed." Ramos discreetly watched her nocturnal behaviour. It was rare for her to leave the sanctuary of their home and exceptional to do so after dark. She made it easy for him.

"I bet you think you get to win every battle just because you're big and scary?" That's pretty much how it works, he thought. "I'm not afraid of you."

Ramos grinned, "Is that right?"

"Know why?" Showing bravado, she took another drink. "Because you've protected me since the first day at the market. You spend a lot of money on our security, and you wouldn't do that if you didn't want me to be safe." She seemed proud of her reasoning.

"I know you wouldn't hurt me." She leaned in and whispered conspiratorially. "I might be the only person in London who can say that." Despite her long and winding explanation, Ramos was still baffled about where she was going with all this, but he didn't want her to be afraid of him.

Suddenly changing course, her eyes filled with worry. "I'm not scared of you, but I'm scared." She took another drink.

"Of what?" Ramos reached for the whiskey and poured a large one.

"Being on my own again." She shook her head. "I'm not very good at it." Alice lifted her glass and took another deep swallow she didn't seem to enjoy. Her eyes were glassy as she refilled. She was not a drinker. Ramos knew that tomorrow, she would feel like hell.

"The girls and I will leave when you say. I'll sign whatever you want." She took another drink and seemed to struggle to swallow. "I didn't have to say that, did I? Everyone does what you want."

"I don't want you to go to prison. I have to step aside." She swept her arm in an exaggerated gesture. "I'm going to miss you. Are you going to miss me? Wait, don't answer that." She slapped her hand over her mouth as if she feared what else might escape.

"You didn't know it, but I fell in love with you at the *world-famous* Lightning Rod." In dire circumstances, when Alice had worked as a club whore is where she first became aware of Ramos Santiago. "Everyone looked up to you to lead and protect them. I wanted that too. You walked around so big and confident. I thought any woman you cared for didn't have to be afraid every minute of every day. I was right."

She laughed, "Our magnificent love affair was entirely one-sided. You didn't even know I existed." She giggled. "I probably would have been terrified if you had." She chuckled and took another drink.

"I left the Rod, but I thought about you a thousand times over the months. Then one day, when I was standing in a shabby market, I looked up, and there you were."

She slapped her hand over her heart. "Wow." Alice had a huge, silly smile. "At that very moment, I knew I was crazy in love with you. I still am. She raised her glass, and her wedding ring caught her eye. Pretty sloshed, she kissed her wedding ring with a big smack.

Ramos reached for another whiskey. He remembered the day in the market. She looked at him like he was the most handsome man in the world. He wasn't. He was a big, rough beast of a man, but the look on her face stayed with him.

At The Rod, he knew she existed and did not belong there. Even then, he did subtle things to protect her. Like making sure his men knew he thought anyone who fucked her would be a pussy in his eyes. It worked. None of his hard fucker men approached her.

"Did you ever fall in love, Ramos? Even a long, long time ago?"

Surprising her, "Yeah. I was fourteen; she was an older woman."

There was more to the story. At school in Orlando, he ran a loan shark business. Even at fourteen, he was a big dude, and rarely did anyone not pay up. Once, when a rich white jerk was seriously past due, and Ramos told him time was up, the kid sneered that he better not touch him. Bragging that his father was a lawyer and Ramos would be in big trouble.

Ramos grabbed the little pussy and was about to punch him in the face when the boy shouted to his sister, "Jennifer, call the cops if this nigger hits me."

"No," she replied. "I kinda wanna watch," she winked at Ramos. This distraction awakened his dick and Ramos dropped the wimp.

Jenny was sixteen, a cute blond cheerleader with a big rack for a skinny bitch. Walking to Ramos she drawled, "He's useless." Looking in his eyes she added, "Is it true what I hear about you?"

"Probably." Ramos figured she heard he was a badass.

"Can I see?"

Hum? "See what?" Did she want him to hit someone?

"Your really big ding-dong." She was quite the tease but was poking a stick at the wrong tiger.

"When?"

"Now works for me. That's my new car. Let's take a drive." She turned and walked toward a shiny caramel-coloured Camero. Ramos followed. They fucked for several weeks until her boyfriend, the football captain, got suspicious.

Three months later, she told Ramos she was pregnant, which might be his. When she told her parents, they went mental. She would not have a dark skin baby by the school thug and son of a junkie whore. Within a week, she was gone. Abortion first, then boarding school in Vermont.

Eyeing the newspapers spread on the counter pulled Ramos back to the present. He knew his wife must have seen the latest tabloid story. It quoted Marita saying, "She looked forward to life in Surrey. It's a wonderful place to raise children." The bitch never missed a chance to kick Alice.

Great social debates raged on who would win the affections of the big bad, mysterious, fabulously wealthy Ramos Santiago and the topic of every talk show. While the wife usually gets the pity vote. No one knew Alice or even what she looked like, and Marita was a genius at self-promotion. The majority of public goodwill was directed at Baez.

The circus was endless and an excellent masquerade for the real story. The vast money laundry, bribery, and now tax evasion case building against Ramos. They talked about how the Detective risked her rising career for *love*. Many faulted Alice for not fighting back, saying she probably just wanted the money.

Typically, an officer with a conflict of interest is removed from a case, but Baez informed the Filth that if she were transferred, she would sue for sexism and racism. After all, she was half Portuguese and a minority. The public sided with Baez. The policy implied that a woman couldn't have a private life and a career. That kind of thinking would not be tolerated in this day and age.

"Goddamit, Alice, don't read that shit." He knew the daily drumbeat of the press was eating her up. He ignored it; the case being built and business left him no time for the drama playing out on the pages. Keeping Baez close was an essential part of his plan.

"It's like a two-headed cow. It's grotesque, but I can't seem to look away. I saw her picture," Alice poked at a stack of papers. "Young and pretty is an understatement. She's gorgeous. I can't be that." She shrugged her shoulders. "I always knew I wasn't enough for you. You're important and such a big, sexy man. Lucky me, but I'm boring, too sweet, or whatever." Leaning on her arm, she looked at him with a goofy grin.

"I did ask you to tell me what I could do or show me how to make you want me, but you never did." She took a swig and wiped her mouth with the back of her hand. "I even bought how-to books and sex toys to up my game, but you didn't notice."

Ramos never intended to make her feel less than desirable. He fucked who and when he wanted. Alice always knew this, and he felt no need to explain it further. To Alice, sex was part mechanics and a whole lot of emotion. Ramos's taste in sex was rough, raw, and always dirty. Emotion free. With a calculated effort, he marginalized his wife in that aspect of his life.

Before meeting her, Ramos never imagined knowing a woman he would value, want to protect, provide for, and have his children. Certainly, not an intellectual who played classical piano, wrote books, grew her own vegetables, placed home and family above all, and was rather pedestrian in bed.

"Over the years, I convinced myself what you did with your," she pointed to his package, "you know, didn't matter, but all of this beautiful Marita stuff and a baby feels so personal."

"She means nothing to me." Ramos tried to assure her, but Alice needed not to hear that Marita meant nothing but that she meant something.

"That's not how it feels." Alice emptied her glass and wiped her nose on a crumpled piece of kitchen roll.

Ramos didn't usually extend the courtesy of listening to the inebriated rattle on, but squiffy Alice wasn't an unpleasant drunk, and he put her through a lot. She needed to get some of it out.

"A long time ago, when you took us to beautiful Baylor, I told you I would live with you anywhere. I meant it." He knew she did. "I don't care if I lose all this." She spread her arms wide. "I don't want to lose you." Taking a big gulp of air, "I'm afraid I already have?"

Ignoring her questions, he leaned in, lifted her to the granite edge, and spread her legs. Only a man would think to reassure her by fucking. He paused, "is it ok?" Not asking for permission to fuck, but rather if it was too soon after the baby. She answered by grabbing and pulling at his belt. After sex on the kitchen counter, they went to their bedroom and fucked again.

‡ ‡ ‡

CHAPTER 18

WIDOWS

Ramos' crew are no telly gangsters or kids on corners talking trash but real men with guns, fists, and bottle. These men lived in harm's way, made their living, and cared for their families through crime and violence.

A remarkable record, Ramos lost only one top man from his dirty dozen in more than five years. The Dozen and their families all stood in the rain for the burial. Because of his high rank, Ramos met with the wives and delivered some home truths.

If he was a valued employee, he expressed his condolences, gave the wife a packet with fifty thousand, and promised an additional fifty in one year. Ramos clarified that this is the total life insurance and pension plan. They were required to sign a confidentiality agreement. All eagerly did so in exchange for the cash. Not used to a large chunk of money, the women felt they had won the lottery and often did something stupid like buying a new car or Louis Vuitton handbags and a holiday.

Soon, the reality would set in. The money is mostly gone, and no way to take care of the family. They moaned and cried to the other wives and finally to Ramos. He would show them their signed statements and remind them of the conversation.

If that approach did not work, Ramos used a physical reminder. Rarely did it get to the more unpleasant stage.

⚔ ⚔

Distracted by a bold expansion into North London, Ramos was not pleased when two of his Dozen didn't show up. MIA was not something to ignore.

Two men were sent out to make the rounds and collect answers on men not picking up their phones for nearly thirty hours. Their women would not be helpful; they were used to not seeing or hearing from them for long periods. Where the fuck were they?

Bosco and Charlie looked like brothers but weren't. No one would call the two men good-looking. Bosco was famous for a bullet hole scar on his cheek that reminded all who observed it of a fluffy pink pussy. It started and ended countless conversations. Not as ripped as some on the crew, but sturdy, fierce brutes. Neither man a Mastermind threat but loyal fuckers who knew their job and did it well. Both married, and Bosco had a child. A real puzzler them to up and vanish?

Charlie worked for Ramos for eight years, Bosco seven, unlike them to be lost in the wind? Each hour out of touch made it feel like they were not coming back.

"Boss, still no fucking word." Tyler and Axel followed up on leads that soon fizzled.

"Tyler, you know Charlie's wife?" asked Ramos.

"In a biblical way." The men smirked.

"Go talk to her and press her for anything."

"Will do." Tyler gave a pelvic jerk and a smirk. "A nice long press." Tyler introduced Charlie to his wife three years earlier. Tyler was banging her hard when Charlie entered the room, got a beer, and sat down to watch. Sheila bent over while Tyler stayed busy, her pussy but not her *head in the game*. Eyeing Charlie and he eyeing her back when Tyler finished, she called out, "Next." Charlie fell in love at that very moment.

Not a whore, Sheila, a pretty party girl, was having a night out. She and Charlie hit it off and, within the year, married in a grand ceremony at the Shock Wave. Naturally, Tyler is the best man.

Sheila wasn't concerned with Charlie's occupation. She was marrying up. Her late husband Colin worked for Ramos too, though not as high up in the organizational chart as Charlie. Sheila received one pack of fifty thousand.

# #

Knock, knock. "Sheila, it's Tyler." He waited for her to open up.

"Hi, Ty, a nice surprise." She stuck her head out the door and looked around. "All alone?"

"Yeah, can I come in?"

"Come in what?" Sheila chuckled at her joke. Tyler felt his dick saying hello.

"Charlie isn't home. Only me and my much-neglected kitten."

"Kitten?" He laughed. "You mean pussy? That's a shame. A kitty that sweet should be played with often." The conversation stopped while the two pulled at each other's clothes.

Usually, Tyler wouldn't fuck the woman of a crewmember. Considered impolite not to stay in your own lane, but Sheila and Tyler had history and chemistry and never quit fuckin in the last three years. Both figured Charlie was not unaware.

Sheila, an excellent hostess, offered Tyler refreshments after the fuck. Tyler pulled up his pants, "I'll take a beer."

In the kitchen, in an open robe, Sheila didn't seem to have a care in the world. "When did you last see Charlie?" Tyler asked between swigs of Stella.

"Couple of days ago. What are you all up to that's so important; Charlie can't come home and fuck me and bring me some cash occasionally?" Sheila sat across from him and took a drink of her gin martini. Not yet eleven in the morning; it seemed a little early for gin, but he didn't mention it.

"You need money?" He reached into his pocket, pulled a wedge, peeled off a thousand, and laid it on the table.

"Thank you, baby. Getting paid for a fuck is fun." She attempted to lighten things up.

"You got a gold mine waiting with that money-maker of yours." He laughed. "Charlie, mention what he was up to or where he was going when you saw him last," easy, casual?

"Charlie doesn't tell me shit. Hell, if he were going in for a heart transplant, he would probably walk out the door and fail to mention it." Playing with her olives and not making eye contact, "ask Bosco; those two are usually up each other's arse."

"Know Bosco's woman?"

"Yeah, Bunny, they live a few houses along. You need to tell Bosco to keep his damn hands to himself. She's a tiny thing, and he put her in Casualty twice this year. He was my husband, I would ..." She let it hang.

"Sorry to hear it. Ramos doesn't like that shit. I'll have a word." He got up and got another beer for himself. "She fuck around?"

"You mean like me? No. She's not the fuck around type. She was too afraid of Bosco to smile at another man." *Was* thought Tyler?

"Jealous type, huh?" He wanted to keep her talking.

"No, the mean fucking bastard type!" Tyler hit a nerve. Sheila started to fidget; Tyler remained cool. "He wouldn't leave her be."

"What happened?"

"Nothing. You need to go." She stood and pulled her dressing gown tight around her.

Tyler stayed seated and calm. "What happened?" He finished his beer.

"Get out. I mean it." She stood and kept looking at the bedroom door.

"Talk to me, Honey. We're friends." About to break, her eyes filled. Tyler neared and wrapped his arms around her. "What happened?"

"In there." She jerked her head toward the bedroom, "self-defence, sort of." Tyler calmly walked to the door and pushed it open.

Inside on the floor laid Charlie and Bosco. Both were shot dead. Tyler turned to Sheila. "Sort of?" He was not showing it, but Tyler was impressed; she took down two serious badass professionals.

"Will you help me?" she said.

"Help you what?"

"Get rid of um. You're a killer. Do you have a big hole somewhere you put bodies?" What she said would have been funny in other circumstances.

Walking back to the kitchen, he sat her down and poured more gin. "Where's his car?" Charlie's Range Rover was not out front.

"I ditched it. I left it in a lot at Gatwick. Then put Bunny and the baby on a plane to Aberdeen."

"She in on it?" Sheila nodded.

"Bunny and I were in the bedroom trying new lingerie and making sex noises. You know, girls' stuff, giggling, having fun. Bosco banged in and started knocking her around."

"And."

"I reached in the drawer and got one of Charlie's guns." She looked distressed. "I told him to stop."

"Clearly, he didn't. How did Charlie end up on the floor?" Tyler sort of understood what happened to Bosco, but why Charlie?

"I didn't know he was home. He heard the shot and ran in with his gun, and I panicked. I didn't mean to shoot. It just happened."

Tyler saw the bodies. "Twice, three times?" Sheila started crying.

"Tyler, help me. What do I do?" The shooting happened at least a day earlier. She sent Bunny away and tried to figure out what to do next.

"Get dressed." He pulled his phone and texted Axel.

"Don't tell Ramos." Said Sheila.

"I can't do that? You can tell him what happened."

"No, please don't tell him. We need the money."

"What money?"

"Ramos pays a hundred thousand to the widows of his top men? We need the money to get away."

"Sheila, it's over." She took hold of his arm.

"Please, I am begging you. We deserve the money." Tyler shook her loose.

"Sit down. Don't move." A feeling in his gut was brewing. Walking to the bedroom, he looked at the position of the bodies. Both were strong, solid men, deadweight, not easily moved by two small women. Charlie lay further into the room than Bosco. It appeared Charlie entered first. It made sense, too, because it was his home. Tyler noticed she had shot both men multiple times.

※ ※

Knock, knock. Tyler headed out of the bedroom to the door. Sheila stood. "Sit the fuck down. I won't tell you again." Axel entered.

"Found um." Said Tyler with a head tilt to the bedroom. Axel took a quick look and took photos of the scene.

"Called Ramos?" Tyler shook his head.

"Get dressed and get your handbag. Leave the door open, and don't do anything stupid, or you're dead." Sheila went to the bedroom. There were guns in the drawer and floor, but she didn't dare.

"What the hell happened?" asked Axel. "She fucking both or something?"

"Some bullshit self-defence story. Ramos has to make the call."

※ ※

Tyler called Frankie and told him to let Ramos know he found Charlie and Bosco and was coming in for a sit-down.

Sheila's anxiety was on max. "Tyler, please don't tell him. He might kill me or something."

"He might; don't try to feed him bullshit. It's his least favourite dish."

#

"They're here," said Frankie. Ramos did not know anything about what happened. Tyler wanted him to hear it from Sheila.

"Bring um in." Tyler, Sheila, and Axel entered Carlos's office at the Rod. Carlos stayed on a chair at the side while Ramos sat behind the battered desk, a subtle bow to Ramos' authority.

"Boss, this is Sheila, Charlie's widow." Everyone in the room caught the word, widow.

Ramos did not ask anyone to sit. "You have something to say?"

"Can you send them out of the room? I feel intimidated and want to be sure I remember everything." Worth a try?

"No. You have something to say. Say it."

"It was self-defence and an accident." She gave him the story she gave Tyler. "I loved Charlie. I'm torn up about it." She did not try that approach with Tyler, presumably because she fucked him.

"Carlos, take Sheila out and get her a drink."

Carlos grabbed her arm, "keep stepping bitch."

"Photos of the crime scene bodies that have been there at least a day." Axel handed his phone to Ramos, who checked the photos. He caught the multiple wounds, and Charlie entered first.

"Any of you know if Bosco has been roughing up his wife?"

"I was at his place a few months back, and she seemed scared of him. He knew I caught it and said she needed to be kept in line. I didn't think it was my business." Said Carter.

"Tell everyman who works for me to keep their fucking hands off their women and children. This shit is difficult to contain and brings unwanted attention. I am not having it. Ensure everyone gets the fucking memo," Ramos was furious at the intrusion into business.

"Will do." Said Tyler, but Ramos spoke to every man in the room.

"You know her, Tyler, Sheila believable?"

"I believed her initially; then, she mentioned the money."

"What money?"

"The money she hopes you will give her and Bunny." Said Tyler. "You gave her some last time."

"Yes, I did." Colin died in an armoured truck heist. Job-related. It's hard to know, but maybe the payoff gave Sheila the idea. "Put her in a room upstairs and someone on her door. Axel, give it to Rio and Dingo to deal with clean up." Ramos didn't need additional time to ponder but had a meeting in an hour at the Cairo Club. The grieving widow would wait.

#

Timing is everything, and when Ramos and his men stopped at the Rod bar for a quick whiskey before heading to Mayfair, the timing for a young red-haired man was up.

Carlos was distracted by the widow problem, and a new man on the door let previously bared Rusty inside the club to look for Daddy. Not taking no as an answer from Carlos, he would demand Carlos admit he knew his mother and was his father. This time, Rusty brought a gun to force the claim.

A gun might have been persuasive if Ramos, Tyler, and Axel, all strapped, were not in earshot. With a great deal on his plate, Ramos quickly eliminated the problem. Bringing his gun down hard on the man's skull two seconds after he shouted, "Daddy." The shot grazed Carlos's arm, and the man dropped to the floor. Ramos put his boot on the man's windpipe.

The music banged so loudly that no one noticed the single small-calibre shot. Axel vaulted over the bar and picked up Carlos, who had fallen to the floor.

"Get your fucking hands off me, *pendejo*," said Carlos, who hated getting old and being a gimp. He knew looking weak was the end for a hardman.

"Excuse the fuck out of me," replied Axel with a grin as he raised his hands and backed away.

"Get him to Patel," a surgeon, struck off five years earlier for selling Oxy and was now on the payroll. Ramos kept him busy.

Tyler restrained the ginger shooter as Carlos stumbled around the bar and kicked him in his red head. "*Hijo de puta!*" Carlos didn't often revert to his Mexican heritage, but this shit seriously pissed him off.

Frankie went for a *splash* and returned from the bog after the excitement at the bar but in time to join Ramos on the ride to the Tower meeting.

Roiling with disgust, Ramos spit, "Fucking bitches, wives, and widows. I can't get business done."

※ ※

Late when Ramos returned to the Rod. "Bring her down." With no time or patience, it better not take long.

Unable to sleep, Sheila tried to improve her story, but nothing came to mind. She hoped Tyler hadn't told Ramos about the money.

"Take a seat." Ramos was behind the desk, Axel and Carlos to the side as Tyler brought her in.

"I'm really sorry about what happened. Shooting Bosco was not an accident. The bastard kept hurting Bunny; don't blame her; she couldn't hurt a fly." Sheila hoped her honesty would have value.

"I begged Charlie to stop him, but he said it wasn't our business. I told him I was going to tell you, and he said if I did, he'd kill me." She paused briefly. "If a man like Charlie says he's gonna kill ya, he will. We ran out of options."

"Charlie?"

"It just happened. Charlie never hurt me unless you count boring me half to death." Her joke fell flat. "I couldn't seem to stop shooting." Ramos believed that part of the story. Civilians with a gun either freeze and unable to shoot or are unable to stop shooting and empty the clip.

"What happened to the gun?" said Ramos.

"I drove Charlie's Range Rover..."

"My Range Rover."

"Yeah, yours to take Bunny to Gatwick. We stopped on the way at a McDonald's. I went into the bathroom and washed the gun with soap and water." Thorough, he had to give her that. "I took a shitty nappy out of the trash, wrapped it around the gun, and put it back at the bottom of the bin. Yesterday."

"What about the other guns?" He meant the ones Charlie and Bosco carried.

"Charlie fell on his, and Bosco's gun slid under the bed. I couldn't bring myself to touch um. I left your car in lot C, like Charlie, at Gatwick."

"I didn't know Bosco was hurting her. Bunny will be taken care of." Ramos rendered judgment.

"Thank you."

"You have a choice to make, Sheila. You can whore for Carlos here at the Rod until you have paid me back the fifty thousand I gave you for Colin. Or right now, you can join Bosco and Charlie in hell?"

Sheila felt such relief that she jumped to her feet. "Who wants to be first?"

# # #

CHAPTER 19

RIVALS

A while since Ramos took the time to go to Dorchester for a fuck; fucks were pretty close by in his world. But in the area for a meet, he decided to stop by. Tyler and Frankie were up, and both men were in the front of the armoured Rolls. No one was talking. The meeting had not gone well. Ramos, of course, won the day, but all three men knew it cost him.

Emerging from the car, the snarling paparazzi reminded him of how visible and public his life had become. He hated the fuckers and walked on. "Will your detective girlfriend be joining you?" Shouted one.

"Or your wife?" snickered another.

"No, asshole, your wife," said Frankie as he roughly pushed the laughing photographer out of the way.

The door shut on the paps, and the relaxed, dim luxury of the Dorchester welcomed them. The duty manager stood near but did not speak, a rule enforced in the reign of John Kohl and worked well for Ramos.

Tyler followed him to the elevator; Frankie stayed out front with the car. "The fine ass of Sakeema is waiting downstairs. You want her up?" asked Tyler, who could see his boss was distracted.

Ramos did not answer. "Come in." Tyler walked to the drinks tray, poured two whiskeys, and handed the boss one. It would be a no-no to question the boss, but the elephant was *in the room*. Ramos tossed his drink back and poured another.

"The fucker has to go," no small pronouncement. The fucker in question was a wannabe big-shot and using the current situation to strut and loudly make his desire to entirely rule his district well known. He did not expect Ramos to get the information by rumour and innuendo. Instead, he invited Ramos to join him for lunch and a chat.

# #

"Hey, you brought your girlfriend," said Chelmsford's *loudmouth mini-Face*, addressing Ramos with Tyler at his side. "Take a seat. My chef is a wizard. You eat venison? Shot the big bastard myself up in Scotland."

Shut the fuck up, thought Ramos. He was there for business, not to discuss the domestic staff, menu, or man hobbies. "I'm rushed for time. What's on your mind?" Ramos went right to it.

"No wonder they call you the Lion King. You are always in a big rush to gobble everyone up and move on."

"Yeah, *circle of life*," said Tyler.

"All the rush is bad for your health." Said the fucker with an irritating smile. Fuming, Ramos waited. He pulled a chair and lowered himself without pulling up to the table. Tyler remained standing nearby. "I was hoping we could make this friendly?"

"Yeah, real mates. What's up?"

"I want to give you a heads up. I am going to take drugs and pussy for Chelmsford." He smiled at Ramos. "It's my hometown, and I shouldn't have to buy a bitch or a hit from you." Still speaking calmly with a grin. Chelmsford was a sweet area with plenty of consumers and only an average amount of assholes.

"Take? What does that mean?" Ramos wanted the cunt to make the threat clear.

"Step back. I'll continue to buy from your connects so you will have a slice, but after it arrives in my fair city, it's my business, not yours."

"Sounds like a simple plan. Only one small problem."

"Yeah. What's that?"

"Me. Not going to happen. You are doing fine as chief distro." Ramos stood to leave. "I will forget the conversation happened."

"You seem pretty busy with other things." An apparent reference to the mounting cases and Baez. A perceived weakness. "Give me this, and I will go quietly."

"Are you offering to buy my valuable territory?" asked Ramos. "I am not certain you can afford the purchase price."

"No. Think of it as a gift. Take the easy way. I know you're *dick high* in shit right now, and I don't want to cause you any additional aggro."

"That's real thoughtful." Ramos stood again and headed for the door.

"Relax. You're acting like you've been right fucking grafted." This opportunist bullshit was exactly what Ramos knew would happen when the case went public. "Come on, last chance to keep it friendly. Even Lions get old."

##

Rivals come in all forms. "Girls, you each get to pick out two flowers. Lindsey, can you get a flat from there to put them in." Alice ventured out to a vast garden center with Luna, Stella, Annie, and Lindsey on a rare trip off the Surrey property.

"Oops," Stella dropped hers and burst into tears. Alice picked her up for a cuddle. "You're ok. The flower is fine." She turned to Lindsey, "Better get them home. They are hungry and need a nap."

"Me too," joked Lindsey. Alice tried to set Stella down, but she was not having it.

Annie reached up with tears in her eyes and patted Stella's leg. "Don't cry," she was as loving and caring as her sweet mother, Julie.

"Perhaps this could help?" Said a man dragging a wagon their way. It is usually used to transport flats of flowers and shrubs, but it would be helpful right now for ferrying the little ones.

"Oh, thank … Is that you, Cliff?" Alice looked into the face of a man she was sure she knew. How refreshing to see someone from her previous life.

"Allie, how darn nice to see you. Are all of these yours?" he asked as he looked at the children.

"These and more." She laughed and turned to Lindsey. Please put everyone on the cart and get them to the car." Lindsey hesitated, uncertain if she was supposed to leave Alice alone. One of the few things Ramos told her when she went to work for Julie was not to leave her alone. She worried he meant the same for Alice.

"It's ok. I won't be long." Alice was never really alone. Today, Rio watched from a short distance, and Boomer at the car improperly stationed at the front entrance.

"Cliff, do you work here?"

"I'll tell you a secret. I own the place." He is a rugged-looking man, not gym-fit but healthy in the way those who work outdoors seem to look. His hair was thinning, but he certainly looked a happy man.

"I thought your dreams were working on computers?" she said.

"Yes, and my dream came true. I invented a popular app ten years ago, and I was able to quit and pursue my other dream of being a *farmer*."

"So, this is your farm, huh?" Her smile was broad and genuine.

"Yes. I opened a store near Baylor seven years ago and this one last year."

"The garden centre near the roundabout in Baylor is yours?" He nodded. "I spent a small fortune in there. We moved out here a few years ago.

"I don't remember your interest in flowers back at school. Weren't you and your piano headed to concert stages around the world?"

"All that's old news."

"Do you have time for a coffee?" he asked. "To catch up."

Alice looked toward the door, and Rio made it clear he was looking at them. His lack of tact was irritating. Cliff asked, "Is the scowling man your husband?" Rio was intimidating with or without a scowl. He currently held the War Room and Zoo record for burpees, and his well-tuned physique shouted, *keep the fuck away*. Cliff could hear him clearly, even at a distance.

Alice was relieved he seemed not to know Ramos. "No, he helps out sometimes. Give me a minute, and I will be right back." She turned and walked toward Rio.

"Please take Lindsey and the children home. I will be here for a while." Without another word, she turned to go back to Cliff.

"No," said Rio in a harsh tone. Alice replied with a sharp look.

"Rio, I am having coffee with my friend who owns the garden center. Please go tell Boomer to take the family home. He can come back to get us." She turned again.

"Don't disappear, or I will fucking tear the place apart." She was too shocked to remind him not to talk to her that way. Alice didn't see Cliff walk up behind her.

"Is there a problem, Allie?"

"No, let's get that coffee now." She grabbed Cliff's arm and started walking. Rio pulled his phone for a quick pic of Allie and her *manfriend*.

They were making their way to a private umbrella table on the edge of the tea kiosk patio with coffee and tea in hand. "This Centre must be a gold mine. I have never stopped by when the place is not heaving with enthusiasts."

"Yes, having a hobby that pays for itself is satisfying." He took a drink of his coffee.

"Did you and Joan marry?" They were the sweet sixteen couple at school. "Any children?"

"Yes, and no. We married, but it didn't last. Joan wanted to use the app money for adventure, and I wanted my farm. She lives in Miami now."

"I wanted far-off places, but it has been years since I allowed those thoughts to creep in. I have five wonderful children and a spacious home. I am too busy to even dream about travel. My escape is my garden."

"Do you have a large garden, or what brings you in?"

"Yes, extensive sprawling grounds and a walled garden off the kitchen, where I teach the girls to love it all. With some success. Running across a worm almost closed down business." She laughed.

"My love for gardening started at a young age, alongside my grandmother. Many of my favourite childhood memories," said Cliff.

"By the way, your children's gardening section is fantastic. The girls are fully outfitted. Gloves, aprons, tools, and pads. It's like playing dress-up for them," said Alice.

"Perhaps you can show me your place one day. I might be able to give you a few ideas or tips."

"I would love that. I am also..."

"The man is back looking at us? You sure everything is ok?" Alice refused to look at Rio and ignored his question.

"I want to put in a maze. A proper English garden maze. I have enough room and budget; perhaps you have some ideas?"

"I have several landscape architects on staff. I could set you up. If you buy the plants and installation from me, there would be no cost for their services."

"Sounds perfect. Do you have any books inside that might show me options?"

"Yes, let's take a look." They stood, deposited their paper cups in a bin, and walked inside. Alice did not look to see if Rio followed.

She picked two books to purchase. "The best book is in my office. It is out of print, but I would happily lend it to you. Right, this way." Cliff opened a door marked private. The inside led to an orderly room with a desk, chairs, and a small table covered with blueprints and books.

"Here it is. There is a whole section on mazes. Do you want a maze of flowers or a puzzle for walkers?"

"I need to investigate first. Give me a card, and I will call, and we can schedule a time for you to come by. And perhaps lunch?"

Cliff handed her a card and a smile. "I'd like that."

Alice flinched, walking out the door as Rio leaned casually against the wall only a few feet away. "Allie, you sure everything is okay? " whispered Cliff, who leaned in to give her a chaste kiss on the cheek. He was concerned that the menacing man seemed to be watching her every move.

Yes, I'll call you." Alice rushed toward the exit, with Rio following with intentional casualness. Rio raised his hand as a faux gun, pointing it over his shoulder as if shooting Cliff.

By the time she reached the car, Alice was fuming mad. "You are as subtle as a water buffalo."

"That hurts." Mocked Rio.

"Don't ever do that to me again." She felt she had given him a stern dressing down.

"Or what, Allie?" Unblinking, Rio replied, his eyes hard and his mouth in a smirk.

Alice looked at him with astonishment. She knew she could not be tougher than Rio, but perhaps she could be cleverer. Her face softened, and she smiled at him. "I'll send you to Boots for Tampons and haemorrhoid cream." She often gave the men lists of things to bring to the property but never anything intimate. She didn't have haemorrhoids but thought he would hate the idea of buying the items.

"Haemorrhoids, Ouch. I never clocked you as the assgasam type. Though I guess to be the woman of the beast, you have to be up for whatever it takes." Then he winked at her.

Alice was horrified that the conversation had become so personal. What did he mean by the beast?

"Maybe you should ask your new boyfriend." Rio pulled his phone and showed the photos, one where she held Cliff's arm and one of his innocent goodbye kiss.

Alice wanted to scream. Considering the hell Ramos was putting her through with Detective Baez, she was steaming. She could not have a cup of tea with an old friend without it being turned into something ugly. Because of anger, she was tempted to push it but did not. She remembered an incident years ago when Ramos and Joe mistook the handsome gay Curate from St. Barnabus for a man caller, and to her horror, Joe worked him over.

She did not want anything to happen to Cliff, and anything was possible in the lives of bad men. In the back seat, arms folded across her chest, she did not speak again until they reached the edge of the Surrey property.

Rio is a pig, but she knows not to make him an enemy. Alice knew there was no way she could ask Cliff to her home; the men might pat him down and demand his cell phone, and heaven only knows what else. She would return his book, but no further contact. She would not miss Cliff but would miss the garden center, the best in the area.

# #

Riding along the long driveway toward the imposing gates while returning to the Surrey Estate, Alice noticed a raggedy young woman. It was not unusual for people or the press to be outside the gates, but the girl looked lost and desperate. "Rio, Boomer, please stop. I want to see if the girl needs help." Neither man looked her way and kept on driving.

Alice leaned forward and spoke again. "Stop. That girl needs help." When neither man acknowledged her request, she hit the back of Rio's seat. There was nothing from the men as the gates closed behind them.

"What's the matter with you? When I ask you to do something, please…?"

"It would be a security risk." Said Rio.

"Could be a trap," said Boomer.

"Or maybe it's someone who needs help? You…" there was no use in arguing with those two.

"Water buffalo," said Rio as he and Boomer smirked. He shared with his colleague what she had said earlier. Both thought it was hilarious.

"I am sorry, I shouldn't have said that," Alice felt foolish. "But…"

"When we get you inside, we'll check it out." Said Boomer.

Snarky now, Rio turned in his seat to face her. "What the fuck do you think Ramos would do to us if anything happened to you?"

Frustrated, she knew she needed to calm down. Her head was spinning with the very long list of things over which she had absolutely no control. It was no surprise she couldn't sleep.

# #

Late, Ramos arrived at Surrey and found Alice alone in the kitchen, reading one of her fat books. Looking up, she smiled.

"Book too good to put down?" He asked.

"My usual porn. The Belgian ship Belgica's 1896 expedition to Antarctica. Restless, I guess." Ramos was not the man who would come home and give her a kiss and hug, which she would have welcomed tonight.

Alice stood and poured her husband a whiskey. Needing an extra moment to consider her approach to the subject, she poured a cup of tea for herself and took a sip. What would she say, if anything, about Rio? Ramos took her quietness as a problem, "What's up?"

"Is there some other place Rio can work? I don't like him."

"That's not surprising. Rio is not a likable man. What's on your mind?" Ramos took a chair and topped up his whiskey. Alice was not a complainer; he would hear her out.

With a deep sigh, "I called him a water buffalo." Alice felt embarrassed that she resorted to name-calling.

"Water buffalo?" Considering the vile and nasty way his crew communicated with each other, Ramos suppressed a chuckle. "He's pretty tough. I doubt he went to bed crying in his pillow."

"It wasn't nice, and I apologized, but he's quick with a snarky retort and always smirking."

"Smirking?" Alice nodded yes, but saying it aloud made the whole conversation sound absurd. She walked over and straddled her husband.

"He is good at his job, but I have a strict no-smirking policy." He grinned. "Guess I'll have to shoot him?"

※ ※ ※

CHAPTER 20

BILLIE

"Fucker of a day," said Ramos. The four men were hitting it hard for nearly seven hours, in and out of a car. Overdue for relaxation and refreshments, their last stop took them near Isle of Dogs.

"Boss, I need a piss?" said Frankie, driving the armoured Rolls Royce Ramos *inherited* from Johnnie Kohl.

"Speaking of piss, Claire, the bog bitch at Lotus must be a hundred. Boss, can you get someone who is not a pensioner in there? That face of hers makes my pecker wilt."

"After all those years, she must have seen at least a hundred thousand cocks," said Ajax.

"Hell, I should be working in the Bitches. Think of all those lovely cunts I could be assisting."

"The pussy whisperer."

"Yeah, and I still need a piss," said Frank.

"You little girl. If the day is too tough for you, why don't we drop you at the Westfield mall, and you can go shopping with your girlfriends," laughed Billie, riding shotgun. He loved these men and being a part of his dad's world.

Ajax, in the back with Ramos, chuckled. "Hold your little peepee, Frank. I vote we hit the Shock Wave."

"Why don't you blow my little peepee? I need a piss." The conversation was meant to be light-hearted, but the men were tired and grumpy, needing drink and a fuck fairly soon.

Ramos wasn't listening but barked, "Play nice, ladies." Focused on today's meet with *Devo*, Dion Shore, a piece of shit from Shepherds Bush. The asshole kept telling him, "Things were going to change," with a heavy hint that it would not be in Ramos' favour.

Ramos was here to explain that nothing was going to change. Not the weight they were required to move and not the weekly nut. The ass-wipe did not take the news well.

The team leader for drugs, Ajax, was good at his job. He also spent several years with KDI and the arms business. Ramos needed a formidable presence in London for the drug side, where many of the dark-skin persuasion were gainfully employed. Ajax was the only man on the elite squad larger than Ramos. Only slightly, but it provided fodder for many jokes and jibes. Today, they double-teamed the idiot Devo.

"Boss? The Wave?" Ramos looked up and nodded.

"Yeah." The men continued to bitch at each other, and Ramos kept his mind on business. Everyone but Ramos made a cheer, pulling up to the side of the Wave and unloading.

"Amen," said Billie.

"Stand aside, girls, or get splashed." Announced Frankie.

Ajax made a show of throwing his hands in the air and jumping back as the men laughed. "Remember to change your tampon while in there."

In an instant, time went into slow motion. Billie stepped out of the front as Ramos stepped from the back suicide door. From the corner of his eye, Billie saw the glint of a gun. With youth's astonishing speed and strength, he threw himself on top of Ramos. A five-hundred-pound pancake of men dropped suddenly to the pavement as shots rang out from a drive-by.

Ajax and Frankie pulled automatic weapons; it was all over almost as fast as it started. The driver took the hit, fell over the steering wheel, and drove the car at speed into a brick building. One man running from the assault car caught one in the leg and one in the back. If anyone else was in the car, it was unknown.

Following the explosion of gunfire, people were screaming and running. Ramos pushed Billie off, expecting him to stand. When he didn't, he turned and could see Billie was hit. Hit protecting his dad, his boss.

"Get him," shouted Ramos as the men shoved Billie in the car, and they sped away.

In the back of the Rolls, Billie was coming around. "You, ok?" asked Ramos.

"Ah yeah, but my arm stings like a son-of-a-bitch." He held his left arm, which was bleeding through his shirt.

Without instruction, Ajax jumped behind the wheel and headed for the closest Doctor on Ramos's payroll, which luckily was nearby. He was well paid in Shock Wave booze and pussy, which had been why he lost his medical license in the first place. The old goat possessed a great deal of experience in dealing with the results of gunplay.

"I hope to hell he has a toilet," said Frankie. He did, but the Doctor explained that his wife was bathing, so he would have to wait.

Ramos did not comfort or thank Billie for doing his job. Business first. "Frankie, call Surrey and up security. Jax, get the men to the Rod. We will meet um there."

Ramos knew who was behind the attempted hit. No competing gangs took credit, and none were expected to. The ass-wipe Devo was *Dead Man Walking*.

Driving away, they heard sirens. Ramos was unconcerned about leaving the scene. He owned the Wave and knew there were no cameras. An alibi would be of no difficulty. With a number of the Filth in the area on Ramos's payroll, he would be surprised if they mounted much of an investigation. Relying on the Filth to get it wrong was not a bad strategy.

# #

All the neon lights outside were off. Inside, payday Friday night at the Rod, the place was rocking even with the supposed rolling shutdown. All the poles were active, and plenty of bitches roamed the rooms. Ramos walked directly through to Carlos's office; Ajax and Billie followed. When the door shut, Ramos asked, "Where the fuck is Frank?"

When Frankie walked in, the three men all looked right at him. "What? Even the World Court in the Hague says I occasionally get to take a piss." Ramos shook his head as Ajax chuckled.

Groggy from the doctor's meds for pain, Billie stretched out on a distressed brown sofa. As he rested his head, Ajax spoke, "You know how much nasty naked ass has sat on that leather?" Billie closed his eyes.

The response to the attempt would be swift. Ajax would lead the posse. Ramos would get Billie home. When Axel and a couple of heavyweights walked in, Ramos changed his mind. He wanted to do Devo himself. Alice could wait.

"Boss, the Calvary has arrived."

# #

The fucking tabloids got the story but no names, only speculation based on the location and the ID of the dead in the car. The headline was impossible to ignore: Gangs Vs. Gangsters. A bad feeling tugged at Alice. It happened yesterday, and surely someone would have told her if Ramos or Billie were involved.

A smaller second-page story and few details did not ease her worry the following day. She had been through it before when Ramos was shot protecting John Kohl. She decided to try to get information.

Alice pulled Luna, Stella, and Annie in a wagon across the stone driveway from the main house toward the men's quarters called the Zoo. She had never been here and never imagined she would be.

Passing the main electric entry gates, the girls waved to the two men on duty. Arriving at the Zoo, Dingo and Jet walked out to greet her. No doubt she was seen on camera approaching.

"What can I do for you?" Dingo asked.

"Hi Dingo, Hi Jet," said Luna as Annie and Stella waved.

"Hi there," replied Dingo without taking his eyes off Alice. Jet remained silent as he leaned against a pillar.

Alice wished she thought to plan what she was going to say. "Hi," It was about a hundred hi too many. "I was hoping to see Billie. Is he around?"

Dingo shook his head. "No, but I'll let him know you stopped by." The opposite of forthcoming confirmed to Alice that something was going on. His stance blocked the entry, and his message was clear.

She tried again, "Ramos?" Dingo shrugged and looked at Jet, and he shrugged. Alice wanted to slap both; instead, she smiled.

"Do you know anything about the shooting? The one in the paper?" another approach.

"Haven't had a chance to read the papers in a while," said Dingo as Jet shook his head.

You ass, thought Alice. I wish you could read my mind. I might as well be asking the dog lying in the sun. "Could someone drive me to the Tower?"

Dingo's face remained unreadable. "Ramos would have to approve it first."

"What? The Driving or the Tower? I know how to drive; I need a car." Alice was frustrated as hell.

Dingo said, "No offense, Alice, but why are you busting my balls? I am just following orders."

There was nothing else to be gained from the conversation. "When Billie gets back, have him come see me. I don't care what time of day it is." She turned to leave.

"He might be out of town, but I will let him know when I see him."

Alice kept walking. "Bye Dingo, bye Jet," hollered the girls. Passing the almost completed chapel, she looked forward to going inside and lighting candles for her husband and son. Her thoughts were interrupted, "Mummy, I'm hungry."

She was furious when she was back in the kitchen, soon replaced by apprehension. Worry no candle would cure; she had to live with it. Walking to the piano in the grand room, she sat down and played a furious round of Beethoven.

⚐ ⚐

The swift retaliation was a bloodbath but a great source of satisfaction to Ramos. He would use it as a *teaching moment* for other fools thinking of making a move.

It wasn't long before the Shepherds Bush event and the Shockwave deaths were connected. Boomer created a grand diversion by blowing up a bank in the City and knocking all other stories to the back of the papers.

With no promise of peace imminent, Ramos told Billie to stay at the Tower and clear of his mum while his arm healed. Only a graze and covered easily with a shirt and jacket. However, the area where the skin was ripped away was tender. When he moved his arm, it was clear something was amiss.

While at the Tower, Billie would occasionally see Julie. She was a lonely girl and too timid to make new friends. A few times, he joined her for some sunshine and lemonade on the roof terrace.

By far the youngest on Ramos's elite team, Billie proved himself worthy of the fast track in a record time. He calmly and efficiently killed Johnnie Kohl. His reason was personal, and that's usually a no-no, but all the crew at the time, except for Titus, thought Alice was ace and Johnnie a prick for bringing up her Rod days. To the men, Johnnie went from the coolest man alive to a paranoid piece of shit after his father's death.

Billie took a bullet for the boss, the most critical job of any enforcement and protection crew. He may have been motivated on a personal level. After all, Ramos was his dad, but no one would again question Billie's courage or loyalty. He carried himself with confidence, and the respect level for Billie Santiago soared.

#

One beatdown never solves the problem, and several other gang patches fomented challenges to management. Ramos did not want the distraction and destruction of all-out war and took *the cut-off-the-head-of-the-serpent* approach.

A precision strike on two of metropolitan London's notoriously vicious gangs flipped the local leadership. The new bosses scrambled to make Ramos their *bestie*. Ramos knew it was a short-term solution, but only so much time in a day with the fucking Prosecution Case and the Baez cunt sucking up the hours.

#

Nine days passed, and no word from Ramos or Billie. The papers were back to the Ramos and Baez saga. Alice felt anxious but unwilling to humiliate herself again and return to the Zoo to beg for information.

Sitting at a massive scrubbed oak table in the kitchen, Alice enjoyed the peace; the children and others were all in bed. Hearing the back door rattle, she looked up, and in walked Ramos and Billie with exaggerated nonchalance.

"Hi mum, anything to eat?" Ask Billie as if not a care in the world.

"No." Both men did a double-take and exchanged glances. A first, she must be pissed. "I have been crazy with worry about you," she turned to Ramos and pointed, "and you." The men knew of her visit to the Zoo. "I lit so many candles I practically burnt down the house."

In Ramos's style, Billie swerved the question. "Mum, I'm a growing boy. I gotta eat." She stood, walked over to him, shook her head, and leaned in for a big hug. Billie glanced over her shoulder and grinned at Ramos.

Earlier in the day, Billie approached Ramos for permission to have Boomer teach him bomb-making and demolition. It was a slow and exact skill and one of the world's most deadly professions. Ramos told him he would consider the idea; Alice would disapprove, but she would not be consulted.

After she fed them, Billie said goodnight and headed to the Zoo. Ramos poured another whiskey and expected Alice to question him. Dingo reported her request to go to the Tower. When Alice said nothing, he asked, "Where would you rather be fucked? Right here, or shall we go up?" He gave her a friendly face, or as friendly as his menacing mug could muster.

Alice walked over, straddled him, and put her arms around his neck. "Are you slowing down? I didn't use to have to pick. I would get both."

# # #

CHAPTER 21

CARLEY

"Hi, Billie," said Carley, a girl he went to school with in Baylor a few years earlier. She was stacking loaves of bread on a Tesco shelf.

"Carley Walsh, what are you doing, working here after school?"

"School didn't work out." She looked sad.

"How so? You get in a catfight and get thrown out?" he chuckled. Carley was a nice girl, part of a trio of girls Billie and his formidable mates called "the Sweeties." There was no chance she was ever in trouble.

His joke made her smile. Billie liked her, and his dick stirred as it always did when he looked at her pretty, freckled face. She was one of the girls in school who had her homework done, didn't sneak off to clubs, and never let anyone touch her. She wanted to go to school, be a teacher, get married, and have babies in that order.

"No, my dad lost his job, and I need to help out." She completed most of her training but had a few courses left to finish.

"When do you get off? Join me for a drink."

"A coffee, maybe." She looked at the cheap watch on her arm. "I get off in about twenty minutes."

"I will be at The Bull, on the corner. Don't worry; they have coffee." He clicked a wink and walked out, not waiting for an answer.

#

Looking up, Billie saw Carley glancing around the Pub as her eyes adjusted to the dimmed light. "Over here." He was not a fancy gent, but with manners, which he knew his mum would appreciate, he stood. He noticed she put on lip gloss and brushed her wavy, light strawberry hair.

"Hi." Carly sat at the small table. Billie was having a pint, but coffee was waiting in a dainty cup.

"Been a minute," his voice deep and smooth.

She giggled. "Are you talking gangster? Am I supposed to be afraid of you?" She sat back in her chair and smiled. "Just so you know, I'm not."

"Is that right?" He threw her a cheeky grin. "Not even a little scared of a big black man with tats?"

"Nope." She shook her head. "I remember you made that horrible bully, Little Ray, stop hurting your brother and the other kids. A bad man wouldn't do that."

"Got me all figured out, have you? Okay, let me start over. Haven't seen you since we moved to Surrey."

Billie was a fit, handsome lad with an effortless sense of confidence. "Surrey, that's posh." She remembered he lived in the exclusive area of Baylor as well and was slightly anxious when the conversation turned to money.

Carley heard stories about him and his dad. Ramos was super-rich and famous, constantly in the papers.

"You were my favourite at school," said Billie, taking a good look.

"Favourite what?" she laughed at him.

"I'm not saying it would probably get my face slapped."

"You could always make me laugh."

"What happened to your dad?"

"He ran Ribizzi's Garage for thirteen years; when it burnt down, he and the other seven mechanics lost everything. My Dad is a wonderful man. I love him to bits, but he has an artificial leg, and people think he is not capable. Now he sits in his chair, drinks Guinness, and hardly ever says anything." Her eyes became glassy.

"Sorry. Is Ribizzi rebuilding?"

"No, he is moving to Sicily. It's what happened to school and my dream of being a teacher." She quickly composed herself, reached over, and lightly patted his leg. Nothing sexual, at least not for her, but Billie perked right up.

"Ah, come on, you are destined to be a teacher, a great one. You want anything besides your coffee, which is probably cold?"

"No, I have to get going. I watch the neighbour's children on Tuesdays so the parents can go to quiz night. *Every little bit helps.*" She straightened her skirt and prepared to stand, "It's nice to see you."

Billie shot forward and put his hand on her arm, stopping her departure. "Carley, you know I always thought you were a blinding girl. Will you go out with me sometime?"

She gave him a gentle smile. "You're the best-looking guy, whoever knew my name. I can't believe I am sitting here with you right now. I had such a crush, but…."

"You did? Hell, why didn't you say?" Things are turning promising.

"I liked you, but I was kinda scared."

"Of me? Hell, I'm a teddy bear." Billie was puffed up by her confession.

"No, of me. Afraid I wouldn't be able to say no."

"You saying I'm irresistible?" His grin was enormous, and his boner threatened to be as well.

"Every Monday, we girls would weave romantic stories of our weekends with our *pretend* boyfriends. You were always mine."

"Go on."

"Macy was crazy for Arty, and she had them going on weekend hunts in Scotland and racing at Cheltenham."

"Arty? The only thing he ever hunted was his next pint," he chuckled. "Who else?"

Holly would tell us all about her fabulous love life with Theo."

"Theo? Theo's a baboon."

"We tried to dissuade her, but she was having none of it. She said it was true love and told us about her weekends in designer clothes and dancing at trendy clubs. And how she and Theo made passionate love at the lay-by on the way back to Baylor."

Theo knew nothing of passion or love; he was a rutting dog, but Billie kept it to himself.

Amused at her gentle stories, Billie knew neither Theo nor Arty knew they were in the crosshairs of the *sweeties*. "Ok, give it up. What was your Monday story?"

"I probably shouldn't tell you; you will get a big head." A big dick is more like it. "You were my Monday *confession*. Naturally, you adored me."

"Naturally," he said with a grin.

"You bought me loads of expensive presents."

"Naturally."

"My favourite was the ultra-elegant silk lingerie. I modelled it for you, and we behaved, ah, very naughty as often as we could." She blushed slightly and put a hand to her mouth as if giggles were about to escape.

"You should have let me know. I was always watching you." He gave her a serious look.

"No, you weren't. You were watching Hailey." He was fucking Hailey, but he was watching Carley.

"Billie, you're the perfect *pretend* boyfriend, but I'm not the girl for you. Believe me, lots of girls want to be your girl, but I'm…."

"I know," he chuckled. "Keeping your knickers on."

"Yeah," she smiled sweetly as she prepared to leave.

"Best looking, huh?" He laughed as Carley looked back at him, smiling.

# #

"Hi, Dad," Billie didn't call him Dad anymore unless they were alone.

Ramos didn't spend much time in Surrey these days. He seemed tied to the Tower, Mayfair, and Soho as his late boss, John Kohl, had been. He was at his desk in the Zoo, the men's quarters, when Billie walked in.

"What's up?" Ramos leaned back in his chair and rolled his broad shoulders. After sitting a while, he was ready for a break. In front of him were tall stacks of money. It rolled in and rolled in. Always in cash and dealing with the sheer physical quantities was an ongoing challenge. Here sat one million, one hundred thousand, taken over Bank Holiday weekend.

"I have a business idea. Is it ok if I tell you about it?" Billie was finding his way in his new world of villainy and opportunism.

"Talk to me." Ramos would give him a chance to make his pitch, but business was about money, and he would not just rubber-stamp any wild idea.

"Remember Ribizzi's garage outside of Baylor?"

"Heard it burnt down." Ramos's crew arranged the Insurance arson job for 30%, but he didn't say.

"Yeah. I talked to Ribizzi. He is not going to rebuild. He's moving to Sicily and left his crew up *shit-river*." There was always collateral damage in the wake of the actions of bad men.

Ramos could see more here than business, but Billie was young and would be allowed a few mistakes.

"He has the lease, brick building, and most of the tools, but the place is a burnt-out trash heap. I asked what he wanted for it; he said fifty-thousand. I offered him twenty, and he came back with thirty." Billie waited, but Ramos stayed silent.

"It's a handy location and was a busy place. It could be an earner?" Billie was anxious but presented his case well. He had done his homework, spoken to the owner, and negotiated a fair amount. "Ah, what do you think?"

"Not generally in the garage business," was not strictly true. Ramos owned and operated numerous parking structures and car care facilities around the city. "I remember the place. It was usually full. Motorcycles, too, if I recall?" A possible money laundry and Ramos always needed places to move cash and drugs.

"The mechanics are still available and used to hard work. I believe they could be up and running soon," his enthusiasm showed, and when he realized it, he pulled it back in.

"What are your plans for financing the opportunity?" A fundamental issue, and Ramos wondered how far Billie thought through the crucial details. To a man like Ramos, thirty-thousand was pocket money, but he wanted to know Billie's plan.

"I am anticipating ten thousand from the Horwich jack job." The crew was splitting the bounty from a high jacking of electronics off a boat from Germany. Naturally, Ramos, the boss, first got his sizable cut. "I have thirty saved, and if I could borrow another twenty, I would pay interest. You are the biggest money lender in London. I would pay you interest and…."

"You said." Ramos settled back; he wants it badly, and it's back in Baylor? "What's her name?"

"Oh, hell, Dad, is it that obvious?" He chuckled with relief. "Carley. She's a great girl, and before you start wondering if I'm thinking with my dick, my dick has never been near her knickers." Ramos knew but didn't say; to a young man, a *virgin-Carley* was far more influential than a *slag-Carley* would ever be.

"It's a lot to pay, even for a great girl. Are you sure? I'll want my money back." Ramos moved two stacks of cash toward his son. "Take fifty," said Ramos, knowing that with zoning and union payoffs, everything on a building project took more money than a rookie would hope.

"Thanks, Dad. I'll work my ass off. Oh, and don't tell Mum."

Ramos laughed. "I am not in the habit of discussing business with your mother." Billie practically skipped from the room.

※ ※ ※

CHAPTER 22

HACKERS

At four AM, Billie drove like hell to the Tower in Belgravia, a far shorter trip from Surrey in the early morning hour when the roads were less clogged. Calling the War Room, he learned Ramos had arrived an hour earlier and was presumably in bed on the 7th floor.

Laptop under his arm, he called from the house phone, which Ramos promptly answered. Ramos was an expert at falling asleep in an instant and, in an instant, being fully awake. His life depended on it.

"Dad, I am downstairs. I'm sorry to wake you, but I need to see you now." The panic in Billie's voice was compelling.

"I'll buzz you up." No one knew the lift code except Ramos. Bare-chested, wearing only sweatpants, he walked from the master suite as the elevator door opened into the grand foyer.

"It's bad."

"What's up?" asked Ramos as he walked to the bar and pulled out a cold Fiji water.

Fumbling to set up his laptop, Billie was clearly shaken. The Mac burst on, followed quickly by a cartoon image. There was nothing funny about it.

The creepy animation began, "These images will be sold to the press if I do not receive one million US dollars by midnight Friday. Wire to this account." There was a photo of wire transfer info on the screen, and then images of Danny began to roll by.

The first image was more than enough. Danny was sucking the cock of a man whose face was turned from the camera. Six more images of similar activity followed.

Turning to Billie, Ramos asked. "Are these images legit?"

"I don't know." Billie's face was worried.

"Could they be real?" Ramos first wanted to establish if Danny was gay. He was a slight, effeminate man who showed no interest in girls or sex before he left for University in America.

Billie looked pained, "Maybe. Probably," as he began understanding what Ramos wanted him to acknowledge.

"Do you recognize anyone other than Danny?" Several face shots showed different men, though it was clear no one knew they were being recorded. Billie shook his head in reply.

"Dad, what can we do? This will kill Mum. Can the papers even print this stuff?" Billie loved his brother, but his first concern was protecting his mum.

Ramos opened a drawer full of burner phones. He called Niall, the man he charged with protecting Danny during his stay in America, a big Irishman familiar with the Boston area.

"Niall."

"Oh, hi boss," Clearly, he had been awakened. "I…"

"Where's Danny?"

"In his room, asleep." Ramos purchased a house near the campus and put surveillance equipment and security locks in place.

"Check." Niall walked across the hall and opened Danny's door. He was sound asleep.

"Is Danny gay?" Ramos went right to it. The photos could still be damaging if altered, but how Ramos proceeded would differ.

"I think so, but I never saw him with anyone's dick in his ass." Niall did not know he was on speaker, and Billie heard it. "He looks like a ponce. Figured you knew." The idea crossed Ramos's mind early on, but he didn't waste time on something that made no difference.

Ramos could see the conversation hurtful to Billie, but he needed information. "Billie received photos online and a demand for money. Anyone around Danny who might be up to this?"

Niall laughed, "They're poofs; no one with the balls for a shake-down. You need me to do something?"

"Keep an eye out for anyone different who doesn't fit with his usual mates. Sweep the house for bugs. I will get back to you."

After he rang off, Ramos turned to Billie. "I am calling the 6th floor," the domain of the spooks, the investigators, and IT geniuses on the Kohl payroll. Tops in their field, and if anyone could find out who was behind it, they could. The time constraints were a problem.

"Get Nolan and Todd to the 3rd-floor office now." Ramos hung up. It would probably be an hour before the men could get to the Tower, and the clock was ticking.

# #

"Are you going to pay?" Billie felt anxious and desperate.

Ramos ignored the question. His next call was a summons to Tyler. As the top man in Ramos's elite security and enforcement team, he would be brought in early.

Billie was gutted. His brother's private life was about to go public among the crew and possibly very public if the photos went online. "I wish everybody didn't have to know, not this way," said Billie as he lowered his head. "Danny is the best and smartest person on the planet. Now everyone will just remember this." He fought hard not to get teary.

Not a man concerned with feelings, but Ramos took a moment for his son. "Everyone has secrets."

# #

Danny did not intentionally hide his sexuality. A late bloomer, prior to leaving London, he had not explored it. There was also the fact that his dad and twin brother were *poster boys* for masculinity. He heard both make disparaging remarks about homosexuals. Truth be told, they made disparaging remarks about everyone. It was how these hardmen communicated.

In Boston, free from their shadows, he allowed his curiosity to become a reality. Niall was nearby; fortunately, he kept a discreet distance, allowing for some privacy.

# #

Ramos met in the third-floor offices and showed Nolan and Todd the animated message and demand. "Can you find out who and where?"

"Probably, but a lot will have to do with how sophisticated it is. If this is the work of a fellow student, it will be fairly easy, but if it's encrypted from a government or corporation, it will take time and may not be possible."

"How much time?"

Nolan and Todd were high-value employees of the Kohl Empire. The business and *shenanigans* done online are astonishing. This was not the first extortion attempt and would not be the last. But it was personal and needed a more delicate hand.

"Get it done. I want to hear back an update from you by noon." Nolan and Todd looked at each other with undisguised doubt.

After the men departed, Billie asked, "Can I go see him?" The brothers were twenty-three. It's not odd for Billie to ask his father's permission. In the world of bad men, you first and foremost, follow orders.

"No. Danny needs to come here and talk to his mother. There is a fair chance we will not be able to stop it from going public."

"Dad, please pay them. I'll work my whole life for no money if you just pay them." Billie was trying not to beg, but he would if he thought it would help.

"No. Blackmailers are not to be trusted. They always want more, or they do the damage anyway. The way to stop them is to find them."

"But what if we can't? Friday is only three days away." Billie's eyes were glassy, and his voice was catching.

Ramos ignored his distress. There was nothing more to do until Nolan checked in at eleven. Ramos went to seven to catch a few hours kip and Danny to the War Room men's quarters.

⚡ ⚡

"What have you got?" asked Ramos.

"Nothing yet," said Nolan.

"Keep going. The clock is ticking." Ramos hung up and considered the following things needing to be done. Talk with Alice? It was piling on an already messy time. She would not want to hear it or see it first in the press if it got out.

Billie had come to seven to be there when Ramos heard from Nolan. Not sleeping a wink, he felt fuzzy-headed. "Dad, please let me go to Boston."

"Shut the fuck up. Do as you're told," said Ramos, utterly without feeling. He knew this was not an emotional crisis; it was fucking blackmail and needed to be handled with clear thinking and precision force. He was not happy to issue orders more than once.

Billie collapsed into a chair and put his face in his hands. Ramos offered no comfort. "Let's roll." Ramos stood and headed to the door.

⚡ ⚡

Ramos and Billie pulled through the electric gates of Surrey when Nolan called again. "You caught some luck. It's not too complex, and the attempts at encryption are sloppy. It's definitely a US server. The bad news is it's backed up offshore and proving stubborn."

"Can you break it?" asked Ramos.

"Don't know yet. It looks like it's run out of Nigeria. They have sophisticated shit there. World's best hackers outside of China and Russia."

"Keep trying." Ramos hung up. Looking at Billie, he offered a bit of reassurance, which was usually not his forte. "Nolan and Todd are genius at this shit. Give them some time."

# # #

CHAPTER 23

LOYALTY

Approaching the Surrey property, Ramos changed his mind about telling Alice what was happening. She was dealing with enough right now. And she still seemed to be losing weight and sleep. "Keep your mouth shut," he said to Billie. "Go to the Zoo and wait." For now, he was keeping Billie from his mother.

#

Ramos stopped at the garden gate to watch, finding his wife, daughters, and Annie making daisy chains. Each wore flower crowns in their hair, creating more for the teddy bears on a blanket nearby. Alice's goodness brought a moment of respite to a man who lived in treachery and brutality. She was going through a lot but would not cheat her children of her gentle best.

"Daddy, Daddy," squealed Luna, Stella, and Annie, who also recently had taken to calling Alice Mummy. They jumped to their feet and ran toward him.

Ramos is not fatherly, at least not with girls. He didn't know what to do with them except to prioritize their security. He tried to ignore them, but Luna forced it. "Daddy, I need a cuddle."

"Daddy, I give you my flower hat to make you pretty," said Annie as Luna tried to place her daisy chain on her father's head.

Stella held a small soft toy, "Daddy, my tiger is my favourite. He *go growl*. If someone is mean, show this scary tiger and make them run away."

Alice could see he had something on his mind, "girls, take your toys upstairs and put some flowers in your room."

Alice stood and dusted grass from her knees. "Is something wrong?" She pulled the posey crown from her head and let it fall. Can it get *worse?*

She looked frightened to Ramos, who ignored her questions. "Just business." He decided not to speak with Alice about the blackmail and Danny's sexual preferences and how they may be revealed. He did not want to soil her world any further. If he could stop the blackmailer, he wouldn't have to. He felt he had one job regarding family: protecting them from all outside enemies.

#

A day later, Ramos received word via Tyler to call Niall. "I went back and checked the log. I remembered a punk who didn't seem to fit in. Sammy, I think. He's the brother of one of Danny's butt-fuck buddies. Didn't look dangerous, just not a fag." Part of Niall's job was to make notes on contacts.

"When?"

"A couple weeks ago, the 14th. He came in loud, talking shit about the mess in London." He referred to the Gangster and the Detective saga playing out in the international press and telly. "Talking up how much money Danny was worth. He demanded Danny lend him five thousand."

"Danny laughed and said he didn't have it. The asshole saw me walk in, and he backed off but kept his mouth going. 'Sure, you don't have money. You live in a four-million-dollar house with a pool and a fucking monkey with a gun babysitting you.' Shit like that. Ten minutes later, he left."

"He shares a place with his brother. I've seen him there a couple of times but haven't seen him here since."

"Might be useful, but seems too easy? Find out who he is." Ramos hung up.

#

Ramos waited for information from Niall but knew he needed to get Danny to London to let his mum know his secret. If he could not contain the cluster-fuck he wanted Alice to be prepared.

#

Billie walked through the kitchen door and found his mum frosting cookies with help from Luna and Stella. At least they were helping lick the spoons. "Hi, Mum."

"Hi Billie, hi," his sisters beamed. They were such joyful cuties. To them, everyone was a loving visitor.

"How nice, come hug me," said Alice, happy to see her son. It had been a while.

"Got a big surprise for you, Mum," he said as Danny walked in behind him. His sisters and mum burst into noisy cheers.

Alice and the girls went to Danny with arms wide. "Oh, I am so happy to see you. Look at you, all grown up." Her eyes were glassy with joy. "You look different. Not my little boy anymore. Come sit and tell me everything."

"Girls, you go up with Sissy. It's bath and story time." After another round of cuddles, Luna and Stella scooted off the counter and took off with the dog. The girls were exceptionally well-behaved. They were loved and well cared for with no worries in the world.

"Mum, you look skinny. Are you ok?" Alice dropped her eyes and nodded.

"I have missed all of you. Even you, Billie." He said as he gave his brother a playful elbow.

Ramos explained to Danny what was happening. Previously, the shakedown attempt and the photos were unknown to him. Ashamed and horrified, he apologized to Ramos, who said, "It's your life, your dick, but you need to get out front of this and let your mum know."

"Did she see the pictures?" Danny was worried about his mother. They all were. Ramos didn't want Alice hurt and would keep Danny's secret, not about his being gay but the ugly blackmail attempt.

※ ※

"Mum, it looks like you built a church by the pool house?" Danny reached for a cookie.

"And ballet studio," said Billie. "What next, a roller coaster?"

"You didn't come all this way to discuss home construction. How's school? What is it again you are becoming?" asked Alice with pride in her voice.

"A long list of mumbo-jumbos."

"Is it difficult?"

"Yeah, Mum, it's killer, but I love it."

Billie knew Danny was home to tell his mother he was gay and soften the blow should the story explode. Both boys knew their mum was already going through hell with the Baez shit, but life does not give you nice tidy timelines for disasters.

"Mum, I need to talk to you," said Danny, looking down at his sweaty hands, hoping for courage.

"You can always talk to me. Billie, give us a minute."

"No, Billie can stay."

"Is something wrong?" she asked.

"It's sort of up to you. I'm gay." Danny swallowed and waited for her reaction.

"I know," she said quite matter-of-factly.

"You do?" Danny and Billie said in surprise.

"I'm your mum; of course, I know."

"I wish you had told me when I was trying to figure it all out. I kept quiet because I was waiting around to become Billie."

"You could never be Billie. You're one of a kind. And so is he." She said, looking at each boy with pride.

The relief on her son's face made her sad. It should not have been a burden for him to carry. We are all different, and while she knew Danny's life would be more difficult and some might love him less, she forever loved him wholeheartedly.

Alice held her son's hand. "Is there someone special?"

"Sort of, but it's early days. His name is Doug." They paused when Alice turned slightly and saw Ramos in the door.

"So, I am the last to know, huh?" She laughed and broke the tension in the room. "While we are all together, let's take a family photo." While we are still a family, thought Alice.

"Sure Mum, just say cheese." Laughed Danny.

"Cheezy," said Billie.

"You are all in time for a fresh batch of chicken soup."

"Ah, music to our ears," sang the men.

⚓ ⚓

They sat at the large kitchen table in the room filled with the aroma of hearty soup and freshly baked bread. The men were eating as if they had been marooned on a deserted island and finally rescued. The scene filled Alice with happiness; for the first time in a long time, she felt like eating.

Between bites, Danny slowed down. "Hey bro, how did it feel to get shot?"

The room instantly fell quiet; there was no clanking of dishes or cutlery, no sound at all. Alice jumped to her feet, and her breathing quickened. She glared at each of them, knowing she was right when she suspected someone had been shot. She asked for answers, but no one bothered to tell her.

"Lies, it's always lies. Danny, you lie about who you are. Billie, you lie about what happens. And you," she looked at her husband. She didn't raise her voice, but her frustration was in no doubt to the men. "you lie to me about..."

Billie jumped to his father's defence in a powerful vocal show of loyalty. Standing, he reached for his mother, but she pulled away. "No, Mum, that's not fair. Take it back." Billie's tone was serious. "Dad always protects you. We all do." He knew Ramos was moving mountains to keep her and others from the vile blackmail information.

Danny knew, though he was surprised by his brother's actions and subdued by the strength of Billie's defence of their dad. He previously had not witnessed him challenge their mum.

The men could not understand how demeaning it was for her to be treated this way. Looking at Ramos, she spoke softly, "If that's your plan, it isn't working."

"Yes, Mum, it is." Billie's adulthood seemed to explode into the room, a man with a man's opinions and allegiance. Still standing, he refused to let his dad be faulted. "Every day since Dad took us out of the miserable shithole in Hackney, he works hard and spends a lot of money to care for you and keep you safe. To keep us all safe and in fucking luxury." He spread his arms as if to remind her of the surroundings.

"You know why he doesn't come home? He works twenty hours a day, every day. He is a remarkable man and an awesome dad." He conveniently omitted a thief and a killer.

Alice was astonished, and it showed on her face. Billie's voice was stern and commanding, his support of Ramos robust. She knew her son idolized his dad, but he had never before spoken to her in this manner.

Danny did not want to be part of the conversation, but Ramos was paying for his expensive education and now saving him from a humiliating situation. He owed it to Ramos to step up. "He is mum."

"I am grateful, of course, but I'm not a child." She looked at her husband and then at Billie, "I deserve to know what's happening," she said, unwilling to concede.

"No, you're not a child. You're a woman, and you don't need to know how the sausage is made," said Billie. "It can get goddamn ugly." He started to sit and abruptly stood again. "The Baez shit is my fault." He felt guilty about bringing her into their lives, "so you can quit being mad at him for that."

Ramos spoke softly, "Enough." Ramos was proud of Billie and how he addressed her need to know, but it would be hard on his mother.

Nodding at his dad, Billie sat down and reached for a bottle of whiskey on the table. He didn't drink whiskey in front of his mother, but nothing about the meal was ordinary. Everything was changing fast.

Dazed by Billie's outburst, Alice slowly dropped her napkin on her chair. "I'll get the dessert." She walked past the puddings and out of the room.

# # #

CHAPTER 24

BOSTON

The blackmail attempt was time-sensitive, but Ramos had other business that needed his attention. After the contentious family dinner, he decided to let Alice calm down. She had been pushed pretty hard these last few months.

Walking toward the Zoo, Ramos gave a silent chuckle, recalling Billie's outburst of loyalty. He was a hell of a kid. Both of the boys were, in their own ways.

Dingo and Jet drove through the front gates. He hoped they delivered a resounding message to a miserable shit in Bristol.

Three days earlier, the shite attempted to lower his business cost by giving Ramos thirty-six thousand a key instead of the agreed thirty-eight. The manoeuvre would cost Ramos a quarter million a year if allowed to stand. It was a ballsy gambit; Ramos had to give him that.

In London, a kilo of uncut would go for forty. Ramos was already giving the asshole a price break. Possibly, Mr. Bristol felt that with Covid driving up the price and appetite for drugs, it was worth a try. He needed to learn his error in that type of thinking. The connect sets the price, not the distro.

Not only were Jet and Dingo to beat the hell out of him and pick up the balance due on the previous delivery, but they let him know the price of his standard drop of five keys a week would now each cost him thirty-nine.

##

Through Boston contacts, Niall found significant information on the Sammy character. Sammy was a local with a brilliant brother at school with Danny. Sammy, a 24-year-old asshole and rubbish gambler, was into the sharks for nearly fifty thousand.

Tully O'Shae was a formidable man, and no one would sleep nights owing him money. Sammy ran out of options. After one more beating, he begged to see O'Shae and explain how to pay him.

"You have five minutes. And don't get blood on my new fecken carpet, or I won't have to kill you; my wife will."

"Tully, ah, Mr. O'Shae," Sammy ran his sleeve across his bloody face. "I can get your money, but I need some help."

"Oh, you do? So you want me to help with your problem? No."

"I need some assistance; IT help. You see, there is a super-rich kid my brother fucks. They're a couple of fags."

"And this is of interest to me; why?"

"I want to blackmail him. His Dad is a real macho badass and probably doesn't want the whole planet to know his son is a fairy cake."

"I'm listening." O'Shae wanted to know how far along the plan was and more about the boy's dad.

"I have been reading online, and his dad, Santiago, is worth billions. That's with a B."

"Santiago? Is this Mexican or Columbian cartel shit? They can be scary bastards."

"No, the guy is like the King of England or something. I figured I could get photos, anonymously send pictures, and ask for a million dollars." Sammy sat back with satisfaction at his bold plan.

"It is a decent budget. Do you have the photos?"

"Not yet, but I know Danny comes over to me and my brother's place to study and fuck. I'm going to place a few cameras around. I just need help setting up the computer so it can't be traced back to me. And an offshore account to have the money wired."

"Could work," said O'Shae. "Only you forget an important factor. If you get caught, this badass, as you call him, will most likely kill you. And if he doesn't, I will because I want my goddamn money. Now get the fuck out!"

# #

"Boss, how do you want me to proceed? Do I go to O'Shae, or will you contact him? Makes sense he is behind it or somehow involved?" said Niall.

"It's almost the day the demand is due. He hasn't contacted me, but I expect it any time now. I have a call into Ryan Doyle," the Irish *Capo de Tutti de Capo* of Boston. "I'll get back." The line went dead.

Doyle was infinitely more powerful than O'Shae. Doyle would have dozens of men like O'Shae on his payroll. Forty minutes later, Ramos receives a call on a clean phone. "Santiago?"

"Doyle?" said Ramos.

"What's on your mind?" asked Doyle, a regular customer of the KDI arms business. He and Ramos met three years earlier in London.

"A douchebag who's into O'Shae is shaking down my son Danny. He has photos I want. And don't want his mother to see."

"It'll cost ya."

"Name it?" Ramos meant to name your price.

"One fifty in weapons delivered to Boston for the photos plus the debt amount. I'll throw the *douche* in as goodwill."

"There is a time issue," said Ramos.

"Ok, when?"

"Today."

"Make that two. I'll be in touch."

# #

If the information Niall provided was accurate, it might solve the problem. The waiting game would mean tense hours ahead.

# #

Billie and Danny were upstairs when the laptop on Ramos's office desk lit up. The creepy animated character came to life and repeated the original demand.

Nothing new. Ramos hoped to hell the bastard was using Boston time because there wasn't a hell of a lot left of Friday in the UK.

The phone rang; Ramos thought it was Doyle, but it was Niall. "I don't have all the details, but it seems something is in motion. I've been sitting on Doug's place. Sammy rushed out the door with a rucksack. I followed him to a large home, the O'Shae place. The ass-wipe must be ripe by now; he hasn't changed his clothes for three days."

Sammy requested that he be present for the money transfer and happily ran to Tully in anticipation of the million dollars. Buzzed into the home gate, Sammy thought, I'll have a place like this someday. A few more wins, and I'll be the big shot. He was lost in his fantasy of the million as he stopped his car.

Two men he didn't remember from his previous visit protected the front door. Hum? They failed to stand aside as he hit the doorbell. Sammy felt the hair on his neck stand up. "You smell like dog shit," snarled one of the men.

"Ah, guys, I have business with the boss," ignoring the insult, he attempted to sound important. "Can you give me some space?" He tried a chuckle, but it rang hollow. The door opened, and two even more menacing men greeted him. One grabbed his arm, the other the backpack.

"Wait, what's going on? I have business with O'Shae." Sammy's fear level was astronomical and failed to improve when escorted to the office. O'Shae and his wife were tied up, and guns aimed at their heads.

"Are you the fucker trying to shake down Danny?" asked one of the men pointing guns. "If so, you are one enormous dip-shit. And you stink." The man with the weapon pinched his face and shook his head. "Danny's dad is a bad man on good days and on bad days; he's a very bad man. This Sammy is a bad day."

"Listen. I haven't done anything. It was only a threat. No one has the photos," Sammy pats his backpack. "Right here." He gave the photos to no one because he wanted the money, and he didn't want to hurt his mother, who might see them of his brother. "I guess I panicked, and well, it's all in my laptop." Sammy could see he might need another tactic. He stuck out his arm and pointed to O'Shae.

"He made me do it." He sighed slightly. By shifting the blame, he hoped things would not go as badly.

"You lying piece of shit," said O'Shae.

It was not up for negotiation. The man pointed his silenced gun and put one front and center in Sammy's head. "A terrible day."

Turning to Tully and his wife, his gun still high. "Oh, hell," said O'Shae. "At least let her go."

The shooter smirked. "Aren't you the noble mutherfucker? She's not on my list. Neither are you." He nodded to another man who untied the wife first.

O'Shae's wife shot up and slapped her husband as hard as she could. "You bastard!"

"What the hell did I do?" he replied, shaking his head.

"You two mind if I interrupt?" said the hitman. "All you have to do is forget what happened here and get rid of the garbage." He poked the body with his boot. "You don't want me to come back."

Stepping over Sammy as he bled out on the carpet, "Looks like the Mrs. is gonna want a new rug," said the shooter, who carried the laptop and bag as they departed.

#

Niall followed the men. One was driving Sammy's car. They ended up at the house of the dead gambler and his brother Doug, where the photos were taken. After the men entered the house, Niall could see the gun flash in the windows but no sound from the silenced weapons. Doug, the *fruit-loop* brother, is what you call collateral damage.

Walking on the property, when the men emerged, Niall introduced himself. The hitters were told to give him the Mac, phones, cameras, and anything else they found of interest before they lit it up.

Niall called, "Boss, it's done." Ramos rubbed his meaty palms into his eyes. I fucking hope so.

#

CHAPTER 25

YOGA

"Mr. Walsh, nice to see you got the garage running again. I wanted to stop by and ask if you still do motorcycles?" Billie decided to keep his ownership a secret but wanted to take a daylight look around.

"Sure, anything with a motor. Shay here'" he pointed to a pair of legs sticking out from under a car, "does appliances after hours. We're grateful to have the garage back in business. The new owners have given us all new specialized equipment. We can repair the newest cars or classics. We're all working our tails off."

He looked at the large lad and thought he recognized him as the son of the big shot Ramos Santiago. When Rio walked in, Walsh worried they might be there to shake him down for protection money. "Better get back to it. Bring your bike in."

Rio and Billie were about to drive away when Billie saw Carley walking up the street toward the garage. "I'll see you at the Rod. I need to make a stop."

Rio saw the girl and smirked. "Give her one, but make her happy by nine. We got business in Tottenham."

⚹ ⚹

"Carley, hey," Billie waved.

She broke into a cheery smile. "Hi, what are you doing here? Your car break-down?"

"No, just checking about a motorcycle I might buy," a total lie. Billie had access to top-of-the-line bikes and cars but needed a cover story.

"Have dinner with me?" he asked.

She looked toward the garage. "I am taking my dad something to eat. They have been working late every night. Reopening the garage has made him come to life. I'm not sure when he sleeps." The happiness showed on her face.

"Dinner?" he repeated.

"It's short notice," she teased. "Maybe I have a big date already?"

"That would be unfortunate. I'd have to beat the hell out of him for making moves on my girl."

"Ha-ha, your girl?"

"Yeah, Carley, from now on, you're my girl."

# #

Four months on, Billie made the trip to Baylor as often as possible. "Mum, I told you we are just friends. Don't worry."

"Friends, huh? Do you believe I don't know what you are up to? The Santiago family are villains, and Billie will get what he wants."

"Mum, don't be like that. I really like him."

"What about school? Are you still planning to go? Or be one more stupid slag with a belly full of arms and legs?"

"School, of course; you know it's my dream to be a teacher." She grabbed her jacket. "I have to go."

"Why doesn't he come here to get you? What's he hiding?"

"Nothing, Mum. Sometimes, he can be late with all the London traffic, and it saves time to meet him at the restaurant." She put her jacket on and moved toward the door as the bell rang.

Carley opened the door, and there stood Billie Santiago. "Oh, I thought…."

"You going to leave me out here?" said Billie, though he could see he was a problematic surprise. "Holding flowers," a lovely bouquet of roses and orchids and not the cheap kind from the market, but an expensive florist-made arrangement.

"Ah, sure." She looked to see if her mum was nearby.

"For heaven's sake, Carley, ask him in," said Mary Ellen Walsh. She had not seen him in three or four years and wanted a look at the boy. She devoured the tabloids with her morning coffee and the many stories about Ramos Santiago. The fame and money titillated her, but she was a mum, knew her daughter was a good girl, and wanted her to stay that way.

Billie walked in, and Mary Ellen was slightly startled by his size. No longer a boy, he dressed and held himself like a hardman. Walking up with a playful smile, he held out the flowers. "These are for you."

"Thank you. It's quite a bouquet. Have a seat. I'll put them in water." It was clear he was charming her.

"That would be nice, but we have reservations soon and should be going." He kept his smile but was suspicious of hers. Carley took the hint and headed toward the door.

"Reservations? You young people seem to have a grand life these days." She was hoping for details.

"Bye, Mum."

"Bye, Mrs. Walsh."

#

"Your mum seems nice?" Said Billie as they drove away.

"She is usually, but I haven't dated much. Now she thinks I am out all the time and worries."

"Saving yourself for me, huh?" Billie was a playful man. "I got you a present." He reached behind the seat and brought out a beautifully wrapped box.

"Wow, but my birthday isn't until September." She was thrilled.

"Go on, open it." Billie was making stacks of money and wanted to buy her nice things. He knew he needed to go slow.

Fluffing the tissue paper, she wasted no time tearing into the package. "Oh, Billie, it is all so beautiful. It must have cost you a fortune?" She raised a hand full of elegant silk lingerie and held it to her cheek. Soft, pretty colours, nothing red or black. Billie knew that for Carley, it had to be elegant, not trashy; it must be the best. "Thank you."

"I don't get it?" She sounded anxious. "You won't get to see me in these things. I know you are a man, and honestly, are you sure you don't want a more willing girlfriend?"

"No worries, Red, I'm the patience type." She didn't know he had free ready-made fucks available anytime with the whores in his dad's clubs.

She laughed out loud. "No, you're not."

"Sure I am. I have been waiting for you since I was fifteen. Now, can we eat?"

# #

"Hi Billie, can you pick me up at the leisure centre?"

"What's up?" He and Carley were having a quick dinner, and she was excited about her new goal of getting in shape.

He pulled up in a shiny black Range Rover. Carley jumped in and kissed him. "I'm taking a yoga class. Have you ever tried yoga?"

Yeah, right after fucking and cage fighting, my favourite way to spend an hour. "No, I haven't been able to find yoga pants in my size," he replied with a grin.

"They offer one each Tuesday and Thursday afternoons. "I don't usually want to do anything to get sweaty, but yoga seems so civilized." She was grinning ear to ear.

"I could take a self-defence class. They teach girls to protect themselves from men, even as giant as you. I could learn to flatten you with one fast move." She flung her arms wide. "Watch out."

I am shitting myself with worry. He chuckled at her enthusiasm. Girls were easy prey for men, bad men. He wished she could learn to protect herself when he wasn't around to take care of her, but he didn't believe for a minute it was possible. Protecting Carley was his job. He now understood how Ramos felt about his mother and all the restrictions he put in place.

# #

Billie checked out the yoga venue and spent the last ten minutes waiting for Carley, enjoying the parade of pussy in their tight yoga pants. Carley walked out in a group of young women. Some were lookers, but he only had eyes for her.

Waving farewell to the others, she went over to him. "What a fun class. Everyone is nice. My body is so goofy I kept getting the giggles, which is a no-no."

# #

The next time Billie was supposed to pick her up at the Centre, he was tied up with Frankie. Carley kept her phone off in class, so he asked Cody, who was in the area, to pick Carley up and let her know he was delayed.

Carley and two women walked over to Cody. The girls were smiling and looked at each other conspiratorially. She previously met Cody but was unsure why he was there. He was a fit, nice-looking man but did not have a friendly vibe. She was hesitant but reminded herself that Billie would not put her in a scary situation.

In the car, Carley started, "Cody, isn't Kelly cute? She's twenty-four, the one in the pink pants." As usual, he said nothing.

I could get busy up in that tight little yoga ass. Silent.

"Poor Kelly got dumped by her boyfriend, Simon. He is going to Canada for a job and didn't ask her to come too. She feels rejected."

Fucking Tragic. How does Billie put up with her mouth?

"I told her I know the very best revenge." Carley was wide-eyed, waiting to share her idea.

Slit his throat and throw him in a landfill?

"The best revenge ever is to have a hunky new boyfriend."

What is she blabbing on about now?

"I'm wondering if I can take your picture with Kelly looking cozy, and she can put it on social media? Simon would be green. I told her you are shy and maybe wouldn't go for it."

Slit some asshole's throat, sure, but a cuddle on Instagram, no fucking way. Not going to happen.

"What do you think?"

I think Billie has no idea the shit I am putting up with. If she keeps on much longer, I'll slit my own fucking throat.

"Shy," he replied. Cody was not in the least shy, but he was not known to waste conversation.

"I warned her it might be the case. If you change your mind, she is pretty cute." He stopped in front of the Walsh home, and as she got out, she said, "Thank you for the ride. I shouldn't tell you, but all the girls said you're dreamy."

I have been called a nightmare, never dreamy.

##

People move in and out of classes, and apparently, Kelly got the long-awaited call from Simon and is no longer taking the yoga class, but Billie noticed a man who always seemed to follow Carley out.

The first couple of times, walking along with the group, but today Billie saw him hang back, pull his cell, and begin taking photos of Carley's ass. Carley's ass was his, and no doubt Roger is a fucking predator.

The prick caught up with Carley before she got to his car. "Bye, Roger, see you Thursday."

Billie asked, "Who's your new friend?"

"He's in the class." He looked mid-forties. "He's amazing at yoga and helps me get into difficult positions. Honestly, one time, my feet were over my head. I couldn't have done it without him."

Feet over your head is precisely where he wants um. Billie started a slow burn. It was time for a chat with Roger.

#

Next yoga class, Billie did not intend to pick up Carley.

He waited out of sight around the corner of the building. Right on schedule, outwalked Carley and Roger. She stopped at the bus stop, and Roger waved to her and broke into a jog. After six blocks and a few twists, he stopped in front of a door.

Pulling out his keys, Roger turned to go in as Billie pushed past him into the dim stairwell. Roger wondered, is he the guy who sometimes picks up Carley? Reluctant to look like a wimp but not liking the look of the enormous dark man, Roger was fast becoming aware of imminent danger.

Turning, Roger headed up two flights of stairs with Billie only a few paces behind him. Roger started to unlock a door and instead, with a surge of manhood, decided to hold his ground.

"Hey, brother, give me some space."

"Open the fucking door, brother, or I will destroy you." Not a lot of ambiguity. As fast as his shaking hand could, Roger keyed the lock. Billie pushed him inside, and Roger almost fell to the floor. His agility was first-rate, probably from all the fucking yoga, and he was able to right himself before he sprawled on the parquet.

"Hey, take anything you want. I don't want any trouble."

"Phone." Said Billie in a voice dripping with menace.

"Sure, all yours." Terrified, Roger handed over his phone and stepped back.

"Password? No, let me guess, yoga?" Roger nodded. Billie scrolled through his photos.

The fucker secretly took photos in the yoga class. He logged dozens, plenty of tits, and crotch shots. Without looking at Roger, Billie hit him like a hammer, and the bastard splatted to the floor.

Holding up the phone, which showed a photo of Carley. "Stay away from her, or you're a dead man." Billie kicked him hard in the ribs.

Tucking the phone in his pocket, he looked around the room.

Billie spotted a laptop on the dining table and grabbed it. With vicious anger, he stomped both of Roger's kneecaps. Reaching down, he grabbed Roger's right arm and snapped it. Billie never used his might for personal matters, and Roger was a civilian, but he would always protect Carley, and this fucker has to be stopped.

"No more yoga for you."

# # #

CHAPTER 26

MARBELLA

"Next week, I have a few days off. How about taking a short trip with me?"

"Where?" Asked Carley.

"So that's a yes?" teased Billie.

"No. I just don't know what you have in mind."

"How about Marbella?"

"Are you serious? My mum would never let me go."

"Babe, you're twenty-one. Do you need her permission? Besides, tell her you will have your own room, or don't tell her anything."

"It sounds fun and sunny, which would be most welcome, but...."

"Come on. I need a holiday. I have been working hard, and we will get a ride on one of my dad's jets."

The Marbella trip was planned to move diamonds south to a Moroccan connect. Billie was part of the trio to take it down and planned to use it as the start of a brief holiday.

"My mum will probably let me go if I tell her about the jet. She loves all the glamour stuff. Can I let you know on Wednesday?"

"You're killing me. Ok"

⚡ ⚡

"Marbella. That is where all the gangsters take their sluts," Mary Ellen was in a temper. "No, I forbid it."

"Dad, please talk to her. Nothing is going to happen. He's really good to me. Please, Dad." Her father walked silently to the kitchen and retrieved a Guinness.

⚡ ⚡

"You're coming with me? That's bloody good news. So, you talked her around?" Billie and Carley were having a quick bite in Baylor.

"No, she thinks I will come home a fallen woman."

"Gee, I hope so," he said with a chuckle but could see it worried her, so he changed the subject.

"Tell you what, come to family lunch at my house on Sunday. We're normal people. My mum is a terrific cook. She could make Gordon Ramsey shut the fuck up and eat."

What he said was funny, but the whole idea made her anxious. Carley had seen the Hello photo spread of the Surrey estate. When the place was for sale, public photos were taken. All exploded into huge tabloid celebrity news when it was learned Ramos was the new owner. He tried to handle the purchase anonymously, but there was always some fucker willing to sell photos or information.

"You mean the huge house? Where they built a Church?" The tabloids got hold of the information about a Chapel, and there was much speculation about why. Perhaps for a wedding?

"Yep, home sweet home," he played it casual. His Carley was timid, and he had to keep reminding himself she lived a sheltered, quiet life, and the bigness of his life scared her. "It's Mum, Dad, my noisy little sisters, and sometimes Julie Kohl. Everyone is friendly and hungry. It's a feast. I'll throw in a house tour."

"Does everyone dress up?"

"No, not fancy."

"We probably should wait. Your parents might believe we are …."

"Are what? Fucking?" He was a bit miffed. "I promise to tell them we are not."

"Don't be angry. I'm just nervous." Her hands were balled and fidgety.

"Come on, let's go." He stood and threw money on the table. Carley followed him out.

Billie promised to be patient, but he felt short-tempered and wanted a fuck. He knew it wouldn't be her. He would take her home and head to the Rod.

He pulled up in front of her home in his shiny new black Range Rover. Stopping the car, he did not look her way. "I'll call you," he said. She slipped out in silence.

# #

"You're home early," said Mrs. Walsh.

"I need to study." She was able to restart her teaching program with Billie's financial contribution. She didn't slow down and went up to her room. She felt awful. Billie was always so generous and kind to her; tonight, she could tell he was angry. She didn't blame him. He offered her a fantastic holiday and a chance to meet his family; she just *hemmed and hawed.*

Taking her jacket and shoes off, she sat on her bed and reached for her laptop to work on a school paper when she heard noises downstairs.

Billie pounded on the door, and when Mr. Walsh opened it, he walked right in. "Where's Carley?" he asked in a less than friendly way.

"She's gone to bed. Call her tomorrow." Said her father.

"Mr. Walsh, no disrespect, but I am going up those stairs with or without your permission."

"Now, wait a minute and calm down. You best leave."

"You can't come in here and…" said Mrs. Walsh as her back stiffened.

He looked from one to the other, then glared. Billie was a fit hunk of a man looking fierce at the moment. The Walshs didn't know what to do. Rory Walsh knew there would be even bigger trouble if he called the police on Ramos Santiago's boy.

"I am going up those stairs." He softened his voice slightly, "Just so you know, I own the fucking garage. Do you think I would have bought the place and brought it back to life if I wanted to harm your daughter?" Both Walsh watched slack-jawed with astonishment as Billie headed up.

Opening the first door, he saw it was a boy's room, her brother. The next he opened, he saw Carley sitting on a fluffy pink bed, looking shocked. What is it with girls and pink?

"Carley, you are a great girl. I don't want you to worry about my family or going to Marbella or however long for a fuck. I know you love me, so let's get married."

"Is there a proposal in there somewhere?"

"Yeah, though I made a *dog's dinner* of it." She stood, and he grabbed her in a close embrace, kissing her like it was the last one ever.

They turned, and her parents were standing in the doorway. Billie, with a huge boner, didn't give a shit if they could see it or not.

Mary Ellen lapped up the prospects. Billie's family was stinking rich, and he could provide their daughter security and a luxurious life. She couldn't wait to tell her friends. "Welcome to the family."

Bile rising, Rory turned and walked away in shame. This young punk was his boss, now taking his lovely daughter from him.

⸸ ⸸

"You got a minute?" Billie walked into the Tower War Room, hoping for a chance to speak privately to his dad.

"What's up?"

"Could we go to your office or something?" Anxious, he mumbled.

"Take a seat," said Ramos as he jerked his head to dismiss the three men at the table. He was busy but could see Billie needed a minute.

"I sort of asked Carley to marry me. Mum will go crazy. I love her. I want her in my bed every night when I get home."

Billie was raised surrounded by the warmth and love of his mother and brother, not the violence and hunger that brought most men to villainy. Ramos did not question his son's loyalty, but a successful hardman was a man who was not sentimental or romantic and didn't worry in the least about getting home or what was waiting when he did.

Ramos knew Billie wanted the gangster life and was coming along nicely, but this was not a positive development. He should have put a stop to the Carley business weeks ago.

His reply is cold. "No. Your focus needs to be business. You said it was what you wanted. It's way too early for a family. Stick to whores and follow orders."

Ramos knew the training required to navigate the violent and unpredictable world of crime. Many Criminal entities were erupting all over the city; Albanian Cocaine cowboys in East London, Somali street gangs in the North East, Bengali Machete thugs in the East End, Russian hit squads, Jamaican yardies, Nigerians, Chilean, Turkish, it was a fucking United Nations of danger and evil. He did not leave Billie room for continued discussion.

Billie knew he had blown it. He made a fool of himself with Carley and the whole Walsh family. Now, he looked weak and sappy in front of his dad, his boss. He knew Ramos was telling him to choose business or family, the choice all hardmen are required to make.

Heart thumping in his chest, Billie took a breath and looked at his dad. "Understood. I'll take care of it."

"Get the crew back in here and join us. We have business." The *Agony Aunt* session was over.

# # #

CHAPTER 27

CHINA

"Just this once, can you use a different post office? It's twenty minutes in the wrong fucking direction to visit your girlfriend," said Dingo as he and Frankie left a meet with Ramos at the Tower.

Frankie did not bother to answer. He was driving and was in the mood for his weekly peek at his *China Doll*. He sent money to his gran in Ireland weekly and intentionally waited for her window at the post office.

Dingo once suggested Frankie send Gran enough for a month instead of weekly, saving them the many trips to the post office. Frankie told him to fuck off. Frankie sent funds in small weekly doses because he knew if Gran got more than she needed to get through the week, she would give it to the fecken priest. Bitches didn't know how to handle money.

Pulling to the curb, he left Dingo to deal with the lack of legal parking. Fucking payday for the spongers, thought Frankie. The dole checks arrived, and the clot of losers were getting pub money and paying bills. He finally made it to the head of the line and his lady Winnie.

"Hi, beautiful." She looked up, and he could see she was sad, or afraid. He wasn't sure; he was not too sharp on emotions. "What's up?"

She shook her head. "No problem."

"Come on, something is wrong? Where's your smile?"

"No smile." She shuffled a stack of papers. "Your Gran need money?"

"I take care of my gran, my family." Frankie was trying to figure out what was wrong. "Four hundred."

"I wish four hundred for my family. They have hard life in China." She made out the check and handed it to Frankie. "Lucky Gran."

"When do you get off? Have a coffee or tea with me."

She forced a slight smile. "Not allowed. Nice girl does not go alone with man."

"We won't be alone. What time? I'll be out front."

"Five. Go, my line too long. I get in trouble."

"Five." Said Frankie as he departed. While he waited for her, he went into a small used bookstore and found a book on Ireland.

# #

Winnie was tiny and very thin, and it surprised him as she headed his way. Previously seen only through a glass window, Frankie wondered if maybe inside she was standing on a box.

"Hi, beautiful." She was lovely, with porcelain skin, sleek black hair, and always scarlet red lips.

"You no say to me; not allowed. My family be shame. You be nice man, please."

"Sure. Let's go in here."

"Not place for tea." It was a pub.

"They have tea. Come on." Frankie was confused about continuing, but he waited almost a year to get her out from behind the glass.

Winnie sat with a pot of tea and a single shortbread. Frankie palmed a Guinness and a double shot of Jameson. Not a talker, his beauty, so Frankie tried. "How long have you worked in the post office?"

"Two years. I got papers to work in England four years. Come with brother."

"I came seven years ago. I used to miss Ireland; now I don't think about it much."

"You think Gran, you take good care. Generous son."

"Grandson, she raised me. What's the problem with your family?"

"Hard life in China. Need money to come to England. My brother sends money, me too, but not enough. I try to get loan at bank. They say not possible."

"How much do you need?" asked Frankie, who knew the top money lenders in the city.

"For my family come, need many Pounds." She shook her head. "Not possible."

"Would five thousand be enough?"

"No. Not possible." She changed the subject. "Tell me you favourite dinner? I cook you some time."

"Sounds nice, but why don't I take you out? You hungry?" She was a bag of bones.

"No, must go home. Fix dinner for brother, or he be angry."

"What about on Friday? I will pick you up after work?"

"Not possible. Brother very strict. I go now. He not happy me late." Winnie stood. "You good man. Thank you for book."

##

CHAPTER 20

LING

Frankie tried not to think about Winnie, but she kept popping into his head. He knew after their brief conversation that he would not fuck her anytime soon. Time to send money to Gran but today, Frankie skipped his time with his China doll and hit a post closer to the Rod where he planned to fuck Peaches, a new girl.

When he did make it back to Winnie's location, she was gone. "Hey, what happened to Winnie," he asked the woman making the postal order for Gran.

With a gimlet eye cast in his direction, the sour-puss behind the glass replied, "family problems. She's taking personal time. Do you need anything else, or perhaps you want to know what happened to my colleague Charlie over the weekend? Got bit by his dog." The nasty bitch glared, and Frankie wanted to punch her in the face.

Walking out the shop door, Frankie's eye caught a girl motioning to him. Slowing down to catch him, she looked furtive and spoke softly. "I know you are her friend. She told me. Winnie is in trouble. Someone beat her up. She looks awful."

"Sorry to hear it; she's a nice gal," said Frankie.

"I think it was her brother. He hits her when she doesn't do as he says."

"You know where she lives?"

"Yes, but he does not let her have visitors."

"Where?" said Frankie.

"Islington, over the Fortune Cookie café on Grand Street. I don't know the flat number, but it doesn't face the street. Tell her Judy said hi."

#

"Who is the girl?" Asked Rio as Frankie returned to the car.

"We need to make a detour."

"That's unwelcome news. My dick is already on its way to the Rod." When Frankie did not reply, "Mind if I ask where?"

"Islington."

"Why the fuck would we want to go to that shithole?"

"I gotta check on Winnie."

"Who the fuck is Winnie?"

"Fuck you," said Frankie, gaining anger with each stoplight.

"Ok, what the hell? Let's go to beautiful downtown Islington."

#

The Fortune Cookie was in the local Islington, China town, and a 6'3 ginger and a 6'2 spic stood out. "I'm looking for Winnie," said Frankie as he approached a man sitting on a stool on the terrace of the Fortune Cookie.

The man replied with a shrug. Not acceptable. Frankie grabbed the man by the throat and jerked him to his feet. "Winnie?"

"Up. Up there." The small man pointed to the sky. Frankie dropped the man and headed up the stairs. At the top were two doors. He hard-shouldered the one on the right. The door split, and he stood in a small room with five women sitting on the floor eating bowls of rice and broth.

"Where's Winnie?" The six lowered their eyes, and no one replied. From the back walked a small but tough-looking Chinese man.

"Get out."

"Where's Winnie?" The man's posture stood firm, so Frankie pushed past him. The man rotated to kick him, so Rio pulled his gun.

"Back off, Jackie Chan." Some of the women began to weep. "Shut up and don't move."

Frankie approached a door covered with a sheet. Pulling the fabric aside, he came face to face with Winnie. Covered with bruises, she rested on a mat on the floor, nursing a baby.

Frankie was stunned but recovered quickly, "You ok?"

"You go."

"You ok?"

"You go, brother, be angry."

"Is that asshole your brother?" Winnie nodded yes as her eyes kept the door in view. "Is that your baby?" She nodded again. "Is your brother the father?" Winnie dropped her eyes in shame.

Rio kept eyes on the brother. With the smallness of the room, it was not difficult.

"You want to get out of here?" Frankie wanted to carry her out right then.

"No place to go. Must stay with family."

"I got a better place. Grab some stuff. Let's go."

"My baby and sister, too, please?"

"She out front?"

"Yes. Please, for Ling to go?"

"Sure. Come on." Frankie took Winnie's arm, and she flinched with pain from her injuries. In the front room, Winnie said something to Ling in Chinese.

"Rio, take them to the car." Rio's face showed shock, but he did not argue. Instead, he led them down the stairs.

"Asshole, you're mine." Frankie stood tall, and the brother rounded on his heels and kicked him right in the ribs. Frankie bent with pain, but his anger kept him going. Grabbing his opponent by the arm, he twisted it behind him, and it snapped.

The brother looked stunned but kept going. He dove headfirst into Frankie's abdomen, landing a powerful gut punch.

"Enough of this shit," said Frankie as he pulled his gun. The brawling stopped, and Frankie backed out the door.

Rio put the two women and baby in the back seat of the Range Rover. "Where to? I take it you have a plan?"

"Greentown." Frankie was referring to a shabby area near Gatwick with no green at all. When they arrived, Frankie pointed out a modest hotel and café.

First stop, the café. "What's going on, Winnie?"

Winnie and Ling looked at each other. "Brother, bad man. He makes us do bad things to make money for family." Frankie figured the brother was pimping them all out. Ling was skin and bones and couldn't be more than 14. The irony of a strong, bad man preying on vulnerable women was entirely lost on these two gangsters.

"He found book you give to me. He made me tell him. Make very angry. He hit me many times."

After a meal, Frankie got them settled in the hotel. He returned with five thousand cash, a box of nappies, and plane tickets. "Here you go. That bastard won't find you in Ireland. Here is money and a letter to give to my Gran. I'll call and let her know you are coming."

"The plane is at eleven-forty in the morning. I will pick you up at eight-thirty if I am detained and not here by nine. Get a taxi and go to Gatwick. OK?"

"Thank you, Mr. Frankie. You good man." Said Winnie as Ling nodded.

"You are going to be fine. See you in the morning."

Frankie returned to the car where Rio waited. "If you're done with the Social Services work, can we get to the Rod while I am still young enough to get a boner?"

"Come on; they're nice girls. I feel like going back and finishing that fucking brother."

"You need to relax. They're fine. Let's get some pussy, and we both will feel better." Frankie was still steaming, but Rio was correct; there was nothing more to do tonight.

# #

Frankie and Rio rolled up at the hotel at eight AM and kept rolling. The place was crawling with Filth and a couple of ambulances. It was easy to see the action was in the room where he left the women and baby. It was not difficult to find out what happened. The area was swarming with gawkers. "A real blood bath in there," said one observer.

"Killed a baby too, or a dog because I saw them carry out a small body-bag."

Frankie turned the car toward Islington. "Hey, this is fucked up, but you can't fix it now, and you need permission to kill the bastard. You know Ramos wants no civilians touched."

"Fuck that. He's a pimp. He's dead. You don't want to come along; get the fuck out."

"I'm in. Just don't wreck the fucking car." Rio sat back and pulled his gun to check that all was ready if needed.

"She must have called him," said Rio.

"Or he has a tracker on her phone." As they pulled onto Greenway, they could see the Fortune Cookie and flats above were engulfed in fire.

"Goddamit!" Shouted Frankie as he slammed his hand on the wheel.

"Hey, brother, chill. He's running. We'll find him."

"He has five thousand to get him gone." As Frankie turned the car toward the Highstreet, he looked in his rear-view mirror and saw the brother watching the fire from across the street. Slamming the brakes, he jumped from the car and took off running.

Rio pulled behind the wheel and followed. Frankie surprised the brother and quickly had him by the neck. Rio slowed. Frankie threw the brother in the back seat and jumped in. Placing his big arm on the brother's windpipe, he was quickly unconscious. Frankie relaxed.

"Where to?"

"The Scrapyard." Sherry's, Sheridan's Scrap Yard was a one-way trip. The *old faithful* where used cars and major appliances went to die, and occasionally, other pests vanished.

"Oh, we are going to have some fun. OK." Rio was always up for violence. The location was used for torture. When Ramos needed information, the uncooperative person was taken to the scrapyard, thrown in a portacabin, and awaited a wide variety of options for pain and abuse: fire, electricity, tools, and all means of misery.

⚜ ⚜

Forty minutes later, the men drove out. "Some of your finest work, Rio." Frankie's smile had returned. "Having him watch as you nipped off his dick in three snips was a nice finishing touch."

"Let's hit the Rod. I need a fuck and a nap." Just then, Frankie's phone pinged. He read the message. "Duty calls, next stop, the Tower."

"Better call your Gran and let her know your girlfriend isn't coming."

⚜ ⚜ ⚜

## CHAPTER 29

JANELLE

Hardman's job description: dangerous career, long hours, dirty work, high tension, and a high probability of getting hurt or worse. The ones good at it love it and usually survive.

The most delicate tasks were not the most fatal, but anything could turn deadly. The uncertainty and edginess kept the men alert. It takes a unique man to do this work and a rare kind of woman to love them.

# #

"Janelle, open up." Tyler banged on Axel's family home door.

"Why? You want to hit me too." Ramos and all of his men would hit a woman without pause, except perhaps Axel, who was not raised in a home where violence against women was commonplace.

"No one hit you, Janelle. Come on, open the door." He pounded again.

"You better not touch me, or I will tell Axel, and he'll kill you." Tyler rolls his eyes.

"Yeah, he would, but no one will touch you. Open it, or I am going to take it down."

"OK, I will open it, but stand back because I am going to film you. Don't try nothin'." The door opened. Tyler stepped through, grabbed the phone, and tossed it on the sofa.

"You're an asshole." She was not angry, just her usual feisty handful.

"Yeah, I've heard. You got a visitor." Ramos stepped inside.

Janelle went quiet as she looked up at Ramos' face, and he digested the fucking gorgeous woman who stood in front of him. Not surprisingly, Axel is a handsome fuck, but his woman is beauty pageant beautiful.

"You're Ramos, right?" said Janelle. He nodded. She recovered from the surprise visit by her husband's boss. "Did he tell you Axel got arrested for beating me?"

"Hell, Janelle, he didn't hit you. You threw the remote at him, and he grabbed your arm," said Tyler. Bad timing is the only reason Axel is arrested. The minor family altercation occurred as the police took an incident report next door of petty vandalism and heard the commotion. It was a decent but imperfect neighbourhood.

She started to point out her bruise but thought better. "He had it coming." Talking to Ramos, "He doesn't pay any attention to his family and pushed me too far. I snapped. I'm no whore; we're married."

Ramos calm. "Look around, Janelle. Nice house, nice car, nice things; bet you have a closet full and plenty of food and cash. Axel works his ass off, taking care of his family. You want him home or working making money?"

Ramos was impressed with the place. Top-quality and immaculate. Well paid, Axel clearly spent on his family, often rare in the villain game. Axel inherited a sizeable amount when his Argentinian grandmother passed. Ramos knew because Axel told him in confidence. He did not want his lifestyle misinterpreted as a skim. After the windfall, Axel never considered retiring from crime. He was having too damn much fun.

"He does take good care of us but only comes home a few times a week. I don't know when he will come through the door or walk out. He comes in smiling, plays with the babies, watches football, and tells me what he wants for dinner. We have a great fuck then he's gone."

"I have been with Axel since I was sixteen. No sex with another man. Ok, I fooled around, but no man's cock but his. He taught me all kinds of fun things to do when we're fucking. What is the point if he doesn't come home? What am I supposed to do with my expertise, write a book? She was not mean or bitchy, just spunky as hell. Ramos let her keep going.

"Sunday was my 25th birthday. My hair and nails were done, my pussy waxed, and I was ready for a big celebration. Does he bring me flowers and a nice gift and take me out on the town? No. He never showed." Ramos knew Axel was in Manchester, making a political payoff to one of the many politicians in his back pocket. His pockets were getting pretty crowded.

"My friends called all day yesterday. "What did Axel get you for your birthday? *Nothin*. It was humiliating." She hoped she convinced Ramos with her thorough explanation of her actions. Mostly, he was astonished at how long she seemed to be able to chatter without taking a breath.

"When Axel and this one," she jabbed a finger in Tyler's stone-hard abs, an action that would get most a broken arm or more, but Tyler, practically part of the family, just snorted at her, "walked in, what do you think my man said? "Oh, Baby, I am so sorry. Oh, Baby, I got you a fabulous present. He walked in with a sexy smile and said, " Baby, I want pork chops."

"Pork chops! Hell, if I had a pork chop, I would have hit him with it. I didn't, so I used the remote."

"It's over, Janelle. Axel needs to be back at work. You need to get dressed up pretty, go to the Nick, and explain it was a misunderstanding and you do not want to press charges."

"And they will let him out?"

"Yes," said Ramos.

"Tyler!" She knew Tyler well and seemed determined to tear him a new one. "You knew and let him sleep with a bunch of paedophiles?"

"What the hell?" Tyler shakes his head and shrugs. Ramos was puzzled too, but knew she would have some explanation.

"My Axel is your best friend, and you should have told me I could get him out yesterday. I barely slept last night. I saw a show on Channel Four about the kind of people in prison."

"He's not in prison," Tyler tried to stop the rant with some factual information, but she wasn't having it.

"Whatever, but he spent a night with paedophiles, rapists, thieves, and killers because of you."

"Janelle, it was because..." His voice tapered off.

Ramos was tired of the conversation. "Here's a thousand. Get him out and get yourself a birthday present, or take your girlfriends to dinner, but Axel needs to get to work."

Finally, out of gas, she went quiet and gave a slight nod.

"The ink, Janelle." Ramos let it hang.

"Oh. You know?" Ramos nodded. In her snit, Janelle went to a tat studio and inked *Fuck Ramos* over her ass hole. She did not question how he knew. Several girlfriends went with her to get it, all with husbands who worked for Ramos.

"No disrespect. I figured if Axel would rather spend my important birthday with you, and well, I was kinda drunk." Ramos saw fear cross her eyes, and she was right to be afraid; his take-no-shit reputation was clear.

"It has to go, Janelle," he doubled down. He attempted not to scare her but to make his message clear.

"It hurt like hell and is really tender. Can I wait a while?

Ramos, at the end of his patience. "No. It's disrespectful to my woman, and she will be the one humiliated." Furious, but he wasn't burning the damn thing off her ass right now because Axel was a vital team member. But it better be sorted quickly; no one is irreplaceable.

"Don't tell her," She added.

"You know things get out. I am sure you told your girlfriends all about it." He saw photos taken by them. Ramos knew Alice would not hear of it but used her to make his non-negotiable point. "You have till the end of the week," three days away. Axel would get it done.

Back in the car, Ramos looked at Tyler, and both men howled. "Holy hell, what a handful."

"A beautiful handful. Axel probably goes to work to get some fuckin rest."

"Boss, those two are crazy nuts about each other. Axel spends every minute he's not working with her and his kids. Janelle loves to fuck and is damn good at it. Says she wears him out."

"Write a book." Both men laughed.

Ramos heard about Axel. Most of his men, even the married ones, spent time at the clubs and bars with whores, but if not work-related, Axel was not around. Not saying he didn't ever swerve the wife and fuck away from home. Any man would, but one look at Janelle and a fine fuck, pretty much explained why he didn't wander far.

"Will she do it?" Meaning, going to get him.

"Oh yeah. I'll drop you at the Rod and go get him."

"Poor bastard probably got a peaceful night's sleep with the paedophiles."

# # #

151

CHAPTER 30

MICK

"You're telling me no one thought it a wise idea to inform me of Cantrell's arrest? Fucking imbeciles." The city was opened up from the Covid. Last night, the bars and clubs were booming, and the streets were full of drunks. Good for business, but it was never that simple.

"He didn't seem significant enough to matter to you'" said Tyler.

"He knows way too much about the card rooms and the drops to be sitting in an interrogation room waiting for a deal."

"Only holding him for now. His wife says he hopes to be home later today."

"Isn't she the fucking optimist? He's probably not going to be home for three to five years. Who are the detectives on the case? Tell me they are on the payroll."

"Yes and No."

"What the hell does that mean?" Ramos was beyond irritated.

"It's Peterson and Jones. Jones, of course, is a friend, but Peterson is new. All about getting the bad guys."

"I guess the only question is, whose family is at risk now? Cantrell's or Petersons?"

"I say first we have a chat with Cindy Cantrell. Her father is one of the Latte brother's collectors. She grew up in the life she knew to keep her mouth shut. She can get a message to Cantrell."

"If he's on a 48-hour hold, it will be expensive, but get her in. She has one try, then Peterson's wife is going to casualty."

"Problem, boss, sources tell me Peterson is gay."

"Even better. Find Peterson's partner; nothing quite as sentimental as a poof and his favourite butt-fuck."

Four hours later, the message was delivered. Cantrell loved his wife and three stupid children and would not say anything or take any deal. He knew if he grassed and Ramos didn't kill him, his father-in-law would. A big boy, he could do his lump if it came to that.

Every day brought Ramos a series of near misses. You could not predict who would be the one to bring you down. It could take its toll.

"You heading to the Rod?" asked Tyler.

Slap on his happy face and go to a fucking birthday party? That is not going to happen. Ramos decided to give the festivities a swerve. "Get the fuck out."

#

Sitting in his Surrey office, Ramos pushed his desk chair back and stretched his long legs. The children were sleeping, and he appreciated the stillness.

The case being built against him was growing, and his efforts at containment and dismissal were, so far, falling flat. The case and COVID were making shit-hash out of his ability to do business. There seemed to be little he could do about any of it except wait. Making a man like Ramos feel powerless was rare and filled him with anger, but right now, he just felt knackered.

#

"Youngblood, it's time you showed up to the party." Billie walked toward the bar at the Lightning Rod. "Frankie is celebrating his birthday and has bet me he fucks ten bitches tonight. I have five hundred that says no way with his stubby dick." The messy lines of cocaine and empty glasses showed that the party had been raging for a while. IV drips with *recovery-fluids* sat nearby; the party was not expected to slow down anytime soon.

"Ten? That's some bullshit there," said Carter.

Someone handed Billie a vodka. He tossed it back, smacked his lips, and countered, "I've seen the *crimson mick* in action. He has at least ten in him."

"Thank you, my fine young friend, for the vote of confidence," slurred Frankie.

From age fifteen, he refused to touch a drop of alcohol in a bargain made with the good Lord Almighty if God would spare his beloved Gran. Being a solid Irish Catholic, it was a vow few could keep. But Frankie never broke his solemn oath until two months ago when dear Gran, age eighty-four, passed peacefully in her sleep. No, it wasn't the fucking Covid.

"You think with Carlos in the hospital, we should be celebrating?"

Carlos was Ramos's partner in crime since their mid-twenties. A decade ago, he moved to club management after being severely hurt and crippled by an auto crash. He missed the danger of a gangster's life. But bar life has its risks; Carlos has cirrhosis.

"Carlos has been unkind to his liver. What's left of his shrivelled organ is on strike," explained Carter, managing things while Carlos was away.

"I always say, better a shrivelled liver than a shrivelled dick."

"I hear you, brother. Slainte!" Frankie raised his glass in solidarity.

"Slawn-what?" Asked Billie.

"Some Irish thing he has been saying," replied Rio.

Frankie slapped his leg. "Tell bitch number four to back that ass over here." Carter held up three fingers.

#

Long hours of work and blurry nights became routine for Billie, but nothing washed away his feelings for Carley. And his shame at what he knew he had to do. He had put it off long enough.

#

"Hey Carley, where are you?" He was calling from his car, already in Baylor.

"Hi, I am heading to St. Barnabus."

"Confession?" Clipped in his delivery, Billie alerted Carley to something wrong.

"No, to light a candle and say thank you. I am..." Billie cut her off. The Walsh family were faithful Catholics.

"Meet me out front in twenty minutes." Then the line when cold.

#

Waiting at the curb, when Carley walked out, Billie remembered St. Barnabus. When he lived in Baylor, his mum and brother attended Mass and all the social functions. His mum often played piano for events.

Carley slid into the front seat and leaned in for a kiss, which didn't happen. As she withdrew, she felt a sense of concern. "Is everything okay?"

He could not look at her. "Yeah, but we need to pump the brakes. I'm just starting business, and you are returning to school. I know you want to be a teacher and…."

"Not more than I want to be your wife. Tell me, what's wrong?" Her confidence was failing.

Billie looked at her lovely face he was about to spit in. "It's not a good time."

Carley was a bright girl and went right to the moment's reality. "Are you calling off the wedding or breaking up with me? Or both?"

"Both, I guess, it's just not the right time and…."

She lunged at him, hitting him with her small, soft hands. He made no attempt to stop her. She wasn't hurting him; he deserved whatever she wanted him to feel. "You promised me. You lied. I will never trust you again." She stopped hitting him and sat back in her seat as her eyes became teary.

"You got what you wanted. I told you I didn't know how to do that stuff. I must have been a big disappointment to you?" They spent the night in a nice hotel together after the proposal. He had sex with her every time they were together since. Now, she felt used and dirty.

"I meant everything I said. Holding you and being inside of you is the best feeling in my life."

"I never want to see you again or hear anything you have to say." She tried for the door, but the safety locks prohibited her from exiting. She hit out at the locked door, then leaned her head against the glass and cried.

He was torn up seeing his sweet Carley this way, but he made a commitment to Ramos, which came first. He knew she would never again feel the same about him. The loss felt enormous.

In front of her home, he released the safety locks. She opened the door and got out without looking back.

Billie felt awful, but the fact he did meant Ramos was right. He was acting like a weak-ass fool, and that shit needed to stop, or he might as well get a job in a chippie.

#

CHAPTER 31

POPS

Ramos returned from Surrey, went to the War Room, and boisterous guffaws instantly surrounded him.

"Sinbad's woman, Monica, comes out during the night and sees he is on his computer with his dick out. She figures he's watching porn, and well, this bitch is always up for it. She creeps up and looks over his shoulder, and he is looking at a dick-flix. Just brothers fucking and sucking.

She is so offended; that she goes to the bedroom, gets Bad's silenced gun from the bedside, and shoots him in the dick till the clip is empty, and there is not much left to shoot at." Loud moans and groans from the crew as the complete scenario sets in. Several men grabbed their packages in solidarity.

"He dead?" asks Ramos as the men turn to look at him.

"No, but he probably wishes he was. Bitch damn near shot his dick off. Gone."

"And one of his legs is mince," added Jet as the men continued to laugh.

"Filth on it?" asks Ramos. Bad is one of his tier-two crew, and he wanted to pre-empt any blowback.

"She called her girlfriend Sabrina, Colum's wife."

"Colum Bell?" Colum and Sinbad were partners on a major protection crew. Ramos was trying to see how close this shitstorm was to him.

He remembered when Sinbad was promoted to the second tier. He asks the boss for a private word. "Guv, so you know, I like pussy, but I ah, well, I sometimes like dick.' It was quite a confession for a hardman. Sinbad waited for all hell to break loose, but Ramos surprised him.

"You have a woman?" Bad, waiting for the hammer to fall, cautiously nodded his reply. "It's your life and your dick. Don't do anything with it that brings shit into my world. You clear?"

"Colum called Tyler. He's on it. He and Frankie took the computer, staged the room to look like Bad was stoned, and cleaning his gun when it

156

went off." Nine times? "They made a call saying they were neighbours and thought they heard shots. Now they are outside the Royal. Bad is in surgery.

"They arrest his woman?" asked Ramos.

"No, Monica and Sabrina went out for pancakes." Sounds about right, thought Ramos.

"Ok, Ladies, let's wrap it up." Ramos would head to seven.

# #

In the years since her mother's death, Julie had desperately wanted a family and had built one with Ross. Now, he was gone, and she was once again terribly lonely. The tabloid stories and envy of others who imagined her wonderful life were hurtful. Why was having a family so impossible?

Julie knew classmates from Sacred Hearts school who could trace their families back a thousand years, but she didn't even know who her grandparents were or where. Are they still alive? Where were they now?

# #

"Move along. You are not coming in," said the enormous well-dressed bouncer. Julie wondered where her grandparents were. Grandpa was at the Cairo Club's door trying to get in.

"Watch who you are putting your hands on. I'm Sir John Kohl's father-in-law."

"Sure you are, but Sir has parted his earthly life, now shove off."

This was the third club he tried to enter, and again was refused. The slight elderly man stood brushing his shabby lapels. Tonight, ready for rejection, he wrote his name and number on a piece of paper. He insisted the man on the door take it and give it to Ramos, whom he had read in the tabloids, was in control of the Kohl organization. The hefty man crumpled the paper as he put it in his pocket.

"What's your name? I am going to tell Ramos how you treated me." He stumbled backward into Frankie, whose first instinct was to hit, but not at the door of an elegant club.

Frankie looked at Kimbo, the doorman. "What's up?"

"Says he's the Kohl children's grandfather."

Frankie gave the man a fierce look and walked directly to Ramos' office. Not about the old git but with a message from one of Ramos' Captains who requested an urgent meet in Camden. Ramos hated drama. When Frankie mentioned the grandfather, he was already in a foul mood.

"Another fucking relative?" Rhetorical, Frank didn't answer. Through the years, dozens of letters arrived at the Tower with people claiming to be long-lost dads, cousins, or best friends of John Kohl's late wife. Ann nor the Kohl children were shown the notes from these fools. The Tower's sixth-floor investigation team, Kohl-Mine, censored, intercepted, read, catalogued, and destroyed their mail.

"He show up before?" asked Ramos.

"Couple other clubs. I've seen the old guy's face on the screens."

"If he shows up again, take him to meet Sherry." The remaining Kohl children were a mess and they did not need the complication of grandpa showing up. Or another goddamn chapter for the tabloid saga.

"Two evenings later, Rio spotted the man near the front entrance of the Sahara Club. After signalling Frankie for backup, he walked over to the man.

"Ramos isn't here tonight. He's in Essex at The Lightning Rod. He got your message and told us if you showed up to bring you to him."

"I told you he would want to see me. Let's go." The man all puffed up as Frankie smiled at him and held the door of the black Mercedes.

"Front or back?" Asked Frankie.

Smiling broadly, "The back. You got one of them driver hats?" As Kohl's father-in-law, he could get used to VIP treatment.

Riding toward Sherry's, the man could not contain his mouth. "Yeah, my little Annie, she was a sweet one. Calls me Pops." Ruffling about in his pockets, looking for something, "Here you go," he said as he shoved a handful of photos toward the front seat. "Take um."

Frank reached back and took the photos. He looked and passed one to Rio. Neither man had ever met Annie Kohl, but Frankie had seen pictures of her. Sure enough, a picture of Annie, John Kohl's wife, standing with a woman and the man sitting in the back seat. She looked about ten years old but hadn't changed much when she died.

"Always tiny and smiling, like Annie's Mum Julie too."

"What took you so long to get in touch?"

"Ah, well, I had a little trouble and.."

"Inside?" Asked Rio.

"Yeah, but it is not what you think. I didn't do it." Frankie and Rio exchanged glances. Prisons are full of people who didn't do it.

Gramps might be a relative. Rio is uncertain if Ramos wants him gone either way. He looked to Frankie for guidance as Pops spoke up. "I thought I might have to go to the newspapers to see my grandchildren." Rio could see Pops would not be returning from Sherry's. No one threatens to go to the paper and survives.

The car bounced on uneven stones as they pulled into the scrap yard. The old man in the back asked, "What's going on? Why are we..." He didn't finish. Looking at Frank, old Pops started to see the light. He panicked and grabbed the locked door handle, but it wouldn't budge.

"You have me all wrong; I don't want nothing from the Kohls. I just want to see my grandchildren." Let me out, and I'll get lost."

The two men in the front ignored him as Rio killed the engine. Out of the car, Frankie reached in, grabbed Grandpa, and with a quick shift, cracked the old man's neck and shoved him to the gravelled drive.

After removing Pop's wallet and phone, he tossed the cash on the body and added a few hundred more. He looked up as Bruno Sheridan emerged from his Portakabin office and waddled across the yard toward them. "He's all yours."

Pulling out through the gates, Bruno's daughters gave a wave. A trio of crazy-ass, lot-lizards with serious *titage*. All three fucked the noxious Bruno and adored the fat slob. Business was brisk with the men who visited Daddy.

One was pretty, but the other two dogs, though these men didn't much care how they looked. They fucked them all, but none could keep their mouth shut, and today Frankie was not in the mood. He drove on.

Rio laughed, still pumped up from the kill. "Let's find Rita and that big redhead. My balls need a cuddle."

"I hear you, brother."

#

Ramos and Jimmy were working in the Cairo Club office when Rio and Frankie returned. Jimmy looked up, "Dear old Pops resting peacefully?" Frank replied with a slight nod. Reaching into his jacket pocket, he brought out the old man's phone, wallet, and photos.

Not DNA, but it looked like the douche-bag might be Annie's father or her brother's father. Ramos did not need any new headaches, and Julie did not need further emotional upsets. It pleased him that Pops was out of the picture permanently.

Ramos opened the bottom desk drawer and put the photos through a cross shredder. Isolating Julie was the only way he could protect her from the evil, corrupt world of bad men. Ramos was fairly certain that *ol* Pops wanted something. Everyone does.

Urgent Camden would have to wait. "Get out and send in Vicki," a new Smoke whore. The grandfather issue is as finished as the old man himself.

# # #

CHAPTER 32

IAN

Rio returned from a pick-up at Ribizzi's garage. Even though it proved an excellent investment, these days, Billie tried to avoid the place.

After Ramos's weekly cut, he quickly repaid his dad and enjoyed a nice earn. With additional income and amounts from the crew work and poker, for a young man, he was raking it in.

Not that he had anything to spend the money on. He drove new cars, lived in a beautiful place, and had unlimited free fucks, alcohol, and blow. He was saving his money, and while he wouldn't admit it, he wanted to save enough to marry Carley. It might take a long time. Right now, he was pretty sure she hated his guts.

Ramos put in a money drop and moved stacks of cash through the books at Ribizzi's. No one would question the figures because the place was continually busy. Walsh added three more mechanics and a girl to make the bookings. There was talk of enlarging the building and going seven days a week. It was a roaring success.

Walking into the War Room at the Tower, Rio grabbed a beer and took a seat. "Been out to Baylor, saw that girl you're sweet on."

Billie tried to look nonchalant but was all ears. "I heard she was at school or something?" a casual reply.

"She was talking to Walsh." Rio took a pull. "Had a baby in one of those cart things." Rio didn't look too concerned as he picked up a tittie magazine from the table.

"Didn't hear she had a kid," Billie disguised his shock. "Was it hers?"

"Didn't have a chat, did I?" Rio smirked at Jet and Dingo sitting there.

"What did the kid look like?" Billie didn't like having to ask, but he wanted to know.

"You mean, is Daddy black?" Rio was giving him a hard time.

"You prick." Said Billie. Getting your shit handed to you was how these men operated. But fuck it; they could be a hateful bunch.

He hadn't seen Carley in months. He needed to do the math. No way he could have a kid? Fuck, what had he done? He drew his phone to call her and stopped.

No, he told himself. It is over. Leave her alone. But what if she has his baby? His mind was racing. Worst of all, he still loved her so damn much. Some fucking tough guy.

#

"Hello, young man, who are you? You look like my son, but I haven't seen him in a while," teased Alice. She did not want to jeopardize her close relationship with Billie by holding on to hurt feelings about his outburst of loyalty to his dad.

"Ok, Mum, point taken." He had intentionally given a bit of distance from the family dinner after Danny accidentally revealed he had been shot. Things felt normal again.

Luna and Stella ran in. "Billie, Billie." Their joyful chatter filled the kitchen. He leaned down and picked them both up, one in each arm. They hugged his neck and gave him messy kisses. "Did you bring us a present?" He never came home empty-handed.

"Yep, it's in my jacket." He set them down, pulled out two lollypops, and held them high as they jumped. "Ok, here you go."

"Mum, you got any food?" Billie stuck his head inside an enormous chock-full side-by-side fridge-freezer.

"You'll find a few of your favourites," she laughed and walked toward him for a hug. "Come on, hug me, and I will fix what you want."

"Mum, you're the best. Can I have the roast beef from Sunday lunch? Yum." Alice resumed Sunday lunches, but only family, Julie, Annie, Sissy, and occasionally Tyler, but none of the other crew.

"None left after you and your dad finished. I was lucky to have a bone to give the dog. Both turned to each other in a serious tone.

"Mum, did you hear about Carley's brother Ian?"

"Oh, son, it's horrible. You can't feel safe even in a nice area." Alice had been mugged on her doorstep in Baylor a few years earlier.

"The funeral is Tuesday. Will you go with me?" Billie wanted to go but was unsure of his welcome if he went alone.

"Of course. Have you spoken to Carley?"

"No, Mum, we didn't leave it too good." Billie was looking down. She knew he loved the girl and was uncertain why it hadn't worked out. She did not know Ramos had intervened.

#

Billie received word through Dingo that Mr. Walsh wanted to see him. He asked if he could come by the garage on Sunday near five. Billie hoped he did not want to leave his employment. It was Walsh who kept the place thriving and the money pouring in.

Ten minutes to five, he pulled up. He could see Walsh's car but waited until five sharpish. The shop was a veritable beehive of activity most days but closed on Sundays. Today, the place seemed eerily quiet.

The small office was the only light in the place, and when Billie entered, Walsh stood. After all, Billie was the owner.

"Hello, Mr. Walsh." Out of respect, Billie never called him Rory.

"Billie." Walsh was quiet, almost timid. Billie thought something was wrong. Had an employee been skimming? Was a customer hurt on-premises? The drugs? Or, maybe Walsh wanted a raise, and in fairness, he was due.

Billie started. "Mr. Walsh, I'm sorry about what happened to Ian."

"I saw you and your Mum at the funeral. Sorry I didn't say hello, but my Mary Ellen was in a bad way." He continued not to make eye contact. "She's still not able to go out of the house."

"I am sorry to hear that." Billie could not figure out what this was all about. As far as he knew, Rory and the whole Walsh family hated him for what he did to Carley and probably for owning the garage. "Have the police found the fucker? Excuse me. Have they?"

"That's just it. I don't think they are even looking. Coppers figure it was just another drunken Pub fight. It's been four weeks and nothing. My Mary Ellen is not doing too well." His face pinched with pain, "I don't want to lose her too."

Billie felt the hurt and frustration emanating from Walsh. "How can I help?"

Rory hesitated. He scratched behind his ear, shifted his feet, and ran a hand to his shirt pocket, which was empty. Billie waited. "You seem to have many contacts, and I was thinking maybe someone has heard something?"

"No, sir, I have not heard anything."

"I was hoping maybe you could ask around?"

"I would be happy to and anything else if I can. What do you want me to do with the information if I get it?" Billie was beginning to see what Walsh wanted but was unsure how far he planned to go.

"My Mary Ellen needs to know what happened, and well, I guess you could call it some justice." He raised his eyes to Billie.

"I can't promise you anything, but leave it with me," said Billie as he offered his hand. It felt risky, and he was relieved when Walsh took him in a firm shake.

⚟ ⚟

"You wanna do what?" asked Dingo.

"I want to find the bastard that killed Walsh's lad."

"And do what? Slay the dragon, make the fair Princess Carley fall in love with you again?" The men were relentlessly cold-hearted. Not raised that way, Billie found it difficult not to be blindsided by their constant lack of humanity.

"No, asshole, I want to give him a fucking medal. Are you going to help me, or shall I ask Boomer?" Billie knew there was a rivalry between Boomer and Dingo and hoped to use it to his advantage. Being Ramos's son was not always a plus. In this instance, he hoped Dingo would not want to be the one who turned him down.

"Don't shit yourself. I was looking for motivation."

"Motivation, aren't you the enlightened motherfucker," said Rio as he walked in and joined the conversation. It broke the tension as the men laughed.

⚟ ⚟

Billie put a ten thousand Pound bounty on the man who killed Ian. No questions asked. That kind of money generated considerable interest. Within the first hour, calls and texts started rolling in. Most were quickly dealt with as useless, but on day three, things turned promising.

"Hello. You the one?" The caller asked Billie on his nameless burner.

"Yeah."

"Can we meet?"

"You have something to tell me? Or is this a fishing expedition?"

"I have what you want. Is it true, no questions and the ten thousand?"

"Straight up. Ribizzi's garage, Sunday night at six p.m. You better not be wasting my time."

"I'm not. You are going to want…." Billie hung up.

#

Dingo, Rio, and Billie neared the garage. "Did you run this past Daddy?" The men were always willing to goad him. Billie, as usual, let it roll off. "We don't want Dad pissed off at us."

The only time the men didn't give Billie the piss was when he played poker. Billie earned the reputation of being a top-rated poker player and often cleaned the table. The men respected that. He used their condescending opinion of him against them. They consistently underestimated him because of the way he became part of the inner circle. His twin brother Danny didn't get all the brains. Clever as hell, to Billie, card counting was second nature.

"Tyler knows what's up," replied Billie. He intentionally did not tell Ramos. Instead, he went to Tyler, his dad's top man. Tyler reminded him that no one but Ramos can order a kill; *don't write a check; you can't cash.*

"How are we going to play it?" asked Rio. This was Billie's meeting, and Rio let him make the call.

"Not sure. He may be just another asshole who wants money for nothing," said Billie. "In that case, we will beat the hell out of him for wasting our time."

"Now you're talking," said Dingo, who was always more than ready to rumble.

Dark inside and outside of the garage, Billie used the entry code. Shortly after six came a knock. "You in there?"

Rio opened the door. There stood a guy about twenty-five who didn't look much like a gangster and a lot like your average ass-wipe.

"Inside," growled Rio in his most menacing voice.

The visitor kept looking back at Rio as if he expected any minute to be hit with a blunt instrument. Rio was having fun with subtle but clear threats. "Sit over there and don't move."

Billie and Dingo walked out of the office. "Who the fuck are you," asked Billie.

"Ah, I ah," the guy looked ready to bolt.

"Your name too difficult for you?" asked Rio.

"No, I just…, why is it so dark in here?"

"Global warming. We are saving on electricity, and if you don't say your name in ten seconds, I am going to think you're wasting my time."

"Jerod Munns. Did you bring the money?"

"Pump the brakes, Jerod. What do you have for me? What the fuck do you have that's worth ten thousand."

Jerod relaxed a bit. "I know who killed Ian and why. Is that worth ten?"

"You have proof?" asked Billie.

"Absolute proof," he puffed up.

"Tell me."

"How can I be sure I will get the money?"

"You can't. Start talking, or this ugly beast will offer some persuasion." He pointed to Dingo.

"First, I have a couple of questions."

The men chuckled at the guy's balls. "What are you going to do with the information? Go to the police?"

"Do we look like men who are helpful to the Filth? Your question should be, what will I do to the murderous bastard who did this evil deed."

"What are you going to do?" Jarod's eyes shot wide. He was losing his attitude.

"It's not your concern."

"I don't want to get anyone hurt."

"Right now, the only one in danger of getting hurt is you. Times up. Say what you know. Or get out."

Jerod started to stand up. Rio pushed him back down.

"No, Jer, not before you tell me what you know."

"I know who did it, but I can't tell you if you are going to kill him or something."

"Whoa, kill him? Hell, Jerod, you've been watching too much telly. No one is going to kill anyone. That would be illegal." Rio and Dingo joined in, nodding and surprised at such an idea.

"And a sin," added Rio as he crossed himself."

"Yeah, that too. Ok, Jerod, you're up."

"You give me your word about no one getting hurt?"

"Yeah, you got my word."

"Can I see the money?"

"Sure, in a nice safe bundle right here in my jacket." Billie patted his chest.

"Do you promise?" muttered Jarod. The men chuckled.

"Yeah, I promise I won't cum in your mouth. Knock off the shit and give me a name."

"Jerod Munns."

"Not your name, asshole, the mugger."

"Ah, it was me. I didn't mean to kill him. Honest."

"You fucking expect me to pay you ten thousand, and you just walk out?" Billie was shaking his head.

"Proof." Smugly Jerod held out a Celtic St. Christopher medal on a chain. "He was wearing it."

Billie took the medal and held it as Jerod continued.

"He was in the Bull showing off his fruit machine win. You see, I owe Aldo. Do you know him? He's a nasty monster."

All the men knew Aldo. A slob who ran a chain of high street butcher shops and was one of Ramos's highly profitable money lenders. No one wanted to owe Aldo.

"I asked Ian to borrow two hundred, and he told me no chance. I was desperate." He looked to the men for understanding and, in return, fuck-all.

"I waited outside to ask him again, but when he saw me, he tried to run me over with his bike."

"Motorcycle?" Billie asks, remembering Ian was not a fan.

"No, his *Boris-bike*." At this, Rio and Dingo start laughing hard.

"Bicycle with deadly force," Snorted Dingo. "Must have been shitting yourself?"

"He came at me, and I pushed the bike hard. He fell against the wall and hit his head. There was blood everywhere. I took off."

"You take the money?" Billie is serious.

"Well, he didn't need it anymore." Billie threw a full-force short uppercut, and Jerod flew off the chair and splat to the concrete. Scared shitless, Jerod didn't try to stand but scooted toward the door.

"No, you don't," said Rio, who put a stiff boot in his ribs.

Fear knotted his bowels, and Munns blew forth with a thunderous bugle fart. Smelly, eye singeing, combustible air hit the men in the face. In a different situation, the men would have laughed. Instead, Rio and Dingo both began to kick the hell out of the windy bastard.

Shaky and sobbing, Jerod whimpered, "I had to pay Aldo. He threatened to rape me Mum." Trying but failing to get a morsel of common empathy.

"Aldo would fuck your dog if it meant he would get paid," said Rio.

Dingo laughed, "No one shits on Aldo." Or Ramos, the men thought.

"Jerod, you little bitch, sack up. The night is just getting started." Billie turned and walked into the privacy of the office.

 # # *#*

CHAPTER 33

DARTS

What does he do now? Kill the idiot? Let Ramos make the call? Let Walsh make the call? Billie pulled his phone and reached out to Tyler, but no answer.

"Mr. Walsh, sorry to bother you on a Sunday. About that issue, could you stop by the garage?" Billie was unsure of what was next.

"When?"

"Now."

"It will be a few minutes." When the phone clicked, Billie realized he could hear his heart beating. Not because of the violence; he lived in that world. Because without approval, he brought a civilian into the mix. A serious no, no. Maybe Aldo's involvement would mitigate the situation. But no guarantee.

Out in the repair area, Dingo and Rio were playing with Jerod. "I need to go to the toilet. These two said no," whined Jerod.

"You're a big boy. Hold it."

"I came here in good faith. We made a deal, and now you're...." Jerod is using up his last ounce of bravery.

"Are what, Jerod? Be patient. Mr. Walsh is on his way."

"Walsh! Why is he coming here?"

"Really, you don't have a clue?"

"Listen, it was all a joke. I thought maybe I could get the money, and well, let me go, and I won't tell anyone about it." Panic firmly set in.

"Tell them what, you tried to extort money from me? You attack me when I wouldn't pay you?"

"That's not what happened. I...."

In walked Walsh. He took a long look at the man cowering on the floor. "That him?" addressing Billie, who held out the St. Christopher. Walsh took it and slid it into his pocket without comment.

"You the one who killed my boy?" Walsh's voice was cold and steely, a side of the man previously unseen.

"Yes, but it was an accident. I only wanted the mon...." Rory Walsh picked up a hefty pipe wrench from the tool tray and, without ceremony, planted it firmly on the skull of Jerod Munns. Blood and brains exploded in every direction.

Dropping the wrench in a bucket of rancid motor oil and entirely without sentiment or regret, "Get him out of here. I'll clean this up."

Dingo and Rio grabbed Jerod under the arms and dragged him to the door.

Billie and Walsh's eyes met. "I owe you," said Walsh.

Billie nodded once and walked out. He knew for him, it wasn't over. The end of Jerod Munns did not solve a problem; it created one. Ramos would need to be told.

⚜ ⚜

Billie wasted no time telling Tyler what happened. "I never saw it coming. Munns said he was the one. I wouldn't have believed him, but he had the St. Christopher." Billie was nervous as hell. "He said he owed Aldo, and that's why...." Billie paused, hoping for feedback. When none came, he kept going. "I called you and then Walsh. I had no idea Walsh would...."

"What did you think he would do when you called? Stop by to forgive the fucker who killed his son? Walsh is a civilian. It could fucking blow up. You don't know if the shitbag told anyone what was going down or where he was headed. This is fucked up and on you." Tyler was pissed-off. Billie was a rookie, and shit happens, but Ramos would be furious.

"I know. How can I fix it?" Billie knew he sounded pathetic but was scared and did not know what would happen next.

"Let's go up and tell Daddy what a bad boy you've been," Tyler said in a way to humiliate Billie, and it did.

⚜ ⚜

"Boss, can we come in?" Tyler and Billie stood at the door of Ramos's Tower office.

After hearing the details, Ramos turned to Billie with a cold, hard face. "Quite the fuck up." Billie stood tall and did not look away. He would take his punishment like a man.

"You're familiar with my policy on what happens to men who break my rules? What I do to fuck ups who cause me agro?" These were not questions to be answered. Ramos jerked his head, and Tyler hit Billie with a savage right hook. He buckled and dropped him to his knees.

Billie struggled for a deep breath, shook his head, and wobbled to his feet, knowing more to come. Blood from his nose and lip slipped down his chin. In an instant, Tyler lay a firm gut punch. Billie doubled over with pain. After a couple of shallow gasps, he stood.

"All the money from the garage for the next six months is mine." Billie's loss would be a considerable penalty of over sixty thousand in pure tax-free profit. "If it happens again, the garage is mine." Ramos picked up papers to conclude the meeting.

Ramos was unhappy about Billie's misstep but planned to give him a fair shot at the outlaw life.

Tyler shoved Billie toward the door when Ramos spoke. "Stay away from your mother until your face heals."

#

Billie felt like hell returning to the War Room. He wanted to go to bed and sleep, but there was no peace in the men's quarters. All the men knew what had happened and why.

"We were about to deal the cards. You want in?" asked Dingo as the men viewed the condition of Billie's face.

Rio added, "Or were you wanting a bubble bath and a cup of hot cocoa?" The men snickered.

Hell, yes, thought Billie, that sounds lovely. He forced a chuckle while trying not to vomit. "I'm in if you wankers have enough in your pockets to make it worth my time."

#

"What do you mean it's over?" Mary Ellen Walsh was holding her dead son's St. Christopher. "Where did you get this?" Her husband returned home after a mysterious call-out on Sunday night.

"It's over." Said Rory Walsh.

"Did they catch him? Is he in jail?"

"No, Mary Ellen. He's in hell. It's over."

Carley walked into the room. Her parents seemed so intense that she stopped short. "Mum? Dad?" Her parents did not look her way or offer an answer. Mary Ellen's arm jutted toward her daughter as the St. Christopher dangled through her fingers. "Is that Ian's? Have the police caught them?"

"It's over." Repeated Rory Walsh as he gave a stern look to his wife. A good man killed a man, and he would be forever changed. He wanted to feel remorse or regret, but he felt nothing. Walking past his wife and daughter to the kitchen, he took a cold Guinness from the Beko, went to his favourite chair, picked up the remote, and turned on the darts match.

# # #

## CHAPTER 34

OXFORDSHIRE

Billie was at the Tower War Room to meet with Dingo and Tyler. The meet was quick and specific. No one got their ass chewed, and they got well paid for a one-off visit to a deadbeat politico.

The big news of the day was the anniversary of the death of Prince Phillip. Alice used the occasion to inaugurate the new Surrey Chapel.

She and her daughters walked solemnly to the beautiful chapel with flowers to light candles for Prince Phillip. Alice thought she would need a blazing forest fire to light enough candles for the problems in their life but lit only one for her husband. Only God himself would know where to start.

#

Standing near the lift, Billie was listening to one of Dingo's worthless jokes when out-walked Julie and her daughter.

Annie. "Hi, Billie." Annie hid behind her mother's slender leg; he leaned down and smiled at her. Usually a timid child, Annie knew him from Surrey and felt safe enough to give him a smile.

"Hi there. What are you two up to?" Billie knew Julie rarely left the tower and then only to visit his mum. Her depression and fear kept her inside and quiet."

"Thought we would see if someone could drive us?" John Kohl refused to let his daughter learn to drive or do many things young women learn as they grow up. His domination was suffocating, and there was a time she pushed back a little, but those days were long gone.

"I can drive you if you want." Billie was upbeat by nature, and Julie brightened to see him. Of similar ages, and she held a secret crush. One of the few things in her life which brought her happiness was seeing Billie.

"Really? That would be wonderful. You don't have to work?" She is such an insecure girl.

"Sure. I do. I work for you," he could see she felt uncomfortable with that approach, though it was true. "Where to, Surrey? I would be happy to take you anywhere you want to go."

Julie offered a gentle smile as she picked up Annie. "Can we take a regular car?" She was asking not to be stuck in the back of an armoured limo.

"How about you sit upfront with me, and we take one of these fine new Range Rovers?" He waved his hands as if he were a game show host. "Pick a colour." The question made her chuckle; all of them were black.

Julie quickly turned sad, "I have never been in a taxi or on a bus?" Her life was abnormal, and it increased her feelings of loneliness.

"Public transport is way overrated," Billie tried to jolly her along as he opened the car's doors.

"Can you put a child seat in for Annie?"

"Oh yeah, I have a lot of practice with the things. Remember, I have three little sisters." He took a seat from her Rolls Royce and attached it to the back seat of the Rover.

"All set for a magic carpet ride." He helped them and motioned to Rio to notice what he was doing. Taking Julie Kohl off-premises was always high security. Two men got in another Rover and stealthily followed them out.

There were no current threats, but Ramos would take no chances with her safety. "I wish they didn't have to go with us," she said.

"No worries, they're just doing their job. You don't want to make those guys redundant?" He was making jokey conversation, but he could tell she was too fragile to push it far. "Where to?"

"Do you have enough time to take me to Oxfordshire?"

"Yep. I am all yours. Maybe even a fancy lunch at McDonald's on the way back?" Billie was feeling good. The earlier meeting was a payday for some *special* work, and he was happy with how well things went.

"Why Oxfordshire?"

"I grew up there. We lived there until my mother died. It was beautiful and peaceful. I hope nice people live there now."

"I didn't know you grew up in the country. I thought you were a city girl." Billie was just making conversation.

"My father didn't want us around." Her voice was flat, without emotion. "I can only remember him coming to Oxfordshire twice in all the years. He didn't love us. He didn't love my mother."

The conversation turned dark and personal, and Billie was unsure how to reply. "Your Dad must have been a workaholic to have achieved such success." He thought of his dad and their meager time with him growing up. Like John Kohl, Ramos moved his family to the countryside.

"I have known Ramos my whole life. He was always nice to me and especially to Johnnie. Do you love Ramos?"

"Sure, he's my dad. He changed our life for the better. I know my mum loves him."

"My father was a bad man. He did bad things, but my mum was lovely. And smart."

"Sounds like you. Lovely and smart." Billie feared saying the wrong thing, but he liked her, and she needed a friend.

"Do you have a girlfriend?" she asked.

"Not really. I had a girl, Carley, but things didn't work out."

"My husband Ross loved me very much." Julie looked in the back seat; Annie dozed in her car seat.

"Of course, he did. I'm so sorry about what happened. That must have been…, be hard to take."

"I worry that my brother Johnnie killed him?" The conversation was heading down a dark tunnel, and Billie wanted no part. He heard the question asked before among the men.

"No. Honest Julie, it was an accident. Cranes kill people every year." She seemed not to hear him.

"Turn here and look for the giant gates." About a mile off the main road, they were met with massive iron gates, which stood open. "When we lived here, the gates were constantly closed. My father's men stood there with guns."

"Security is important, especially for the families of rich and powerful men. Ramos has my mum and sisters protected. She ignores them." He was attempting to make Julie's very unusual life sound ordinary.

"I was never sure if they were keeping everyone out or keeping us in. I was afraid they would shoot me if I tried to leave. It feels that way at the Tower."

"The Tower," she shook her head, "what person calls their home the tower? Maybe it fits? The Bloody Tower," she softly whispered.

"I will drive on in, but we may get thrown out," said Billie, trying to change the conversation.

"I want to see the house."

"Inside?"

"No, I won't bother them. I only want to see it again. We were happy here. Johnnie always wanted to be in London with my father, but mummy and I loved it here."

Driving past a swan-filled pond, the massive house came into view. "Whoa, this place is insane. I thought our house in Surrey was big. Not even close to this mega-mansion. Who did your dad buy it from, the Queen?" He stopped the car so they could take in the view.

"My father insisted we have the biggest and best of everything, except none of himself." It was far more conversation than previously shared and quite personal. Billie felt uncomfortable and concerned.

"I loved being married." She seemed to be having a conversation with herself. "Do you plan to get married?"

"Yes. I like the idea of having someone to come home to."

"I am so alone. Billie, would you marry me?" Billie was stunned.

He was looking right at her. "Jules, you're beautiful, and any man would be lucky to be your husband, but you are still grieving for Ross." He took her delicate hand.

"Please don't say no. I need someone to love, Annie, too. Please marry me." The sadness in her eyes was heartbreaking.

"Julie, you are easy to love. But you're like a sister to me." He would take a bullet for her, but not this.

"You're not like Johnnie or my father. You know how to love because of your mother. Just think about it, OK?"

Billie started the car and headed back to Belgravia. He wished the conversation had never happened and wondered if he should tell his mother or Ramos.

♯ ♯ ♯

CHAPTER 35

TWINS

The phone bludgeoned a heavy sleep, but Ramos was alert in seconds. "Yeah?" The house phone call from the War Room to Ramos on the seventh floor.

"Boss, Miles called down for an ambulance. I imagine it must be his brother, but." Ramos quickly dressed and headed to the Tower's fourth floor, where Miles and Nathan, the twin sons of the late John Kohl, lived. These two were the sad losers of the family. Not bright like the others and lived primarily in their little twin-world.

A luxurious world, to be sure, but in an isolated bubble. The twins and their minders were constantly flying around the globe to Football games and party locations like Ibiza, Miami, and Vegas. John let them get on with it as long as he wasn't troubled. When John died, big brother Johnnie used the same game plan, which was now all in Ramos' hands.

It all came crashing down when a drunk and stoned Nathan wrecked his Lamborghini and survived. He currently resides on a ventilator. Miles was known to sit and talk to the unresponsive vegetable for hours. In the last few years, except for several trips to privileged Rehab locations, Miles never left the state of drug-induced nirvana.

"What the hell is going on?" shouted Ramos over the chaos. Two paramedics were pounding on the door to the Twin's flat.

"Miles won't open up," said Boomer, who called it in.

"Take it down!" he answered. Quickly, the men had the door open and went in. They found his nurse tied up in Nathan's room and Miles sobbing in his dead brother's bed.

"No, you can't have him," shouted Miles. "Get out. He is staying here. I am going to take care of him. Get out!"

The EMTs and the crew waited for Ramos' orders. "Everyone out. To the other room," he said.

Before untying the nurse, Ramos asks him, "What happened?"

"About eight o'clock, I called Miles and told him to get here. I thought the end was close." Hospice care professionals know the sights and sounds of final hours. "He was out of the building and took about an hour. He walked in, and without saying a word, he hit me. When I came around, I was tied up. I was on the floor, but I could see the clock. He died about ten-fifteen."

Ramos looked at his watch; almost five hours had passed. "Have the EMTs take a look at you." Later, he would have Tyler give him a handsome wedge for his silence.

When the room was cleared, Ramos pulled up a chair. Miles held his brother in his arms. "This is so fucked. I am sorry, buddy, but he is out of pain now," said Ramos.

"Shut up. Just shut up. You didn't even like him, and now you are acting all concerned." Miles was not buying it, and he was right; the boys were not well-liked.

"Let's get you up," said Ramos.

"No," shouted Miles. "I am going to keep him. I want to freeze him or something. Like a stuffed cat or...."

"I know you don't want to let him go, but he is already gone." Ramos knew he was dealing with someone out of their mind.

"I have billions of pounds, and they will not take him." Miles was beyond hysterical; he was mental.

"Do you want me to call Julie?" said Ramos, knowing he was not reaching the boy.

"Julie? No, she is almost as fucking finished as Nathan. No, I am the only one left to make the important decisions. All the money is mine now; you work for me. Do what I say. Get um out of here. And you, too, leave us alone."

Ramos was done. He stood, stepped to the bedside, and punched Miles. Sending him flying from his bed to the floor. Reaching down, Ramos jerked him up and roughly pulled him into a reverse bear hug. He held him tightly while the ambulance drivers lifted and removed Nathan.

"You bastard," yelled Miles as snot and tears ran down his face. "You're fired." He pointed to Rio and Tyler, who were also there, and screamed, "All of you fuckers are fired. We hate all of you. We always have."

Ramos turned to the nurse. "Get him a shot of something."

"Sorry, I don't have any drugs with me. Nathan doesn't take..."

Ramos to Tyler, "Get him something."

⚡⚡

Julie was delicate, but Nathans's death was not unexpected. Standing at the Glenwood family tomb, she held her brother's hand. "I love you, Miles."

He turned to her conspiratorially, "We need to fire all these assholes. The money belongs to us. Go along with me. Ok?"

Julie was puzzled. "What do you mean?"

"I am going to get rid of all those fuckers. They killed Johnnie; they killed Ross and our brother Nathan. Maybe Dad too. Don't you think it's odd that everyone died in the last few years?" Miles was frantic. "We're next. Don't look at them."

"Miles, I don't believe, well, Nathan, the accident." She tried to be calming.

"Maybe they rigged his car and made him crash? They want us all gone so they can steal our money. Dad's money." When the crash occurred, Nathan had been high while driving his Lamborghini at 160 miles per hour.

⚡⚡

The paparazzi were behind a wall of Ramos's men, but the noise and chaos were hellish. Ramos told Alice to stay away because it was going to be rough. Alice contacted Julie and offered to care for Annie until things settled down. She was unsurprised Julie agreed. Lately, Annie has spent most of her time in Surrey.

Miles and Julie followed the casket into the mausoleum as the bearers placed Nathan in an ornate marble crypt. Their mother, Annie, built the magnificent Italian-style marble family tomb when their father was presumed dead after a plane crash. Julie began crying hard as she looked around to see how many of her family were gone. Miles was right; too many died too soon.

While holding Miles' arm out into the sunlight, Julie offered a weak smile as Billie approached. Ramos told all the men to stay clear, but Ramos nodded ok when Billie asked to speak to Julie.

"Hi Julie, Mi…"

"Get the fuck away from us," shouted Miles. Billie stepped back.

"No, Miles, he's my friend." Julie held her hand out to Billie.

"None of these fuckers are our friends. Don't you get it, Julie? They are killing off our family to get their hands on our money?"

"Miles, no. Billie is my friend." Slightly calming Miles with her soft voice.

Billie spoke directly to Miles, "I can't imagine what you are going through, but I am also a twin. Danny is not just my brother; he is part of me. I don't know what I would do if I lost him."

"Yeah, they don't get it. They think that because Nathan was hurt, it is okay if he is gone. I tried to tell them, but they are too stupid to understand."

"I wanted to tell you I am sorry," said Billie as he nodded and moved to leave. Julie took his arm, and he paused.

"You're Ramos boy, right?" asked Miles, who warmed to the idea of a fellow twin and one near his age.

"Yeah."

"Do you love him? He's a bastard; how can you love him?"

Billie did not react to Miles's harsh accusations. "He is a tough man, no doubt, but I love him, and so does my brother, three sisters, and our mum. We all do."

"Does he love you?" Billie snorted. "Our Dad didn't love us. Right, Julie? He only loved money and whores." Billie could see how uncomfortable Julie was with her brother's words.

Ramos and Tyler stood near enough to hear their voices but did not intrude. While it seemed an inappropriate time for the conversation, it slightly calmed Miles. "Ramos isn't like the dads on telly, but he has always been good to us, makes us feel like we matter to him. So yeah, he loves us."

"Let's go, Julie," Miles turned toward the enormous armoured Rolls Royce limo.

"Will you come with us?" said Julie to Billie. He returned a glance at Miles.

"Yeah, come with us. I want to talk to you about something."

Seated in the luxurious automobile, Miles returned to his paranoid tirade. "Are you in on all of it?"

"All what?"

"Killing us off. It's what Ramos and Jimmy and all those fuckers are trying to do. I am going to fire all of them. Not you. You can take over and do what I need. I will pay you a million a year." He sat smugly back in the seat, waiting for a yes.

"It's a flattering offer, but I'm not up to the job. You deserve a real team of pros for business and security. Ramos is very good at his work. Tyler too."

"Of course, you would say that. Do you know what he does?"

"Miles, please don't say mean things about his father. He already told you he loves him."

"Ok. But you still work for me, and I need your help tonight."

"What's up?"

"My brother. I want to bring him back to the Tower."

"Miles, that's wrong he is…" said Julie, who was horrified.

"Julie, I have to talk to him every day, and I don't want to drive out to the fucking graveyard. I will keep him in his coffin and put him back in his room.

Billie knew he was listening to a fucking maniac. "I want you and a couple of the men to get a van and go get him tonight."

"The place is going to be watched pretty closely for a while. Probably not possible right now." Billie was trying to pump the brakes on Miles' crazy plan.

"I hadn't thought of that. The leaches are always watching. Our whole lives, they wait and wait to get a photo of us picking our noses or scratching our nuts. They are fucking disgusting." Finally, all three had something to agree on.

Leaning her head on Billie's chest, Julie closed her eyes. Billie thought Miles was settling down. Instead, he reached into his jacket and pulled out a small zippered case. When opened, he revealed a hypodermic needle. Heroin probably, Miles had been addicted on and off for years.

# #

The weeks rolled on, and Alice continued caring for Annie. She had blossomed into a happy little girl. She was playing and giggling her days away with Luna and Stella. The three insisted on sleeping together in one bed at night, so Alice had a king bed moved to the nursery area.

Julie came to visit every few days. Then, without much conversation, she moved in. The Surrey house was enormous, and Alice welcomed her. She noticed the only thing that seemed to bring Julie out of her sadness was a visit from Billie.

# # #

CHAPTER 36

PEACHES

Ramos' reign at the helm of Kohl Enterprises took a new approach. Instead of top-down management, he took his most skilled men, divided the vice categories, and pursued a delegation style. Very 21st century. To each manager, a percentage of the pot is based on performance. The bank could be substantial. The penalty for not producing was equally as sizeable.

Ramos had offshore men headed by a retired US Army Colonel who handled arms. He had scant patience for the arms business, but it was a huge fucking earner, so he gave the respect deserved.

Posh people didn't want to deal with a thug who resembled a thug. Axel, a handsome fuck, was put in charge of west-end clubs and pussy. His Aryan good looks and educated charms were welcome to their tables and beds.

During Covid, the arms business was booming. Ramos moved Axel to that division, much to the complaints of many society ladies.

Carlos is in charge of South and East Clubs and pussy. Frankie was put in command of protection. Ajax, a man who worked for him for many years, was in charge of narcotics. A man poached from a Southampton Face was on loans and gambling. Second-tier men rotated between the managers, and everyone cross-trained.

Each man had a right hand and crew they picked themselves. The team men could save their lives and make them enormous money. The crew leaders were responsible for the actions of each of their crew, and choosing them wisely was a must. Ramos encouraged hiring from within.

All sectors reported to Tyler; Ramos direct report. Billie was on float between them all; no one asked why.

Monday lunch was a hardman version of a *staff meeting*. Usually held at the Tower, but occasionally moved around to other locations. Today was at Hot Shots, an Essex Gentleman's club. First on the day's agenda is some HR business, Ramos' least favourite.

Ramos lost a valuable man last night, Kevin Pretty. It should never have happened. Dealing with it is annoying because it was not over business but pussy. Kevin was sleeping with the wife of the son of Willie Ball, who flattened Pretty with his new BMW.

Ball ran girls for Ramos on the Union building sights, a damn lucrative enterprise. Apparently, during their meal breaks, a great many masons, painters, and carpenters liked to get blowjobs after their sandwiches and tea.

Willie, a clever one, and his earn impressive but a disruption of business, a colossal irritation for Ramos and answered in spades.

Jimmy sent Ball and his son, who killed Kevin, to meet him at Hot Shots.

Ramos offered no greeting, walking directly through the Club to the back office. Tyler patted down the Balls and escorted them to the front of Ramos's desk, where they stood anxiously, shifting on their feet.

No small talk; Ramos went right to it. "Kevin Pretty earned a sweet wedge, and we must face the reality of lost income. For his family and mine."

The Ball family wisely chose to stay quiet. Willie Jr. wanted to say something, but his father warned him it would be a grave error and to keep his gob shut.

"Kevin's widow will today get twenty thousand, and I will get thirty. Every month after, she will get an additional ten. I will get ten above the usual amount." Willie Senior nodded and smiled happily to learn they would be around to make payments.

"As it seems the Ball family have lost their manners, one of you will need a refresher course," said Tyler. Ramos thought the wife could use a refresher, too, but assumed Willie Jr. had already taken care of her. Any man would.

Willie and his son looked horrified. One of them faced a severe beating. "Decide among yourselves who needs a bit of etiquette refocus, and you let Frankie know." Ramos jerked his head to signal that the Ball meeting had ended.

Ramos paused before calling the animals in, wondering why men got married. It was a never-ending misery to keep everyone happy. He was not a man who would tolerate that shit and thought less of men who would. Conveniently forgetting the hell he was currently putting his wife through.

##

With so much on his fucking plate between the arms business sale, routine vice, the Prosecution case, and the tabloid circus, Ramos relied heavily on his new management approach.

"Meeting called to order," laughed Frankie in a big show of putting aside a stroke magazine.

"Anyone hear from Carlos?" Asked Ramos. Unusual for one of his "team leaders" not to check in.

"I saw Carter at the Rod last night. Said Carlos was *running slow*." Carter was Carlos's backup for a number of years and a capable soldier.

Ramos wondered, not for the first time, if Carlos was due to retire, which was rare in the villain profession.

"Running slow? What the fuck does that mean?" Ramos hated generalities and was concerned but didn't let on. Carlos' overused liver was protesting and landed him in the hospital twice in the last six months. Ramos would take a trip across the river and see for himself.

"Sorry, boss, I don't know. He's not exactly the sharing type."

"Let's get this done." The boss was cross; it was not an easy time to do business. "The fucking China virus," he spat. Boris kept trying to reopen the city, but a new variant would crop up and cause plans to change. Businesses closing meant protection money dropped, many people were out of work, and loan repayments and gambling were down. The massive jump in drug sales to those stuck at home helped offset part of it, but Ramos was in no mood to be upbeat.

For the next ninety minutes, each man reported in, brought payments, got assignments, got their asses chewed, and got paid.

"Ok, girls, let's roll," said Ramos as he stood, signalling the end of the meet.

The next stop was the Lightning Rod, and it was time for Ramos and his old friend to have a sit-down. Previously, without success, Ramos approached the retirement subject. He casually suggested Carlos and a couple of the men take a holiday to one of his villas in Marbella. Carlos pulled his gun and thrust its grip toward Ramos. "Pull the fucking trigger, you son-of-a-bitch, or fuck off."

Carlos proved obstinate in the last couple of years with any reference to his age or fitness. Ramos expected him to be no more welcoming with another attempt at a *stepping-down* conversation. He served the organization well, and Ramos wanted him to take his well-earned rest. Carlos would not see it that way.

#

"*Got the hottest chick in the game wearing my chain,*" blasted Jay-Z. The sea of strippers and whores parted for Ramos, like Moses at the Red Sea. "Hi baby, you come to find me?"

"Been way too long, big man." They threw Ramos exaggerated smiles. He would probably fuck a couple before he left.

"Where's the boss?" Ramos asked Sapphire.

"You the boss, Baby." The hos were flirting and laughing.

"Carlos in his office. Think he's pounding Peaches."

"Honey, that crazy, fat-ass bitch ain't doing his taxes," said Mia, which gave Ramos a chuckle.

Peaches was fairly new to The Rod. The girth of her astonishing derrière had all the ass-men lining up. "Peaches is ah *dick garage,* and she always full," shrieked Saffy as the girls laughed.

The men held no privacy concerns regarding fucking, which Ramos figured Carlos was doing. He walked toward the office and stood ready to turn the doorknob when a ripping scream jolted everyone to attention.

Ramos hard-shouldered the door and found Peaches cowering on the floor in shock. Carlos slumped in his chair, his trousers open, dick out, and quite dead.

"I didn't do nothing, I promise. I didn't." Peaches was trembling and flinched when Ramos leaned in to help her up.

"What happened?" he asked, believing he already knew.

""I was bouncing up and down on his dick like he likes, and he made a funny noise. I thought he was finishing. His dick was still in me," she sobbed, great heaving sobs. "He die in me? No, God, please, no. Am I gonna catch something?"

Ramos patted her shoulder for a brief moment. "You're ok. Carlos died the way he wanted. Hell, the way we all want to go." He nudged her toward the door.

Ramos sat for a moment on a worn leather sofa where he had sat hundreds of times. Looking at Carlos, it surprised him how old his friend looked. He and Carlos, Rambo, and Mitch were the original crew, and now all were gone, even John Kohl. Ramos felt the weight of the years.

Carlos had no family. It is not an unusual story among hard men. Ramos would see he had a hell of a send-off, naturally, at the Rod. He could hear the hos crying and carrying on. Peaches must have spread the news. He would close the place down for all except his men and anyone in the organization who wanted to pay their respects.

"Boss?" asked Carter as he stuck his head in the door. Ramos waved him in. Carter was a reliable fallback for the clubs, but Carlos was a legend. Ramos would ensure he was remembered that way.

# # #

CHAPTER 37

SISTER

The kitchen was brimming with delicious aromas of beef stew and freshly baked bread. Alice stood at the stove stirring the pot when Billie walked through the back door. "You smell this all the way from the Zoo or the Tower?" she asked with a glowing smile.

"Mum, can we talk?" His not thinking first about food was alarming to Alice. She lowered the flame and walked toward her son with her arms out.

Billie was a big man, but he cuddled close. "Let's sit down." As they sat at the table, Alice took her son's hand. "Talk to me."

"Mum, I fucked up. Sorry, I messed up. I didn't mean to; it wasn't planned, but I can't undo it." He shook his head and dropped his gaze to his hands.

"Son, I love you. Let me help." Alice was unfamiliar with seeing her tough and confident son worried and scared.

"I ran into Julie at the Tower. She seemed so alone. When she asked me to come in. I said yes". He raised his head and looked into his mother's eyes. "I had sex with Julie." His mother's eyes did not reveal her shock.

"She gave me a tour of her place, which is fuc…, I'm sorry, it is amazing. We ended up in the home theatre, and she asked me to watch a film. Mum, I never planned, honest I. Oh god, mum, I, what can I do?"

"Son, she was willing?" She asked as gently as she could. She was surprised as Julie was childlike to her.

"Oh yes. We were sitting on the sofa lounger, and Julie was cold. I pulled one of those blanket things over her, and she leaned into me. We watched the film. You would call it a girlie thing, a love story. She felt good, and well, the film was almost over, and she kissed me, and I kissed her back. Mum, I'm so sorry. What do I do?"

"How did you leave it with her?" Julie's reaction was vital to what was next.

"Mum, she was happy. Happier than I have ever seen her. When I was leaving, she told me she loved me."

"She is a vulnerable girl, but you are a handsome man. I am sure she felt safe and cared for. Did you wear a condom?" This a blunt question but important.

"No. I'm sorry. It just happened. She's so sweet it didn't come to mind." Now, he had something more to regret. "I wear them when I, you know, other times." He didn't want to say to his mother when I fuck whores. "It felt good to hold someone lovely again." Instead of his usual steady diet of soulless fucks.

"There is something else. I probably should have told you." He looks pained.

"Did it happen before?"

"No, not that. But a while back, she asked me to drive her to Oxfordshire, where she grew up. She talked a lot about her childhood and her mum. Her Dad and Johnnie too. And Ross. We parked by the pond to view the house. She asked me if I had a girlfriend. I said yes, but it was over. She asked if I planned to get married. I told her I look forward to having someone to come home to."

Alice knew her son missed the love and intimacy he shared with Carley. It could not be replaced with nameless whore fucks in a hardman's life. He, too, was vulnerable and needed affection and explained how the situation with Julie happened.

"Then she, she asked me to marry her."

"Oh. What did you say?" This was a huge complication. Had he given her hope?

"I told her she was easy to love but not that way. Like a sister." Julie spent a great deal of time at the Surrey house, and they all felt she was family.

"You used the word love?" she asked.

"Yes, it came naturally. Like a sister."

"What did she say when you turned her down? You did turn her down?"

"Yeah, of course. She said, please think about it."

Alice stood and walked toward the stove to pause and gather her thoughts as she stirred the stew.

"Have you been in touch with her today?"

"No, I couldn't figure out what I should say. Is it ok to text? Oh, hell, mum."

"You should call her and say how nice it was to see her; she is lovely. And while it's been difficult for a while, you are certain things will be better for her in the future. Wait, she might imagine you are promising her a future."

"Ramos is going to be furious. Mum, it's no small thing. You don't know him. When he gives an order, he never takes shit. Something bad is going to happen."

"Son, Ramos is your dad. He'll understand."

"No, mum, he won't. After Carley, he gave me a specific command, stick with whores and follow orders. Those were his exact words, and it doesn't get any clearer."

"Son, calm down. Nothing terrible has happened. Two young people reached out to each other. It's very natural."

"No, mum, I am supposed to be a *gangster* and not have gooey feelings and shit. If I behave like a weak, sappy punk, I let everyone down. Especially Dad. I have a huge knot in my stomach. You can't let him know I told you first. Please promise me."

Billie was genuinely worried and a far cry from the man who stood up to his mother and defended his dad at the family dinner table.

"You need to speak to Julie. Right now. Call her."

"Mum, I…"

"Do it. You need to get past this."

He pulled his phone, took a deep breath, and called. "Hi, it's Billie."

"I hoped you'd call. Thank you for last night." She was on speaker. Billie looked at his mother as if she might tell him the perfect reply. "Yeah, your place is amazing, and …."

"Maybe you can come by again sometime?" said Julie.

"Sure, ah, but next time, I get to pick the film." Julie laughed. "I have to go, bye." He hung up and looked at his mum. "Did I make it worse?" Alice didn't know.

"You need to eat. Let me get you a nice bowl of stew," Alice stood and went to the stove. He bought some time with Julie, but the conversation was far short of clarity, and Ramos would have to be told.

# #

Billie and Jet were playing video games in the Zoo. Billie looked up to check the monitor when the gate chimed open. Seeing Ramos' car drive in, he almost threw up. Telling the Boss what happened with Julie could be put off no longer.

Billie headed down the path to the main house, formulating what to say and how to say it. He walked around the house, avoiding the kitchen entrance and onto Ramos' office door. He could see his dad at his desk reading something. Tapping lightly on the French door, Ramos looked up and motioned him in. "What's up?" he asked.

"I fucked up, sir. I'm really sorry." Ramos could see and hear the fear in his son.

"Again. What now?" His voice was cold and entirely without empathy.

Billie eyed Tyler sitting on a chair nearby and gave him a quick nod.

"I slept with Julie, and …" Ramos was instantly on his feet and around his desk. He grabbed Billie by the neck and exploded in his face. "You fucking idiot. You're no hardman? You're a pussy in a romance novel, like some 14-year-old girl. First Carley, now Julie. What the fuck did I tell you?" Incensed, Ramos shook Billie hard. It was the first time he ever laid hands on his son.

Unsure if the question was rhetorical, but before he could reply, Ramos spat, "Stick to whores and follow orders. Does that ring a bell?" He shook his son loose, causing him to stumble, but Billie caught himself before falling.

Ramos was unconcerned about a fuck, but he continued to feel loyalty to John Kohl and his job to keep his daughter Julie protected. To Kohl, that meant protection from men.

"Dad, she always seems so lonely, and I…."

"You were going to fix it with your dick?" Ramos was furious. "Has it happened before?"

"Well, I…"

"Goddammit. I what?" Ramos was firing questions but with no patience for answers.

"No, I never touched her before, but…."

Ramos glared. "But what?"

"A while ago, I drove her to Oxfordshire. She wanted to see the house where she grew up, and she, she ah, said she loves me and asked me to marry her."

"Oh fuck," said Ramos as he returned to the other side of his desk.

"I told her I love her but like a sister. She said she wanted to marry me anyway."

"Is that where you left it?"

"Until last night." Billie nodded. "Today, I talked to Mum…."

"You ran to your mummy? I am disgusted with you."

"I needed her advice on how to deal with Julie. I don't want to hurt her."

Ramos returned to his desk chair. "Get your things from the Zoo and leave here tonight. You're moving to the Rod. You can help Carter." A massive drop in status for Billie, from elite crew to assistant club and pussy management. Billie hung his head and nodded.

"It's your last fuck up. Any more weak-ass shit and I will buy a florist shop for you to run." Out of view of Billie, Tyler winced. "Get the fuck out of here."

Full of shame and regret, Billie spoke softly, "I'm sorry I let you down."

When Billie departed, Ramos looked at Tyler and ran a palm across his face. "I never knew a hardman worth a damn who had a sweet mother. It's his fucking problem; a gentle, loving mum. Feelings and shit make a man soft." These men kept their fear, flaws, and doubts unexamined, buried deep.

"You could have him marry Kohl's girl. Keep it all in the family?" said Tyler. Ramos already thought of that. It was unsaid, but both men knew it would mean eliminating Carley.

Tyler moved to lighten the moment, "he tries hard. Hell, it's not all his fault the little *sweethearts* can't wait to drop their panties for the handsome fucker." Both men shared a much-needed laugh.

※ ※ ※

CHAPTER 38

SOOTY

Ramos was home earlier than usual and stood in the kitchen pouring a whiskey as Alice finished dinner preparations.

"Oh no, oh no, Alice, I am so sorry." Sissy ran into the kitchen with Luna, Stella, and Annie following.

Alice thought someone had broken something, but it didn't matter; none were intentionally destructive. "Accidents happen". When she looked up from the bread she was kneading, she saw the problem. The little ones were covered in makeshift tattoos. They had taken permanent colour Sharpie pens and written all over each other. They were an awful mess. Alice wanted to laugh but did not want to encourage the behaviour.

"We got pretty pictures like Daddy and Billie," said Luna, smiling up and holding out her arms for inspection. Sissy had tears in her eyes.

"I am so sorry. I was taking a shower." Alice stepped in to hug her. "It's ok. It is not your fault."

"It doesn't wash off. I tried." Sissy, a sweet simpleton, was in distress.

"It's ok," said Alice as she handed Sissy a tissue.

"Daddy, Daddy, we have pictures like you." They ran to him for cuddles and to show off their *ink*.

"I'll get them changed," said Sissy. They had made quite a mess of their clothes as well. When they had departed, Ramos and Alice looked at each other and burst into laughter.

It was rotten timing and in no way his idea of how to relax, but he set through a rare, noisy kitchen dinner with Alice and the little ones. Alice always made a meal to savour, which was some compensation.

※ ※

After several rounds of giggles with goodnight kisses, Ramos excused himself to his office to work. Three hours later, he stretched his long legs and ran a hand over his tired face. The case against him seemed to keep ballooning, which meant he was stuck with that fucking cunt Marita until it all went away.

The damage to his marriage was not a big concern. He didn't want Alice unhappy, but he knew she loved him, and she was terrified of everything and everyone outside the gates of the Surrey fortress. Her fear worked to his benefit. She wasn't going anywhere.

Jumping to attention, Ramos's reflexes were sharp as he pulled his weapon when he saw movement outside the office's French doors. It was dark out, and there was no reason for anyone to wander around. The grounds were lit by a motion detector, and the zoo and gate sentries closely watched the monitors. Moving flat against the wall, he shielded himself within the thick damask drapery. Peeking out, he saw Alice poking about in the foliage.

"What's up? He asked as he opened the French door.

"Sooty bolted, and we haven't found her. Annie won't go to sleep until I do." She turned to see her husband return his gun to his waist holster and step near her. He heard everything about Annie's new kitten, Sooty, at dinner. Alice stooped and peered under a clot of Peonies as three loud gunshots rang out.

Ramos spread his enormous body wide to shield his wife. Covering her, they dropped to the ground. The following minutes were pandemonium as men from the gates and zoo ran to secure the home's exits.

"Get off me. Go save the children." Alice was pushing against her husband to no effect.

"They are in no danger," he comforted Alice, but he did not know if his statement was true.

When Ramos felt it safe, he stood, his weapon in hand, as he held his trembling wife. "You're ok."

"What happened? Are the children safe? What do they want? How did they get in?" She was frantic at the idea that someone was trying to hurt their children. It wasn't long ago someone had shot Billie.

"We'll find out." Said Ramos as Rio and Jet came around the end of the house.

"Area secure," said Rio. "Dingo and the gate crew are doing the parameter checks. Jet is reviewing the footage." Ramos nodded his approval.

It was a nervy move if one of his enemies struck at his home. Ramos started making calls. He ordered more men to Surrey. No chatter was picked up, and no one had any heads up. The fucking case was emboldening his enemies. He would need to find out who did this and hit them hard.

Forty minutes after the shots were fired, Rio knocked on the kitchen door. Ramos had been trying to depart Surrey, but he needed answers. "Boss, a man drove up to the gate and said his name was Winterburn. He lives in the next property over. He ripped off three, trying to get a couple of foxes. Sorry for the inconvenience."

Ramos responded, "Damnit." He knew it was one more punch in the face to Alice and all for a fucking fox.

#

Ramos entered the War room; Billie, Dingo, Jet, Frankie, and Rio stood. It was a show of respect from the John Kohl and Johnnie Kohl era.

No small talk, "Good job at the house last night." He meant the team's response to a perceived threat. "Rio, Billie, get this to Southampton." Tyler dropped a duffle bag of cash on the table, a payoff for the union boss whose men unload the Turkish drugs. Ramos turned to walk out.

"Ah, Boss, can I go by Surrey first?" asked Billie. "It's Mum's birthday, and…."

"No," he replies as he keeps walking. He noticed a wrapped birthday gift on the side table. He never celebrated anyone's birthday, not even his own. It felt like an annoying intrusion, and he was trying to knock all the family shit out of Billie's head. Business first seemed not yet to sink in.

#

In his third-floor office, Ramos saw a stack of the day's tabloids waiting. Sighing heavily, he reached for the whiskey and sat. What the fuck are they on about today? He flipped the first one aside and halted at an enlarged grainy photo of Alice.

None of the previous stories had a photo of his wife's face, and keeping her hidden seemed like a blessing. Now, it was blown to hell. The article mentioned that she was the Luna and Magic Piano series author. Ramos tried to imagine how they got the photo, which did not look recent. Possibly from the Baylor days, her hair was shorter now. Someone, probably a school mum, sold the photo and information. One more kick in the teeth for Alice. It was too wishful to imagine she had not seen it. Some fucking birthday gift.

# #

Alice saw the photo and remembered it from a day the boys played football with Baylor schoolmates. She consistently kept a low profile, but after Ramos drove them to the game and astonished all the parents with his enormous build and powerful demeanour, the women relentlessly pressed her for details of her life. I bet it was Luanne or Daisy who sold the photo and information. The tabloids paid a great deal of money for photos. Both women were *social mountaineers* and loved cash.

# #

"Girls, it's beautiful. Mummy will feel very special when she sees it." Lindsey said, helping the three girls finish decorating the rather lopsided cake they had spent the afternoon creating.

Alice waited in her writing nook for the ok to enter the kitchen. When she did, it looked like a terrorist zone. How could three little girls make such a mess? "Don't worry, Alice, I will clean it up," said Lindsey as she glanced around at the disarray and laughed.

"Can we eat it?" asked Luna, licking frosting from a spoon.

"Let's wait for a while. Maybe Billie can join us?" She picked up the day's tabloids, poured a cup of tea, and looked again at her photo. Maybe I should let my hair grow?

"Billie, Billie." They giggled and ran out of the room with Sissy to clean up. Alice looked at the cake and the clock and wondered if Billie would make it. She wasn't so sure. In the villain world, business and not birthdays always came first.

# # #

CHAPTER 39

DERRICK

Ramos still had not been to Surrey. He couldn't do anything about her photo, which now was worldwide on the net. In his third-floor Tower office, he took a call from the War Room that Ajax was in the house. Could he come up?

No meeting was scheduled. Ramos wondered about the next pile of shit that was about to drop? "Yeah, send him up." Even he could hear the lack of enthusiasm in his voice.

"Jax, have a seat." Ramos nodded to the whiskey, and Ajax reached in and poured a short one. He sat back in the oversized leather chair but did not look relaxed. "What's up?" Ask Ramos.

"I take it you have seen the photo?" Both men knew he was referring to the photo of Alice. Ramos nodded in reply. "Not sure it means anything, but," he took a pull from his glass. "one of the crew mentioned it?"

"How so?" These men took small steps in conversation.

"I have an older man who works on a small team. They handle weed and H for the whores in Kings Cross. Some on the streets but mostly at the houses. He's Jamaican but has been here a while. Moves a fair amount of weight; worked for me about six years." Ramos was curious about the details but waited.

"Yesterday was our usual meet, and he mentioned Alice. He said he knew her. A long time ago, he was living with her mother and fucking Alice too." That was rather blunt, but these men did not need kid-gloves. "He had her picture from the paper in his pocket." Ajax paused when Ramos didn't speak; he continued.

"I told him if he were smart, he would keep that information to himself. The problem is, he isn't very smart. I wanted to run it by you. He might be full of shit or wishing to make a quid or two, but I don't know."

"What's his name?"

"Brown. Derrick Brown." Ramos's unreadable face revealed nothing. Ajax stood. "Boss, let me know if I can do anything. I have to get back to it."

#

Ramos remembered what Alice told him about her twin sons: At seventeen and a virgin, she was raped by a man from Jamaica who was involved with her stepmother. It was an ugly fucking story.

Two months after her father's death, her Mum's girlfriends talked her into a week-long holiday in Jamaica. It was Alice's first time alone. Mum stayed for three weeks, and on her return, she brought a man named Derrick. She moved him right into the house and her bedroom."

"Derrick was not mean or anything; mostly, he sat on the sofa, smoked weed, and watched football. He and Mum would go out at night."

"My mother is a concert pianist. She was not a superstar but worked steadily with orchestras and events around the UK and Europe. Also, a thriving business in master class piano instructor. She booked a performance in Edinburgh and went a few days early to rehearse with the full orchestra. Derrick didn't go."

"The first night, he came into my room and told me if I didn't fight him, let him do what he wanted, he wouldn't hurt me. I didn't, and he didn't. It lasted three days." She swallowed deeply, her mouth dry with fear. Ramos could see she was humiliated about what happened.

"I was certain he would take off before my mum returned, but he stayed. When she returned, I told her what happened, and she didn't believe me and said I must have caused it." Ramos could see the sadness in her eyes that she attempted to hide.

"He was staying, and I could stay or go. It was difficult to believe it was happening, but I knew I had to leave. Before I departed with my savings of seven hundred and twelve Pounds, she told me she was not my mother."

"I was astonished. I loved her; what Mum was saying seemed impossible. She told me my birth mother and a brother I never knew died in a car accident when I was less than a year old. She was a neighbour and helped my Dad with me between concert dates. After about a year, she moved in. They planned to tell me after I finished school."

"I left home and learned a few months later that I was pregnant. I had lost my father, mother, brother, and stepmother, and when I found out I was going to have a baby, I was happy I would have someone to love again. A month later, I learned I was having twins.

Alice wanted her babies, even after rape, and made considerable compromises to take care of them. One of her soul-crushing choices was working as a club whore at the Lightning Rod for a few months, which is how she met Ramos. After the night she told him, they never spoke of it again. This fucker put Alice through ten years of hell until Ramos stepped up.

# #

Ramos sat in his office and pondered the shit he needed to sort. There was no question Derrick was a *dead man*. That was a given. But who, how, and when were decisions yet to be made?

Billie, without hesitation, shot and killed Johnnie Kohl for disrespecting his mother. It would not take much to imagine his actions upon learning someone raped her. But unknown to Billie, his birth father was the rapist, and news like that could fuck up a man. While killing Brown might give Billie some satisfaction, it was too risky.

Ramos would be happy to give the kill to Alice. Sweet revenge, but Alice was no killer. In his way, he protected her, married her, and protected the children. He would keep the secrets his protection required.

# #

Walking into the War Room, the men stood. Not usual was Ramos joining the men at the table for casual conversation. "I have a question. What would be the worst way to die? What do you not want as your exit?" He didn't know why he asked the question, maybe looking for inspiration.

"Is this a parlour game, boss?"

"Yeah. What about you, Rio?"

"I don't want to fall or be pushed off a tall building. Being near the edge makes my balls shrivel."

Ramos looked at Dingo. "Fire. I had an uncle burnt in a big bush fire in the Blue Mountains last year. My sister said it burned the meat right off his bones. That's scary as hell."

"What about you, Billie?" asked Ramos.

"I don't want to die for some dumbass reason. Like walking down the street, a piano falls on my head." They chuckled. "Or a bus jumps the curb and mows down ten people. Stuff like that is pointless, but you're still dead. Whatever it is, I hope it's not for a long, long time." He laughed, and the other men joined in.

"Hear that."

Now, the men were relaxed and all ready to contribute. "I don't want to die being shot by some pissed-off husband." Said Tyler.

"You, my brother, might need to change your wicked ways. Quit laying pipe at another man's building site, or being shot's a reality waiting to happen," said Frankie as he made the sign of the cross and caused more laughter.

Ramos asked, "What if some fucker raped your woman or daughter?" The men went quiet and then filled the room with a terrifying level of anger. Except for Billie, all the men most certainly had raped someone, but their indignation flared.

"That fucker would pay."

"I would take all day killing the piece of shit."

"I would see his ass was raped until he begged me to end it all."

"Cut the perv's dick off and make him eat it with a side of shit."

"You are a creative fucking bunch." Ramos stood; he noticed the birthday gift remained on the table. "Billie, you and Rio head to Surrey. Let Kelly and Cody know to come here. The men moved their chairs back. It was time to get to work.

"Let's roll."

#

In the back of the Bentley SUV, Ramos called Ajax. "Bring Brown to Sherry's. No make it the new place." Ramos had recently purchased another scrap yard. Recycling was damn profitable and like Sheridan's scrapyard, where a great deal of ugly business was done.

Ramos felt he owed Alice to take care of Derrick Brown himself. While the men in the War Room reminded him of the many ways to die, for a rapist, it had to be only one thing.

#

Walking toward the portacabin, they heard voices. "Hey man, what's happening?"

"Shut up, Derrick." It was Ajax.

Opening the door, they were met with a blast of warm, fetid air. Derrick knew he was in deep shit and jumped up. "Oh, Ramos, I mean Mr. Santiago. I don't...."

"So, you know my wife?" Ramos said menacingly. Looking at Derrick's face, he expected to see Billie, but there was no similarity.

"Ah, I was bullshitting. I guess trying to be a big shot and... No offense, ok. I didn't mean...." He looked to the blank faces of the other men for understanding. None was found.

Tyler shoved Brown back into the chair. "Read the room, asshole. You're done."

"Get your dick out." Said Ramos. "Time to say goodbye."

Derrick was crying, with snot and tears gushing. "Please, no man, I will go away, do whatever you want."

"What I want is for you to get your fucking dick out."

Derrick fumbled with his zipper and pulled his dick. Cradling it in his shaking hands he looked desperate. "Hold him," said Ramos as Ajax and Tyler held his shoulders. Ramos raised the pipe and came down hard on Derrick Brown's manhood. The ragged end of the iron tore through the skin. Derrick screamed. Ramos slammed his meat a further two times before Derrick passed out. Ramos finished by ramming the pipe through his neck and walking out.

"To Surrey." None of the men knew why or what Derrick Brown had done. None except Ajax, who could see Ramos was completing some unfinished personal business.

# # #

CHAPTER 40

MILES

"Get the fuck out here," demanded Miles exiting the lift into the Tower garage. With scant enthusiasm, three men walked out of the war room.

"What's up," said Rio as Dingo & Kelly stood near, looking bored.

"Whatever the fuck I say. Remember who is paying you. That would be me. Not Ramos. You assholes seem to forget that."

"Looks like we are off for another pleasant evening," mumbled Kelly.

"I want to see my brother," said Miles, standing by one of the armoured limos. He did not move to open his door and waited for one of the men.

Dingo opened the door and deeply bowed, "At your service." You punk-ass fool.

"Fuck you," said Miles as he slid onto the seat. Dingo and Kelly were up, and Rio would stay in the War room in the unlikely event Julie wanted to go out.

Miles had not missed a day visiting the cemetery since his brother's death. He still intended to bring Nathan back to the Tower but heeded Billie's warning to wait until the press lost interest.

Arriving at the mausoleum well after dark, Dingo and Kelly expected to wait in the car. Miles surprised them, "Come with me."

"Sure, boss." All the men hated Miles, but it was their job to jump when the miserable shit said jump. So they did. The men followed him to the door and waited as he punched in the entry code. Inside, the ornate place was eerily cold.

"Help me with the lid thing," said Miles.

"Lid?" Dingo and Kelly were unsure.

"Yeah, this thing." Miles pointed to the carved marble top of the crypt. I want to get it out of the way to open it up.

Dingo and Kelly looked at each other and then at Miles, who seemed even crazier than usual. "I don't think…" said Dingo.

"Who the fuck pays you to think. Just get the top off," said Miles.

"Looks pretty heavy, not sure if…." Kelly started.

"Men smaller than you put it on, so just shift the fucker."

Kelly and Dingo tried to get handholds and move the marble, but it was slow going to lift and slide it aside even for muscular men. Miles stepped in to help, but was not any. Finally, after push and pull, the slab slid to the side.

"If we go any further, it will fall to the floor and break," said Kelly.

"Fuck off. Leave it," said Miles of the Crypt lid, which hung on the end and was slightly supported by the back wall. "Now, get the fuck out." The men were happy to go.

#

Dingo reclined his seat in the car and closed his eyes. "Wake me when the nutter is done." It was not unusual for Miles to stay an hour or two. Kelly looked at his watch, a tick after ten, stuck in his earphones, and cranked up some Drake. They knew it would be a while.

Dingo was snoring, but Kelly didn't notice with his earbuds and started to doze himself. He jerked to wake and checked the time. Three twenty. "Hey, Ding, let's go get Prince Dickhead."

Kelly stretched, "what time is it?"

"He has been in there fucking the corpse for five hours. Should be enough time to get his nuts drained." Both men headed to the mausoleum. Neither knew the code, so Kelly banged on the door and shouted.

"Hey Miles, you ready to go? Miles, come on." After ten minutes, "He's probably asleep."

"What do we do?" said Kelly. "Call Tyler, or leave him till he comes out?"

"He was stoned, probably passed out. It's fucking cold out here." Dingo shouted, "Open the fuck up." It was useless.

Back in the car, with the heater on the two men tried to warm up. "We better call it in," said Kelly. Dingo nodded in agreement. "We don't want the fucker to freeze to death."

"We don't?" laughed Kelly.

"Tyler, we are at the cemetery, and the Prince has been inside for over five hours. He has the door locked and won't come out. Do we wait or what?" He did not mention opening the crypt.

"Was he ok when you left him?"

"How the hell do we know? He seems like a fucking lunatic on the best of days. He was stoned and drinking, his usual wonderful self."

"I'll get back to you," Tyler hung up and called Ramos at the Tower to explain what was happening.

"Boss," said Kelly as he answered a call from Ramos.

"The code is 1-9-4-8, John Kohl's birth year". "Check on him and let me know."

Dingo and Kelly returned to the door, put the code in, and entered. What waited inside was another dead Kohl. Miles apparently tried to open the upper half of the coffin, and it slipped to the floor. Dislodging the precariously positioned marble crypt lid, it fell across his upper body and flattened his chest and neck.

Lying on the floor were an empty whiskey flask and syringe. Miles's nemesis was heroin, which would later prove to be what it held.

Near five-thirty, Tyler and Ramos arrived. The sun would be up soon. Ramos needed to decide how to play it. A drug overdose would surprise no one with Mile's rehab history. Or with the added drama of the open crypt. The overdose would need a lot of payoffs and favours called in, but a far less creepy version of his death was the best for Julie. Except for little Annie, Julie was the only surviving Kohl.

After the funeral home van took Miles's body and the crypt sorted, Ramos called Alice. His early-hour call was highly unusual, and she answered with alarm. "Is it Billie?"

"No. Miles. Call the Zoo and get someone to drive you to the Tower. Julie will need to be told. The internet and papers will have it quickly. I'll see you there."

#

The Range Rover with Alice and Dingo pulled into the Tower garage an hour later. In all the years, this was a first for Alice. Not sure what she expected, but it all seemed relatively orderly and non-threatening to her, at least on arrival. When the SUV stopped, four men came out of a room with a large dark glass window. She could not see in, but they could see her. One of the men phoned Ramos in his third-floor office.

Everything felt too quiet, and none of the men spoke, though she assumed everyone knew what was happening. The lift door opened, and Ramos walked into the garage. "Come on. I will take you up."

Alice stepped into him in the lift, and he put a big arm around her. "I have no idea how she will take it. She is totally alone now." Alice tried not to cry.

Walking to a beautiful double door on the fifth floor, Ramos did not knock but opened the door and nudged Alice in. "I'll give you a few minutes."

# #

The sixteen thousand square feet home of ultimate luxury felt cold and empty inside. It wasn't. The heat was a comfortable temperature. Alice found Julie at the kitchen table with a cup of tea. When Julie looked up, she offered a weak smile. Julie did not question her being there.

"Is it Billie?" Julie's voice was soft, and her face was etched in worry. Alice shook her head. "Would you like tea?"

"Yes, please." Julie stood, took a delicate porcelain cup, and filled it from a matching teapot.

It's Miles?" Stated Julie. Alice nodded. "Our family is corrupt. My father did many bad things; we don't deserve to live."

"Oh Julie, no. Everything has happened for a reason. It is too much too soon, but …" Alice looked up and could see Ramos in the doorway. Julie followed her eyes to him.

"You ok?" he asks.

"No. But I'm not surprised. Was it an overdose?"

"Yes. At the mausoleum. He has been going there every day. I tried to get him help, but he refused."

"Can I help you get some things together? Come to Surrey; Annie and Lindsey are already there. You will feel better seeing her precious face," said Alice.

"No. I want to see Billie." She turned, "Ramos, will you ask him to come here?"

"I can have him come to Surrey."

"No. I want to see him here. I'll wait." Her calm monotone felt spooky. Ramos and Alice exchanged glances.

"You wait with her. I'll get Billie." Ramos turned for the door.

"No. Alice, you go. You too, Ramos. I'll wait for him." Julie did not know Billie had told his parents about her marriage proposal and having sex with her.

"Ramos will go, but I will ..." Julie shook her head. "Ok, if you are sure?" Alice slowly stood. Then, with more force, "I can't leave you. I am sorry. I promise I will leave when Billie arrives, but I won't leave you alone." She sat.

Julie smiled at her friend and realized she was happy her friend stayed, at least for a while.

⌗ ⌗

Summoned to his father's third-floor office, Ramos was waiting with Jimmy for Billie to arrive. "The tontine is complete. Julie has inherited all of the post-Johnnie fund settlements," said Jimmy.

"How much?" asked Ramos.

"Plus, what Ross left her, and his Life Insurance, about four hundred million." An astonishing number, but these men were used to big numbers. "The Trust is up to almost sixteen billion." Both men were enormously wealthy in their own right but knew long ago that vast wealth lost all meaning for Julie Kohl-Redmond.

In walked Billie, "I heard Miles OD." He was back in his father's good graces but didn't know why he was here at this hour.

"Julie is asking for you. She refuses your mother's help until she sees you."

"Dad," he shifted on his feet, "what do you want me to do?" He wanted clarity and did not want to mess up again.

"Whatever she needs." Ramos was telling his son to say or do whatever was required at the moment. "Understood?"

⌗ ⌗

The dawn light backlit Julie's slender frame as she stood in the breakfast room window. Billie took her into his arms, lifted her, and carried her to the bedroom. His dad was right; it was like some Romance novel, but he didn't know what else to do.

⌗ ⌗

The day was fully underway when they woke in each other's arms. His heart did not love her as she wanted, but his body did. He would not hurt her, he promised himself. The day drifted into another. On the third day, Billie looked at his phone, and there were a dozen messages from his parents.

"Should I call them back?" he asked Julie.

"It will be the funeral news and sad things I don't want to hear. Let them know I am; we are ok."

"Hi Mum, Yes, I saw your calls. Everything is fine. No, not today. Goodbye, Mum."

"One down, one to go," she said, almost smiling.

"Hi, Dad. Everything is fine. No, not today. Anything I need to know? Goodbye."

"The funeral is Thursday," said Billie.

"What day is today?"

"It's Tuesday."

"Text him; not until Saturday." She reached for him, and his body responded.

⌗ ⌗

Later, they wandered out to the kitchen for food. Billie could see various newspapers spread about the table left there by her housekeeper. The tabloids were banging on about the Detective and the Gangster. The Financial Times splashed: Kohl Empire tops sixteen Billion. Poor Little Rich Girls, said the Mail.

Julie caught his eyes, "A lot going on in the world. Our world."

"Those bastards don't care who they hurt," said Billie.

"No, they don't." She moved to lighten the mood. "What would you do with sixteen billion Pounds?"

"Far too many zeros for my brain to comprehend," he laughed.

"OK, remove a few digits. How about one billion?"

"Nope, still too many." He didn't want to talk about money and tried to keep it casual.

"A hundred million? Or fifty?"

"Ok, fifty million." They were sitting and having coffee. "I would buy an island somewhere warm, with a massive house for the whole family. And a boat. Not a yacht, but one to go fishing and diving. And a place for Danny to build spaceships and…."

Julie interrupted him. "I don't believe fifty would do it." Julie knew money did not equal happiness. You have to be happy first. And you need someone to share it.

"What was it about food?" Billie was an immense man with a huge appetite and was somewhat disappointed with the selection as he stuck his head in the enormous refrigerator.

"Sorry, not much *man* food in there." Julie was also looking in the fridge now. "How about eggs? Your mum has been teaching me to cook."

"Eggs will work. Six eggs, four slices of toast, and anything else you want to throw on the plate."

She laughed. "Six, are you joking? I have never witnessed anyone eat six eggs." She busied herself with breakfast.

"I'm a growing boy. Besides, it's your fault; you depleted my energy."

##

After breakfast and a long, sexy bubble bath, they returned to bed. "Don't worry, I will make something of all this," said Julie. "I know you don't love me, but I love you, and it feels wonderful to be in your arms. You make it easy to forget about the world outside."

"I don't ever want to hurt you. Please stop me before that happens, but believe me, you are beautiful and important to me."

##

Billie left to dress for the small private ceremony, which would not be private at all because of the press. He rode with Julie in her Rolls Royce to the cemetery. Ramos and Alice and all the elite team were waiting. Another thirty men formed a wall of muscle to keep the paps back.

Julie was immune to the shouting, baying mongrels, "How does it feel to be the last Kohl?"

"Were you and your brother close?"

"Did you know he was using drugs again?"

"Will you stay in the Tower alone?" and on and on. Julie remembered that as a young girl, her mother, mercilessly hounded by the press, told her to keep a calm look on her face and look down at her shoes. After so many years, she did it naturally.

Inside the mausoleum, Julie took a moment to glance around the vast room, which held space for many more Kohls. When her mother commissioned the impressive structure, she must have thought that with four children, she would have many spouses and grandchildren and years and years to fill the sad place. None of John Kohl's three sons married or fathered children to carry on the name. All who remained were Julie and Annie.

Billie stood at Julie's side. Jimmy, Ramos, and Alice were the only others inside the flower-filled space. Julie declined a priest. Instead, she walked to her mother's crypt, bowed her head, and said a silent prayer. She kissed the cold marble of her husband's resting place and the tiny crypt of their stillborn son. Looking up with a gentle face, she said, "I never want to come here again."

# #

Julie and Alice were in the garden with the girls, planting bulbs for spring. Julie had been here for weeks, and as the days passed, she seemed to be coming back to life. She never again asked to see Billie, though she saw him briefly when he visited his mother and sisters or occasionally in the Tower garage. Her time with him was a secret gift she did not need to share with anyone.

# # #

CHAPTER 41

MRS. T

An unattached female rarely went into The Lightning Rod, a tittie club heaving with pussy and men seeking that commodity. It is not the type of club to host Hen Parties or GNOs, Girls' *Night Out*. When a rather attractive woman in her early thirties, expensively dressed in a conservative suit, walked up, Beto on the door knew there was trouble brewing.

"Stand aside, please; I am going in," snipped the woman.

"Not tonight," said Beto as he flashed a fake smile.

"Don't be an asshole, move."

"Take off," Beto held his ground and was surprised when she attempted to push past him. No small task as Beto was an enormous brute and not in the least friendly.

"Oh, you want money. Fine, here's forty. Please step aside." She flipped two twenties toward his face.

"This way," said Beto to the men standing behind her. As they attempted to pass into the Club, the woman pushed forward.

There is only one way to deal with a crasher. Beto stepped in, grabbed her around her slim waist, and spun her. Ready to heave her to the pavement, she startled him with a piercing scream. "Tyler!"

Fuck thought Beto and the other doorman Benny. Tyler is Ramos's top man, and she is hollering his name.

"Tyler!"

"Shut up, lady."

"Tyler!" Beto and Benny exchanged glances. Now what? Beto set her down.

"You have business with Tyler?"

"I'm his wife, you big ape. Now let me in," she demanded.

Anything she could have said might have been believable, but not that she was Tyler's wife or anyone was his wife. Tyler was not a marrying kind of man.

"No. Wait over there," he pointed to a lighted corner of the building.

"Is he here? If not, I'll leave."

"Shut the fuck up and stand over there, or I will throw you out in the street." Beto, huge, ugly, and fierce, did not scare her much.

She didn't like it but did as Beto ordered. He made a call and confirmed Tyler was inside. He didn't know if the bitch was someone he would want to see. Hell, he might be inside fucking someone.

"What? Tyler's wife is here? You having a laugh?" said Carter. The line went dead.

Beto raised his phone and took a photo of the woman. "Stay put and don't try to get inside, or Benny, who is not near as old and nice as I am, will knock the shit out of you. Understand?"

"You are not exactly ambiguous," she sneered in reply as she folded her arms and began tapping her foot.

Beto went inside and approached the bar. "Where's Tyler."

"In Carlos's office. Think Sapphire is blowing him about now. Why?"

"His wife wants a word." Beto, let that hang. Frankie and Jet were having a drink and overheard, causing both to laugh out loud.

"No fucking way," said Frankie. The other men joined with a head shake. "Chances are she's someone's wife but not his."

"Let him know," said Carter as he moved to the other end of the bar and poured shots for a couple of punters mesmerized by the bitches slowly twirling on the poles.

Beto knew these men rarely cared about sexual privacy or formality, but he knocked before opening the door and went on in.

Carter was right. Tyler was getting his dick out as Sapphire headed for her knees. Tyler reached down and helped her stand. Such a gentleman, our Tyler. "Later," he said.

"What's up?" asked Tyler.

Beto hesitated while Saffy exited. When the door shut behind her, he said, "Your wife is here, and she wants inside?"

"Wife?" He chuckled. "OK, is this a quiz? Do I guess?"

Beto stepped forward and showed him the photo.

"No shit, what is she doing here?"

"What do you want me to do? Let her in or?"

"Take her around to the side door. Knock twice, and I will open up." Not many knew Carlos' office had an outside entry door. Handy for a quick escape or, as in this case, a discreet visitor. The office was still called Carlos' office out of respect for the deceased legend.

# #

Opening the door, there stood Fiona, a proper Mayfair society lady married to a barrister. They spent a few months fucking early in Covid, but it became too much of a hassle during the lockdowns. Fucks were not difficult for Tyler to find, and Fiona rarely shut the fuck up. What the hell was she doing here?

"Come in."

"What a brute." She smoothed her suit as if she was dusting off Beto's fingerprints.

"Wife?" He cocked his head.

"Oh, I wanted to get his attention."

"It worked. Have a seat." He pointed to a bottle of whiskey. She nodded yes, and he poured them each a drink. He sat behind the desk to give a bit of distance between them. She wanted something, and he needed to know what.

After a few polite sips of whiskey, Fiona still failed to state what was on her mind. "I've missed you," said all warm and coy.

"We had some fun." He took a drink, eyeing her cautiously.

# #

Fiona and Tyler met in the most unlikely way. He was walking along Park Street near Grosvenor Square and the Cairo Club about noon when she stepped out of her Aston Martin Vantage, throwing the door open in his path.

A looker, beautifully dressed, Tyler flashed her a smile and kept going. "Can you help me?" she called out. He stopped and looked back.

"Please." Tyler's sphere of hard men was not a please and thank you world. It put a grin on his ruggedly handsome face.

Tyler was a hunky man with a solid build and confident stride. Unlike many of his brother outlaws, Tyler didn't look too beat and battered from his embraced lifestyle. He oozed testosterone, which lubed up many unsuspecting females, many of whom were wives of someone.

"What's up?" He stepped toward her.

"Something is wrong, and my car won't move. I'm half on a double yellow, and the parking wardens in this area are real bastards."

"I'll try." He went to get behind the wheel, but she didn't give him much space. Far too little room for a man of his size. Was it his imagination, or did she rub her ample tits on him as he was seated?

Turning on the ignition, he could diagnose the problem quickly. "Looks like the butler forgot to get petrol. You're out."

"Butler? Aren't you funny?" And sexy, she thought. "Good timing; I'm desperate for a laugh. It has been a rather shitty morning." Quite the potty-mouth chuckled Tyler.

"Just a bit of gasoline, don't let it ruin your day." He stood to leave, and the woman placed her hand on his arm. Men such as Tyler didn't like to be touched by the uninvited. He looked at her hand, then her eyes, but not with menace, with mischief.

"You are so big and strong." She squeezed his bicep. "Could you push it a few feet and save me from *Council-hell*? I would pay you."

"Sure. Step back." He put the car in neutral and gave it a nudge. "That should do it."

"You must let me pay you. Oops! I forgot my wallet. I live around the corner on Upper Brooke. I have the cash there. I insist you come with me." She took his muscular arm and walked on.

Tyler didn't know if it was a regular game she played, but it was a dangerous one. She was dripping with diamonds. They met up a dozen or so times after that. Always on Wednesdays, the staff day off.

⚡ ⚡

"What brings you by the Rod?"

"Honestly? You're the only *villain* I know. I need some confidential help."

"I'm not killing your husband if that's what you are here for?" He grinned, only half-joking.

"What? I'm not crazy; besides, he is not worth the effort. He is sleeping with his clerk, and he doesn't have enough left to bother me. No, it is more of a financial issue." She took another sip.

"You need money?" Having been to her home, the thought baffled him. Money did not seem to be in the least a problem.

"Don't be silly, of course not. My father is 7th Baron Collingwick, and my late mother was one of the Starling sisters. You know, all that fabulous American pharmaceutical money? I would be willing to pay you."

"For what?"

"To," she waved her hands about, "to hit a person making trouble for me. Would you hit a woman? Or know someone who would? Make it look like an accident."

Tyler had hit plenty of women but needed a hell of a lot more information. "What did she do?"

"Do you have to know that? Isn't it enough to know she is causing me harm?" She seemed reluctant to share the potential victim's misdeeds.

"Tell me."

"Twice, she has pushed in to join a charity committee I am on and insists on being the chairperson and grabbing all the glory. I know it sounds petty to you, but it's a matter of principle. The bitch deserves to have her nose broken or something." She sighed loudly.

"Fiona, I can see you are upset, and I would like to help you, but this is not in my wheelhouse. Find another way to make her pay."

"There is no other way. She's a vain bitch, and messing up her smug face is the only justice."

Tyler refilled his glass and tilted the bottle in offer. Fiona nodded yes.

"Oh well. You want to have sex?" she blurted.

"Sure, but I am not going to hurt your friend."

She turned pouty, "She's not my friend."

"Come here."

⚜ ⚜

Out of the blue, she showed up ten days later. This time, at the lobby door of the Tower and buzzing to get in. The stories in the paper about Ramos made the Tower and many of the clubs well known.

"Yeah, who is it?" snapped Dingo.

"Tyler's wife." It had worked before, so she decided to use it again.

Typically, Dingo would have just hung up, but all the men had heard the story of a woman showing up at the Rod with that claim. Tyler had seen her, though no one knew why or on what matter.

"Wait." The lobby phone went dead.

Dingo called Tyler in his third-floor office. "The Mrs. has stopped by to see you. She's in the lobby. Do I bring her up?"

Almost as surprising as the first wifey visit. Tyler was too busy to mess about, but figured why not? His dick wouldn't mind a few minutes of attention. "Yeah."

Fiona walked into the office looking her usual lovely, confident self. Tyler noticed she dressed considerably sexier than her Rod visit. "Have a seat," he dismissed Dingo with a head jerk. Tyler's office door was open, as was Ramos's office door. Fiona was unaware the boss was in and could hear her every word.

Sitting tall, she gave Tyler a flirty grin. "You going to share the whiskey?" He poured her one and slid it across the desk toward her.

"This is a surprise," he said.

"A nice one, I hope? For both of us."

"What's up?" He could see her eyes dancing as she squirmed that she was bursting to tell him something.

"So, this is the Tower? Your boss is certainly in the tabloids a great deal."

"He's a public figure; his name sells papers."

"The stories are so trashy, yet thrilling. Like it's not real."

"A great deal of it isn't." He was bored with the chit-chat and wanted to get down to it. "Why are you here?"

"Remember what we recently talked about? My little favour?"

"Yes."

"You weren't accommodating, but I didn't offer you anything you wanted. Now that might have changed."

"How so? What do you want?"

"My husband Malcolm, the barrister, QC, and all that; we had a small luncheon in our garden yesterday, and guess who stopped by?"

Tyler felt impatient. "No idea?"

"My husband's Oxford roommate. Judge Campbell of the Serious Organized Crimes prosecution unit. The same Judge in those *Gangster and*

Detective stories in the paper." Tyler was on pointe now. "Well, you know gossip and alcohol are such a vulgar combination. Amazing what comes out."

"How so?" Tyler wanted to shake her but did not divulge his impatience.

"I might have a tiny titbit your boss would find useful. I could help you, and you could help me?"

"We can probably work something out. What ya got?"

Unknown to Fiona, Ramos was standing in the doorway behind her. "Two things. First, that horrible bitch has done it again. She gave an interview about my committee's work to Hello magazine with photos! Photos! She has to be stopped. You positively have to promise me you will smash her ugly face." She slid a photo clearly torn from a magazine across the desk, with a name and address on the back. She waited for confirmation, but none came.

"In exchange, you can prepare your boss; they are serving a search warrant. If you promise I get what I want, I will tell you exactly where and what they have the authority to look for and when they will arrive. Deal?" She leaned back in her chair and waited for his reply.

He smiled at her naivety. Bad men do not let others dictate the terms of an arrangement. Any information she had to trade was his for the taking. "You said two things. One is to waste your rival and the other?"

"Oh, Tyler," she squirmed a bit. "Promise me you won't think I'm a terrible person? I want to fuck your boss. He is such a sexy beast and so famous. I get wet just thinking about him. Fact is, I am pretty moist right now." Tyler gave a small chuckle as Ramos walked in.

"Hello. Am I interrupting?"

⚜ ⚜ ⚜

CHAPTER 42

UNLIKELY

Construction on the ballet studio and chapel was completed. The Children began ballet lessons, and the studio was also used for afternoon yoga sessions. The men at the Zoo enjoyed the tight yoga pants on the ladies' parade to the studio. They often came outside to watch them walk by.

"You are welcome to join us?" said Alice when she spotted the men viewing the procession. Carley, Lindsey, and Sissy grinned as the little girls skipped hand in hand. Julie kept her head down.

Rio and Dingo were laughing. "Sorry, we forgot our yoga pants."

Ramos spared no expense on the chapel. The craftsmen added character and elegance. The small but beautifully designed structure was made of Cotswold stone and marble. The finishing touches were a graceful marble statue of the Virgin Mary at the entry and a towering stained-glass window depicting the crucifixion hanging over the altar. Alice had been astonished by the extravagance.

The chapel held twenty in five rows of double pews. On each side of the altar were stands of fresh flowers, candles to be lit, and padded benches for kneeling. A discreet sound system added to the authenticity. Several times, a local priest arrived to offer communion and receive donations for their latest Parish fundraising projects.

Alice and the children regularly attended Mass and other church activities when living in Baylor. Alice often provided the music for services and events, now impossible with the press intrusion.

"I can never thank you enough for adding something so beautiful to our lives. The chapel feels one step closer to heaven." Effusive in her thanks and excitement, Ramos knew it was the only step toward heaven he would ever take.

The chapel would be the perfect place for the Santiago family to greet police as they served a Search Warrant two weeks later.

⚓ ⚓

It was unusual for Ramos to arrive in Surrey on Sunday morning. Alice and the others were in their pyjamas in the kitchen, having coffee and fresh home-baked cinnamon rolls. The aromas were intoxicating.

"Daddy, Daddy," rang out.

Ignoring them, Ramos turned to Alice, "I need you to get everyone ready and go to the chapel."

"Now?"

"Right now."

Alice understood it was urgent and asked no further questions. "Everyone up and get dressed quickly." She nodded to Sissy, who picked up Sunny and headed upstairs with Luna and Stella following. Lindsey, Julie, and Annie were not here today, making things faster.

Ramos headed to his office. He kept nothing incriminating here and wanted to check the top of his desk where Alice put his rare current mail. He did not hesitate; he quickly read and routinely shredded the contents.

A gun permit leftover from his position as head of security for Sir John Kohl was in place. All weapons were in a locked gun vault. Several in the master bedroom, Ramos hid in four smaller chambers behind light switches. He patted the Sig in his waistband. The Filth did not have permission to check his physical body.

"Is everything okay?" asked Alice as he entered their bedroom.

"Yes, but the filth will be here soon."

"Are you going to be arrested?" Worry flooded her face.

"No, they will serve a search warrant and tear the place apart." He was tipped off about the search by Tyler's rich-bitch and was confirmed by Filth on his payroll. "Relax. There is nothing to find. I want you and the children to be in the chapel. Are you ready to go?"

Ramos already dealt with the Zoo. Nothing was on paper or findable. The only issue was arms and cash, concealed in an underground armoury and gun range under the saintly chapel.

"Yes. Can I do anything?"

"Just go." Alice would not push back. The case and tabloids were entirely out of her hands, and while frustrated, she knew it was no time to take a stand. It was Ramos' show; it was always his show.

Sissy put Sunny in a pushchair and Stella and Luna in pretty matching dresses. Alice was in a simple pale blue frock, her hair loose, and, as usual, almost no makeup.

Alice was surprised to see Tyler, Dingo, and Rio sitting in the rear of the small chapel as the exquisite voice of Andrea Bocelli sang Ave Maria. Hearing police sirens approach, Alice stood lighting candles. She looked up to see Ramos enter the chapel. He walked to the front, took Sunny from Sissy's arms, and took a pew. It was the first time he had ever held his youngest daughter.

After a deep breath, he could see his daughters had been here often and knew what to do. They were surprisingly quiet, sweetly sitting together, holding hands and swinging their legs.

When the door banged open, everyone looked up and froze. "Holy hell! Ramos Santiago and his animals in church?" They had been directed to the Chapel by the men at the gate. "Hope to hell the ceiling doesn't fall on us?" A Detective forced a bellicose laugh as Ramos's men kept their eyes down.

"No one will fucking believe it," bellowed one of the intruding Detectives.

"Neither do I, boss."

"I am DCI Watson. I have a warrant to search your home and garage." Ramos noted he did not say Chapel, ballet studio, or other outbuildings that the police may not have known existed.

"That man said a bad word," Luna pointed at the Detective.

"Daddy, it not nice to make big noise in chapel." Stella shook her head. "You pose to whisper."

"My angels." Ramos passed Sunny to Sissy and leaned in and kissed the heads of his little girls. Walking casually to Alice, who stood, eyes wide by the candles. Placing a muscular arm loosely around her, he softly whispered, "Everything is fine." He kissed her lightly on the forehead and walked out, with Tyler following.

# #

"That was quite a show. You, your family, and your bunch of monsters at church." Said Watson.

"Well, if anyone has a reason to pray," laughed DC Smith.

Ramos remained silent as the Filth tore up his home. They were throwing everything on the floor, overturning furnishings, and pushing things about. "Someplace you got here, Ramos. How much money did you have to steal to get it?"

"Crime does pay, boss. Look at the size of the toilet." Both men feigned laughter, but the long-suffering detectives were jealous and resentful.

Jimmy walked in. "I'm James Redmond. I am of counsel to Mr. Santiago. Please provide me a copy of your warrant."

"Keep your hair on, old man." He flipped Jimmy the paper. Jimmy reads the warrant.

"It says you are looking for tax records and large amounts of cash. Have you found any in Mrs. Santiago's lingerie drawer? If not, it is time to get your hands off her garments." Jimmy, an elegant gentleman, cast a stern eye. "If you take the children's coin banks, I need a receipt for each amount."

"Sure, Redmond, everything by the book. By the way, we found this." Without divulging the contents, Watson held up an envelope "in one of your boy's rooms."

"Detective, there is no law against having cash. Mr. Billie Santiago owns a successful automotive garage. There is no cause for excitement."

"Looks like at least thirty thousand; that's some fuckin petrol station. We'll count it for you."

Ramos noticed a man taking photos with his phone and motioned to Jimmy.

"Photos for the Filth or the papers?" Redmond asked.

"What photos?" said Watson. "I didn't see any photos?"

"Me either, Guv." All the men knew the photos would be worth substantial money when sold to the tabloids.

"I will lodge a complaint to prohibit the sale of any photos. Or you could sell Tyler your phones for twenty thousand?"

The two detectives dismissed the officers doing the search. When they moved to depart, DCI Watson walked closer to Redmond. "Twenty each." He smirked at Redmond, feeling it was a big win.

Jimmy nodded once. "That is ten additional to whatever you have in the envelope." No one believed for a moment that Billie's envelope would ever make it to the evidence file. "You're done here." Redmond pulled ten thousand from his jacket and passed it to Tyler, who gave it to Watson. He then held his hand out for the phones.

"Don't be looking at the pussy shots of my wife on there," snickered the DCI.

"Detective Watson, it is highly unlikely you have seen your wife's vagina since the invention of the cell phone camera."

The Detectives took a second to decide if they would push back, but in the end, both laughed, and wrapped it up. Empty-handed of evidence, but far richer than the morning started. DC Smith grinned at Ramos as he patted his jacket pocket, where Jimmy knew he tucked a pair of Alice's knickers.

"Fuckers!" Spat Ramos.

⚓ ⚓

The Filth was not the only pain in Ramos' ass. Marita Baez wanted to go back to Surrey and see the Chapel. It had not been built on her one brief visit. "Is it grand enough for us to get married there?" she asked him. Convinced she would live in the Surrey house one day, Marita did not like being left out of what was happening.

⚓ ⚓ ⚓

CHAPTER 43

MUSIC

Alice, a bookworm, regularly visited bookstores and the library when living in Baylor, but now even something so simple seemed almost impossible. She loved her home and quiet life, but fame sometimes felt like a prison. She decided to disguise herself and attend a series of seminars *devoted to the study of analytical approaches to modal, tonal, and non-tonal music through careful examination of seminal theoretical treatises and their relevance to music from the early Middle Ages up to the present.*

Gosh, that is a mouthful she thought as she reread it, wondering if she was about to jump into the deep end. But some days, she needed to listen to someone over the age of six.

♯ ♯

"Ramos, the damnedest call? Luke Corbett from the Met has politely asked you to come in at two?"

"Any idea what's up?" Asked Ramos as he stretched his long frame.

"None. He is a DCS and pretty high up the Filth food chain to be rousting you. And it didn't sound like it had anything to do with the other shit that is percolating."

"What did you tell him?"

"I would check with you and get back to him. What do you think? Of course, I will go as legal counsel." Jimmy, a licensed/certified Barrister, and Ramos, with the death of Johnnie Kohl, was his only client. Curious to Jimmy, with many friends, the bought and paid for kind, but no one alerted him to a new problem in the Crown Prosecution office.

"Make it three," said Ramos of the unusual invitation. Usually, the Met would send someone to Kohl for the latest hassle, not someone of Corbett's stature.

⚡ ⚡

Ramos' appearance at the Met was hot news, and the building was all abuzz. After clearing security, including metal detectors and a pat-down, Ramos and Jimmy were shown to Chief Superintendent Corbett's office.

Corbett stood when they entered and directed them to chairs. Not a grand office like all of Ramos' but not a cubicle with a scarred old desk and chairs held together with duct tape.

"Thank you for coming in today, Mr. Santiago," began Corbett. Ramos said nothing.

"Before we begin, I wish to clarify if my client is under caution. At this time, he is not prepared to make any statement."

"You can relax, councillor; we are here as a friend to Mr. Santiago. We have information the department feels he should know." Kohl did not make a sound, but his eyes said quit masturbating, asshole, and get on with it.

"Due to complex and efficient police work, I am proud of; we have uncovered and stopped a plot to kidnap Mrs. Santiago." Ramos, already sitting tall, became stiff and attentive.

"Mr. Santiago demands to know the full details of the plan," said Jimmy. "What, when, where, who, and how you learned of this plot?"

"We learned of it through confidential informants and will not divulge their names to you. Frankly, for their safety, but rest assured, the men behind the plot are no longer a threat."

"Are you saying they're dead?" asked Ramos when he finally spoke.

"I couldn't say."

"You might reconsider your position. Mr. Santiago deserves to know."

"We may have in the past pursued you, Mr. Santiago, but on this issue, we are on the same side. The matter is over."

"May I ask how long you have known the information?" asked Jimmy.

"About ten days."

"You are telling us for ten days Mrs. Santiago has been in potential danger, and not once you thought it might be good police work, as you call it, to let Mr. Santiago know?" Before Jimmy finished his sentence, Ramos stood up and walked out of the room.

He was enraged that the bastard sat there, speaking casually about the safety of his wife. The arrogant cunt would be dealt with, but first, he needed to ensure Alice was safe. Next, whoever hatched the plot needed to be very dead.

Outside Police headquarters, Ramos called Frank. "My wife is in danger. If she is out, get her home."

Frankie called Rio, who walked into the Academy of Music lecture room. Everyone looked startled by the menacing man who entered. No one said a word. Jerking his head toward the door, Alice knew if she did not get up, he would come and carry her out.

"Rio, for fun, can you do something unusual and tell me what's happening?"

"Boss wants you home." He held her close to him, his eyes everywhere. Alice hated him touching her, but now was not the time for that conversation.

A car waited at the curb. Frank stood outside the car on full alert. Alice felt confident; she looked as if she was being abducted, but no one moved to help her. Maybe they recognized her or did not want to tangle with Frank and Rio. Who would?

Sitting close to her in the back of the car, Rio put his hand on his gun.

The grounds of the estate were buzzing with men and activity. Where did they all come from, she thought? Rio took her home. He checked each room and waited outside the front door. Alice stood inside, wondering what was happening.

Jimmy called. "Need to see you; I am at the door." Thirty seconds later, the doorbell rang.

"I take it you are here to let me know why I was spirited away from my class?"

Jimmy seemed puzzled. "What class?"

"What does it matter? Rio brought me back and made it quite clear it was not optional."

"What class?"

"A class I am taking at the Music Academy." You don't care if I am doing pet psychiatry or home watching the shopping channel, she thought.

"How often does it meet, and how long has it been going on?"

"Quit bullying me; please go." Jimmy has very little interaction with Alice, and she is unhappy with his intense questioning.

"How long and how often?" Alice's attempts to be assertive proved ineffective. Jimmy's face and body were fierce; he knew if anything happened to Alice, he would be among those in line for blame. He was fed up with his go-between role and was even more determined to find his replacement and retire.

Alice sighed, knowing, as usual, she would have to comply.

"Every Wed for the last three weeks, but I signed up about six weeks ago."

"Goddammit, you have been told."

"Told. What do you mean? What's happening? Please tell me."

"Stay here until I tell you it is okay to leave the property." He left without further explanation.

Ramos went mental. The idea that cunt Corbett thought he could keep information from him was a severe misjudgement. He would soon have the details, but Corbett was due a penalty of enormous proportions; Corbett's wife was now the one in danger.

Anyone in Ramos' life who matters to him is a target. Kidnapping, hurting, or killing his wife would put anyone on the map. They might die trying, but Mrs. Ramos Santiago was a hell of a prize and, to plenty of scum, worth the odds.

Jimmy worked the phones, as calls and texts were coming fast. Ramos went to his Tower office, closed the door, and slammed his hand on his desk. Just what I fucking knew would happen. He would look weak if anyone killed his wife. That cunt Corbett sitting in his shabby office being the big man and telling him someone wanted to hurt his wife and take his property, and the fucking wonderful police saved the day. He was not having it.

Lots of money and force made all of the information Ramos wanted to flow like a leaky Thames water tap. Less than nine hours later, the informant stood before Ramos in the backroom of a seedy wine bar near Billingsgate Market. The imbecile gave up the information on the simple plan and was beaten and thrown in a ditch near Tilbury docks.

Burton Senior was banged up for years and not going anywhere when he learned Burton Junior, his only son, was killed on a jack-job. He felt Ramos did not do enough to protect his men. The heist was an easy hit, but Junior coked out of his head and fell over a bridge railing to a highway below, his death on himself alone.

Once a respected motherfucker, Burton Senior should have known to keep it in his cell, but now he is a moaning bitch. He bad-mouthed Ramos to whoever would listen. One of those all-ears, an Albanian, was Jako Delmont: a dim face, tats, and body with a penitentiary build his entire resume.

Jako and his brother were struggling to break into the London crime world. The few things they tried to get noticed had not gone well, thus their stays at Her Majesty's pleasure. Jako is out, and his brother is due for release soon.

Jako started watching the Surrey estate, frequently mentioned in the press and easy to find. Having seen Alice's photos in the tabloids, he watched the property, taking care to avoid the numerous cameras.

Mrs. Santiago was always covered by at least one brute, but Jako figured he and his brother would outnumber them. Ramos' men looked tough, but life was rough in Albania, and the Dalmont brothers were unafraid of a bit of pain.

A week before his brother's release, Jako sussed the Mrs. went to the Academy every Wednesday. She entered the lecture room, and the tough guy stayed outside the door. It might be tricky, but not impossible.

Jako got a message to Burton Senior. His brother was out on Friday, and they would grab Mrs. Santiago the following Wednesday. Thrilled Ramos was soon to be spanked; Burton spent the whole weekend jabbering to the other cellblock mates.

Burton's roommate knew the information was valuable and asked to speak to a *screw*. In short order, the Met notified, and a deal was made. The informer considered selling the info to Ramos, but he couldn't get him early release and home to a lovely Sunday roast and fuck with his wife. He told the Guv and the deal was done.

The excellent police work done by the met involved all the cunning and energy of arresting a litterbug. Jako was picked up on a handgun parole violation and back in prison within twenty-four hours. A severe setback to the Armenian brother's plans and a huge fucking disappointment to Burton.

Jako was shived in his cell at Parkhurst. Burton Senior knew they were coming and bid his time.

Corbett was all that remained. John gave him a short bit of distance. Corbett, an arrogant prick, thought being an important man in the police made him an important man. Ramos knew it did not.

Ramos intended to make Corbett a proposition. Join the ranks of the Filth on my payroll or pay a high price for putting my wife in jeopardy by not informing me she was in danger.

Ramos arranged no formal meeting to discuss the options. Instead, Corbett's wife Grace was grabbed off the street when visiting her mum in Greyshot. The speed and precision of the abduction were impressive. No one in the neighbourhood saw anything.

Hooded and tied in the back of a van, Grace could hear breathing and smell men. Frightened, but she remained hopeful and smug, believing the men would be sorry when they found out her husband was a senior police officer. They already knew, which made grabbing her all the sweeter.

The front-page story of the missing woman was a total mystery. Gossip started thanks to Ramos' friends at the tabloids. Grace, a known flirt, perhaps ran off with someone? Others denied such a thing possible; she loved her husband and would not leave her children. The story kept the front pages burning for four days, but with no new information, it was relegated to a small blurb on page eight.

Corbett is no idiot. Ramos was the first to come to mind, but he pushed it aside, thinking not even Ramos Santiago would be that brazen. Would he?

On day five, Jimmy called Corbett and offered to help. "Chief Superintendent Corbett, we were shocked to read about your wife's abduction. So many animals out there. Not for a moment do we believe she ran off." Jimmy paused, but Corbett remained silent. "Mr. Santiago would like to help. With extensive ties in the greater London area, possibly he could find out something your excellent police work has failed to turn up?"

Corbett exploded. "You Bastard, you think I buy his feigned moral integrity? The shit he is selling with photos ops with sick children and big checks. You think I don't know what …." The phone went dead?

Corbett waited twenty minutes to call back. He knew Ramos Santiago was fearless and did not care if he took on a Copper, the Pope, or the Queen. If he wanted you dead and gone, it would be done.

"Mr. Redmond, it's Corbett. Can we meet?"

Ramos did not attend. Jimmy went to the area near Corbett's Met office and a planned *accidental* meeting outside a nearby pub.

"Go to the men's room, and you will be pat down. Come back and join me." Corbett did as told.

At the small table, two pints waited. Neither man drank. "I give up. Tell me what you want?" Corbett asked in defeat.

"Respect. Mr. Santiago wants some goddamn respect. You left his wife vulnerable while you and your merry band of *jerk-offs* got yourselves all puffed up. Damn, disrespectful." Corbett nodded his head in agreement. If Ramos' wife were harmed, Corbett knew he would have killed his wife, children, and probably his dog. Corbett was nearly out of his mind with worry and inadequate sleep. Anything Ramos wanted was okay with him.

"Mr. Santiago is open to friends in all professions, and if he can somehow get your wife returned from the bad men who have her, he believes it will be the basis for a friendship." Corbett nodded his head. He knew Ramos Santiago would own him.

"Good news." Jimmy looked him in the eye, "and more good news. Your wife was spotted unhurt on the M25 at a McDonald's." Relief flooded Corbett's face. He knew Ramos' monsters had taken her, but all he felt now was gratitude.

"We'll be in touch when your friendship is required."

# # #

## CHAPTER 44

RETIREMENT

Jimmy Redmond was putting his ducks in a row. When Ramos suddenly became head of Kohl Enterprises, he committed to two final years, which had passed.

Sir John Kohl had been a business genius, but Redmond's contributions to the Empire were unquestionable.

Jimmy was the nerd, the detail man, and he brought an educated finesse to the business of villainy. But he was exhausted from the decades of adrenalin.

Getting the businesses in Ramos' hands and selling the arms business were almost complete. The only loose end was who would replace him. It was unsaid, but Ramos and Jimmy knew Ramos would need another legal eagle and fixer.

To find someone qualified and willing to be part of the dirty business of bad men was not going to be easy. Bad lawyers and bad men are not uncommon, but they were usually deficient and turned to villainy when more pristine pursuits came up short.

Jimmy's replacement would require top-level skills and a lack of empathy for others. Willingness to control and manipulate with charm, charisma, threats, or aggression. In other words, an intelligent, educated, polished textbook sociopath who could take orders from a beast like Ramos Santiago. This was a rare breed. Ramos and Jimmy had a meeting at the Tower set for late afternoon to discuss the matter.

※ ※

Briefcase in hand, Jimmy walked into the late John Kohl's elegant office, now occupied by Ramos. The men exchanged a nod in silent greeting. Jimmy poured two whiskeys then sank into a plush leather chair. Ramos thought he looked old and slow.

"I may have good news?" Jimmy reported.

"Good news is welcome; what's up?"

"About three months ago, I heard from a former colleague, Richard Post. He started at the Crown Prosecution about the same time I did. While my career was taking off, his was as well. Fucking brilliant, he was my toughest competitor for the next big steps up. Or he was until it all fell apart." Jimmy paused for a pull of his whiskey.

"One morning, we walked into the office, and he was arrested. He was as surprised as I was. He had been drilling one of the clerks, and when he tried to break it off, she accused him of sexual harassment and assault. I believed then, and now, it was bullshit, but by noon he was gone and his career over."

"Sexual harassment was just becoming a big issue. Prosecution Division took the easy way and gave him a choice to resign or face charges. We stayed in touch for a while, but he moved to the US. John wasn't big on holidays, so I didn't see him again until early May this year."

"He stay in law?"

"Yes, but not unlike my change of mind when I left to work for John, Richard became an international criminal lawyer in Miami. A real rock star."

It was long ago, but Jimmy lost his first wife and two young sons to a degenerate drunk driver. A young Jimmy Redmond had loved the law almost as much as he loved his wife and sons. He was obsessed with the tools of the law and his determination to use them against the bad men of the world.

The trial was uncomplicated, and the drunk was quickly found guilty of his crime. He was given only a nine-year sentence, and then the Judge stunned everyone when the sentence was suspended. Jimmy could never again believe the law was a magnificent force for good. The law was a joke. Very soon after, Redmond approached John Kohl to help give him justice and a job.

"Post was in town to see his son, Rich. He went to Yale Law and then was at Oxford. He married an English girl and stayed in the UK."

"At the end of last year, Rich learned what happened to his father at the Crown Prosecution." The charges against his father had happened years before social media and Google, but these days, nothing stays secret. "Richard said he was outraged. He could not believe his father was a rapist and was considering leaving the law over the injustice. He lost respect and the passion that had propelled him so quickly through the ranks."

"Richard knew his son was a damn fine Barrister and urged caution before taking his next step, but he told me Rich is determined."

"Determined to do what?" Asked Ramos.

"To use his brain to make a lot of money and to fuck the Crown Prosecution whenever he got the chance."

"How old is he?" Asked Ramos. He knew this was no job for a young rebel; he needed a solid grown-up.

"Closing in on forty. I met with him for lunch last week. It was promising."

"First, have the snoops on six check him out." Said Ramos, meaning Kohl-Mine, the investigation unit of Kohl Enterprises located on the sixth floor of the Tower.

"I did before I met with him. He checks out to be what his father said he was. I believe he could be a good fit. Want to meet him?"

Ramos knew he needed someone for the details, and Redmond was ready to end his employment. He had amassed a personal fortune of over four hundred million Pounds, but even that held little interest for him these days. His son dead, his wife nearly so, and his other children spread across the globe, Jimmy was an old man, and he was tired.

"Set it up."

#

Hello, Mr. Santiago." Rich Post offered his hand. Bad men did not often bother with the petty gesture, but Post lived in the polite world of phony behaviour, so Ramos took it and returned the handshake. Rich smiled as he pulled back his hand with a comic shake. "That's quite a paw." What he said was unexpected and made Ramos smile slightly; he did have enormous hands.

"Please have a seat, Rich," said Jimmy. Tyler had done a thorough pat down for weapons and wires and taken his phone before escorting him in.

Ramos looked at the man in front of him. Handsome, impeccably dressed with American confidence that might prove useful. The richest, freest country in the history of the world made Americans feel invincible. They weren't.

Ramos was not a man to plan what he would say. He opened without drama with a make-or-break line. "Rich, have you ever killed anyone?"

"In self-defense or because I was pissed off?" Rich held no frivolous tone. He knew of the reputation of the enormous man across the desk and understood why he was there. He also knew a lot of bravado would not go down well.

Ramos was not a man who answered questions and remained silent. Rich knew he expected an answer. "No. It hasn't been necessary yet."

⌗ ⌗

Ramos decided in favour of Rich Post. Jimmy would work with Post over the next months and prepare for his exit.

⌗ ⌗ ⌗

CHAPTER 45

THE LETTER

"We'll hit the Cairo, then head to Waltham," Tyler told Billie, who was driving. The men were making rounds before a meet to discuss a massive new drug drop. Many clubs and cafes closed down because of Covid restrictions and had never reopened, but The Cairo was busy. Pulling into the valet area of the Mayfair club, both men noticed the boss's car.

"Daddy's home," said Tyler, who, like all the men, would not miss an opportunity to goad Billie and subtly remind him how he made it to the top of the criminal crew so quickly. The men closest to Ramos were his bodyguards and the enforcement arm of the organization. "I'll be right back." Signalling Billie that he was not coming inside.

Commanding significant power, Tyler was Ramos's right hand. Billie never challenged his authority. No wise man would. With a deep sigh, Billie leaned back and pulled his phone to check messages and the Instagram of *Titty-Boo,* a stripper and enormous tit model currently making it big in the *influencer world.* Her unique attraction was her third nipple.

"Ah fuck," his phone was dead. Reaching for the cords to juice, he saw Dingo standing by Ramos's car. If ever a man liked crazy monster ta-tas, it was *the OZ,* and he was sure to share the latest photos.

"Cold as fuck out here," welcomed Dingo. "My balls are so far up; I am getting a knot in my throat," Both men laughed and turned to look as Detective Baez stepped from a back door on the blacked-out Bentley.

"Hi. Your Billie, right?" Billie looked at the woman with what he hoped was an unreadable face, then eyed Dingo. What a phony bitch. He fucked her a dozen times. He's the one who introduced her to his dad. All the men knew the details of the Santiago family drama and how much Billie and everyone hated the Baez cunt.

"Thought I should say hello. After all, I am practically your stepmother." Baez patted her baby bump and laughed at her attempt at a joke, but both men met her with stone faces.

"How is your mum doing? Or should I ask, where is she? Word is she left town?" Marita kept a smile. A hateful bitch, she seemed to want a reaction more than a reply. She received neither. "Is she on holiday, or" she hesitated, "has she moved on?"

"Probably should run that by Ramos," said Dingo. Billie turned to go back to his car. Reaching out, Marita put her hand on Billie's muscular arm. "I do hope we can be friends?" Billie shook off her hand and kept walking.

# #

You cannot unbreak an egg. Ten days earlier, Ramos received a letter via his men. He knew it all would be over, but maybe not soon enough to save Alice's trust, if there was any at all left to save.

Ramos,

I found a house on Cape Cod. It's on the beach, about an hour from Danny. I plan to take the girls on an extended holiday. I am not asking you for anything. I have money from my books. I just wanted to let you know.

I am taking Sissy with me. We leave on the 30th.

I will always love you.

Alice

# #

Alice lived in a private and protected world. Her letter made it clear that she did not understand that she was always in danger.

She was badly shaken by seeing her photo in the paper and exposed as the author of her children's book series, but there was no way she could go off on her own.

Billie and Frankie recently escorted Alice and the children to the London Zoo. Someone there recognized her and took photos. The tabloids obtained the images yesterday and placed a picture of Marita Baez alongside them. It looked as if it was a happy day out together.

Baez tried every option to get an actual photo taken with Ramos, but he made certain real photos never happened. He told her to knock it off unless she wanted Alice to end up with half his money. That shut her up for now.

Luna spotted the picture at the breakfast table, "that's Daddy's friend." Luna saw some of the daily images. Alice was horrified. It was relentless, all piling on. Even on paper, she did not want Baez anywhere near the children.

⸻ # # ⸻

Luna patted a pillow as she made a bed for her bear. Stella brushed her doll's long blond hair as they played on the large bed in the master bedroom, with Sunny sleeping nearby.

"Daddy home!" the two little angels shrieked as they stood on the bed to jump in his arms, though he kept his eyes on Alice and did not pick them up.

"Daddy, we have family movie night. Will you watch Frozen *wif* us?"

"No, Stella, Daddy has to work." Luna was passing along her big sister's wisdom.

"Daddy, you can play *wif* Elsa." Stella was trying to up the offer as she held out her doll.

"No, no, Stella, Daddy has to work all the time. Daddy no gets to play *wif* us."

"Thank you, Daddy, for work hard and give us nice things," said Stella as she hugged his leg.

Ramos looked into the innocent faces of his daughters and knew they would grow up to be like their mother; gentle, vulnerable, and too damn sweet. He would do whatever it took to keep the evil far away.

Alice intervened, "Girls, is there something you wanted to ask your dad?" Ramos had not and would not play with his daughters. He didn't know how to play.

"Daddy, can I have chicken?" asked Luna. "*Pleeze?*"

"Me too," said Stella. "I wanna chick."

"Go ask Sissy for something to eat." Ramos finished the family chat. Alice stood at the door of their massive dressing room and walk-in closet.

She softly explained, "They want to get some baby chicks. I told them to ask you." She knew she should give up trying to make him part of their lives; she managed a weak smile.

"Run along, little ones. Billie is downstairs; he has a surprise for you."

The girls grabbed their toys, scooted to the floor, and took off shouting. "Billie, Billie."

#

"How's the baby?" asked Ramos, as he attempted to sound interested without a glance at the sleeping child. He didn't fool Alice; she knew he had not given their youngest daughter a single thought. She was weary of lying to herself about what she or the children meant to him.

"Sunny is doing well. They all are." Exhausted by the fear and humiliation, she did not want to tear up. Today, another flashy, juicy story about the love affair of the *Gangster and Detective* appeared. She knew she shouldn't read it, but like the train wreck that was their life, she could not look away.

"Got your letter." Luggage lay on the bed, and he could see she was packing. Their framed wedding photo was placed on top. "I understand you want to escape, but you need security." Alice made no response as her arms dropped to her sides.

Some nasty villains are aware Ramos is under indictment. He knew many truths he could trade to make deals with the Filth. No one believed Ramos was a snitch, but he would face prison for the rest of his life if convicted. They believed grabbing Alice or one of his children would be sure-fire insurance against opening his mouth.

"I organized a jet, a few men, and a yacht. It will be the best option as many places are still in Covid lockdown, and hotels are closed or restricted. The boat is roomy enough for everyone." Not a man who expected pushback, Ramos gave orders, and others obeyed; not Alice, not this time.

"Thank you, but no." she shook her head without drama, her voice low and lifeless but determined to stay strong.

"You're my family. I will protect you."

"Family? What does that mean? I'm not young and pretty. I can't help you with the case." She paused. "You have three beautiful daughters full of love and joy, but you never look at them." In Ramos's style, he made no reply.

"Thank you for all you do for Danny, but Billie is the only one of us who is part of your life. Because he is like you, his fealty is absolute; not to Carley, not to me, but you. He would do anything you asked. I know he would." She knew Billie would kill for Ramos. Maybe he already had, which filled her with guilt. What had she done to her son?

Alice's voice was barely above a whisper as she licked her dry lips. "You stop by in the middle of the night once a week or less. You have something to eat, and we have sex."

She gave a sorrowful chuckle, "I'm not naive enough to think I am your first of the day." Accurate but incorrect, Ramos did not regard a fuck as an emotional experience, just a body function like eating or taking a shit. It was not going to change. Even after all these years, Alice still struggled with the notion.

"Protecting and providing for you and the children all these years did not make me a good man. The man you want me to be." His steady eyes were focused on his wife. "I'm a bad man, a very bad man. You've always known this." Theirs was not a partnership. Entirely unapologetic, he made the rules.

"Are you trying to convince me you're not loveable? You're not. So, what's wrong with me?" Alice shook her head as if she honestly could not figure it out. "Why do I still love you so much?"

She looked away as if she couldn't face him and snapped back. "I am out of my depth. I'm scared." Her shoulders slumped, and she held her hands palm up in surrender.

"Of what?"

"You. I'm afraid to be without you. You've kept us so protected that I started trusting nothing bad could happen. You warned me a long time ago that I wasn't safe from you, but I never believed you would be the one to hurt us. Never." She shook her head. "Now, I don't know if today, tomorrow, or next week you'll send someone to move us out of your way. I just want to get it over with." Ramos said nothing to comfort her or make her feel secure.

It was unheard of for Alice to argue or challenge his authority. "It's time for us to go." She nodded her head as if she had a good idea. "Maybe she can make you happy?"

"Baez means nothing to me." The same sorry line she heard over and over. He was annoyed to keep having to say it.

"I believe you. That's why it's so awful. You're having a baby with her, and she is nothing to you. Being the mother of your children means nothing." Ramos was unfamiliar with his wife like this: joyless, beaten.

"We're going, and you probably won't notice." Alice pointed toward the zoo, "The men out there are your family." She sniffed softly.

Ramos wasn't sentimental; harm to his family would make him look weak, which would be bad for business. His enemies would try to use this moment in time to take him down, but they would fail.

"You must have protection." Attempting to *play nice,* Ramos did not say, but he would not let them leave Surrey alone, even if it meant forcing her to stay against her will.

"Yes, what a great job you do of keeping us from harm!" Alice threw the sweater in her hand to the floor and charged him with both arms out. She gave him a push that failed to rock the mammoth man. Hitting out at his chest and arms, "How could you allow this horrible mess to happen to our family?"

Anyone touching Ramos would typically receive a painful reply, but she was not hurting him; she was hurting. He waited as she ran out of steam, which wasn't long. He turned her around, taking her in his arms and holding her tightly against him. "No matter how hurt and angry you are, I will not let you put yourself and the children in danger." He knew his wife was terrified and would do as he wanted.

Lying her head on his thick arm, she squeaked her weary consent, "They're hurting our children; I can't make it stop." Holding her close, Ramos nuzzled her head as Luna and Stella stormed the room.

"Billie gave us a toy." Each girl raised their arms to show new soft toys; Luna another for her immense collection of bears, and Stella with a zebra.

Billie smiled when he stepped through the door and saw his parents in an embrace. "Am I interrupting?"

# # #

CHAPTER 46

YACHT

"Hi, Mum, said Billie as he entered his mother's domain. Billie was always hungry and happy in the kitchen, where his mum could often be found. Lately, the relentless Marita Baez story was taking its toll, and she spent more time in her writing room alone.

"What a nice surprise." Billie usually wore his dark hair short, but today, his head was shaved like his dad's. His transformation into his *idol, his hero,* was well underway. "Come hug me. Then you can tell me what you want to eat," They laughed; Billie came out of the womb hungry and seemed not to fill up yet.

Alice rose from the table where she was writing stories for her next children's book series. The real world is pretty ugly these days, and she found her writing and piano a place of escape.

"I saw Julie today at the Tower. She usually seems sad but happy to see me. Guess the ladies can't resist my handsome face and charm?"

"Or your new haircut?" He laughed at his mum. "Julie is happy to see you. Every time we talk, she mentions you. She has gone through so much loss. It's good to know something can still make her smile. I'll call her and have her come for lunch tomorrow. Maybe a picnic?"

Billie cared about Julie, but not in the way she wanted. He made a conscious effort not to hurt her. Hugging his mum, he looked over her shoulder to a vat simmering on the stove. "What smells so good?"

"I take it you are not referring to me." She laughed. 'Your favourite, chicken soup. Sit, and I'll get you a bowl." Ladling a generous portion into a large bowl. She grabbed fresh rolls and sat them in front of him.

"A feast." Said Billie as Alice put a tub of soft butter on the table. Billie grabbed a roll and dragged it through the butter.

"What manners you have," she said as she shook her head. Do you remember Uncle Joe loved this soup?

Billie paused, "I wish we had a chance to say goodbye to him?"

"I figure one of these days I will look up from the stove, and he will be standing here waiting for some soup. He loved you children. I loved him like a brother. He'll be back."

Alice didn't know, and Billie didn't know the details, but he learned on the day he killed Johnnie Kohl that his dad had killed Joe. It was an understatement to say his dad is not an emotional or sentimental man. Billie knew it must have been business.

They both went quiet with the memory. After Billie's second bowl, he pushed back the empty stoneware. "Mum, I want to ask you something?"

"Of course. I hope you are not worried about me. I'm fine. I'm coping." She wished he did not have to deal with the Detective Baez circus, but there was no escaping.

"Mum, no one likes her, and I hate her most. Or maybe Ramos does, but it is all about the case and..."

Alice interrupted, "What do you need to talk with your mum about?"

"I know you are going away, and no one blames you. Dad arranged a jet and a yacht, and he will make sure it is super nice." Alice was not sure why he was *selling*.

"You're probably going to need some help, and I was wondering...."

"Help? I am sure your Dad has a pilot and boat Captain lined up." She tried to lighten whatever was causing him anxiety. "And Sissy is coming along."

"Not that, mum. Carley finished school, Early Childhood Development, and primary teaching. She loves children, and I thought you could hire her to go with you. Be sort of a Governess or something?"

"Is she looking for work?"

"Yes. Her teaching job starts in September, only if schools fully reopen. COVID makes everything uncertain."

"Are you and Carley...?"

"No," his soft reply with a slight head shake.

"Carley is a lovely girl, and I am certain she would be good for your sisters and company for me, but what are you hoping for?"

"Hoping for hope, I guess," he said.

Unsure if Carley was a wise idea, Alice continued. "I know your feelings for Carley are strong, but you have chosen a life that is difficult on families and can be dangerous for them," Her gilded prison was proof of that. "Not all women can accept what it means." She was trying to gently remind her son that Ramos was not exactly a *dream* husband or father.

"Oh, you mean the Baez shit?" he said with disgust.

"No. I mean the day-to-day heartbreaks. Not knowing when you will come or go, missing special occasions like birthdays and Christmas. Little or no time with the children. Knowing you could be hurt or killed or arrested. The tabloid intrusions and well..." she paused, not knowing quite how to say the fact hardmen fucked anyone, any time they wanted, "knowing your husband is always unfaithful."

"Mum, it's just fucking. It doesn't mean anything." Alice was unsurprised but sad that her son had adopted his dad's line.

"It will to her."

Billie dropped his eyes. He fucked whores right alongside his dad on numerous occasions and thought it was cool. He never thought about it as hurting his mum. "I would never hurt Carley."

"Son, you already have." Alice paused. She laid a lot on him for a young man in love. "What it means to work for your dad is business will always come first. Before you open the door to Carley again, ask yourself honestly if she can handle it?" Eyes down, he replied with a nod.

"You don't have to work for your dad?" Alice took her son's hands. "You have a successful business with the garage, and I could help with the money from my books."

"Mum, stop right there." He moved his hands from her grasp. "I love you, but never say that to me again." Billie's face was serious. Alice saw him as a man now, no longer her boy but the man who had fiercely defended his dad at the dinner table. "I made a commitment to Ramos. I will never go back on my word, not for you and not Carley." His loyalty could not be more precise.

Fearing she had pushed him too far, she eased the moment, "Do you want me to call her?"

"Let me check on a few things first, but thanks, Mum, for everything." He knew he shocked her by pushing back. He leaned in to give her a reassuring hug. "I have to get back to the *Zoo*. Tyler, the animal trainer, has called a meet. They will all be jealous when they hear you fed me."

⚡ ⚡

Rory Walsh was the man behind the success of the garage. He was a good businessman who didn't mind getting his hands dirty, and it was no surprise to Billie to find him rolling out from under a classic Jaguar.

He owned the place, but Billie was rarely seen at Ribizzi's garage. He was ashamed of his behaviour toward Carley.

"A word, Mr. Walsh?" respectfully asks Billie. Walsh made no reply but walked toward his small office. Once seated behind his desk, Walsh waited for Billie to speak up; the boy had something on his mind.

Clearing his throat, "With all the stuff going on, my Mum is going to take a long holiday. She is going to need help with my three little sisters."

Walsh remained silent, and Billie continued. "I heard Carley is looking for a job, and I wondered if she might want to work for my mum. Sort of a Governess or something. She would pay her, and ..." he let the sentence drop.

"When?"

"She leaves in three days."

"Where?"

"Somewhere warm. My Dad is making all the arrangements, one of his jets and a big yacht. All private, and safe, no COVID worries or masks. I know it will be super nice."

"You going on this holiday?" The suspicion in his voice was unmistakable.

"No, sir, I have work to do here."

"I can't promise you anything, but leave it with me," said Walsh as he stood. The exact reply Billie used when Rory asked him to find Ian's killer: *Quid pro quo*.

"Here is..." Billie pushed a piece of paper with his mum's phone number across the desk toward Walsh.

"I owe you one." Walsh's face was unreadable, but Billie's wasn't. Walsh knew Billie loved his Carley.

# #

Dinner was simple. Rory Walsh worked hard and dealt with people all day. Usually, he was ready for peace and silence at home. After Mary Ellen said grace and the plates were filled, Rory startled Carley and his wife by opening the conversation. "Girl, you still looking for work?"

"Yeah, Dad, I am trying." Carley was disappointed, but the effects of the Covid lockdowns were working through the country's economy. No one was hiring the young and inexperienced for temporary employment.

"I might have something for you," said Walsh.

"You?" said his wife with shrill skepticism.

"Until you start work at the school in Sept."

"If it reopens with all the Covid Tiers and the virus changing."

"They need sort of a Governess for three young girls. You'll have to travel."

"Wow, Dad, it sounds amazing." Carley's face was happy and hopeful.

"Travel where?" asked his wife.

"Someplace warm," Rory smiled at his daughter.

"Warm, what kind of answer is that? The Sahara Desert or the Caribbean, can you narrow it down a little?"

"Mum, it doesn't matter. I want to go."

"A wealthy family. You'll be on their yacht." Rory Walsh knew the way to win over his wife was to lay out the posh bits.

"A yacht? Am I dreaming?" said Carley.

"I have read about these things. Usually, American celebrities want someone with a British accent to teach their children. Manners and such." Said Mary Ellen, titillated by the proximity to glamour.

"Oh, Dad, I am so excited. How do I get an interview?"

"No interview needed. You leave in three days."

"What's going on? Who are they?" Mary Ellen grew suspicious.

"Alice Santiago."

Slapping her hand on the table, "That trashy bunch! No, I forbid it," said Mary Ellen, who reads every word written on the *Gangster and Detective* saga playing out in the tabloids.

Ignoring her, Walsh decided to sweeten the pot. "You'll be going by private jet." Carley jumped up and hugged her father's neck as his wife's mouth dropped open. He knew he won this one, or did Billie Santiago?

# # #

CHAPTER 47

AWAY WE GO

The arrangements were made: Alice and the children would take a Kohl company jet to Athens and a helicopter to Piraeus to catch the largest of the Kohl yachts. The Lady Ann is a 125-meter, meticulously maintained, stunning masterpiece. Elevators, pool. Spa, gym, ten VIP suites, six additional cabins, gourmet kitchen with chef, and a crew of twenty-three. And all the toys imaginable.

Four days before the departure, Lady Ann was requested for Charter by a Middle East zillionaire at three hundred thousand per week for six weeks. It did not include food, petrol, or gratuities.

The charter changed Alice's arrangements to the Miss Julie, a slightly smaller but equally opulent vessel. Sadly, there is no onboard helicopter.

⌗ ⌗

Alice still hoped Billie would join them, but she knew it was all business when six brutes entered her kitchen. Dex, Rio, Jet, Cody, and two men, Kelly and Ali, whom she had not previously seen. Did Ramos pick the biggest and fiercest of his crew, she wondered? How would they ever fit in?

Ramos, the last to enter, knew the little ones would be bouncing. "Dex! Look Stella, Daddy's friend Dex. He my favourite." She smiled and ran to him, her skinny arms held high for a hug. It was universally agreed that Dex was the least cuddly person on the planet and nobody's favourite, but not to Luna.

Dex had been one of the Baylor in-home security team and a hardened man. He was the oldest of Ramos' men but not to be confused with old or incapable. He swept Luna up in his massive arms. "How ya doing, Cupcake?" The hardmen were having a robust chuckle, as Dex was the scariest man they ever knew, and Luna thought he was a teddy bear.

Days earlier, Alice asked Ramos, "Can Billie come with us?" She hoped that if they needed men to accompany them, Billie could, and they would have a holiday together. Perhaps Danny could join them, as the boys were sure to miss each other.

"Billie has work here," said Ramos. If anyone made a move on Alice or the children, the response would be swift and violent. He would not want Billie's mother or sisters to witness him kill anyone.

⚜ ⚜

"Sissy, take Luna and Stella in one of the other cars," said Alice as the logistics for the holiday were now in action. "Carley, can you hold Sunny while I go back in and make certain we've not left anything or anyone behind," Alice laughed.

Walking in, she looked around and suddenly thought we might never return. Maybe Ramos was using the holiday to move them out of the Surrey house and out of his life? She had no proof; perhaps it was a tiny bit of wishful thinking. She shook her head clear of the thought.

⚜ ⚜

"Away we go," said Alice. The Rolls and eight fully loaded Ranger Rovers pulled out through the electric gates. An ever-present pod of paparazzi snapped away. She hoped they were lazy and not too curious to follow.

The private jet made for an easy ride, though Alice didn't enjoy the proximity to the men who accompanied them. She understood there would only be three, and with no advance notice, additional men she did not know showed up. Ramos made all the arrangements, and she would not argue the point. Getting out of England was all she wanted.

⚜ ⚜

Alice hoped Ramos would come to the airfield to see them off, but he sent word that he was detained. The Ukrainian war had heated the arms business as massive orders for weapons and mercenaries flowed in from every vulnerable hot spot across the globe.

Billie came, and he and Carley exchanged a few polite words, but it was far from relaxed.

"Hi, Carley. You ready to go?" Billie tried to sound casual.

"Yes. It's an exciting opportunity for me. I probably have you to thank. So, thank you." She held her hands at her sides and tried to seem nonchalant.

Looking at her, Billie thought, you are so pretty, and I'm an idiot. "No, my mum needed ..." he let the thought go. Alice stepped in and hugged her son, and Luna and Stella, who adored their big brother, ran for cuddles.

"Bye, everybody," he looked at Carley one last time before driving off.

# #

Reaching the yacht took the whole day, but it was a sight to behold. "That's for us?" asked Carley. "We're like Royalty."

"No, they had to sell their yacht." laughed Alice.

"Thank you for including me. I feel like I'm dreaming." Carley hugged her host.

"Me too," said Alice.

Sissy held a sleeping Stella, Alice, with Sunny asleep on her shoulder, and Carley held Luna's hand, and they boarded the ship. The Chief steward and service crew lined up to greet them while others loaded the luggage and provisions. Luna insisted on bringing a whole army of teddy bears, and Stella brought every animal in her soft toy menagerie.

The crew escorted them to their cabins. Everywhere they looked was luxury and opulence. Alice recalled the first day Ramos took her to Surrey and the wonder of it all. As always, he took very good care of them.

# #

With no set date to return to London, the holiday in the Greek Islands was well underway. The women confined themselves to two or three of the nine levels on the enormous yacht. One of the security men was always close at hand as others patrolled the decks. Alice told Carley to ignore them as she had been doing for years.

The men were also enjoying the cruise. Several of the steward crew were nice-looking bitches who were happy to be well-paid for fucks.

On the tenth day, Alice wandered into the yacht's galley and marvelled at it all. Chef Nico was bored or cranky; she wasn't sure. Too many chicken nuggets and mac and cheese orders seem to be the cause. Alice would allow him to surprise them with a special dinner.

The days drifted by with the sun and the easy pleasure they found in each other's company. The beautiful Mediterranean ports were a bonus.

They stopped on Patmos Island to visit a famous monastery devoted to Saint John the Devine. It is believed that the caves of the nearby hills were where he wrote the Book of Revelations. They lit candles, and Alice lit several as she needed a great deal of help these days.

Indulging herself in the pleasure of writing several hours each day, Alice felt inspiration everywhere she looked: the sea, the islands, the children. Alice thought how right Billie was about bringing Carley along. She was wonderful with the girls.

A special surprise was the beautiful grand piano in the main lounge. Alice treated herself to classical music and the others to fun show tunes and children's songs. She had not been this relaxed since, since when she thought? Since her daily joy dissolved into tears, and her fear level shot off the Richter scale. The day before, Ramos walked into the garden, and her world exploded.

Initially, Alice did not want a yacht but a typical house on an ordinary beach, but it was perfect. She would remember to tell him.

⌗ ⌗

"Lady Julie is named for John Kohl's only daughter. I read it in the booklet of facts I found," said Carley. "They have beautiful monogrammed stationery and postcards of the ship on the writing desk of each cabin. Is it ok if I keep them as a souvenir?"

"Yes, of course. It's quite a boat. Or is it a ship?" laughed Alice. "Julie is a beautiful girl inside and out, but much sadness and tragedy in her short life. People often feel the mega-rich have no sadness or trouble, but it isn't true," said Alice.

"You have given me an idea. I'll contact Julie and ask her to join us. Her daughter is a favourite playmate of Luna and Stella. Hope you don't mind; it will mean more work."

Carley laughed, "I don't call this work."

⌗ ⌗

Good news, while it took persuasion to assure the fragile and frightened girl, Julie agreed she and Annie would join them.

Julie had never been anywhere. Her father had never allowed it. Everyone was excited and on deck waving as the yacht tender brought Julie and her entourage from the Venice Marco Polo private jet terminal.

With Julie's security team and hers, Alice thought they looked like the family of a third-world despot with their army of goons. She kept the thought to herself.

# # #

CHAPTER 48

HIGH SEAS

Cruising the Adriatic with no immediate port in mind was pure bliss. Carley, with her hands full of children, loved every minute. They were having a light breakfast on a deck as the sun danced on the water and the children played tag, "I believe the Chef is fattening you up," said Alice as she looked at Julie.

"He's hard to resist," she replied. Changing the subject, "Carley, you're a natural with children. I wanted to be a paediatrician. So did my mother," said Julie. "But life got in the way."

"That could be true about most of us," said Alice. "I imagined I would be a concert pianist. Oh brother, these days, I would be lucky to get a job in a Pub playing on a Saturday night." All laughed together and abruptly stopped.

Five men with guns were walking toward them and wearing grotesque face masks. "Inside, on the floor bitches!" The women each grabbed for the children. "Now. Do it, or I will shoot these two assholes." He pointed to Rio and Dex, who were battered, bloody, and handcuffed.

Alice felt a wave of guilt. Once, she tried to remove Rio from her protection team, and he looked to have fought hard for them.

Dex lurched at one of the men in a swift head-butt. The spokesman turned and kicked him in the balls, and he went down.

Luna screamed and ran toward Dex. She loved him and was hysterical seeing him hurt. Luna grabbed hold of Dex and petted his face with her tiny hand. "Dex, wake up. I will make you better." It was heart breaking to see her try to help the beast. Right in front of them, two of the intruders jerked Dex up and threw him overboard.

The horrified women screamed as the man who seemed to be the leader raised his gun and fired once. "Shut the fuck up."

Alice held Luna, who was inconsolable. Stella hugged her leg, crying. "What do you want?" asked Alice.

"Shut up bitch."

"You must want something. Tell us so we can get it for you." Considering the circumstances, keeping a cool head was difficult, but their lives might depend on it.

"Shut the fuck up!" The man stepped toward her and grabbed Stella. Alice lunged at him and tried to pry her sobbing daughter away as the other women continued screaming.

Raising his gun, the man fired again, stunning the women into silence, but the children wailed. Still, he held Stella tightly in his arm as she tried to kick and struggle free.

"You," the masked man pointed to Carley. "Get a bottle of whiskey from the bar over there and don't do anything stupid, or I shoot the kid."

"Please, we are going to do whatever you ask. No one needs to get hurt," Alice reasoned, "Is it money?"

"It's always money, you stupid cunt." He jerked the whiskey from Carley's hand and gave her a filthy leer.

"E, K take the one with the ugly puss," he pointed at Sissy, "and all these brats below and lock them in."

"There is a girl who is unwell in cabin four," said Alice. Julie brought Lindsey, who had been seasick for most of the voyage since Venice.

"I'll keep this one to remind big mouth here not to do anything she'll regret." Stella sobbed hysterically, but the man seemed heartless and unconcerned.

"Sit down," he commanded the women. Looking Carley over, "Tasty. Hey R, what do you say we party a bit with this one?"

"Ah... *suckin diesel* now!"

B turned serious. "Maybe after business."

##

Alice was terrified, but her behaviour did not divulge her fear. She walked casually toward the table where the man sat with Stella and poured herself a whiskey. After two deep pulls, she leaned in and gently took her daughter in her arms. Walking toward Carley, she winked. She placed Stella in Julie's arms, returned to the table, and finished her drink. The alcohol hit her quickly, and she thought she might have overdone, but she couldn't undrink it now.

"If you intend to hold us for ransom, you may be on the wrong yacht. If you read the papers, you know I am not exactly priority one to my husband. Probably should have grabbed his girlfriend, Marita Baez."

"Julie Kohl has money," she pointed to Julie, "but she can't get it for you, and pretty Carley has no money."

"Is that right," with sarcasm, the masked man replied.

"Forget the children. Men like my husband, and you, do not value daughters."

"You finally done? No wonder your husband doesn't come home. Try shutting your fecken cakehole." Snickered the man Alice believed to be the leader and seemed to have relaxed his urgency.

⚜ ⚜

The hours ticked by. "Please allow us to use the toilet and check on our children, who will be hungry," Alice again took the lead. "You have guns and…."

"Oh hell, she's starting up again," said the spokesman. "K, J, take um one at a time down to where they put the brats."

"Thank you," said Alice as she stood. Before joining the men and taking Stella below, she gave a reassuring smile to Julie and Carley. Julie was shattered. Carley held her in her arms, and Alice feared for Julie's delicate nature.

They fed and comforted the children for the next hour and learned a bit more. The intruders entered the yacht through large cargo crates marked as food and beverages brought aboard in Bari by the chandlery service.

Ramos' men were poisoned at gunpoint by Chef Nico. One died, and the others were ill with violent gastric outbursts. Others might die if they do not get medical attention soon.

The yacht's crew were tied up, and the boat was at anchor near shore within cell tower range. The Captain waited under armed guard.

Sitting in the expansive lounge, the women were slightly refreshed. Julie was trembling and refused Alice's offer of Brandy.

"It's 2:15 in London. Showtime". B, the spokesman for the thugs, stood from the table where they were playing cards and pulled his phone.

"Since you like to flap your mouth, you can be first." He threw a quick head nod to Alice. "I will be taping you. Don't try to be clever, or I'll hit the little bitch next to you." Julie cowered as Carley held her close.

"What do you want me to say and to whom?" asked Alice, not wanting to give him any reason to hurt anyone.

"So now you can't find anything to talk about? Just talk bitch." He held the phone up and pressed record.

"Ramos," she said, believing this must be about him. "Some horrible men are on board. They sound Irish but wear ugly masks, and it's difficult to tell. They have hurt your team, and the ship's crew are restrained." She looked at the man the others called B for assurance that she was not saying the wrong thing. He nodded.

"The children and Sissy are locked in a room downstairs. They have been fed and are mostly unharmed. Julie, Carley, and I are in the lounge with the men. They have been on board for almost four hours and have not told us why they are here or what they want." Alice looked to B for instruction. He nodded again, and she kept going.

"I love you, Ramos, and I always will." Alice's eyes were teary now. She asked Julie and Carley, "Do you want to say something?"

Julie looked like a beaten animal and surprised Alice by nodding yes. Sniffling, she began, "Ramos, my father trusted you to look out for us. And I do too." Julie turned and wept. "Carley, you are a wonderful girl, and I know why Billie loves you and could never love anyone else." That seemed odd, but they were all under terrible stress. Carley spoke last.

"Please tell my father and mother I love them." She paused. "Please tell Billie I love him very much, and I'm sorry I didn't tell him before we left."

"Ok, all that love shit ought to do it," said B. "Now, I send it to Rich Post." He pushed a few buttons, sat back with a fake sigh of relief, and reached for the whiskey.

# # #

CHAPTER 49

THE CASE

The Crown Prosecution revealed the case they were building: bribery, money laundering, and tax evasion. Rich Post, now acting as Ramos's legal council, told him to be ready for an offer to make a plea deal. Any deal would require Ramos snitching, not just a few tidbits, but to give them something meaty. Big names and empires would have to fall.

Ramos was no rat, but any man facing the rest of their life behind bars would face pressure they had never previously encountered. Many of the top Faces in Europe would be losing sleep with the information Ramos Santiago possessed. None more so than the "king" of Ireland, Declan Gulliver.

The summons by the Crown Prosecution for an under-oath deposition arrived. Post held it out to Ramos, "It's here. 3:00 on Thursday."

Ramos didn't look too bothered. "Oh, hell, looks like I'll have to fuck Marita tonight and see what she knows." Both men laughed. They despised the bitch and the *shit-show* she thrust them into, but she did have information, and even pregnant was without reservation a damn good fuck.

#

Waiting in the prosecution office's outer chamber, Rich got a text ping. He looked at his phone with the intent to turn it off. The number was unknown, but the face was Alice.

Ramos, reading documents, looked up as Post played the video. Five seconds in, he stopped the play and stood. Two armed police officers were standing near the door.

"There's an emergency. We must be shown to a private room now." Neither officer moved. "We walk." Ramos looked at Rich and stood. He did not know what the hell was going on but could see it was important.

Ramos and Post reached the exit as two Crown Prosecution men entered from a far door.

Rich knew the private room was recorded and had two-way glass. He demanded that the cameras be turned off and drew a curtain across a small window.

Rich pulled his phone and played the video for Ramos.

His reaction was cold and calm. "The fucker is dead. Let's get this shit done."

Seated in the Chief of Serious Crimes Prosecutor's office, Post began. "My client has nothing to say and looks forward to his day in court to clear his name of all charges. The case, or rather these charges, are outlandish, unprovable, and at the very least stinks of taint."

Rich and Ramos stood and walked toward the door. Ramos saying nothing barely contained his rage.

"Santiago, this is not going away. Perhaps we can help each other..." said the prosecution team leader, but the door was already shut between them.

The prosecutors looked at each other. "That went pretty well," chuckled one man as they used phony laughter to conceal their concerns about their deteriorating case.

"The fact he showed up is a win."

"Lunch at the Swan? I need a drink."

⚊ ⚊

"Which one of you bitches is the best cook? I am fucking starving."

Alice stood. "What would you like? The kitchen is well stocked."

"Surprise me, but make it fast."

⚊ ⚊

Entering the kitchen, Alice was shocked. Chef Nico seemed unconscious or dead, and the vast galley was in chaos. She asked her escort if she might look in on her husband's men, and he refused.

After cooking endless meals for Ramos' crew, she knew you could never go wrong with a rare steak and potatoes.

She grilled five hefty beef steaks and roasted an enormous pile of chips. She doubted they would miss the veg but stirred up sprouts with bacon, onion, and honey. While cooking, she tried to think of any move which would benefit the situation. Nothing reasonable or doable came to mind.

The food was ready; Alice grabbed a pack of soft rolls, a tub of butter, and a chocolate lava cake the chef had prepared earlier for their dinner. Piling all on an elegant trolly, she rolled it to the lounge.

#

"This is fucking perfect." Said K as he finished his plate and a second piece of cake.

B patted his belly, "must be why Ramos keeps you around even with that motor-mouth you got on you." All the men laughed.

"Ah, here we are, a perfect day on a big yacht. Sun is out, good food, good liquor; the only thing missing is a good fuck." B looked right at Carley. All three women recoiled.

"No," Alice spoke up. "Your boss did not give you permission to rape us." Carley hid her face in her hands.

"So, you know my boss?" B sneered at Alice. "No, you don't. If you did, you might know he fucks anyone anytime he wants, and so do we. Sort of like your husband." He was mocking her and the tabloid drama and hardman rules, gaming her to shut up.

It didn't work. "You have not been too stupid so far. Don't start now. The young woman you keep leering at is the fiancé of Ramos's son." It was quite a stretch, but it made her point. "A rape would not go unanswered no matter what else happens here today."

"Holy fucking hell, you have diarrhea of the fucking mouth." B turned to his men and shook his head.

"The crew all have the squirts," from the poison, "at least hers don't reek," said K as the men laughed.

"We need to use the bathroom again." Ignoring the insults, Alice continued. "Please."

"No, shut the fuck up and get another bottle of whiskey." Alice retrieved a bottle from the extensive bar selection. When she placed it near him, he grabbed her wrist. "Sit down and join me."

Alice wanted to be nowhere near him, but she would do as told if she could keep his attention from Julie and Carley.

B took two dirty glasses from the table. Tossing the remaining contents onto the rugs, he drew heavy whiskey pours into each, sliding one to Alice.

Looking at the glass, she knew she could not drink that much but took a polite sip. Alice abruptly stood, and B jerked to attention.

"I need to clear the table before it starts smelling up the room," said Alice as casually as she could muster.

"No sudden moves bitch. You almost got yourself punched."

"K removed this shit," said B as he settled back in his chair.

"I'm leaving the cake. I want more later," said K.

"Boyo, you fucking pig, look at that gut on you. Gulliver is going to fire your ass if …" B abruptly stopped. He inadvertently revealed the boss's name. All of the men were slightly stunned.

"Please, the bathroom?" Casually asked Alice as if she didn't catch his error.

# # #

## CHAPTER 50

GULLY

A nasty, vicious villain, Declan Gulliver rose to prominence years earlier by walking into a gentleman's club and slitting the throat of the reigning Irish Face. In full view of the dancers and punters, no one dared remember a thing.

After two-plus decades of hard graft and brutality, he climbed over the bloody bodies of anyone who stood in his way. Gilliver resented the Rockstar treatment the late John Kohl received but never moved on Kohl or his nearest rival, which, if the papers were correct, had his hands full of Garda. Gulliver's restraint proved Declan was a covetous bastard but no fool.

Gulliver, or Gully as he was known, heard rumours that Ramos was open to selling the arms division. He didn't want to deal with the shites who wanted guns, but if Ramos wished to downsize, he would be happy to acquire Kohl's vast vice business.

##

A few months earlier:

"That's odd," said Jimmy to Ramos and Rich, "That was Josh Brenner, Gulliver's man. Gulliver wants to meet?"

"Why?" asks Ramos, leaning back in his office chair.

Jimmy shook his head. "Didn't say."

"What do you imagine is on his mind?"

"How to knock you off the top." Rich Post, there learning the ropes, laughed with the other men. Gulliver was to vice and villainy in Ireland as Ramos was to England. Both men with private domains rarely bumped up against each other.

One of Ramos's primary money machines was arms. He didn't like the arms unit or the people he dealt with nearly as much as his predecessors had in their quest for world domination. However, credit due, arms brought in staggering sums of money, as did vice.

Ramos was looking to sell the arms division and had several powerful offers on the table. Some were in cash, and others in Bitcoin, a currency that made Ramos uneasy. Maybe he was just too old to go crypto? A thought he pushed aside.

No way did Gully have the backing for a purchase of that size. "Maybe he's interested in expanding. Smart enough to avoid a war and wants to make me an offer?"

"You could be right. Are you interested in selling? Pros handled the legitimate Kohl business empire in the city. Jimmy never heard Ramos express interest in dropping the vice side, only the arms business.

"Don't know? You want out, Jimmy; maybe you have the right idea?" The men had agreed on two final years for Jimmy, which were up. Ramos paused. "Naw." The men chuckled.

"Set it up. If he has a problem, we don't want to find out about it on the street."

#

The Kohl Empire Hotel, Mayfair.

Security preparations were extensive, even as Ramos knew of no particular curdled blood at the time. When Declan Gulliver, Josh Brenner, and Brody James entered the penthouse, no one was introduced, no pat-downs, and no petty gesture of a handshake.

Jimmy brought Rich Post. He had introduced Post to many aspects of the business and many very bad men preparing him to step into the Consigliere position. Tyler flanked Ramos. After discreet nods, Tyler and Brody stood tall as the other men sat.

"Welcome to London," said Jimmy as a tension breaker. It didn't work.

"Hate fecken London, too many foreigners." It might have been funny if Gully cracked a smile. He was wearing a very British Burberry tie, which seemed out of place with his attitude and scowl.

"What's on your mind, Mr. Gulliver?" asked Jimmy. The meeting was off to a pissy standoff, and Jimmy knew Ramos would not put up with it for long.

"You selling up?"

"You sound informed, you tell me." Ramos dealt with assholes like this for forty years. Full of bullshit and bravado, they never disappointed.

"No interest in arms. I have my fill with the IRA and that bunch of nutters". The way Gully was talking, he didn't think much of the Irish either. "Give me gambling, drugs, loans, and pussy any day." He left the idea hanging. Both men knew the Covid pandemic wreaked havoc on many small businesses, but the real world of vice was big business, big business indeed. And it was unstoppable.

Ramos knew better but asked, "You want to sell?" At this, Gulliver broke into a loud, phlegmy laugh.

"Why Santiago, you not *happy out* with your billions? You want my humble little patch too?" His eyes were hard, as if Ramos was the predator. "No offense, but can you see Ireland run by a nigger?"

Ramos ignored the insult. "I have nothing for sale you can afford," Ramos stood, signalling the meeting was over.

Gully stayed seated. With an exaggerated relaxed posture, he poured another whiskey from a bottle. "So, you know what I can afford? You sound like my wife." Eyes steely, no one thought for a moment he was making a joke.

Ramos would not sit again. It would put Gully in control, which was not going to happen. Rich Post jumped in. "Mr. Gulliver, either say what's on your mind or ...."

"You're a fecken tetchy one." He laughed a deep belly laugh that was entirely phony. "Just having a drink and hoping to lay out a few things of mutual interest. Have a seat, Ramos; join me."

"Join me, huh? In my fucking hotel? You having a laugh?" Hard to believe, but Gully was more of an asshole than Ramos expected, and he headed to the door. Before he made it, Gully spoke.

"Five hundred million, cash." Even between men of means, it was a hell of a number.

#

Over several months, Ramos feigned negotiations with Gulliver, but no sale. Additional bids also came in for the arms division. While it was all hush-hush, the sale to a shady Russian oligarch was already in progress. That is, if his assets were not seized as others were in personal punishments dealt out to friends of Putin by do-gooders such as EU and the bumbling old crook in the White House.

The sale would net more than a billion cash into Ramos's pocket. He was far past pleasing the likes of Declan Gulliver and his nebulous offer.

During all this, Ramos came into possession of a significant amount of inside information on the Irish operations and Declan Gulliver's fiefdom. And why Ramos had pretended to be interested in selling to Gully. It has often been said, "Information is power," and in this case, very much so.

Gully kept trying to impress Ramos and ensure he had sufficient money to complete the *vice* deal. The one thing he failed to do was convince Ramos he wanted to sell.

# #

Gulliver showed impressive stones, making his move on Ramos by way of his family on the yacht. Immediately, Rich contacted Danny's protection team in Boston and Frankie, who was babysitting Billie this month, though Billie was unaware. Neither man reported suspicious activity, but both were put on red alert.

The problem was not simply that Gully found out where Alice was; he knew when and what was happening in Ramos's legal case. To be informed of the exact time of the meeting today? Hell, maybe he was fucking Marita too?

"The expedient way to handle it is to give Declan Gulliver his props. Let him know he was on the mark and that his message was clear. Best case, he pulls his crew from the yacht ASAP?" Jimmy was looking for the go-ahead.

Ramos replayed the video, and his rage grew. "Give him one hour to have the men gone."

"A good first move." Jimmy, as always, the man of reason.

"Once they're safe and in the air, put a five-million-pound bounty on the head of Gully and one million for every member of his family."

"What about that fucker Brody?" Asked Rich. Gulliver's top man had been a total asshole during the attempted possible sale negotiations.

"Tyler will want the kill."

"For that kind of money, the Garda will take them out."

Rich added, "For that kind of money, their mothers will take them out."

# #

B pulled his phone, read a message, and stood. "Ladies, we will leave you now." He took a bow and then headed for the door. B turned to look back. "Damn good meal, but ginger there still owes me a fuck." Laughing, the hijackers departed the salon as quickly as they arrived. Alice followed.

As the men went down the gangway, Alice put her hand on the gun in her pocket. She found the weapon while in the kitchen, looking for steak knives.

The man, B, the talker and the man who shook and squeezed Stella, was last to depart the yacht and first to depart this life. Halfway down the gangway, he turned back and offered a departing sneer. Alice raised the gun and shot him three times before taking her finger off the trigger.

The other men seemed unsure of what to do. They had weapons, but she had a far better angle. They would have to return up the narrow ramp, and she might shoot again. Maybe others with guns as well. The men did not move to escalate but instead grabbed B and dragged his body toward the pier.

# #

The relief of their exit was overshadowed by Alice's shock at what she had done, but it was no time to relax. "We need to help the crew. Let Sissy know everything is ok but to keep the children in the room until we search the ship."

Ramos's men were sick, and two were dead. The women brought water and bread and tried to clean them up. Wading through the vomit and excrement was sickening, but they needed help. It was made slightly more manageable as they were confined to one room.

All of the men, bloody and battered, went down fighting. Dex was dead and thrown overboard, and Ali and one of Julie's men were missing and presumed dead and overboard.

The Captain was released and unharmed. His engineer and co-captain were locked in rooms. The steward staff was locked in the enormous walk-in pantry, well-fed and half-drunk from the provisions at hand.

As *Lady Julie* belonged to the Kohl Corporation and was controlled by Ramos, the Captain did as ordered when he called. He took the ship to nearby Brindisi.

Ramos called on the assistance of a local leader of a major criminal organization in the area, rumoured to be the Sacra Corona Unita. In exchange for a shipment of arms, he secured medical attention for his men, and all were quietly taken to the private terminal at Salento airport.

Four hours later, Ramos' men and family were on a large jet heading to England.

So far, word had not reached the press, but with no guarantee that the silence would last.

⚔ ⚔

When the jet landed in London, relief was heard in sighs and laughter. "Amen," said Alice as the women and children hugged each other.

The men, some of whom were in precarious shape, struggled to stand, and Alice went to help. Ramos's men boarded the plane and told the women to get the children and exit.

Looking out the door, Alice hoped to see Ramos, but he wasn't that man. She had not told the others about shooting someone.

Billie stood waiting, and the moment Carley hit the ground, he swept her up in his arms. She was crying with joy as they kissed.

"Carley loves Billie," teased Luna as Stella and Annie eyed the couple. Yes, she does, thought Julie.

Carley shouted, "Yes, she does!"

⚔ ⚔ ⚔

CHAPTER 51

SAFE HARBOUR

It was agreed that everyone would stay in Surrey, and no one would contact anyone outside with news of their return or what had happened. Ramos explained that it was necessary to keep quiet until the police found the men who did this. He did not want to add to the circus continuing to play out on page one.

Carley wanted to see her parents, but with no one, Julie was grateful to be with Alice and the children. Lindsey was a god-send in her kindness and caring toward Julie and Annie.

⌗ ⌗

Surprisingly to Alice, their lives were returning to normal. She used her time writing while the young women were outside in the sun, taking the children to a playground Alice had designed, and Ramos had built. It seemed anything she wanted on the property, no matter how expensive or unusual, Ramos was willing to provide.

"Good morning, ladies," said Rio, nicely recovered from his beating on the yacht. The girls smiled as they walked through the loggia near the Zoo. The men were sitting in the sun at a table on the terrace.

"Tomorrow is World Naked Gardening Day; if you need help in your *patch,* let us know?" said Dingo. The girls shook their heads and kept walking. The men would have kept their mouths shut if Alice had been along.

It was typical for young single girls to chat about men; these women now saw the brutish men differently. They fought hard on the yacht and took punishing beatings on their behalf. Pushing the little ones on the swings, Lindsey asked, "Do you think Dingo is nice?"

"He's good-looking but has a scary vibe," Carley replied.

"Oh, it's because he is big. But I like big men. It feels like they could protect you, and anyway, I like his Ozzie accent."

"Have you seen Frankie? He looks goofy, like he is always smiling. I like that. And his Irish accent, too." Said Carley.

Not always smiling, thought Lindsey as she recalled the night he and Billie drove her to The Chambers to pay off Hirsh.

"Tyler is the most handsome," said Sissy, his simple sister, in a rare attempt to join the conversation."

"Tyler is handsome, but he looks serious. Like he is doing something important and doesn't want to be disturbed." Lindsey said while not saying he was too scary for her taste.

"The serious one is Ramos." Carley shivered. "He walks into a room, and everyone shuts up."

"Not everyone. Those *monkeys* never quit giggling," said Julie, pointing to the children and gently trying to change the subject.

"Ramos has been good to me," said Lindsey. She did not share with the others how she came to work for Julie. Ramos told her never to speak of it or her relationship with Nathan. She was enormously grateful to him for making her part of his world and saving her from Hirsch's world.

"Rio is sort of hunky but so intense. I don't like him at all. He sneers and seems angry," said Carley.

"You only have eyes for Billie; your opinion doesn't count," laughed Lindsey as Carley blushed.

"Julie, I have seen pictures of your brother Johnnie," said Lindsey. "He was dreamy handsome."

"Yes. So was my father, but they were bad men." The others were only having a laugh, but Julie seemed so sad that they went quiet. "I have known men like these my whole life. I say stay away." The woman did not challenge her take because Julie was fragile. Lindsey was unconvinced and flirting with the idea of Dingo as *boyfriend* material.

Julie was right; these were bad men, and the lovely young women would be horrified to know who, in truth, they were. They would also be shocked at the reality of Billie and Ramos Santiago.

# #

Nine days after their return, Alice awoke in the dark of Ramos's office and knew he was home. She often slept on the sofa, where she felt close to him.

Ramos promised to protect her. At times, in their dangerous world, he had not. Years ago, in Baylor, when thugs, for a fee from a rival, abused her and Luna. And now the raid on the yacht.

Most in the Gulliver family and chain of command were dead. Gully was still alive, but he wouldn't last much longer. Ramos intended his *scorched-earth* approach to send a message to others who might imagine the case weakened him and perhaps heading to prison.

Alice sat up, and Ramos moved nearby. Snuggling closer, she buried her head in his chest. With his heavy arm around her, he knew he failed her and the others, a rare feeling he resented. Neither seemed to want to be the first to speak. Finally, Ramos asked, "You, okay?"

"I thought we were all going to die. I had the ugliest thoughts." Her voice was shaky, "one man was hurting Stella." Alice sniffed, "Please, make Billie redundant. Or whatever you call it." Alice sounded urgent. "I don't want him to be one of the men who follows orders and does awful things." Ramos did not reply. A man, not his mother, decides his future.

"They killed Dex. Luna loved him and tried to save him. She patted his face and told him she would make him better." Tears rolled down her cheeks. "It was heart breaking." Ramos was certain Luna was the only one in Dex's long, hard life who ever loved him. He was unsurprised Dex died trying to protect them. "They threw him overboard right in front of us."

"I'm sorry about the mean things I said about Rio. He was so brave. They all were." Shaking her head, she said, "You were right about us needing protection. I didn't understand what was happening." In his usual manner, Ramos gave her nothing back.

"I was an idiot wasting my time worrying about your dick when you were worrying about us. I wanted you to quit saying she means nothing to you and tell me I mean something."

"I'm not proud of myself. After all that you do for us, I was petty and jealous. Baez is young and pretty and having your baby. I can't help you with the case, but she can. It made me feel useless to you and scared."

"You are the man I want you to be. You're the only man I will ever love. Thank you for not throwing us to the wolves." Ramos knew his wife was terrified by the reality of his violent world.

Alice looked into her husband's eyes. "I'm not ok. I did something horrible." Ramos knew Alice killed Brody Gulliver or B as he was addressed on the yacht. "I wanted to kill them all," she confessed. "I have never felt like that before." She was trying to convince him of something he knew well.

"Fear will do that," said Ramos.

"I shot one of the men and don't feel anything. What's wrong with me?" She paused, "are you shocked?"

"You protected your family," he said.

"No, they were leaving, but I shot him anyway. The others didn't see me. Oh, Ramos, he might be dead." Ramos knew he was but didn't say.

"He won't hurt anyone else." Ramos tried to help her accept what she had done, but he could see his wife was in shock.

"I don't want to be the kind of person who could kill someone. It's too scary." Her voice was catching. "I don't want to be you."

A direct statement: Ramos understood where it was coming from. Showing unusual tenderness, he cupped her face in his big hands, "You could never be me." He kissed her forehead.

Alice put on a brave face for Julie and the others, but it was a façade. She was severely shaken seeing her children in danger and killing a man.

"You got everyone home safely. You were brave and strong. It's what you told me you wanted to be." He was not a talker, but Ramos attempted some flimsy assurance.

All of Ramos's crew thought Alice was a *badass momma bear.* They knew what she had done because Gully called during their flight back from Italy.

Ramos, Jimmy, Rich, and Tyler were in the Tower office when the call came in. The assault on the yacht was not simply business; Sissy was Tyler's sister. Julie was Jimmy's daughter-in-law, and Annie was his grandchild. Alice and the other girls were Ramos's family. Gully's move on the yacht was an outrageous over-step and very personal.

"Santiago, your fecken wife shot my nephew. Brody was a son to me, my brother's only boy. My top man is dead. Do you think I am going to let this go? Think the fuck again!"

"Bring it, you bastard." Ramos hung up. He knew it must have cost Alice a great deal to take such an action. He ordered that no one, including Billie, ever mention it to her.

Alice took a breath and relaxed a bit. "What about you? How is the case going?" Without mentioning the beautiful detective.

"Making progress…" he stopped. He believed if he told his wife, *it would take time*, or it would *be okay* one more time; she would probably shoot him too.

"Was what happened on the yacht about the case?"

"More or less." He did not elaborate and could make no promises until Gulliver was dead. Gully was unlikely to be the last to come after him. The sharks were circling and hoping for his demise.

Ramos and Alice's eyes were drawn to the doorway of the dimly lit office. Stella walked toward them in her soft kitty-cat pyjamas, a small crumpled blanket in her hands and weeping softly.

"Come here, little one. What's the matter?" Ramos held out his arm, and Stella crawled up in his lap. It was a special moment, a first, nothing like it had ever happened.

"I can't find my *scary tiger*. The bad man gonna get me." Sniffing as she dragged the crumpled blanket across the tears on her precious face. "He gonna get me."

Ramos looked at Alice as he softly patted Stella's delicate back. "Badman?"

"She's been having nightmares since the man on the boat grabbed her. The one I, you know? It was horrible. He shook her and yelled in her face. He squeezed her till she threw up." Alice let out a sob.

Anger instantly burned in Ramos, but he remained composed. Those fuckers touched his wife and daughters. They believed he was weak and had made their move.

"Daddy won't let anyone hurt you." This, too, was a first; Ramos referred to himself as Daddy.

Resting her head on his shoulder, she snuggled into his neck and sniffed. "Daddy, you be my scary tiger?"

"Daddy's your tiger. Don't be afraid." He kissed her warm, sweet head. Stella soon drifted off to sleep in his arms. Ramos could genuinely feel what was at risk.

"The sun is about to come up," said Alice as the rays began slashing through a gap in the heavy drapery. "Let's go to bed."

※ ※

Ramos carried Stella upstairs and gently placed her in the king-sized bed with her sister and Annie. Looking at them holding each other's hands, he felt the weight of their innocence and vulnerability. And his fury at the breech in their protection.

Alice put out the *Do Not Disturb* sign, and they slept many heavenly hours.

Lying in bed and snuggling into her husband after a fuck was something Alice feared might not happen again. Moved by his gentleness with their daughter, Alice's shaky resolve to leave vanished. "I said I didn't want to be me, but it's not true. I was afraid you didn't want us anymore. I never want to leave you or leave here. Can we stay with the *scary tiger*?"

"You're pretty scary yourself." Alice killed a man who threatened and harmed her children. "I bought this place for you to be safe and have nice things." Alice knew it was as much an answer as she would get and sighed with relief.

"Julie is so fragile. I don't know if she can take much more. I honestly don't know if she can ever be alone again. She needs to stay here. Nine of us females all depend on you. We must be costing you a fortune. Please know we're grateful."

Ramos was old school and knew the blackness in the hearts of men. Women were their prey. He believed women needed a man to safeguard and care for them. He saw the devastation and damage done to women without a protector. In his view of the world, none of the five women and four little girls would ever be safe on their own.

He understood why his late boss, Sir John Kohl, isolated his wife and daughter. One might even describe it as *solitary confinement*. It was the only absolute way to protect them. The toll on their mental health was not his concern. He left that to the women to sort.

"Whatever is best." Technically, as head of John Kohl Enterprises, both legal and illegal, Ramos Santiago's first job was protecting the last surviving Kohls. Leaving Julie and Annie in Alice's caring hands was the best he could do for them, no matter the cost.

Luckily, the secured Surrey Estate had nine bedrooms with staff quarters, outbuildings, the Zoo, pool, gym, ballet studio, tennis, two guest bungalows, playground, beautiful gardens, and a chapel; everything to fill a family's life with security and happiness. If needed, he could expand the compound. Julie could stay as long as she wanted, which looked like it might be forever.

Ramos waited with another gut punch for Julie Kohl, "Renee died yesterday."

Jimmy Redmond's wife of almost forty years, Renee, became close to Julie when she married her youngest son Ross. Renee died of kidney failure due to a severe beating years earlier at the behest of her husband's employer, John Kohl.

Very few knew, but Renee was the one to put the infamous misogynist in his grave. He never saw the shot coming because, to John Kohl, women were only to be fucked, not feared.

"Oh no. I thought the transplant was…?" Ramos shook his head. Jimmy told him Renee gave up the fight when their son Ross died. "Please don't tell Julie, not yet. We have intentionally not brought in papers. Tell everyone not to mention it." Alice felt motherly and protective toward the broken young woman. Alice had her own secrets now.

Ramos knew Alice would do what was right for Julie. "Any chance of breakfast?" He looked at his watch. "Or lunch or whatever damn time it is?"

Alice didn't want to allow Marita Baez into their cosy moment but felt grateful to Ramos and wanted to do her part. "Is there any way I can help? With the case, or her?"

"Care for Julie and some breakfast. I am running on empty." Ramos, with business waiting, was at the end of his quotidian of intimacy.

# # #

CHAPTER 52

BIG C

Ramos and his men live in a violent world and often die violent deaths. It was easy to forget that people died for all kinds of non-violent reasons.

"Boss," said Jax as he entered Ramos Surrey's office. It was rare for Ramos to do business there, but news just arrived that Gully, the filthy cockroach, had been exterminated.

Ajax asked to see him, and it sounded important. "Have a seat. Whiskey?" said Ramos, pointing to the decanter and glasses on his desk. "I told Alice you were stopping by; she insists you stay for dinner."

"Tell her thanks, but I...." It was a bright sunny day, but Ajax looked pained as he ran his hand over his shaved head.

Usually, the men were hard to read, but it was clear to Ramos that something was seriously wrong. "What's up?"

"My Sheera. She has cancer."

"How can I help? Your boys?"

"No, my grandmother has come from Cameroon to care for them. She's old, and I don't know how long she will be able, but for now, she is here."

"If you run into problems, let me know. Alice loves children, and we have plenty of bedrooms." This gave Ajax a weak smile.

"Sheera doesn't have much time left, and there is not a fucking thing I can do about it." Jax's head hung in the shame of his weakness, his inability to help his wife.

Ramos saw John Kohl lose his young wife Annie to a brain aneurysm and understood the powerlessness Ajax felt.

"When I committed to you, I agreed business would always come first. I'm sorry to ask, but...."

"Take some time off. Be with your family. Do you know who you want to put in charge?" Ramos thought he knew but gave Ajax the respect of his opinion.

"Frankie. He knows the territory, drops, distros, and connects. He's the happiest-looking badass I ever met." Both men chuckled. Frankie was known for his goofy grin and his huge fucking balls. Ramos fully agreed with the choice.

"You'll let him know?" Both men stood, and Ramos came out from behind his desk and extended his hand. "Take care, brother."

※ ※

The funeral was nine days later. Ramos and Alice, in a rare public appearance, attended together. Alice wept at the sight of the three now motherless young boys. With Ajax for a father, she feared, as with Billie, they would go into the family business.

The elite crew was all present and respectful. It was a minor miracle on a sad day; the press did not manage to learn of it and were nowhere to be seen.

※ ※

After the funeral service, Ramos directed Billie to take his mum home. It was time to see Marita. Driving to Baylor, he thought of life's layers. He was not much for introspection, but funerals can do that to a man. Few of his men enjoyed what you called traditional marriages as Ajax had. Solid but low-key, and today, he buried her.

Jax had not been able to save his wife, and Ramos had not protected Alice and his daughters from fucking Irish pirates. Very little made *big-dick* men feel impotent, but today, failures weighed heavy.

The Baez bullshit complicated things further. It would all be over, is what he kept telling his wife. He was as sick of hearing it as Alice must be.

※ ※

Ramos and Marita lay on the bed after a fuck, "I want to use the decorators at Harrods. They are the best, and you can afford it." Marita felt confident in dethroning Alice. After all, her Instagram followers told her so.

"Whomever you want," said an unenthusiastic Ramos. He hated the bitch; but an excellent fuck, and he was stuck with her until the case officially closed. He hoped to hell it was soon.

"Where are we going to live? I don't fit in at Baylor. It's boring. We should have a city home. I want to live in Mayfair or Chelsea, with designer shops and top clubs. What about the Tower?"

Ramos used the Covid lockdowns to spend as little time as possible with Marita. She wanted to go to his clubs and play the reigning princess. Ramos kept reminding her that many were closed, but COVID was done, and that excuse had pretty much played out.

"We must move slowly until the case is…," said Ramos.

"What case? It's practically in shreds. You seem to care more for the case than your baby son or me." She was pouting. It took great restraint for Ramos not to belt her.

"Shreds?" asked Ramos.

The OC (organized crime) chief opened a case against Angus Farland. Can you believe it? He thinks he might have been wrong about you. The Solicitor General denied any more wiretaps or surveillance."

"Sounds like good news," said Ramos. The bribes and extortion seemed to be paying off, and at least she shut up about getting him to divorce Alice, one of the cunt's favourite topics.

"Worse than that, some moron lost nine boxes of case files from the evidence room. If the Chief finds out who, they can kiss their pensions goodbye."

Ramos paid fifty thousand for the boxes to vanish, and it was his first confirmation of a result. Marita was useful. The good news made him ready for another fuck. "Turn over."

# # #

CHAPTER 53

WILL

Julie seemed to be doing better. The events on the yacht took their toll, but she grew even closer to Alice. Annie spent long periods in Surrey in a happy, upbeat environment.

Since her brother's death, Julie was occasionally seen smiling and out shopping or walking in the parks. She moved easily and often between the Tower and Surrey. She happily put on some much-needed weight.

#

Waking suddenly with sharp pains in her lower abdomen, Julie instantly knew what was happening. She lost her second child shortly after her husband Ross's death and knew it was happening again.

She was filled with joy when she learned she was pregnant with Billie's baby. She planned to tell no one until the last minute because she did not want Alice to make him marry her.

No one would or should ever marry her. They would become part of the *Kohl-curse*. She just wanted another child to love so Annie would not be as lonely as she was as a girl. Even with three brothers, after her mother's death, she lived alone in the massive house with only a few servants. It was horribly lonely, and she feared her precious angel Annie would feel the same way.

She struggled from her soiled bed and retrieved a letter she had prepared. Previously, she wrote a meticulously researched holographic will to deal with her astonishing fortune.

The hundred million Pounds of cash from each of her twin brother's estates came to her at their deaths. With her own hundred million and eighty-plus million more inherited from her husband Ross, plus interest, Annie's fortune had grown to almost half a billion Pounds. The numbers were so large they had no real meaning to her, but she knew they would to others.

Feeling weak and faint, she took a few small sips of water, went to the roof terrace, and pulled herself onto the block and glass fence. The motion detectors in the War Room turned the monitors on. Jet and Billie were astonished by what was happening. They ran to the lift and headed to the roof but were too late.

# #

Dear Alice,

Please take my precious Annie. She will inherit the entire Kohl fortune, recently valued at about sixteen billion, but I want her to have what money can't buy. She deserves the love and family I know you will give her. You shall have full access to any of the capital.

To Annie: My beautiful girl, you deserve a long, happy life and a loving family. Your father, Ross, was a fine man, loving and kind. We were so in love, and you were our cherished child. I wish you had known your grandmother, Annie, for whom you were named. She was full of love and grace, and so are you. Renee was your other grandmother and a beautiful soul. She loved you very much.

Julie intentionally did not mention her father, brothers, Jimmy Redmond, or Ramos.

Alice will be your new mother and is the most loving person I know. I always wanted a sister, and lucky you will have three. Stella, Luna, and Sunny will be your sisters. Billie and Danny are your new brothers.

I bequeath from my fortune:

Fifty million each to Alice, Luna, Stella, Sunny, and Danny Santiago.

I give one million pounds each to Ramos' top twenty men in hopes they will be able to spend more time with their families.

Thanks for all the years of trying to keep me safe from the outside when what was inside the Kohl family was most corrupt and dangerous.

I want to give Lindsey, who has been so helpful to me, two million pounds.

To Ramos: Please continue as head of the Kohl Empire as long as you wish to serve. I am sure there is money I don't know about, and it is all yours. There is plenty to go around.

To Billie: Thank you for making me feel alive again and giving me a reason to live and laugh for a while. I leave the balance of my fortune, one hundred million or more, to buy your island. I hope you and Carley will be forever happy. She is wonderful. I understand why you love her and why she loves you because I love you too.

I look forward to being with my mother again. I have missed her so.

Julie Kohl Redmond

⚔ ⚔

As he stood at the bloody mess on the pavement in front of the Tower, which was once the sweet Julie Kohl, Billie's eyes were teary, and he felt sick. His head pounded as he waited for Ramos and the police and shouted angrily for the people to stay back.

When it was all over, he slowly followed Ramos into the Tower. He wanted to cry like a baby but knew he could not. Not in front of Ramos or the men who rarely showed any humanity.

"What now, Dad?"

"Head to Surrey. It will be big news quickly, and your mum will need you. Go on." Ramos knew Billie and Julie had become close, and this tragedy hit him hard. Getting used to violent death was part of being a hardman at this level, but this death was very personal.

⚔ ⚔

Ramos went to the fifth floor to Julie's magnificent home. He looked in on the staff. The three women were in front of the telly watching Coronation Street, with no idea of what had just happened.

He walked to Julie's bedroom. Her death was no accident and not spur of the moment. Ramos was confident there would be a letter. He stopped abruptly at the bed linen, bloody with clots and an unmistakable mass about four inches long, and he immediately knew what had happened. She miscarried Billie's baby.

Shaking a case from the pillow, Ramos wiped the blood and tissue into it and threw it in a bin in the bathroom. Placed on her pillow was the letter. Hearing voices, he quickly tucked it in his pocket and tossed the duvet over the fouled sheets.

"Find anything?" asked Jimmy, whom Tyler had called. Retired now, he was not simply the family legal expert emeritus, but Julie's father-in-law. He knew suicides often leave notes.

"No," said Ramos. "You see the film?" He attempted to change the subject.

"She took more than most of us could ever handle. It is no surprise, but it is so damn sad. I am glad my Renee is not going to have to know."

Ramos walked by him, "I need to get to Surrey. It will hit Alice hard. Annie is already there."

#

Alice became hysterical when Billie told her. By the time Ramos arrived, she was no longer screaming in anguish and mellowed to stunned disbelief. When Ramos walked in, she began sobbing again as he held her in his massive arms.

"Why? Why did she do it? She was doing so well. They are all gone. All the Kohls are gone. All but precious Annie. She is ours now to love and …."

"And protect," added Ramos. "Lay down and rest while the little ones sleep."

"I want to close my eyes, sleep, and wake up, and it's all a bad dream. Why, why did she do it?"

"Come on, let's get you to bed." Ramos guided her up the stairs. He noticed the light under Billie's bedroom door.

Billie did not want to go to the Zoo tonight and be a tough guy and hear hateful shit from the animals. He wanted to put his head on his pillow and cry. But he felt he had to be strong for Carley, whom he held in his arms.

After settling Alice, Ramos told Sissy and Lindsey, who were severely shaken, to deal with the girls, then retreated to his office.

# #

Sitting in his chair, he sighed deeply. They were all gone. He lived with the Kohls in their lives day after day for years. In a way, Alice was right. The Kohls and his men were his family, his world.

Ramos respected and admired John Kohl and learned a great deal from him. John Kohl gave him purpose, self-respect, and, ultimately, the keys to the castle.

He mentored Johnnie through the years and thought a lot of Kohl's son until after his father's death when he disintegrated into a piece of shit that everyone was happily rid.

Ramos chuckled at the memory of Billie blowing the fucker away. A huge fucking surprise, maybe the biggest ever, and the outcome placed the entire Kohl fortune in his hands. Well done, Billie. He took another long drink of whiskey and eyed the day's newspapers.

Liz Truss and Boris Johnson had gone to Balmoral to see the Queen and deal with the change of Prime Ministers. The changes also meant another queue of politicians with their hands out. He hated these leeches. He tossed the papers aside and reached inside his jacket pocket for the envelope he had found in Julie's bedroom.

Julie's first wish was for Alice to take Annie; no question, it would be seamless. Jimmy would make arrangements for Ramos and Alice to formally adopt her.

The bequests of fifty million for his wife and each of his children were not going to happen, and neither were his top twenty animals going to *win the lottery* for a million each. Julie had no idea; the men would do nothing positive with the money, and it was unlikely that those with families would have loved ones who benefited.

The two million for Lindsey would not happen, but he would give her a pay raise and cancel her debt, which she had no chance of repaying. He would throw in enough to get her Dental Hygienist certification at a later time. He wanted her to stay in Surrey and help with his children.

Then there was Billie. Julie was in love with Billie and knew she would never take Carley's place. She kept it secret that she was expecting his baby.

What was this about an island? No, Billie would not know of his one hundred-plus million.

Ramos demanded control and obedience, and the bequests would explode it all to hell. He lit a match and burned the letters in his fireplace; one more secret in a life full of secrets.

⌗ ⌗

Queen Elizabeth II died a day later. It was a lucky break for Ramos as Julie's passing was quickly old news and replaced with the ten days of mourning, remembrance, and magnificent pageantry of the Queen's state funeral.

⌗ ⌗ ⌗

CHAPTER 54

A RESULT

Adjusting a soft pink blanket, Alice leaned in to kiss the warm, downy head of her baby girl, Sunny. Looking up, she saw her husband silently resting against the door frame. It had been a while. It had been a hellish and exhausting year for both.

It was almost four AM, but as the years passed, there were unpredictable hours and random days. It was a challenging year, especially the months since Ramos came home one day and blew up their life in one brief conversation.

"She keeping you up?"

"No, she's a good baby, just hungry." Alice leaned into her husband as he circled a muscular arm around her shoulder. It felt like they had been through a war together, and she finally felt safe again.

After the hijacking of the yacht and Julie's suicide, Alice put aside her hurt and anger about Marita Baez. She made the decision to get on with it. She loved her children, home, and husband and accepted everything it meant.

Not a romantic man, Ramos was a villain. She didn't stop wanting him to be a better husband; she finally quit expecting him ever to be, which gave her peace.

Alice was no longer the hopeful young woman who thought of Ramos as her *Knight in Shining Armour*. Though he had swept in and changed their lives for the better. She averted her eyes and mind from the reality of theft, drugs, brutality, and treachery until she, too, changed over the years as a gangster's woman, though she hadn't seen it happening.

If Alice was aware of her gentle slide in his direction of criminal behaviour and thinking, she didn't acknowledge it. Yet years earlier, she had successfully alibied him for four grisly multiple murders by beheading, for which she knew he was guilty. Having shot a man retreating from the yacht hijacking, she too had blood on her hands and could kill without regret.

As for the money laundering and bribery cases, considering his actual sins, those were tame charges. The penalty, if convicted, would be a monster lump in one of His Majesty's resorts. And confiscation of much of the visible wealth.

In an astonishing show of trust, Ramos gave Alice the details for accessing the millions in cash hidden on the property and hundreds of millions in offshore accounts. She was surprised to learn of the vaults below the Chapel. Laughing, she thought how through the centuries, across the world, the church used its hidden vaults to conceal wealth and sinister deeds.

Was it possible her husband was going to prison? A villain for forty years, his family would be hit hard. Ramos's children, including Annie, would not know him. In his sixties, he would possibly die in prison.

"Join me," he said. "Champagne?" She smiled. He must have good news, which would be most welcome.

"I'm not supposed to when I am nursing, but yes, please." Ramos followed her into their massive kitchen. Renowned for her cooking, it was her domain. Previously, she prepared sumptuous Sunday lunches for the family and crew but stopped when Baez came into the picture. Maybe they would resume after tonight?

Couples who have been together for years move about in harmony. Ramos reached in the wine refrigerator for an expensive bottle and opened it while Alice poured him a whiskey.

"Why are we celebrating? Another new Prime Minister?" She laughed as she joked and tipped her glass.

"The charges were dismissed in their entirety. It will be announced tomorrow morning. There were many errors and problems with the cases. The Judge warned them to be cautious about doing anything like it again."

Rich Post had proved himself useful through his contacts and was able to get this information in advance.

Alice threw her arms around him. "I was so worried we would lose you." Ramos would never have gone to prison. He would have vanished before any trial. Early on, Alice offered the family's option to run.

"It was damned expensive and risky, and finally, it all paid off." Alice did not mention the *elephant-Marita in the room.*

"You did what you had to do for your family." Ramos did what he had to do to stay out of jail, but she gave his concern for family credit. "What is the look on your face? I can't quite make it out?"

What she said to him was amusing, as his face and demeanour were almost unreadable. It was essential in the villain's life, and he was at the top of a very big pile of evil. "My face?" he laughed. "Remind me not to play poker with you."

"Marita's dead. She had a seizure; she stroked out and died when she got to the hospital. It's called eclampsia or something. The baby is fine."

Alice met his eyes and did not look away. Ramos wondered if Alice suspected a doctor on his payroll supplied the seizure. "All those months with that horrible woman was quite a sacrifice. I'm not happy she died, but I won't pretend to be sorry." Her gaze at him was unemotional.

Men and women must answer for their sins. She understood her husband, his life, and the life she ultimately chose. It was all about risk and reward and not about good and evil. The evil was a given.

"No one will be sorry she's gone, except perhaps the tabloids." Said Ramos as he drained his whiskey, reached for the bottle, poured another, and then returned his eyes to Alice. "You didn't believe I would let anyone destroy our family, did you?"

"No. I never did. Though you were right, I did get my feelings hurt." They were both firmly on the same page. Maybe more than ever before.

Alice lightened up and shook her head. "The things we do for family. I was horrified at The Rod and about as qualified and comfortable as you were when picking out wallpaper at Harrods?" Laughing out loud together felt good after the strain of these months.

"In my defence, I only paid for the damn stuff." The tabloids went into elaborate detail about Marita's trip to Harrods and the outrageous expense of the paper she chose.

Alice took a drink of bubbly. "Does she have a family?" The conversation turned serious.

Ramos shook his head. "None here."

Alice could allow herself to feel nothing for Marita, but now with a baby to consider. "Years ago, you welcomed my sons into your life, and I welcome your son to ours."

"He's not mine. The DNA test said no." He insisted on a DNA test before Mirita put his name on any birth records. She balked, but Ramos was adamant. His face turned serious, not as happy as the news he gave her would imply. "He's Billie's."

"Oh no, he hates her. He's too young. He loves Carley." This was horrible news. "Does he know?" Ramos knew she would not question if what he said was true.

"No. No one knows." Both Alice and Ramos fell silent.

"What's his name?" she asked.

"Doesn't have one yet."

"The baby is blood," she took a deep breath and spoke up. "He's family. He should be here with us."

"As Billie's son? Or mine?"

"Ours. It's what we do for family."

You are a hell of a woman, thought Ramos. To open your heart and home to the child of a woman who put you through hell. "Our three girls, Annie, and another baby would be five under the age of seven." and a massive house. "You have enough help?" She looked at him with surprise. At no time before had he concerned himself with such issues.

"Sissy and Lindsey are terrific with the children, and I hope Carley will accept my offer of full-time employment." Alice had decided that schooling the children at home would be best for a few years. Alice reached for the whiskey bottle and poured him another one.

"She would probably work for nothing just to be near Billie." Alice hoped Ramos would relent and let them marry, but she would not intrude on what he believed to be a business matter.

Ramos smiled, "You warned me. Remember?" He took a pull of his drink. "Years ago, you said I would wake up someday and the house would be overrun with children."

"That's not the worst of it. You know it means we're grandparents?" chuckled Alice.

I value this woman, thought Ramos. Her loyalty to our family and me is stellar. He was pleased he married her. "We can keep that to ourselves."

"We'll go to her funeral together and then out for a fancy lunch." Never once in all the years had they gone out for a meal. "It will give the papers a real story to write. Oh, and I want a new dress."

Ramos laughed as she had never asked him for anything. Maybe it was her price for the hurt feelings? He did not remember seeing his wife this upbeat in a very long time.

Alice's face lit up. "Let's call him Joe."

Joe had been Ramos's top man for years, and she and the children adored him. But the life of a villain is no fairy tale, and Joe was a murderous criminal. On the day he married Alice, Ramos killed Joe for violating his rules. In the world of bad men, you are unforgiven.

Retreating to his world of secrets, Ramos raised his glass in salute, "Joe, it is."

# # #

CHAPTER 55

MINDY

Business and not grannies in care homes was the victim of Covid, the fucking China virus. Keeping the Clubs, bars, and fuck-pads closed, or the appearance of being closed, had cost a fortune. Ramos was fed up. Downing Street spent two years talking about "Freedom Day," but none of the promises had been soon enough. Schools had reopened, and confusing and conflicting efforts were made to save the tourist and hospitality industry; bans were lifted, and businesses reopened, at least those that didn't shut their doors forever.

Marie Antoinette was right. Soothe the masses with *"Bread and Circuses."* The Queen's Jubilee was a much-needed distraction from rising inflation and street crime, but that good feeling was long over now with the death of the Queen.

Ramos paid large sums to politicians who made these decisions and the Filth who enforced the policy. Inflation and the eyes of the world were making it a challenging and costly period.

Britain seemed to be going through Prime Ministers at a rate that would make the Italians blush, and it did not help that the leadership of America was currently in the hands of the woke and senile.

Bitcoin, a currency Ramos was reluctant to use, was now dropping faster than the ass of an aging ho. Due to the downturn, one of his most promising buyers for the arms division had now rescinded the offer.

Ramos pushed his chair back, stretching his long frame. He was feeling fatherly. Not about Surrey, but he had given four elite crew permission to go to the World Cup in Qatar. Providing a jet, accommodations, and VIP tickets. His men worked hard and had little time off. Billie would have loved to go; he had played the game for years but had not earned his place on the jet. Ramos never let his son skip the queue.

The four were chosen based on their time in service, excluding Tyler and Ajax, who were too valuable to leave Ramos's side. Frankie, when offered a spot, replied, "Ireland is not going; why the fuck would I?"

Ramos eyed the stack of daily papers on his desk. There was a shit load going on in the world, Britain, and his life. He reached for one from the stack, and the headlines screamed it was costing Britain fifty-seven million annually to house Albanian criminals. Ramos figured the Albanian criminals were costing him at least that much. He tossed the papers aside and checked his watch. He spent far more time at a desk than in the field these days, and it was not going to change now that he controlled the whole fucking enterprise.

He recalled the reign of his former boss and mentor, Sir John Kohl. A genius, who loved every minute of the *theatre* of being a villain. A well-dressed, handsome, smart-as-hell outlaw. The memory made Ramos chuckle. But he was a different cat. Ramos liked the dark. Unlike Kohl, to him, time spent with tarted-up fuckery and those who think they run the world was a giant source of aggro and consumed far too much of his life.

Tonight, he spent sitting at his desk at the Pink Lotus. All the bans were lifted, but the Lotus remained closed for renovations. It was transitioning to an upscale gay dinner club. Kohl's empire had numerous gay establishments, but none of this level of elegance and prestige as the new Pink Lotus would command.

It made a handy place to meet and greet the assholes who wanted money. Every person who walked through his door was working some version of graft. Not wanting an actual loan, they would be required to repay, but with big ideas of how they would make money magically appear if Ramos would partner up. No one who entered stopped by to give him money.

Ramos looked at his watch and unfolded the late edition of the Daily Dispatch. The *human-interest* story was on "Cocky" Curtis Warren, the infamous Manchester gangster who was released after a long stretch in a high-security prison in Worcestershire. A reporter wanted to *enlighten* the public on how well he was adjusting to his new life.

Bullshit, thought Ramos. It was widely speculated that Warren had two hundred million hidden, awaiting his release. How much adjusting would that take? Much had changed in the world of criminal business in the last thirteen years, but Ramos had no doubt, if interested, that a clever man could catch up quickly.

Another story blowing up was a major Europol bust: forty-nine arrests and six countries rumoured to control the soaring production levels and importing a third of the cocaine in Europe. The press hinted at ties to the alleged Irish Kinahan organized crime group currently based in Dubai. They offered nothing of substance to actually link them to these raids.

Ramos was familiar with the press using famous names and zero evidence to sell papers. The public loved stories of bad men, whether true or untrue.

Tyler entered the office and plopped in a leather chair across from the desk but first poured a whiskey for both men. Ramos hoped the night's business was coming to a close and thought he might head to Surrey.

"Jimmy and Rich are on the way over. Redmond is shitting himself about a new will and letter from Julie that some Nun gave him. But first, you lucky bastard, you got a surprise waiting?" Tyler grinned ear to ear.

"Who's up?"

"Mindy. She looks as fuckable as the first day she walked into the Lightning Rod."

"Yeah, that ass is as good as it gets." He chuckled. "I'm ready, so get me some." Tyler stood as he knew Ramos was telling him to fetch her.

"Boss, my dick turned to Nelson's column when she walked in. Have pity and save some of that fine ass for the rest of us."

"No promises." Both men laughed.

#

Mindy had been a one-of-a-kind whore. Ramos and Joe had picked her up on the M25 the day after her 18th birthday. She was looking for a ride to London to start her new life. They took her to Carlos and The Lightening Rod.

Ramos quickly knew she was no lap club ho; she had top-trim potential. He took her from Carlos' middle-of-the-road east end Club to John Kohl himself. After one fuck John hired her for the top-of-the-line Smoke Escorts in Mayfair and Belgravia. The highest paid in England. A natural, Mindy was soon the most requested escort in all of Kohl's options. She booked months in advance and travelled the globe in private jets and yachts, making John Kohl and herself a fortune.

She always had a soft spot for Joe, Ramos' late top man.

#

Mindy made her entrance in her usual *look-at-me* style. "Hello, handsome. How's my favourite big brown bear?" She purred as her stilettos tapped softly on the marble floor.

"Mindy." He nodded to the chair, but she ignored him and moved slowly to his side of the desk. "I thought you moved to Moscow." Leaning back in his chair, "Or was it Singapore?"

She knew; he knew exactly where she had been. Mindy did not bother with a reply. "Married life seems to agree with you," he said. She had accepted one of her many proposals of marriage and left Smoke and London. She was still an exceptional piece of ass.

"I'm a widow." The conversation was intentionally slow and coy.

"My condolences. You back in London, looking for work?"

She laughed softly. "No, Uri took good care of me."

"I am certain you took good care of Uri. He die in the sack?"

"You mean like Carlos?" Mindy had been asking around. "No."

"Covid?" After all, Uri was not a young man. She replied with a head shake.

"He fell down the stairs." Pause. "Twice."

"Twice? Very careless." She perched on the edge of his side of the desk, crossing her perfect legs.

"Big Man, you look a little older." It had been years since Mindy departed London. During that time, John Kohl and his son Johnnie died, and Ramos ascended to the throne of the Kohl Empire. "Uneasy lies the head that wears the crown?"

Fuck me, a whore quoting Shakespeare. What next? Ramos made no reply, letting her finish because they both knew he would fuck the hell out of her in about two minutes.

"How is that big cock of yours? She purred. "Please, tell me that's not getting old?"

Ramos laughed. "All the Viagra I need was looking up and seeing you walk through the door."

"I know." Mindy was confident of her skills and effect on men, and why shouldn't she be? She raised her skirt and straddled him. Ramos opened his pants as his hard cock saluted hello.

There was no rush. These two seemed to be in a battle to outlast the other. Both are at the top of their game. Ramos flipped her over, pausing a moment to enjoy the view. Running his large rough hands over the soft peachy skin of her ass, he leaned in for a taste. Mindy moaned, and they kept going.

They pulled apart and sighed when both proved themselves worthy of their reputations.

"Lucky me, you sure know what you're doing." For a second, Alice stepped in Ramos's head. He recalled a time she said the same thing to him.

"As do you, Mindy. Are you sure you're not looking for work? I hate to see that money-maker idle." He put his happy dick away.

She laughed as she picked up her handbag. "You got a light?" digging in her bag for a cigarette. Instead, she pulled a Glock and aimed it at Ramos's face.

"Whoa. Slow down," said Ramos.

"You bastard, you killed my Joe. I know you did."

"Put the gun down," Ramos spoke calmly.

"I loved Joe. We were going to get married; be a family." With sadness on her face but no tears, she steadied the gun.

"You left. You married Uri. Joe didn't know you were coming back."

"I married the asshole to make money, so Joe and I could get a nice house. Uri gave me a million cash upfront and a couple of million in jewellery. His first wife gave me another half million to leave Moscow. The Arab and Hong Kong pigs were all generous. I came back with over six million. To be with Joe."

"You did real good. Quite a long way from the *StopnGo* on the M25."

"None of it matters now. Joe is dead, and you did it." Anger overtook sadness, and her danger level spiked. "Don't lie and say you didn't kill him. You're the only one who could get the drop on my Joe."

Both glanced as the door opened, and Tyler stepped through with his gun out. "Put the gun down," said Tyler. She did not and kept it aimed right at Ramos's head. Ramos had stepped on an emergency button to alert Tyler to a problem via a discreet red light outside the door.

"It was business, Mindy. Joe understood and accepted the risks."

"Goddammit, he loved your wife and children. He loved you like a Daddy, and you killed him. I am going to kill you." Hers was a rather *fanciful* recollection of Joe, a stone-cold killer.

"I named my new son Joe. That shows you my respect for the man. It was business."

"Is it true about the name?" she asked, seeming to hesitate but did not lower the weapon.

"Yes. It was in the papers." Tyler nodded.

"I didn't mean to hurt you, Mindy. I always liked you and helped you when I could. Took you to where the real money is made." It was no surprise to Ramos that she amassed a small fortune.

"Like me? No, you like my pussy, not me. Only Joe really liked me. As a little girl, no one loved me; they just loved my pussy. I know the difference."

She barked, "Back off, Tyler." Mindy could see he was moving in. Tyler stopped. She stood just out of arms reach to both men. Her finger was on the trigger and within the *will-not-miss* range of Ramos's face.

Ramos didn't want to kill her. She had been the one who found out who hurt Alice and Luna when they lived in Baylor. He killed Joe as a result of putting all the puzzle pieces in place. The knowledge of his family and whereabouts, and who had the opportunity to divulge the information, even if unintentional.

The list was very short. When he figured out it was Joe, Ramos' leadership required the ultimate penalty for such a breach. Now, the same goes for Mindy. Ramos could not allow anyone to live who attempted to threaten his life. First, he needed to get her gun.

"You have all those children and a woman who loves you, and I got nothing. Joe loved me. Now I got nothing." She stood taller and refocused the gun. Her arm was steady, and one well-placed bullet from the Glock was all it would take.

Ramos tried again. "Come on Honey, put the gun down. You kill me, and Tyler kills you. It doesn't have to end this way."

Mindy winked. "Yeah, it does."

# # #

THE END